Other books

The White Wolf Prophecy
~ Mating ~
Book 1

The White Wolf Prophecy
~ Hall of Records ~
Book 2

Reviews

WOW! what a book! I thought that the 1st and 2nd books were great, but this Author just keeps getting better every book. Once you pick this book up, you can't put it down. Mystery and time travel together. LK Kelly really knows how to write about us Vampires. A must read and love story. Someone needs to make a movie after these books.

Happy Nightmares Deadgar Winter.

~~~

LK Kelley has created another masterpiece! Scroll of Time is a multiple mindbender with twists, turns, and plots – and is brilliantly captivating to the hilt! Revisiting, remembering, and merging times pasts and repeating events that were previously lived, while reminiscing over recurring love spells, in which love and timings are impeccable! Deja vu runs rampant throughout this book and moreover throughout the entire trilogy folding over into multiple layers of alternate realities. The bad guys will play, but good always prevails in the end. The main character Kaitlan is more powerful than ever, both wolf and wizard, and has a key role in the Scroll of Time. Time for the final chapter in the book -- time for the epilogue -- time for the end of everything -- merging the old with the new and the beginning of yet another chapter into something even greater and newer! A grand replay of the old to set things right again. A definite mind engaging read!

Author Anita Meyer -
Criminologist
Cryptologist
Religious Procurement Specialist
~~~

Reviews

The White Wolf Prophecy
~ Scroll of Time ~

Book 3 of The White Wolf Prophecy Trilogy

By LK Kelley

DragonEye Publishing

~ **Prologue** ~

In the Hall of Records the Scroll of Time waits, which is an ancient, and the single most powerful scroll ever written by the Wizards. So powerful that they even fear it. However, their arrogance would not allow them to destroy it, so they hid it in the Hall just hoping that no one would ever find it. Unfortunately, Zanack found it quite by accident, and it's just what he needs.

While everyone begins suffering from repetition, a surprising secret has been kept from Kaitlan, and her family, since the beginning, and the discovery of who she really is will stun her beyond belief. Dahll warned her about a power so great, that she could not give into that power, or she would become evil. Kaitlan had no idea what he meant by that, but she won't let it happen. But, this power is beyond anything she has ever felt. Will she give into it, or not? And, what happens to the world if they succeed in stopping Zanack? Will any of them have been born? Exist in some form? Or, will Kaitlan take what she feels is her right?

"It has been found, Ali'on?" Sandra asks.

"It has."

"What now? It should never have been found," she says with horror in her voice.

"Perhaps. However, we have another problem," Ali'on says.

"What?"

"Kaitlan."

"I do not understand, my love?"

"It is who she is, Sandra. What she really is. And,

the power that is hers."

"I thought she already had the power of The White Wolf?"

"True. She does. But, that is not the power I mean. She is about to inherit a power than can destroy her. Could make her evil. Zanack is not the worst thing that could happen. If Kaitlan embraces that power, Sandra, she could be seduced to use it. And, if that happens…" he stopped.

"What?" Sandra was shaking with terror.

"Let's just say the evil would be far worse than any that has ever been unleashed on this world, or all the others," Ali'on told her, and his face told her enough to scare her to death.

And, thus…

The White Wolf Prophecy Concludes…

~ 1 ~

Stall, Stall, Stall…

Six months! Zanack had waited *six, damn, long months* to recast his curse! What the hell had happened? He had it planned down to the second, but it would seem that fate was interfering with his triumph! The trouble was that he had not factored any interference into his plans, because he anticipated nothing happening of any lingering consequence. The Supernatural world rarely, if at all, didn't change! Granted, it was a mistake on his part, but it wasn't his fault. It was theirs! How had his plans gone so wrong?

Zanack shoved his hands down into the pockets of his jeans as he walked to an abandoned warehouse just outside the city limits. Months earlier, he had been lucky enough to find it, and buy the building. He had an unending supply of money stashed all over the world. Since supers lived so long, they all had amassed great wealth over thousands of years. And, Zanack was no different. As he walked, his mind worked overtime on his dilemma.

The discovery of the hiding place where he stored his food scraps put the first crimp in his plans to recast the curse. Unfortunately, the scroll he had used the first time was forged, and he had no idea that anything was wrong. At least until the appearance of the White Wolf in the form of Kaitlan Seneca O'Hara, daughter of Canaan O'Hara, leader of the O'Hara Clan. The curse had begun unraveling due to an obscure Prophecy known to the supernatural world as The White Wolf Prophecy. And, why? Because, the Earth Elemental had been ripped from the other three Elementals in which all four of them were necessary for casting the curse. But, he had proceeded anyway with the curse not knowing it could unravel time itself.

Zanack huffed as he walked along. According to the real scroll, he had recently found in the Hall of Records, he was required to cleanse his body by gorging on blood and flesh followed by fasting for seven days. Unfortunately, the scroll also said that he had to recast it not only in the very same place as he did thousands of years ago, but he had to do it in the *same time period* as well. In addition, it mentioned something about another scroll with a time travel spell! He had yet to find that scroll, and this had also delayed his plans.

He kicked a rock on the sidewalk sending it sideways into the road. He had collected live beings, draining their blood, and using their flesh for his food storing them in a basement of an old, deserted building in downtown St. Louis, Missouri. That was his next complication. The building was bought by a corporation, and they would be tearing down his building. Before they imploded it, though, they had revealed his monstrous habit to the authorities. At least that's what the papers had said. Zanack clenched his teeth, and growled. People passing him looked up at him in surprise, but he just smiled sheepishly, and continued walking. With his food supply gone, he had been forced to find a new hiding place, and he had to work faster in order to replenish his needed food. That just posed another problem. What had taken him years to accomplish had to be replaced in just a few months. No one really noticed a few missing people over the years, since he hadn't hunted anywhere but in the red-light districts. He was always cautious, and gathered his food slowly choosing them from prostitutes, drunks, and criminals.

However, now he was running out of time, and time

was his biggest enemy right now.

Seizing more food was imperative, and that meant Zanack had to branch out into neighborhoods. However, he had to bring that to a stop temporarily, because the police were noticing the missing people. Zanack, then, decided to take people from the slums of downtown combined with his original stomping grounds. And, that worked - for almost three months. No one cared, or noticed that anyone was missing. At least he was almost finished, but with more people missing, the authorities were very worried, and put out bulletins telling people to be vigilant. Zanack knew he was taking far too many people, far too fast. Therefore, he had no choice but to bring his kidnappings to a virtual standstill, causing him to waste even more of his valuable time.

If that wasn't enough, other complications began to appear. Three months earlier, the vampire leader, Stefan Rico, had decided to step down. He had declared Anteros de Angelis his successor whose induction would take place on the first day of celebrations in Italy, and that was more time lost. Whenever a new leader of the supernatural world was chosen, the Master Council consisting of the four leaders from their world were required to attend the festivities in the country of the new leader. Thus, Cordone and Kaitlan, as well as Sam and Sarah, would be leaving for Italy today for the week's celebration as was custom. More crimps in Zanack's plans! As long as they were in Italy, he couldn't proceed! He had to time his gorging and fasting down to the second according to what he had read! There was no room for errors, and he had made several already!

Making things even *more* difficult, Richard and Lynne had disappeared over a month and a half earlier, and Zanack had no fucking idea where they were! All he knew was that they had still had not returned, and no one seemed to know where they were - or they just weren't telling! His guess was the latter, and that Cordone was not telling the council. The only way he could keep up with what was happening was because he was on the council. Zanack began to suspect that Cordone believed that someone on the council was not to be trusted, and therefore, he was keeping secrets from the council. Zanack didn't know what they were up to, and without that knowledge he, and everyone else on the council, were in the dark.

Dan and Anita were running the company and the Clan in everyone's absence. The more Zanack thought of his delays, the angrier he became, and made no effort to be nice to people if he bumped into them as he walked. Ignoring the grumbles of "Hey!" or "Watch it jerk!", Zanack continued on his way. His entire life was a mess, and he had no idea how to make everyone come back home! How could he if he didn't even know where anyone was? And, Cordone and Kaitlan sure weren't coming back any time soon! He had heard Anita tell Dan that after their trip to Italy, the two of them were going to spend several weeks traipsing about Europe visiting new authors! Since when did they do business that way? The answer was…"What is they didn't?" Alex for $2000 - his favorite show being Jeopardy. It was just another stall tactic, and he had to come up with some sort of plan to get them to return!

Zanack turned down the side street that led to his warehouse. It was musty, filthy, cobwebs everywhere, but he didn't care. He thrived in this environment, and it was "home" to him. Walking across the dirt-strewn floor, he reached the padlocked door hiding the stairs to the basement. While he almost had enough corpses, there were still not quite enough to gorge on for the curse. Now, he was forced to be patient against his own will. He had no choice but to wait until the Elementals came back home. If they were trying to stall him…well, let them!

They didn't know he couldn't cast the curse yet, anyway, so that just gave him more time to build his stores. Therefore, he was going to have to kidnap more people faster than he wanted. Fuck! If he just had a bit more time, maybe he could enjoy a couple of them. He had been terribly horny for over two months. His sexual desires were a distraction, and he had to end it by burying himself inside a woman soon!

It was still harder to get his food where he was at the moment. Unlike his former hunting grounds in the red-light district, the location of the warehouse had little foot traffic. While it was not as convenient as before, he had to knock the person out in the middle of the night in order to carry them back to the warehouse, and he had to use his two idiots, Beta and Mu, to help him.

He threw the padlocked door open, slamming it against the wall, and stormed down the stairs. As per his instructions, his minions had strapped a girl to the metal table, which he had acquired in the basement of a nearby hospital. They were such cowards! They never had the stomach to stay around to watch him play and feed! Well, he wouldn't need them much longer.

Zanack was done with his "cloaking" magic for the day. He'd just thought of the word after watching an episode of the old "Star Trek" series the other day. He thought it was apropos. Anyway, without enough food, it was getting harder and harder for him to maintain his "cloaking magic". Keeping his human form constant was getting harder by the day. It required a great deal of energy, and he had to expend more energy that he just didn't have any more. And, right now, he had to take out his anger and need for sex on someone. This woman was the lucky winner! So, he let her see what he really was as he approached her. Human women never wanted to play with him, and he had no idea why! He was gorgeous, and his cock was amazing! His mouth drooled when he saw her eyes widen in terror, screaming bloody murder as he approached. He was about to give her something she had never had on this Earth, and at least that gave him a huge boost of pleasure only increasing the size of his penis. He stalked toward her holding and rubbing it so that she could see what he was going to give her. His long, slimy tongue slipped out, and she screamed louder. Too bad, she was wasting her breath. But, still she screamed.

"That's right, baby. Scream all you want. There is no one to hear you, and I'm going to give you a thrill that other women enjoyed!" he hissed at her while licking his lips.

She screamed even louder. Hmmm. Zanack had a thought. Maybe this area had its attractions after all. After all, no one could hear his prey scream here! His elongated mouth grew wide with glee as he began to rip off her clothing, so that she lay before him naked. Then, savoring every second, he crawled onto the table between her legs, and thrust into her.

The best thing the Clan ever did was to buy a second jet. Cordone had two bedrooms and baths installed into the new one a few months earlier. The flight to Italy would take several hours, and the children would definitely need to rest. Milon and Muriel had delivered Canaan and Tara to the airport. Cordone and Kaitlan seized every moment they could to be with the twins. It had been almost a year since they were born, and Kaitlan was missing them constantly. They were already just about to hit the two-year-old mark by human standards, but their minds were equivalent to the age of six, and they were absolutely adorable. Even though they loved their great aunt and uncle, they were totally thrilled to be with their Mom and Dad, as well as Aunt Sara and Uncle Sam, again.

Before they boarded the plane, Kaitlan picked up

Tara, and Sara took Canaan. The children kissed Muriel and Milon, before they left. Even though Sara was still sad at having lost her child, she loved these little devils unconditionally. They were so darned hilarious! Sara and Sam always enjoyed entertaining them, making them roar with laughter, tickling them, and playing games with them. That was good, because Kaitlan and Cordone still had work to do. Kaitlan sat in her chair editing, while watching the four of them play together. After Zanack had killed Sarah and her baby, Kaitlan found her heart had expanded larger than even she ever thought possible. Because of it, she didn't mind sharing her daughter and son with them.

A shuffle from the front of the plane, and Tim entered the cabin tearing Kaitlan's eyes away from her editing. He was transferred to this jet for the flight to Italy, because he was their best pilot. Along with both Cordone and Sam, who could fly as well, he would be able to take a few breaks during the long flight.

"Hey, y'all!" he drawled exaggerating his southern accent. "Time to buckle the youngsters up! Oh, and that means the kids, too!"

Canaan and Tara broke out into wails of laughter, because he called the adults kids! Kaitlan and Sarah buckled them into the cushy, leather seats. Well, they *attempted* to buckle them into the seats! They wiggled and squealed.

"Will you two wiggle warts stop squirming?" Sarah's face was trying to be stern, and she failed at it miserably!

"*No!*" they both said together giggling.

"Uh, Aunt Sarah?" Canaan asked.

"Yes?" she answered while finally succeeding in buckling Canaan in the seat.

"What's a 'wiggle wart'?"

Sarah just stared at him, then looked at Kaitlan who

just grinned and shrugged.   Just what *was* a "wiggle wart"?   She'd never given that a second thought!

"You know?   I don't know what one is!" she laughed, and the kids joined her.

But, trust Mommy to rain on their parade, and to make sure they were on their best behavior. And, if it took threats, well….

"OK, you two. Do you want to stay home, or go with us?"

"Wanna go with you, Mommy!" Tara said for both of them.

Canaan just glared at her. Tara was always speaking for both of them, and he didn't like it. However, Canaan had a lot to learn about when talking to a girl. And, like most men, he couldn't keep his mouth closed, and decided to say something. It began an argument that might have lasted until they grew up - if there was to be a tomorrow.

"You just wanna get on Mommy's good side!" he complained.

"Do not!" Tara answered back.

"Do too!"

"Do *NOT*!" yelled Tara.

"Do *TOO*!" Canaan yelled right back at her.

"You're just an ole' poo-poo!" Tara squealed.

"Am not!"

"Are too!"

"*AM NOT*!"

"*ARE TOO*!"

Oh, great! Kaitlan rolled her eyes at Sarah, while biting her tongue to keep from laughing. Like most adults who really want to laugh out loud at some of their children's antics, Kaitlan and Sarah struggled to keep their faces straight. OK. So. At least they *tried* to keep their faces straight. Kaitlan and Sarah were biting their lips from turning up at the corners.

For about three hours, Cordone and Kaitlan worked on Publishing House business while Sarah, Sam, Canaan, and Tara sat on the floor playing a game of monopoly. A plus for being a werewolf was that their minds developed quickly, and it didn't take them long to understand the game. It took about ten minutes of Tara and Canaan arguing about who was going to get what token, before Sarah settled it by making them use two tokens they didn't want. And, she and Sam, of course, took the ones the kids did want!

Finally! A couple of hours later, Sarah and Sam's plan worked! The children's eyes fluttered as they tried to keep awake. Sarah and Sam scooped up both of them, and placed them in one of the bedrooms, so they could sleep for the rest of the trip.

The jet landed earlier in Rome than they had expected, the children were still asleep, and the de Angelis cars had not yet arrived to take them to Anteros' home. Tim walked into the cabin.

"Ya sure you don't need anything, Boss? Help? Whatever?" Tim asked before he left to go to the Excelsior Hotel.

"I don't think so, Tim. We'll be here for a week or so. Why don't you take a vacation while we're here? Anything you need, just let me know, and we'll take care of it," Cordone told him.

"Wow! Thanks, Cordone! Italy has places I haven't explored yet!"

"Great. You have a good time. Don't get in too much trouble, and there is a car waiting for you at the airport counter, so you can go anywhere you want. I'll call you when we are ready to leave."

Tim made a mild salute, muttered "Y'all have fun!", and waltzed off the jet to claim his car. There were definite perks working for Seneca Publishing, and this was just one of the biggest! He loved it! And, his paycheck was damn good, too!

As he drove away from the airport, he hummed a tune, and made plans where he would go in the next couple of weeks. He pulled out his phone to make a call to someone he just happened to know.

"Hey, gorgeous! I'm in Rome!" he paused to listen to the woman on the other end. "I didn't tell you, because I wanted it to be a surprise. So, baby. Are you up for some real fun? Gonna be here for at least a week!" He paused again. "Now?" he asked in surprise. The other party said something, and Tim's eyes bugged out at what she said to him. "I'm on my way, baby! Set the wine on to chill!"

He steered his car in the opposite direction with a great big smile on his face! He was going to get some tail tonight!

A couple of hours passed, and finally, the cars arrived to escort them to Anteros' "castle" (so christened by Canaan and Tara after seeing it for the first time). It was a three hour drive into the countryside outside of Rome. Once in the car, Sam took it upon himself to keep Tara and Canaan busy, and the two shot all kinds of questions at Sam while Kaitlan, Cordone, and Sarah spoke.

"How long have you known Anteros, Cordone?" Kaitlan asked.

"A long time. A *very* long time! He and Canaan's Dad were great friends. Of course, that was long before the countries existed, but it's how Canaan and I met him. Sam and Dan as well."

Kaitlan turned to Sarah.

"Don't know about you, but do you ever get the feeling that you and I have missed a whole lot?"

Sarah nodded. "Yeah. Almost every time any of the guys open their mouths!" she answered with a grin.

Kaitlan laughed, rolled her eyes, and that just made them both laugh stopping when Cordone narrowed his eyes at both of them.

"Do you two want to know about Anteros, or not?"

Both girls gulped, nodded, and then broke out into laughter again. They'd had so little to laugh about, for so many reasons, this just struck them as hilarious.

"I-I'm sorry, honey, b-but my giggle box must have turned over!" Kaitlan gasped between laughter.

Sarah erupted into gales of laughter when she heard Kaitlan say 'giggle box', and Kaitlan followed right behind her.

Cordone kept staring at them. They were such girls! He tapped his fingers against the door handle waiting on them to finish! Finally, he just had to say something.

"You two done, yet?" Cordone complained, raising his right eyebrow signaling he was getting annoyed.

They both nodded with a hint of amusement in his eyes. He knew it wasn't over. Not by a long shot! The girls broke out into all new gales of laughter knowing it would be a long time before their "giggle-boxes" would turn right side up, again. Cordone leaned his head back, and closed his eyes in a huff.

The girls tried to catch their breath after their "laugh-a-thon". Kaitlan finally found a way to talk - but not without sucking in air between her teeth as she tried to stop laughing.

"We're sorry, honey," Kaitlan apologized as she swallowed. "Go ahead. Now, tell us. Why did Stefan choose Anteros for his successor?"

Raising his head, Cordone looked at the girls to see if they were ready to listen.

"Well, he was always the choice. He is Stefan's adopted, step-nephew."

"Wait. What the hell is an adopted, step-nephew?" Sarah asked while gasping for breath, still trying to get her laughter under control.

"Well, it's a really, really complicated story."

"Give it a try anyway," Kaitlan told him rolling her eyes. Geez, Cordone's stories were always "complicated".

"I'll simplify it, if I can."

"Yeah, babe. You get right on that one!" Kaitlan thought, when oops!

"Watch it, mate!" Cordone growled at her, then aloud, "OK. So, I was already great friends with Nico Ricci who is Anteros' adopted brother from another mother."

He stared at the girls whose mouths just gaped. He grinned wickedly.

"When I met Nico and Anteros, neither had been sired, yet, and both were grown men. Nico introduced me to his Mother, Nicola, and his Father, Carlo, as well as his friend, Anteros de Angelis. Anteros had been an orphan, and he was a bit older than Nico. Nico begged his parents to let him live with them making them not only friends, but brothers. Nicola was also Stefan's baby sister. A vampire named Fawn, turned all of them, and afterwards, Nicola Ricci became mate to Carlo, even though she was still his wife. Stefan considered Anteros his 'step-nephew'. Now, Stefan, in the meantime, took Fawn as his mate. Fawn became Nico and Anteros' step-aunt."

Cordone leaned back in his chair completely oblivious that Kaitlan and Sarah were already totally lost with what he was telling them. They glanced at each other seemingly in a daze, while Cordone continued down his own memory lane.

"What no one knew was that Fawn was crazy as a loon. She was insane. She killed Nicola about six hundred years later. Carlo became hysterical, and accused Stefan of letting his mate kill Nicola, which made no sense whatsoever. Since a sire's blood courses through their veins, it was inevitable that insanity was going to come sooner or later. Carlo wanted retribution on Fawn. Stefan was furious at Fawn, and stood aside to allow Carlo to enact his revenge. Both inherited her crazy gene. To keep them safe, and before she was killed by Fawn, Nicola begged me to hide Nico and Anteros from all of them. They came with me, and I hid them well. I was glad that they never showed the same insane behavior. But, unfortunately, that was not the case with Carlo and Nicola, as I said. The two of them killed each other, and Stefan was finally free of Fawn. It was discovered a few years later, that Nico was not really the son of Carlo and Nicola, nor was he the nephew of Stefan. They had adopted him the same as they had done with Anteros. At that point, Stefan didn't care, because he cared for both of them equally. Anteros was older, so naturally, Stefan named him his successor. Nico agreed. They wanted nothing to change, and they have been brothers to this day."

Cordone ended his story, and looked at the girls noticing their eyes were glassy. Well, they had asked for it, right? Sarah and Kaitlan's eyes had glazed over about half way through his diatribe. Now, their eyes were totally glazed over. They both blinked.

"Huh?" Sarah finally had a comment. "Nothing you said made one bit of sense!"

"Well, I told you it was rather complicated. It gets worse, though, but that is the best explanation, and the easiest. Er…want to hear the rest of it?" Cordone asked as he laughed at their confusion, knowing their answer.

Kaitlan shook her head.

"OK. That was so not helpful, Cordone!"

"Let me try to explain," he continued, his eyes crinkling in laughter.

But when he opened his mouth to explain further,

she held up her hand.

"Never mind. I have enough in my life without adding more confusion!"

Sarah just nodded in agreement, and Cordone dropped the whole damn subject with a huge snort.

The drive was almost over, and it took them ten minutes to reach the house after they turned into the gate! As the car approached Nico and Anteros' home, the girl's eyes widened to a point Sam was certain they were going to roll out of their sockets!

"There's the house," Sam told them unnecessarily while pointing at the huge castle in front of them.

"House? What do your mean house, Hunkalicious? Hells bells! Who, in their right mind, would call that a 'house'?" Sarah squeaked.

Cordone and Sam watched the girls and the children gape in astonishment as they drove up to the house that belonged to Nico Ricci. If they only knew the truth about who he really was, they would pass out from the knowledge!

"What the hell? That's not a house! That's not even a mansion! It's a frickin' castle!" Kaitlan exclaimed.

Tara crawled onto her Mom's lap pressing her nose against the car door window with her eyes wide.

"Frickin' Princess castle!" she squealed in delight.

Kaitlan slapped her hand over her mouth when she heard Tara's parroting, and Cordone turned to look at her! She really needed to curb her language! A second later, she rolled her eyes. Right then, she decided to shut her mouth, and let Cordone take over.

"Does a frickin' Prince live there, too, Daddy?" Canaan asked.

"Well, as a matter of fact, a Prince does live here, Canaan. He is our host and owner of the 'frickin' castle', Nico Ricci. I wish you could meet him, but he is out of town. I think you would have liked him."

Kaitlan huffed, and stared at Cordone for using the same word. He just laughed at her fake outrage.

Both Canaan and Tara's faces fell. Especially Tara. She had so wanted to meet a real prince! She sighed with what seemed like disappointment. She liked his name, too. It sounded so "princey"!

"Don't worry, Tara. I'm sure you will meet him someday. It'll be hard for the two of you not to meet at some point."

He glanced at Kaitlan knowing that wasn't going to happen. He could never see a reason for Tara to meet Nico Ricci at all.

Well, that wasn't good enough for Tara, but she filed it away for the future in her mind - somewhere. Her excitement at getting to stay in a real castle couldn't be contained. When she got out of the car, she started bouncing up and down with unlimited energy. Canaan just rolled his eyes at his sister. She was *such* a girl! This despite the fact that he was just as excited, and bouncing as well. But, *he* would *never* admit it!

The double door opened, and a huge man almost floated down the stairs. Tara and Canaan stopped bouncing to stare in awe! Cordone and Sam were amused at their reaction, and saw that their mates were staring with the same, stunned look as the children.

He was commanding in his stature, and gorgeous. Not just gorgeous as in man gorgeous, but gorgeous as in an ethereal-god gorgeous! How did a vampire look like that? Neither woman had ever seen a vampire like this one.

His hair was coal black without a speck of gray! His skin was heavily tanned with an olive complexion, sporting a slight glow. His neck was long, sleek, and his lips were absolute perfection. Dark blue eyes, the color of the night sky, held flecks of various colors of "glitter" that reminded them of stars. Taller than any other vampire they had ever seen, he had to be six foot six at the very least!

Cordone approached with his hand out, and he clasped forearms with Anteros.

"My friend, it is good to see you again. It has been too long." Anteros deep voice spoke in a formal tone.

"It has been, Anteros. Far too long. I want to offer my congratulations on your new status," Cordone replied just as formally. They never knew who might be listening, so they continued their charade in public.

Turning to Sam, the two men also clasped forearms.

"Thank you, Cordone. Sam, it is also good to see you as well, my friend."

"As am I, Anteros. Cordone is right. It has been too long."

"What is it with the formality?" Sarah wondered. *"It's as if we stepped back in ancient times!"*

"Is there some reason why we should not use formality, Tink?" Sam asked her.

"I guess not, but it's just damn weird to those of us who never lived back then!" Sarah sighed.

They released arms. Anteros turned back to Cordone, and smiled. If the girls were not enamored before, all three dropped their mouths when his smile lit up his face. The three couldn't help but stare at him.

Cordone covered his mouth to keep from laughing, and introduced the women. Anteros had always had a way with women - married or not, young or old. Guess he still had it!

"Anteros, may I introduce to you my mate, Kaitlan Seneca O'Hara Valon."

Still smiling, Anteros bent at the waist, and took her hand to kiss it. Sam and Cordone's lips twitched in amusement as they watched Anteros charm both Kaitlan and Sarah.

"It is, indeed, a great honor to meet the daughter of

Canaan O'Hara. He was a great man, and a great friend. May I call you Kaitlan?"

Kaitlan stammered so badly, she was almost tongue-tied.

"S-sure. T-thank y-you."

Grinning with amusement, Cordone continued.

"And, this is Sam's mate, Sarah Collins Knight."

Again, Anteros took Sarah's hand.

"I am most pleased, and happy, to meet Sam's beautiful mate," and like Kaitlan, he kissed her hand.

Sarah couldn't speak, but her eyes held a dreamy expression. That's when she made the same, dreamy sound as the Widow Paroo did in "The Music Man" when Professor Harold Hill had charmed her.

"Uhhhh!" she groaned.

Anteros grinned at her when he felt a tug on his pants, and looked down at a tiny little girl. Tara held out her hand, too.

"How charming!" Anteros thought in amusement, and knelt down. This tiny little girl was a beauty!

"Hello," he said.

"Hi! I'm Tara!" she said to him.

He took her tiny little hand just as reverently as he had Kaitlan and Sarah, and everyone around them broke out into huge smiles watching him charm even a one-year old as he stared into her brilliant green eyes.

"And, most especially, it is my great honor to meet Tara, granddaughter of Canaan and Tara O'Hara, daughter of Cordone and Kaitlan Valon. It is so nice to meet you, little one," he told her, and gave her a tiny little kiss on her hand as well.

Tara copied her aunt. "Uhhhh!"

Laughter and happiness trickled over everyone while Canaan just rolled his black eyes at what he thought was just stupid.

Anteros, then, turned to Canaan, and held out his

hand. Canaan automatically held out his, and Anteros grasped his small forearm as he did the grown men while Canaan's hand barely sat on top of Anteros' massive arm. Canaan perked up, and pretended to be a grownup.

"You are Canaan Valon, grandson to Canaan and Tara O'Hara, and his namesake. It is truly a great honor to meet you, young sir!"

"Thank you, Anteros. It is an honor to meet you as well," Canaan said in his most grownup voice,

Tara narrowed her eyes. She would never - ever - let him hear the end of this!

Cordone was never more proud of his children than right then, and Kaitlan grabbed his hand with a teary smile.

"That's just so cute!" she used her thoughts to Cordone who just nodded.

After the formalities were over, Anteros led them into the castle behind him.

Again, Kaitlan, Sarah, Tara, and Canaan stopped as they walked into the entry. Stopped and gaped, again. It was huge with a capital *HUGE*. Multiple staircases led to multiple floors, and two large Duncan Phyfe tables were in the center of the entry with at least four large Waterford crystal vases sitting on top of them holding fresh flowers.

"As you know, the castle is half mine, even though it rightfully belongs to my brother, Prince Nico. I do wish he was here to meet all of you, but he was called away for business last week, and I fear he will not arrive home in time. Please feel free to explore the castle all you want. Especially Tara and Canaan."

A man with dark brown hair entered the room, and bowed.

"Ah, Gio!"

Introductions were made to Giovanni and his mate, Millicent Morisi who had followed behind him. They were more than servants to both Nico and Anteros. Giovanni was a great friend, and was like a Father to both Nico and him.

"Will you please show our guests to their rooms, Gio? Millicent?"

"Of course, my lord. We are very happy to do so," he replied bowing to Anteros, again. Turning to the guests, he asked them, "Please, follow us."

~ 2 ~
The End of a Reign

Millicent took the children's hands in hers with Tara on one side, and Canaan on the other, and led them up the stairs following Gio with the rest of the adults tagging behind her. She was very patient while the children made their way slowly up the magnificent black, white and green marble staircase. Two of those staircases were on either side of the entry hall and curved upward meeting in the middle ending at a large landing. Stairs in front of them, as well as stairs to the right and left led to the different wings of the castle. Gio and Millicent led them to the stairs on the right, and into the west wing of the castle.

"The left staircase leads to the East apartments for Prince Nico while the South Wing holds the apartments for Anteros," she explained.

It seemed as if they walked forever. The hallways seemed to go on forever. After walking for a while, Kaitlan wondered if the castle was actually adding rooms just before they would turn the next corner like in Stephen King's "Rose Red". Finally, they stopped in front of hand-carved, massive and wooden double doors. Gio opened both, and stepped aside for Kaitlan, Cordone, and the children to enter the room. All four of them stopped dead. It was not just a room. It was a massive suite!

"I do hope this will be satisfactory? The suite has three bedrooms, so the children will each have their own rooms, and they are on the right. Your rooms are on the left. Each bedroom has its own bath, and of course, this is the central living area. You will also find a small kitchen is behind those doors." Gio pointed to their left at a couple of smaller doors. "When master Nico heard the children would be coming, he ordered that their rooms be decorated especially for them.   Shall we see Canaan's room first?"

He walked to the first room on the right followed by Canaan. Canaan had an insane love of science, and he had declared that he wanted to become a doctor for the Clan like his Aunt Anita. While everyone just rolled their eyes, he knew he'd prove it to them eventually - when he was interning with his Aunt!   Canaan, like most boys, also loved sports, and anything to do with sports, but he really loved NASCAR the best. And, that's when Gio beckoned him into his room.

Canaan stood in the doorway with his mouth open.

"Holy freakin' cow!" he exclaimed with excitement.

It was decorated like a racetrack! There was a track, a small stand for "people", and his bed was a car sitting on the track! He ran over, and automatically tried to spin the wheels.

"Wow, Dad! Look! They really spin!" he squealed.

Across from the bed was a 32" TV screen, and at the window a "shop" table with chairs designed like tools along with a small red sofa facing the TV. The table was loaded with every type of digital gadget anyone could want!

"Checkout the bathroom and closet, young Master Canaan," Millicent suggested.

Canaan went to the bathroom.

"The bathroom looks like a pit!" he squeaked.

The adults started to laugh hard when he described it as a "pit". But, of course, they knew he meant a pit stop in the center of a racetrack. For some reason, however, it just struck them all as really funny!

It was in a black and white checkerboard tiles for the winning flag, with random blue, yellow, green, and red tiles mimicking the different colored flags in racing. The cabinet was actually sitting on multiple tires laid end to end in a square with a green glass sink sitting in the center clear glass top that was just his size. The sink faucet had handles resembling car doors, and the tub and shower were actually made from tires, jacks, sockets, and other things needed for a pit stop!

"Oh, MAN! This is so cool!"

Kaitlan glanced at Cordone.

"Well, maybe he'll want to get clean?" she asked hearing her mate's hearty laugh.

Next, it was Tara's turn. Leaving Canaan to explore his room, they walked into Tara's room. Tara just stood in complete awe - along with the adults!

"It looks like a fairy-tale!" she whispered breathlessly.

Tara's room was like an enchanted forest. There was a bed in a "tree" complete with a winding staircase leading up to it! Three "trees" with fat trunks having open, irregular, arched doors were scattered around with something different inside each one of them. One had a child-sized table that looked like a toadstool with matching toadstool chairs. Another had a small, forest green sofa with a large 32" Flat Screen TV. In addition, the third one had a desk where she could pretend to write or draw complete with everything she would need to do so. Tiny rope lights mimicked the lights emitted by fairies and lightning bugs were strung throughout the room, and green, plush, and carpeted pathways led to everything. In the back, a large rock with an opening like a cave stood in the corner.

Millicent jumped up and down grinning.

"See the rock with the opening? Go see what's behind it!" Millicent leaned down to whisper to her.

Tara looked up at her, and then excitedly ran to the rock. She followed a short path in an "S" curve, and came out into….

"MOM! You gotta see this!" she screamed in happiness.

Kaitlan and Cordone knew she wasn't going to be happy unless they followed.

When they exited the "S" curve, even their mouths dropped open! It was like walking into a place for pixies. Everything was a bit larger than normal, but still child height so Tara could pretend she was a pixie. A sink cabinet was a "leaf" pedestal, and the sink was a pink glass flower sitting on a green glass top with wings for faucet handles, and the faucet was a branch. Her shower was not enclosed, but sunk into the floor like a small pool one would find in a forest. It had nothing more than a tiny trickle of water flowing off a rock, but to Tara, it was a massive waterfall! The tub was a green leaf, and she was in heaven!

"Hey, Mom, I'm going to take a shower!" Tara squealed, and began to undress.

Laughing, the adults left the kids to explore their rooms supervised by Millicent, while Gio led Kaitlan and Cordone to their room.

"Gio, Nico didn't have to go to all this trouble for the kids. We're only going to be here for a week," Kaitlan told him. She was still reeling with shock at his generosity for her children.

"I know, but Nico and Anteros so rarely get to see children, they were just excited to make their stay magical. Children love to have their fantasies fulfilled. And, we love fulfilling them!"

"Well, we truly appreciate the attention. Their rooms are incredible!" she said, just before she entered their room.

"Oh!" Kaitlan gasped.

"Right behind you, babe!" Cordone told her as he, too, gaped.

"Nico loves to make adult's dreams come true, too," Gio laughed.

It was beautiful! The same fairy lights graced the room, but the bed was larger than any king bed they had ever seen. Draped in blues and golds, the room had the colors of royalty. Various shades in blue and creams decorated the oriental rugs, which graced the hardwood floor. The walls were painted in gold, and the molding was mahogany. The ceiling was rather surprisingly plain. Gio walked to the table by the bed picking up a large remote control, which had all kinds of buttons, and handed it to Cordone.

"Press the gold button in the center," he told Cordone.

Both Kaitlan and Cordone jerked their heads upward at the noise above them. The entire ceiling slid back to open the room to the sky! No wonder it was so plain compared to everything else!

"It's beautiful when the stars and moon come out," Gio told them. "Both Nico and Anteros designed the ceilings. They like to feel as if they could fly into the sky."

"Holy freakin' cow! A convertible bedroom?" Kaitlan muttered sounding just like her son.

"Now, in there," he pointed to the door on the left side of the bed, "is the bath. I'm going to let you explore it yourselves. If you think that this is incredible, just wait till you see that room! If you don't need me any longer, dinner is at eight p.m. Millicent and I will serve the children's food at seven in their rooms, and she will stay with them. If you will excuse me, I will take my leave to show Sam and Sarah their rooms."

Gio bowed, and left. Sarah and Sam were led to a suite of rooms on the other side of the hallway, which contained two bedrooms, two baths, and a living area with a small kitchen as well. Their rooms were no less elaborate decorated in reds and golds. Sam watched his mate explore the rooms in awe thinking how beautiful she looked with her red hair against the red of the room!

Meanwhile, Kaitlan was drooling over their bathroom! It was unbelievable! Like the bedroom, the ceiling retracted. It was at least half again as large as the bedroom. The colors of blue and gold continued. Two, royal blue pedestal sinks stood side by side continuing in the tiles that were also royal blue. Looking closely, Kaitlan realized that the faucets were gold.

"Do you think they're…?" she started to ask Cordone.

"I have no doubt," he answered.

"Real gold, not gold plate!" she breathed in shock.

The tiles matched the pedestals. Turning, she saw a bathtub. But, what a bathtub! It was sunken into the floor instead of raised as was the style of today. Two steps led down into the gold tiled tub, and there were gold jets all around for a whirlpool bath. It was big enough for at least four people! A drain was placed into the corner of the tub near the shower, and a waterfall faucet completed the effect. What was really interesting was that the shower was also sunken, but one step up from the tub. It led into the gold and royal blue tiled shower! It was the ultimate spa with water heads all the way around. One could take a shower, and the other a bath, and the water ran down the one step into the tub!

It was at this point, they heard the children's squeals piercing the suite. Cordone and Kaitlan ran into Canaan's room following the sounds.

"Mom! Look at this!" Canaan grabbed her hand.

"Daddy! Come see the tiny toilet in the bathroom! It looks just like a flower, and is just my size!" she squealed grabbing his hand.

"I can't believe that they did this for the kids and us, Cordone! It must have cost a fortune!"

"Well, they have a fortune," he informed her in a matter-of-fact tone.

"Are they really that wealthy," Kaitlan whispered.

Nodding his head, "That doesn't begin to describe it, Kaitlan. Wealth is reserved for the very rich. Nico and Anteros are so far above that they haven't invented a word for their type of wealth!"

"Wow!" Canaan said in a whisper. "I'm never gonna wanna to leave this place!"

Tara's head nodded in total agreement. The thought of living in this castle, mated to the gorgeous Anteros, became her secret dream. She really didn't need a "prince". Anteros was prince enough for her!

Lynne and Richard finally returned after being absent for two months, but both were mum about where they had been - at least to the council. They strolled into Dan's office holding hands where they found Lon McClain and Roland Turner sitting across from Dan.

"Crap! Well, those two just ruined my day!" Lynne told Richard through their bond.

He merely nodded his head in agreement.

Roland turned around. He was obviously irritated.

"Where the fuck have you two been? You just leave without a fucking word, and don't tell anyone where the fuck you were going, or when the fuck you would return? That is fucking unacceptable, Richard!" he roared at them.

Dan slammed his hand down on his desk.

"That is enough, Roland! First, it's none of your business where they go on their vacation, which incidentally, neither have had in a very long time, and second," Dan told him, "well, it's still none of your damn business!"

Roland's face shot back at Dan. He had never been so angry!   How dare Dan tell him it's none of his business!

"It is my business to know where council members are at every single moment! You have no authority over the council, Dan!"

Lynne, Richard, and Dan looked at each other. Did Roland just *really* say what they thought he said? Besides, what reason did Roland have for being angry anyway? Dan glared at Roland with the face that he used to scare anyone he interrogated.

"I am third, Roland, or have you forgotten that already? I do have the authority, and I also have the authority to kick someone off the council if they show that they are unstable! And, right now, you are damn close to that happening!" He rose to his full height to stand over Roland. "I am quite certain you did not mean what you just said. Am I right?"

Roland glared daggers at Dan. He had been overly aggressive lately. More so than usual. Dan wondered why.

Gritting his teeth, Roland answered, "No. I did not mean it. I apologize, Daniel."

"Good," Dan told him, standing to his full height. "Now, my patience has worn thin. Both of you get the hell out of my office!"

Both Roland and Lon slunk out of Dan's office. Once they were gone, Dan fell back into his seat, and ran his fingers through his hair.

"Those two get on my nerves more than any other people I have ever met!" he told Lynne and Richard. "I just spent the last hour cooped up with their complaints, yelling, and demands!"

Richard sat down across from Dan, and Lynne gave her mate a very heated and sexy kiss. Richard slapped her ass as she turned from him to return to her desk. He watched as she took that luscious ass out of the door, then settled back to speak to Dan.

"So? Do you think that they are real suspects?"

"I don't know Richard," he sighed, grinned, and asked, "So, how was 'Dad'? And what did he think of Richard, Jr?"

"You're really funny," Richard grinned back at him. "Odin was a bit pissed off when he found out I was mated, and had a son, but there is little he can do. I think, in a way, he was happy to find he was a grandfather. His new wife, Zira, was thrilled to be a grandmother as well. If it hadn't been for Richard, Jr., I doubt if we would have been welcomed. Anyway, Odin insisted that we leave him with them after he heard what was going down. I know he'll be safe there."

"That's a good thing, right? Dahll?" Dan asked. "And, by the way … he kinda creeps me out!"

"Dahll is...well, is Dahll! He's one of a kind, Dan. He sees everything."

"That's what I mean! He's a strange bird. How does he not go insane?"

Richard shrugged.

"I don't really know, but he's always - been. He doesn't even remember his own origin. He's old, Dan. Very, very old. Even older than Odin, or his father, or his father's father."

"Wow! It must be miserable to have lived that long!"

"Not to him. At least until now. He confided in me that he cannot see any future at all. And, that is truly a first, Dan. That terrifies him - and for the first time in his entire existence! So, if he is scared, well…"

"That doesn't instill confidence in anything."

"Yeah," Richard answered.

Dan leaned back in his chair so hard, it rocked backward while he flailed his arms trying to keep the chair upright!   It caused Richard hoot out loud. Dan managed to keep upright, but glared at Richard, who ended up pretending he was coughing instead of laughing his ass off!

"Very funny," Dan growled.

"Why yes...yes it was!" Richard stopped pretending, and laughed hard.

Dan kept glaring at him sitting back to wait for Richard to stop. But, he didn't, and as we all know, laughter is a "condition" that is highly contagious. Both men laughed.

"OK, I see we are still stalling," Dan gasped between laughs.

"Yep. I mean we can stall Zanack for only so long, obviously. At least it's given the girls more time to deal with their elements."

Dan agreed. Each of the girls almost had total control of their element, and that's more than the original Elementals had been able to do, apparently.

"Well, Lynne and I are back. You and Anita can take off, now, and do your part to stall, stall, and, did I say stall? We have to keep Zanack from pulling all this shit off until *we* are ready. And, the best way is to make sure we split up as much, and as often, as possible. If we can keep from gathering together in the same place until then, well...." he let his thought trail.

Dan nodded, stood up, and stretched. He was so looking forward to having his mate in his arms for the next two weeks.

"Well, I'm so for interfering with his plans for as long as possible. OK. Richard. I'm outta here, and off to our secret destination. You're in charge of the Publishing House, now. It's yours! Call me if you need anything."

"Will do."

Dan darted off to Anita's office, grabbed her, and the two of them had a driver take them to the airport - by way of changing vehicles about four times just in case Zanack tried to follow them. It was getting harder and harder to keep out of Zanack's way.

At the airport, they boarded a plane that Dan had chartered under a different name. His flight plan was filed under a different name, so that they could pick up Rachel.

The constant changing of cars, planes, and even boats when necessary, served to keep them under Zanack's radar so he couldn't figure out where any of them were at any given time. Anita had purchased special cell phones, which had nothing to do with business, allowing the couples to keep in touch with each other. Now, if Cordone would just *stop* crushing every damn phone he held, the office might get into the black, and Kaitlan would be so much happier!

The "Meeting to Delay Zanack" at the "monster castle", as the kids called it, was a success. Their constant avoidance of him worked for quite a while, and that was good.

Ali'on had not been able to join them for the first week since he had to attend to Elven matters, and for once, when he did arrive, there was no arguing - especially when Stefan came to announce his shocking news.

Stefan had joined up with them at the castle outside of Rome a few days after Kaitlan, Sarah, Cordone, and Sam had arrived at Anteros' home.

"Well, it seems our diversion of disinformation worked - again," Stefan told everyone.

"Yeah, but for how long?" Sam asked crossing his arms over his massive chest. No one answered. Well, he hadn't asked anyone anyway.

Stefan looked around. He had originally lied when he said he would step down to help stall Zanack. The plan was for him to announce his leaving office, and then, after a couple of weeks of pretend arguing, he would agree to stay. However, during the lie, Jennifer had discovered that she loved having her mate all to herself after thousands of years. Even Stefan had been having fun making love to her constantly without interruption. Freedom was precious, and he was ready for it! Now, he wondered why in the hell he'd been hanging onto the leadership for so long! He had told her of the lie, but later, asked her if she would be upset if he truly did step down. Jennifer had been so thrilled when he told her of his actual decision, she'd given him sex for hours on end without stopping! He could stand that for the rest of his existence! His mind drifted back to their last act before he left for Rome.

Creator! His mate was sexy! She had met him in his office in the middle of a conference call, and locked his door. Nothing was unusual about that, because she had done that many times. But, this was a bit different. Normally, she would have waited until he was off the phone, or finished whatever work he was doing at the moment. But this time, while he was on the phone, she had stripped naked, kneeled in front of him, and unzipped his pants. She pulled out his dick, and gave him a blowjob that he wasn't likely to forget for the next millennium! He had a very hard time concentrating on the call watching as she sucked and licked his cock for several minutes, bringing him almost to a climax. And, then, he lost all track of the conversation widening his eyes as he watched her use her breasts to catch the massive amount of semen that exploded from his cock. Then, she took her hands and spread it over them! Male vampires had semen, but it was a clear liquid. It could never take root within a vampire female, of course, but it was as close to an orgasm as they could get. It was all visual for them. He had quickly finished his call, and attacked Jennifer, throwing her to the floor and thrusting it into her. Unlike other supers, though, vampires could have sex for hours on end without stopping! There was no need for sleep, or other bodily needs. He so wanted to get back to her as soon as he could. He planned years for her on her back, her legs spread, and his legs between her legs. In addition, he also had plans for him on his back with her straddling, and impaling herself with his cock! So, now, he was ready to make his huge announcement, but before he could, Ali'on butted into it with a stupid statement.

"Well, we must have a party! When was the last time we all were together, and we didn't argue?" Ali'on laughed.

"What? So, you want an argument?" Kaitlan joked.

"Of course I do! I mean, after all, we can't break tradition!"

Even Stefan laughed, and that was something unheard of with him. Cordone's eyes narrowed. Something was up, but what?

"OK, Stefan. Give. What the fuck is wrong with you? You are never this cordial, nor happy. What's the deal?"

Stefan's face became sheepish as he answered.

"Well, you see? It's like this. I will be breaking tradition. I mean. Jennifer and I had a lot of sex, and made a decision."

"TMI, Stefan! We don't need to know! And, that would be what decision?" Sarah asked.

"Well, the original idea about stepping down was to throw Zanack off, and delay his plans. But, I have an even better idea that will delay for at least another week."

Everyone's face turned toward Stefan. He was really enjoying this attention!

"The truth is I am stepping down for real. I am

finished leading the vampires. Someone else can have the damn headache!"

There was a complete and collective silence while all heads turned to him, and mouths fell open. You could have heard a pin drop. Finally, Anteros spoke.

"You are not serious, Stefan? You've been in control for thousands of years - at least ten. Why now? You had better have a really good reason."

Stefan didn't really want to tell them the real reason, but he didn't see anyway out of it. He was so finished being leader. He had loved the power, and perks that came with his position, but Jennifer was more important, now. It was time for him to be a free agent.

"I'm as serious as I can be, Anteros. You are my successor, and that has not changed. But, frankly, both Jennifer and I are ready for some fun - if you know what I mean, since little Sarah doesn't want me to give you too much info!" He waggled his eyebrows to the groaning and rolling of eyes. "I know. TMI, right Sarah?" He grinned at her scowl. "Well, tough shit! We have been having fun for the last few weeks since I announced my fake leaving. For the last ten thousand years, I've not had one, single vacation. But, the fact remains that we don't want to stop. I mated Jennifer about five thousand years ago, and we haven't really had a 'honeymoon', for lack of another word for it. She and I are ready for one, and I plan on making it last for thousands of years more - or as long as it takes to take Zanack down and you girls change the time line. Whichever comes first. One way or another, when it does happen, I plan on being inside of her!"

He stood, turned to Anteros, and knelt in front of him.

"My dear nephew, today I step down, officially, from being leader of the vampires, and I name you as my successor. In front of all present today, all will be held as witnesses thereof. I, now, hand over the reigns of the Vampire Nation to my successor, Anteros de Angelis. Do you, Anteros, accept my resignation, and my allegiance to you as leader of the Vampires?"

Anteros answered, "I, Anteros de Angelis, do accept your resignation and your allegiance. From this day forth, until I step down, I will serve my Clan, and the Vampire Nation, to the best of my ability, and honor."

Stefan, still kneeling, removed his ring, and took Anteros' right hand.

"Then, as is the custom, I pass this ring down to you as my predecessor did to me. The ring is ancient, and is sacred to the Vampires. It is, and always has been, the symbol for all leaders of the vampires. Only three have ever held this office prior to me, Anteros. You will be the fifth leader of the Vampire Nation. As it is with the silver and Tourmaline ring of the Elven Nation, which Ali'on wears, and the silver and Tiger's Eye ring of the Werewolf Nation, worn by Canaan, I wear the ring of Proustite - a blood-red stone symbolizing the unification of all Vampires. Only the leader is granted the right to wear this ring, and now, my nephew, it is yours!"

Stefan slipped the ring onto Anteros' right middle finger, and swore allegiance by kissing the ring. While the actual ceremony would have been longer, this was every bit as much an official transfer of power as it would be with the longer ceremony. Anteros was, now, leader of the Vampires. Stefan stood, and bowed to his nephew.

"Have your week's party, I wish you good speed, and I know that you will lead the vampires into a whole new age. You have been groomed all your life for this, and now, I pass on to you all power that is granted by that office. I will be around should you need to consult me, but you are ready. And, I am ready for an extremely long vacation, and a lot of sex with Jennifer!"

Everyone laughed and applauded. Anteros stood,

and bowed his head to his uncle.

"Go in peace, Uncle. You have deserved your vacation. Tell Jennifer congratulations."

"I will. So, everyone, I take your leave, and I'm outta here, stage left!"

Stefan was gone so fast, no one saw him leave, and in his stead, a new leader of the vampires stood in front of everyone.

Truth be known, everyone was going to be a whole lot happier with Anteros as leader anyway. Gio entered with glasses of different drinks for everyone to toast the new leader.

~ 3 ~
Why Must the Shit Always Hit the Fan?

After their "fake" business was concluded - well, except for the "real" change in vampire leadership, which gave the entire meeting true verification - Cordone and Kaitlan discovered another way to stall Zanack by visiting ten different authors who were eager for the Seneca Publishing House to publish their books. That meant that they had to cover the entire European continent, and each could take a minimum of one day to a week, because they would have to read those that had not been submitted. Well, really, they didn't *have* to read anything, but it was a great excuse to use for another delay! In the meantime, Sarah and Sam took the twins with them delivering them to Muriel and Milon. Cordone's aunt and uncle were two very busy adults! They had it all down to a science: when they would get the children to their parents; where they would take them; and how to bring them back, was becoming their specialty.

Taking the jet to their next rendezvous with author number nine, everyone was trying to come up with more ways to put the inevitable off for as long as possible. And, that's what Kaitlan was telling Anita when she was speaking to her on the phone.

"We have to stall as long as possible, Anita," Kaitlan was telling her.

"Well, you certainly don't have to tell me! So not eager to see the shit hit the fan, yet! Anything at all no matter how trivial will work," Anita agreed. "Hmmm. Let me see if I can come up with something. My big brother have any ideas?"

"Don't know, but I'll ask him, and hey! We'll try anything! Girl, I'm so on edge right now, I feel as everything is in slo-mo. By the way. How is your element?"

"Oh, it's been blowing up a storm!" Anita joked. "How about yours?"

Catching on to Anita's attempt to bring a bit of levity into their serious lives, Kaitlan laughed back.

"Dirty, of course."

"Talked to Lynne yet?" Anita was laughing harder.

"I did."

"And, her element?" Anita shut her teary eyes. She was afraid of what Kaitlan would answer, and she didn't disappoint!

"Wellll…she told me that she was just *hotter* than the 4th of July! In fact, she claimed that she was…and I quote…'so, damn, fucking hot for Richard'!"

Anita groaned. That was just so bad, it made her laugh that much harder! And, then, Kaitlan pulled out the big guns!

"Oh, and Sarah says she is leaking a lot, and wondered if she should get some incontinence pads!"

Face it! When women are trying to change direction in their speech and mind, they joke about sex and bodily functions! Men were so clueless! They were not the only ones to joke about sex!

"So, when are you two coming back?" Anita asked when she managed to calm he laughter.

"Soon enough, I guess, unless we can come up with another stall tactic." Then, Kaitlan asked, "Anita, are we really doing the best thing? I mean stalling like this? It's only putting off the inevitable."

"Yeah. I know. I honestly don't know the answer, but one thing is sure. It's going to happen. Should we force his hand?"

That was something Kaitlan hadn't thought about

yet. Force Zanack's hand?

"You mean just get it over with? Maybe you're right, Anita. No matter what we do, it doesn't matter. It's gonna happen. Do you think we should?"

Neither of them knew what they should do.

"I guess it's time for a meeting of the minds. It's obvious that Zanack wants to control the contact, and time of our confrontation. Let's meet at the house. We all need a run, and it may clear our thoughts."

"Run. Right. Suuurrre you mean 'run'!" Anita rolled her eyes. "You and I both know you don't mean run. You mean 'get it on'! OK. We'll leave, and pretend to go other places to keep Zanack off the track, and then meet up there."

Their stupid puns seemed to be never ending. And, they were just so damn bad! She shrugged, and turned to tell Cordone that it was time to have a meeting, and to go home.

"Good idea, Kaitlan. A wolf run is just what we need!"

Kaitlan started to nod when a thought hit her. Anita had told her that Zanack wanted to control the contact point. In other words, Zanack wanted to control the entire situation of when, where, and how. She grabbed Cordone's arm as he stood. He turned to her.

"What?" Cordone asked.

"Cordone. We've been trying to stall Zanack's control of the situation, simply because we are trying to put it off for later, but since we don't know when, we just keep stalling."

"Yes, and…?" he asked puzzled.

"It's not Zanack who needs to control it!" She looked up into Cordone's frowning face. But, before he could speak, she was excited as she told him, "It's not him! It's us! *WE* have to control the situation! The where is already a given. All we can control is the when and how!"

Cordone sat down across from Kaitlan, leaned back into his chair, nodded his head in agreement, and smiled.

"Agreed," he said. "Let's see. The children's birthday is soon, and I'm pretty sure that he won't attack then - especially if he is on the council as we suspect."

Kaitlan leaned back in her seat.

"Then, we all meet at the house for their first birthday, and celebrate."

"OK. Afterward, we make sure that Zanack knows we are there. It's time to finish this!"

"It's past time to finish this, Cordone," Kaitlan told him, and he nodded.

It was another three weeks, though, before Cordone and Kaitlan arrived at the house in the Rockies. Richard and Lynne arrived first, followed by Kaitlan and Cordone an hour later. The next day, Sarah and Sam came in the morning while Anita and Dan waited until the evening. Each couple came from different places, different directions, and different methods. Once there, Milon and Muriel, again, brought the children. There was no way that they would miss Tara and Canaan's first birthday with the birthday of Rachel and Richard, Jr. a day later. Odin had relented to let his grandson see his Mother and Father once more, and brought him over the Bifrost personally to Muriel and Milon.

Everything was ready when they arrived, and the five couples watched as the children opened their gifts, and sat down to play. What surprised them most was the kids' willingness to share. Tara and Canaan's pissing contest was over, and they played together happily, as if nothing had ever happened between them. It made Cordone shake his head in confusion. His glance at

Kaitlan just made her laugh.

"I just don't get it!" Cordone told her.

"I know. I don't either, but apparently, they do. I guess we just don't need to make a big deal about it."

"You're right. If we do, they do."

Kaitlan nodded in agreement, and joined the other girls in the kitchen to help prepare the birthday dinner.

Cordone and Sam spent their time outside on the deck grilling hamburgers, hot dogs, and racks of ribs for the men. There were colas for the kids, and beer for the grownups. Since Lynne had a different palate, there was also wine. And, then there was a huge, 4-tiered cake in the colors and flavors each child liked the best.

Rachel loved strawberries and pink, while both Richard, Jr. and Canaan liked chocolate with chocolate icing, and chocolate ice cream with chocolate chips covered with chocolate syrup. Tara, however, preferred plain, simple, white cake with her favorite color of icing in purple.

"Hey, Mom! Look! The cake is like 'Neopolitan' ice cream!" Richard exclaimed.

"Yep, and we have the ice cream to match!" squealed Tara.

When it was time to eat, Rachel stood on her toes so she could survey the spread before her.

"Ewww! Mommy? I don't eat meat! Why doesn't anyone ever remember? Aren't there some veggies and fruit around?"

Richard, Jr. whacked her upper arm.

"Ouch! What's the big idea?" Rachel squeaked rubbing her arm.

"What's wrong with you? You're a wolf! Wolves eat meat!"

"Shut up!" Rachel glared at Richard, Jr. "I don't care if I'm a full wolf! I still like vegetables and fruit better!"

"You're weird," Canaan said.

"Stop picking on Rachel!" Tara said, putting her arm around her. "She likes veggies! So what if she's a wolf? Who said wolves only eat meat?"

Rachel and Tara stood hand in hand against the two boys. The boys glared daggers at them. After all. *Everyone* knew wolves ate meat! Girls were just stupid!

Sarah shook her head. The others didn't know what to do about this.

"Hey, guys!" she yelled. "Put a sock in it! Rachel, I made sure there were plenty of vegetables for you. They are in the fridge. Come on. You can help me put the trays on the tables. Trust men to ignore anything, but meat!"

Tara and Rachel followed Sarah to the kitchen, and opened the refrigerator door. There, stacked high, were several types of vegetable and fruit platters! Rachel's mouth watered.

"Yum!" she grinned.

Helping their aunt, they pulled out the trays, and put them on the table. Other delicious non-meat foods were potato salad, coleslaw, chips, baked beans, corn on the cob, and more. It was a spread big enough for a regiment! But, then, werewolves *ate* as much as a regiment!

After the food was ready and waiting on the large table, Rachel said, "Now, this is more like it!"

Then, she slapped Richard, Jr. on the arm the way he had slapped her. He had been turning his nose up at the vegetables and fruit. He looked at her raising his hand as if he was about to get her back for her getting him back when his eyes met his Mom's. Ooops! He lowered his arm, and shrugged. He could be big about it! He'd just find a way, later, of getting Rachel back!

After the feast, the cakes were cut, and the kids ate their fill. Then, the grownups settled back, drank their beers, complained they'd eaten too much, and watched the kids play together. They sure didn't act as if they were full! No more arguments cropped up for the rest of the day, and even late night was peaceful.

The children were growing so fast, and even though they were the equivalent of two years old in human years, their minds had progressed far beyond that of a two year-old. They stayed with their parents for a week, before they were kissed and whisked off with Muriel and Milon, again. This time, the couples knew what was happening, and tears stung Muriel's eyes knowing that the children would never see their parents again, and that they would never see their relatives again, either. She hugged all four women, and Milon grasped arms with the men. Trying to keep the children happy, they wiped their sadness away, and drove away for the last time.

The couples stood and waved bye for a long time even after the kids were out of sight. That's when all four women began to cry, and there were tears in the men's eyes as well. They knew it was the last time that they would see them - at least in this timeline. The plan was that Muriel and Milon would meet Odin at the Bifrost site with the children, and he would take all six of them back to Asgard - just in case timeline changed, and it might only be on Earth. Or, in case they failed altogether.

"It's best this way, my love," Cordone said with pain lacing his own voice, and tears in his eyes as well. He was holding her on the sofa as were the other men holding their mates in the various overstuffed chairs.

"I know, but it's just so hard!" Kaitlan wailed.

"Kaitlan's right," Lynne sniffed.

Richard had no idea what to do with this side of Lynne. He had never seen her this sad, nor this emotional before, let alone see her cry! He, too, was sad, but his upbringing as a warrior taught him to push it to the back when danger was present. Richard wrapped his arms around his mate, and kissed her head. Maybe he was more "human" than he thought after all. And, he was discovering that it was not such a bad thing. Lynne snuggled into his neck.

Though not crying, Sam held Sarah. She had no child, but she was sad for her friends. Maybe it was better they had no child at this point.

Finally, Sarah sat up, dried her eyes, and slapped her legs as she stood.

"Come on girls! Let's go clean up. There's never anything better than physical work for the blues."

Dan who was holding Anita on his lap, nodded silently, and standing up she joined Sarah who had already started for the kitchen. Kaitlan and Lynne followed.

"Come on, guys. We need to do some Clan work. Let's head for my office," Cordone leaped up to the landing in front of his office with the other three men following.

The truth was, it was all "filler" work. There was really no reason to clean, or work on Clan matters, but this is what people do when faced with finality.

Later that night, Cordone and Kaitlan phased to go for a run. With the wind in their fur, and the ground under their paws, it was exhilarating to be outside under the stars. After hours of running, the two wolves circled each other, sniffing. Remembering her words to Anita earlier, she realized that Anita was right. Kaitlan may have said "a run", but what she *really* meant was sex. Lots of it!

"The smell of your arousal is intoxicating, Kaitlan!"

She cocked her wolf head, pointing it in a downward manner. She took a good look at her mate's underbelly. Eyes wide, she still could never get over the size of his cock in his wolf form!

"Well, the sight of your humongous cock is equally intoxicating, Cordone. It's just so damn big!"

The two wolves nuzzled muzzles.

"Present yourself for me, my beautiful White Wolf!"

Cordone ordered playfully.

Kaitlan pretended to think by cocking her head at her mate, again. She pranced back and forth as if she was considering his suggestion.

"Well, I don't know. I mean, just what are you planning?"

Cordone leaned his head back, and howled. The howl sounded like laughter to her, and her wolf eyes narrowed.

"You want me to come out and say it, don't you?" he told her.

"Yep. I'm in the mood for dirty talk!" she laughed.

"OK. Then, I want you to stick that gorgeous pussy in my face so I can slam my giant cock into it!"

"What is it with you and the word 'pussy', Cordone? You use it a lot lately! And, how can I have one when I'm not a cat, but a wolf?" she giggled as she pranced in front of him, turning her butt toward her mate.

"Details, schmetails! I'm not interested in debating my use of words with you! Just put it in front of my face!" Cordone ordered again.

And, with a huge wiggle, Kaitlan had no problem at all with Cordone's "order".

Hours later, and dawn arrived. They had gone to their private pool, and dressed in the hiking clothing they usually left there, Cordone left Kaitlan. She had asked for a few moments alone to contemplate what was coming. He understood that she really wanted to say a prayer, and giving her that honor, went to the house.

Kaitlan sank down to one knee, and bowed her head in prayer to the great Creator.

"I do not know what is to come, but I ask that you give the eight of us the courage to do whatever is necessary to stop Zanack. And, stop him, we must. It is in your design to have us set things right. I do not know why you chose the other girls and me, but it does not matter. We will follow your will."

Kaitlan stopped a moment thinking about what else she wanted to say.

"I ask only one thing. That you give us courage, and the presence to deal with Zanack. Lots of blood will be spilled. Many of us, if not all of us, will die in this. It is certain. If we succeed in reversing the timeline, and reverting it to the way it should have flowed, none of us even knows if we will exist. Oh, Great Creator! Please give us courage to do what we must no matter how terrible it might be. I pray for us to succeed. Zanack needs to be ended - forever. He has done enough damage. It's time to stop him. Amen."

Kaitlan stood, grabbed her purple jacket that matched her purple workout clothes, and sauntered slowly toward the house. Knowing their time was limited, it was decided that they would begin to control Zanack instead of him controlling them. They were ready to end it.

"We have to get this over with, *now*. We all know what is at stake. We all know sacrifices will be made. But, we have to end this," Cordone told everyone seeing Kaitlan walk into the room. "Girls, you have all pretty much mastered your powers, and we are only delaying the inevitable."

"So. We go back." Dan stated the obvious.

Cordone shook his head. "Yes, to prepare. We are going to control the when and how. We already know the place, so, we will force *him* come to *us*."

"Ah, but only *when* we are ready! I see. No problem, then," Dan answered.

OK. No problem. Just take your time, but hurry it up!

They headed back to St. Louis to begin their final plans. It was important that they still kept Zanack "hopping" around until they were ready. The council room was probably the worst place to meet, but it was the only one. Or, so they thought. Of course, knowing the penchant for surprises with this group, naturally, there was another surprise! This one from Kaitlan.

"So, just how do we accomplish getting him to come to us, Cordone? Up until now, Zanack has had the upper hand. How do we force him to come to us?" Sarah asked aloud what everyone else was thinking.

They were still in the jet and eight pairs of eyes just looked around at each other, while Lynne was on the phone discussing some small problem one of the employees was having. The council room was no longer safe for the council, or anyone else. Even thought they thought the jet was safe, it was not totally secure. A place was needed where they could lay out their plans where no one would know where they were. Even Richard's destroyed city didn't fit the bill. They needed a place no one knew existed. Several ideas bounced around between them, but none of them was good enough.

Kaitlan solved the problem when they gathered in her Father's office in the Seneca Publishing building.

"Well, there is a place we can go," Kaitlan had said.

One that no one knew existed - except for Kaitlan. She had been hesitant to tell them, and she shrugged when she did tell them about it. Surprise was evident on their faces.

"So? what? Everyone has at least one secret! And, it wasn't really mine to tell anyway until I needed to do so," she had told them.

"One?   Just one? Seriously, Kaitlan?" Richard sneered.

Kaitlan had turned to stare at him in surprise.

"That's rich, especially coming from the great god,

Thor, who told everyone everything about himself up front and center?"

Richard just grinned at her.

When someone had asked if one of them should remain behind in case someone was suspicious, Lynne had volunteered.

"Just in case something comes up, and we needed a fast answer," Lynne had said to them. Richard would fill her in later.

Kaitlan led the way to the elevator. It was specifically designed not to stop on the secret floor - ever. There was nothing on the panel inside the elevator indicating anything was hidden. Only Kaitlan had the key to it, and knew the combination to press in order stop the elevator at the hidden, thirteenth floor. Cordone narrowed his eyes at her while they were in the elevator, but said nothing. Again, Kaitlan just shrugged as she stepped back to let everyone exit, and, of course, everyone rolled their eyes at the "thirteenth floor" cliché.

Kaitlan, periodically, had used it for quiet when she had a school project, or just wanted to be alone. When she was young, she could just "disappear" whenever she wanted. Through the years, though, she had made sure there was furniture on the floor. She had added things like a desk, desk chair, comfy chairs that her Dad helped her with late at night, and even a nice large bed in case she wanted to sleep, or she needed to pull an all-nighter. The windows were dark, but you could see out - just not inside the floor. In fact, the outside was designed to make sure that there were no windows indicating another floor existed. And, that's how her Dad had hidden it! The design was ingenious.

Kaitlan remembered the day her Father took her to the "secret thirteenth floor" of the building. It was completely deserted, and completely empty. And, her Father had told her why. Even though she was almost seven at the time, and she didn't know that she was a werewolf at that point, her Father declared that she was his heir At that point, he had told her that if anything should ever happen to him, and danger was imminent, this is where they could meet in secret.

"Why Daddy?" Kaitlan had asked him at the time.

"Kaitlan, call this our 'secret battle plan' floor. And, while I have never had to use it, it is possible that some day, you will have to do so. I show this to you, so that you know that even in the midst of great danger, it is a place of safety that you can lay out battle plans if ever need be."

"Geez, Daddy? Battle plans? That's for war!" Her nose had wrinkled.

"Yes, it is, sweetie, but even 'the best laid plans of mice and men' can get really messed up!"

"That's really funny, Daddy! Where did you get that one?"

"From Robert Burns."

"Who?"

"Robert Burns was a poet who wrote 'To a Mouse'."

Kaitlan had giggled. "Why was he writing a poem to a mouse?"

Canaan had given his daughter his best imitation of a cartoon character with huge wide eyes.

"Huh?" he had asked mockingly. "I shudder at what the educational system is teaching you kids these days!"

"Did you know him?" Kaitlan had asked.

Canaan had answered, but not completely.

"Kaitlan. He lived in the eighteenth century," he answered dryly.

And, that had been that. Now, she realized that maybe her Dad had met him - in person!

"So, this is a shocker. Why didn't you tell us about it before, Kaitlan?" Dan asked.

"It's called a 'secret floor' for a reason, Dan. Good

grief!"

The floor was very plush. Canaan had decorated it per Kaitlan's design, and was for someone who wanted to "disappear" for a while. While it was totally empty at first, there were several basic bedrooms, a full kitchen, no less than four baths, and a gigantic meeting room with a huge table and chairs.

"*This* is where you disappeared to those times I couldn't find you, and your Dad told me you were visiting relatives?" Sarah asked in surprise.

"Well. Yeah," Kaitlan told her sheepishly.

"Why you little bitch!" Sarah said to her bestie, but laughed.

Kaitlan grinned at her.

"You sneaky, little bitch!" Sarah said, again. "You knew all the time about this floor, and didn't tell me? Your bestie?"

"What about it? Daddy warned me that if I ever told, I'd be sent to boarding school. I wasn't about to let that happen!"

"Ewww! And, that would mean we wouldn't see each other?"

"Exactly."

"Enough said. You're forgiven. 'End of Line'," Sarah hugged her best friend while Kaitlan shook her head at the line from "Tron". Well, she had to admit. It was very apropos in this situation.

They gathered around the table in the meeting room. Like the main floor, two walls were open to a lovely view even though no one could see into the floor at all.

Cordone propped his left hip on top of the table, dangling his left foot just above the floor while everyone else pulled out a chair.

"So far, more research in The Hall of Records has been fruitless, so I guess we need to stop trying to find anything there," Cordone stated.

"Well, it's obvious why, isn't it? Zanack must have found what he needed. If we can't find anything, then he must have it, right?" Sarah questioned.

"Not necessarily, Sarah, but we have to assume he has found whatever was left to find given the fact he seems to be about ready."

"So, we have no idea how this is going to happen, right?" Anita reasoned aloud.

"That's about right. I think we can also ditch the 'how'. So, that leaves only the when. Anyone have any idea how to force Zanack's hand? Speak now, or forever shut the hell up," Sarah declared.

As usual, everyone looked at her in puzzlement.

"What? I'm just sayin'! "

"I just realized something. You know, Johnson hasn't been around for the last two days to help in the Hall. Anyone know where the hell he is?" Anita asked.

Everyone was silent, and all had the same question. Just *where* the hell *was* Johnson?

~ 4 ~
Missing? Missing isn't good

Apparently, Canaan had even thought to install an intercom and phones on the thirteenth floor, and Cordone pushed the intercom button that went straight to Johnson's office.

"Xavier, here."

"Xavier, this is Cordone. Do you have any idea where Johnson happens to be?"

"No, Alpha. I don't. We noticed he was missing yesterday, but no one seems to know where he was. Personally, I haven't seen him in a couple of days. It's kinda strange. We thought we would check it out before contacting you. I was just about to call you."

"Did he tell you anything about where he was going?"

"No, Alpha. I'd like to help, but honestly, we've all been wondering that ourselves."

"You haven't heard, or seen, him in at least two days?" Cordone wanted to verify what he had just heard.

"No, Alpha. He just took off, and we haven't seen him since. I think we were all thinking that you had ordered him to go somewhere?"

Cordone didn't want to reveal too much.

"Hmmm. Well, if he returns, have him contact me immediately, will you?"

"I will, Alpha."

"Thanks, Xavier."

Cordone let the intercom button go, and leaned back running his hands through his hair.

"Cordone," began Sam, "I've never known him to

just disappear before. Something isn't right."

"Agreed. I don't know what's going on, but we need to find out. Excuse me a minute."

Cordone pulled out his cell phone ignoring Kaitlan's growl of warning. Making sure his location services were off, he made a quick call to McClain, who said he would get on it immediately. Shutting his cell phone down, Cordone was getting a very, very bad feeling about this. It wasn't like Johnson to take off without telling anyone.

Before Cordone could walk ten steps, his cell rang. It was McClain? That was fast!

"What?" Cordone snapped, then, "Sorry, McClain."

"Don't worry about it. We are all under stress. I found Johnson. You are not going to like this, Cordone. He has left The Hall!"

"Left The Hall? Who gave him permission to do that?"

"I was with Lynne when you called. She informed me that she had just gotten off the phone with Johnson. Said he told her that he had some business to attend to, and he wouldn't be back for a while! Didn't give her any explanation as to where he was heading at all. When she pressed, he just hung up on her. You know what this might mean? This could confirm your suspicions, you know?"

"Agreed. It's too coincidental, McClain. Way too coincidental."

"Wait…Lynne wants to talk to you," interrupted McClain.

McClain handed his phone to Lynne.

"Cordone. I don't know if it was, or wasn't, Johnson," she said looking at McClain.

"Why?"

"I don't know. Something didn't sound right with his voice. It just didn't sound like him, yet it did. He sounded raspy - as if he was getting a cold. I asked him where the hell he was, and that is when he hung up on me!"

Cordone's eyes shut as he dropped his head. Damn! No one had ever thought of Johnson as a traitor, but maybe…? Little did anyone else know that there was one other person with access to the Council Chambers, and that was Johnson. He was given the right to the room, because he was always leaving information that he had researched for the Council. The council members didn't know about it. Even Kaitlan didn't know. At least he didn't think any council member knew. Maybe he was wrong! His hand squeezed tightly on his phone, and there went another one! He saw Kaitlan shake her head at him - again.

"Shit!" he said to no one in particular. Then, he ordered, "Lynne. First, get me another phone, and second, can you get a trace on where his phone is?"

She looked at McClain who shook his head, and took his phone back. Lynne already had a new phone in her hand, and headed into Cordone's office to put it on his desk.

"We already tried that, Cordone. I asked Lynne to check on it. Nothing. He obviously turned off his location services. Hang on a sec. Lynne says she just got an idea."

Cordone heard a lot of tapping on a keyboard of the computer.

"Yes! Man, I'm good! Got him!" Lynne exclaimed.

"Lynne found where he was before he turned it off. He must have thought of it afterward, but Lynne found a last location on him," McClain told him.

"Where?"

Cordone asked, and McClain handed the phone back to Lynne.

"You definitely are *not* going to like this, Cordone. He's in Colorado! I am calling Tim, now, to get the jet ready!"

"Right. Thanks."

Cordone shut the phone down. He turned to the others.

"It seems that Zanack has anticipated our actions. Let's go to the airport! I'll explain on the way!"

They all left the building in what Sarah termed, afterward, as "super-duper werewolf speed". Lynne joined them as they poured into their cars, and proceeded straight to the airport where the plane took off within minutes of boarding.

"I can't believe it!" Sam was shocked. "We all trusted him!"

Sarah was thinking hard. This was just too easy, or maybe just too convenient.

"I have a very bad feeling about this!"

Everyone turned to look at her. OK. She was nervous, and she wasn't about to let a perfectly good quote from Han Solo in "Star Wars" go to waste!

"What? So? Sue me!" she said aloud. Then, "*Too convenient,*" she muttered in her mind.

Sam turned to her. "*What, Tink?*"

"*It's just too convenient, Sam. Too coincidental. There just is no such thing as coincidence. You know I don't believe in it. Why would Johnson head to Colorado? What possible reason could he have?*"

Sarah turned to Cordone, and spoke aloud. "Has he ever been to your house?"

Cordone said, "No." He stopped. If he had, Cordone certainly didn't remember it. "Not that I know of, but honestly? I have no idea."

Sarah drummed her fingers on the seat arm. Her mind worked fast and quick. Finally, Sarah unbuckled her seatbelt, and jumped up from her seat.

"Of course! I don't know why I didn't see this before!" She turned to everyone. "It makes sense! Look.

Everything has happened on Cordone's land, right? Kaitlan became The White Wolf, there. We mated there, got pregnant there." She whirled to Cordone. "*Is* there something special about your land, Cordone? Something else you forgot?"

Everyone looked at her. They'd been on this seesaw over and over without answers.

"OK, look. I know we've batted this idea around before, but maybe it is far more important than even we thought. Is there? I mean…is there something that maybe you forgot? Maybe magical? Supernatural? Anything at all?"

Cordone frowned. His land. Something special. They already knew there was something there, but he didn't remember what, if he had ever known in the first place. He shook his head.

"I just know it's my ancestral home, Sarah. I mean, it's always been magical to me, but to anyone else? I don't understand why it would be. I mean, I can't think of anything. And, if I ever did know? Well, as I said before. I just don't remember."

"History, man, history! What's the history?" Sarah pressed with the same question. If she could press Cordone hard enough, he might remember something.

Cordone tried to remember what little he did know.

"Sarah, you're like a huge bug!" Cordone replied. She just grinned at him. "Well, let's see. The house was commissioned by my parents, and they hired the Elves to build it, for one thing. The Elves were adamant that it be carved into the mountain - to keep the pristine look of nature. I guess you could call them the first environmentalists. As for carving rock, well, only the Elves have those kinds of skills. Hmmm. They use their supernatural abilities, so I guess, if you think about it in that way, well, I guess it would be magical. To tell you the truth, though, it's kind of hard to remember that far back."

Kaitlan frowned. What did Cordone mean, he couldn't remember? After all the stories he had told her, and he couldn't remember about this one thing? Because, it was "too far back"? That was truly odd. He remembered everything else. So why couldn't he remember this one part of his life? She narrowed her eyes. She wished that they had time to figure it all out, but they just didn't.

"Cordone. What do you mean you can't remember that far back? You remember everything! Your stories about your past have all been highly detailed. I know. You've told me about them. For the Creator's sake! Why the hell can't you remember something momentous like the carving of your house?"

"*OUR* house, Kaitlan," he reminded her, again, absently. "I have to admit. That's a really great question."

"*Please, my sexy mate,*" Kaitlan used her mind to him. Aloud, "You have to try to remember! There is something just not right about all of this. Something we are missing."

Cordone nodded, and shut his eyes. But no matter how hard he tried, it was as if a brick wall was blocking his memories from that time period. He was just a boy, of course, but he was a werewolf boy. It was as if his mind had been blocked. But, why? Did someone deliberately block his memory?

"Well, take your time, but hurry it up, will you?" Kaitlan sighed.

Sarah looked at her friend, and did a double take. Then, she grinned.

The land. Cordone was trying to wade through all those years back when he was a little boy. Memories of happiness, and loss when his parents had been killed in the Vampire Wars. And, the last time he actually remembered ever seeing them alive. The house and land had always been a haven for him. A place of peace, and contemplation. Then, suddenly, he was able to move one of those bricks, and he remembered a conversation that he had heard when he was about four or five. He closed his eyes to try wading through the hazy muck. He opened his eyes, again. Why was this part of his life so hazy? He remembered everything else so damned well. He closed his eyes again, and tried to bring up the words that were just barely coming back to him.

Everyone watched as Cordone struggled. Finally, Kaitlan put her hand on his shoulder.

"Cordone, let's go to the bedroom. You need quiet away from everyone.

"No. No. It's not necessary," he told her. "Some of it is coming back to me. I just need everyone to be silent for a minute."

There was dead silence except for the hum from the jet engines.

Ten minutes went by, and everyone decided it wasn't helping the way they were staring at him constantly. So, Lynne pulled out her iPad to read. She was way past catching up with her Facebook. Dan slithered to the coffee pot, and poured himself a cup of coffee with cream and sugar. Anita and Richard pulled out the cards. No one else ever wanted to play with them, because they were such great con artists! Sam pulled Sarah onto his lap, and they curled up together deciding to take a quick nap. Kaitlan sat quietly beside Cordone gently stroking his temples. She could see he was struggling to remember. She could feel his struggle, and her heart broke for him. Who in the hell had done this to him? It must have been so bad that Cordone had blocked it out. But, what?

Cordone's mind was wading through a very murky haze - like London's fog. He couldn't see even a hand in front of him. There was a way that he hadn't used but once, and he had not put himself in a trance in years. If they had enough time, and as a flat out last resort, he would call Nico Ricci. Nico was not just an ordinary vampire. He was one of only three Mind-Manipulators in the world. He could delve into people's minds to find even the tiniest detail. But, Nico was the best! He was the cream of the crop! He could do things the other three could not, but it was extremely dangerous. If one mistake were made, feasibly, it could kill the subject! If Nico pressed into his mind too fast, it could erase his subject's entire memory forever. When Nico was ready to pull his mind out of a person's mind, he needed to go slowly. Too fast, and it could erase memory. If only he were here, now. But, he wasn't, and there just was not enough time. He would have to do this alone.

"I'm placing myself into a trance. It may help me to remember."

Without waiting for anyone to answer him, Cordone closed his eyes, and in seconds, was in a trance. Patience was the key to this. He came to what looked like a brick wall. He looked for a hole, or a gap in the wall for a long time. Finally, he saw one, and broke through a tiny part of the haze, and pushed through it. His stomach clinched as a small, memory invaded his mind. Kaitlan could see that whatever he was doing, it was causing him much pain and agony. She tried to use their bond, but his mind was closed to her. She reasoned that it must be the trance.

At first, he heard voices in his mind that blurred into each other, and finally, he was able to distinguish his Dad's voice, which was extremely angry. Then, the more he concentrated, the clearer the voices, and he heard his Father talking. But to whom?

" 'NO'!" his Father had yelled.

His Father's voice was so loud, it startled Cordone, and he almost lost the trance.

" 'I'm not asking you, Zoar. I'm *telling* you what

you are going to do!' "

Cordone began to speak aloud softly, and everyone stopped whatever they were doing. Sarah hopped to attention as she bounded out of Sam's lap, and ran to kneel next to Cordone. Something had happened to her while she had been asleep. Another power had been given to her, and this time, she wouldn't fight it. She would go with it.

"Don't fight it, Cordone. Let it come naturally. Let your mind hear nothing but the words. Let them flow like a slow stream. Concentrate on that, and that alone. I will be able to help you if you get stuck, OK?" Sara told him.

She took over from Kaitlan who moved aside to let Sarah take over the massaging of his temples.

Cordone nodded, then he began to repeat what he heard aloud.

"I remember something. It's not much, but my Dad's voice was damned angry. I don't know who was on the receiving end. I don't know who the other voice belonged to, but I do remember it was a man."

He continued with a frown as he tried to drag up a memory of thousands of years ago. Another memory popped through. Johnson *was* there! What the hell had Johnson been doing in his house? He voiced it aloud.

"Wait a second! Johnson? Johnson really *was* there!" Cordone said in surprise as he voiced his thoughts aloud.

"OK. My Dad was angry. Very, very angry. In fact, I had never heard him so mad!"

"Who was he angry at, Cordone?" Sarah asked in an almost whisper.

"Johnson. My Dad was angry at Johnson. But, it wasn't just Johnson. Someone else was there, too." He shook his head as he frowned trying to bring the vision into focus.

"No. Can't remember who it was, damn it!"

His head was beginning to hurt - badly, and as he tried to rub his own temples, Sarah brushed his hands away as she continued to apply gentle pressure to his head.

Kaitlan frowned.

"Headache?" she asked.

He nodded.

"Yeah."

"I'll get you some aspirin," she said as she stood to go into the bathroom.

"No, Kaitlan. We cannot afford him to be under the influence of any drug. Even aspirin. Anything that might block his mind."

She turned back to Cordone.

"The headache is there from whatever, or whoever, tried to wipe your mind. The headache is the sign that your mind is breaking through. Your subconscious mind is trying to push through your blocked memories. Just relax, and pay attention to only my voice."

"Sarah is right, Kaitlan. I can't be under any drug, or everything I'm remembering might stop."

"But…" she began.

"No."

Kaitlan pouted as her mate was adamant about not accepting some aspirin, but she sat back down.

"I remember my Dad yelling at Johnson," he began, then stopped as some more of the conversation broke through.

"Hang on a moment! I remember more, now!"

His eyes closed, but his head came up as he spoke.

"Let's see…Dad said…." He paused for a few seconds, then continued.

" 'Johnson, you go too far! This is my land, not yours! I will not allow you to take it from me, or my family! And, most especially from my son!'

'You have no choice! You agreed to it when Ter'act

built this house! You gave part of your land to me!'

'No, I did not agree to any of that! We agreed that once the house was built, the Elves would be given the right to use this land on occasion, because its properties is one of ten places on Earth that greatly enhances the powers of supernatural beings! But, I certainly did not sign anything over to her, or to you!'

'Then, I will take it, Zoar!'

"Who is Ter'act, Cordone?" Sam interrupted.

"Oh," Cordone blinked his eyes coming out of the trance. "She was…she was…. YES! Now, I remember! She was Johnson's mate! How could I have forgotten that all this time?" Cordone asked himself. "Right. Let's see, where was I? Oh, right. I remember Ter'act screamed. It was the first time I had ever heard an Elf scream, and believe me! Once you hear it, you never forget!"

Everyone else nodded except for Kaitlan and Sarah who had never heard one scream. Lynne just grinned at everyone.

Cordone concentrated hard, but heard nothing else…just total silence. Damn! He couldn't remember one thing after that! Nothing else.

"Who was Ter'act, Cordone," Anita asked returning from the bathroom.

"What? Oh. She was Johnson's mate," he absentmindedly answered, again. "And, I have to admit that she was strange to put it mildly. Fuck! That's all I really remember. Why didn't I remember that before this, and why the hell can I not remember anything else?" Cordone wondered aloud.

Sarah took his hand in hers. She was about to show off her newest power that none of them had, and one they would never forget!

"Cordone, listen to me. You must try to remember more if you can. Please. You just confirmed to us that Ter'act told your Father that the land has properties to enhance supernatural powers. Finally, we have part of the answer."

Sarah turned to Anita.

"You were right, Anita, about the land, but only partly. There is no doubt, now, that the land is the cause of the reversal. The White Wolf appeared upon your land, Cordone. Kaitlan was the catalyst just as the prophecy said! And, because it happened there, it enhanced her, and her wolf's supernatural powers. I feel as if I am close to understanding more. But, I'm still missing something."

She turned back to Cordone, holding his hand.

"Cordone, think. Give me your other hand. Show me what you see."

"What?" Kaitlan demanded.

"It's a new power that I received. I don't really understand it, but I know that my mind can push into his, and manipulate his memories to release them fully."

Cordone's eyes opened, and stared at Sarah.

"Holy shit! You are a Mind-Manipulator!"

"A what?" Lynne asked him.

"What the hell is a Mind-Manipulator?" Kaitlan asked him.

Sara was still holding his hands as his face came up to meet hers.

"How is that possible? There are only three in the entire world!" Cordone was stunned to say the least.

"A what?" Sarah's eyes were wide, adding, "What Kaitlan asked?"

"A Mind-Manipulator. It's one of the most powerful gifts anyone can ever receive, Sarah. It basically means that you can enter a person's mind, and help them draw out whatever is keeping them from remembering. I was just wishing that Nico Ricci were here. He is the most powerful Mind-Manipulator to ever have walked the Earth!"

Everyone gasped, and a couple of them dropped

their mouths open in shock.

Sam had known of the three, but now, his own mate was one?

"Well, holy fuck!" Sam gasped.   A Mind-Manipulator! What else was being given to her?

"How do I work it?" she asked everyone.

Shrugs all around, then Anita spoke.

"All our powers seem to come naturally to us, Sarah. Perhaps this specific power is the same?"

Sarah thought about it a moment, then closed her eyes. In her mind, she saw how to manipulate the mind - of anyone. She could unblock, or block memories. She could destroy an enemy. She could help put a mind back together that was lost, or erase all memories from a person forever. Whoa! What a power! Yes. She knew what to do.

"I know what I need to do, Cordone. Will you submit my mind to manipulate yours in order to unblock what is blocked?"

Her mind would connect with Cordone. Maybe she could unlock what he couldn't remember.

"OK. Cordone. It is time. Give me your hands. I have to touch skin to skin to do this."

Cordone took Sarah's hands, and nodded once.

"Let's do this, Sarah. I'm sick of not knowing."

"Then, if you are ready …" Sarah began, "close your eyes, and open your mind to mine."

There was complete silence on the jet from that point forward, and not even a breath could be heard.

Yes. This time, Cordone was confident he would know the past that had been blocked, and his real past during this time with his parents. As hard as it would be for him, Cordone would face what his mind had conveniently forgotten.

~ **5** ~

Mind Manipulation is Powerful

Sarah closed her eyes as well. Sarah felt her mind pushing into Cordone entering his mind.

"*Oh my! The mind is so complicated!*" Sara said to herself - and to Sam.

"*Really? Who would have thunk?*" joked Sam.

"*Ha, ha, Sam. Please, just shut up right now will you?*" Sam answered with a grin that Sarah didn't see, but felt.

Concentration was her main goal. Relaxation was the next. Finally, she began to push through his memories slowly, startling both of them.

"Whoa!" Cordone exclaimed.

"Just relax, Cordone, and know I am with you. There is nothing to be afraid of, and you need to relax. Whatever you do, don't let go of my hands, do you understand? I will push through your memories until I reach the block. This may take a great amount of time since I'm new at this, and I will need to go very, very slowly. I do not want to hurt you, or erase your memories."

Cordone had seen Nico work his "magic" once before, but never on himself. Quite frankly, watching him work had terrified him. Now, here he was allowing a brand new Mind-Manipulator to poke around in his mind. Maybe he shouldn't, but he would allow it. He had to know why he couldn't remember anything about that particular period of his life. Too much was at stake.

"First, can you remember how old you were, Cordone? Just a guess, I mean?" Sarah asked him.

"Well, I guess I was, maybe, four or five in wolf years? I'm not quite certain, but that sounds about right."

"OK. So, I need to go further back than I thought. Are you ready?" Sarah asked him.

"After what I have seen of Mind-Manipulation, no. Of course not! But, it has to be done."

Sarah began by holding his hands lightly stroking them. Cordone was so damn tense that he found it almost impossible to relax. He'd seen enough of manipulation that it was dangerous. But, he concentrated on Sarah's gentle voice, and bit by bit, Cordone began to relax. It allowed Sarah to begin moving through his mind searching for the block that prevented Cordone from remembering. Sarah slowly pushed through his mind.

When she felt his body tighten, she stopped until she felt Cordone relax, then would proceed.

Time passed slowly for everyone else, while both Sarah and Cordone lost all track of time. For a while, they just watched Cordone and Sarah, until they realized nothing was going to happen any time soon, so they decided that they might as well do something else. Kaitlan and Anita began to talk about the latest books that they had read, and when the Seneca Publishing House was going to publish the books of their newest authors. Dan and Sam decided to make sandwiches for everyone putting two of them into the small refrigerator for Cordone and Sarah. Lynne and Richard took up their card game, again. Except for the roar of the jet engines, it was relatively quiet.

In the meantime, Sarah kept pushing gently. It was amazing! The mind! It was so complicated, and because of Cordone's age, his knowledge was vast. As much as she might like to poke around to learn some of them, tempted even, it just seemed so wrong, somehow, to wander around in someone else's mind!

Time just seemed to stand still for both of them.

But, when she found the block, she was stunned. It had a physical appearance in the form of a locked and bolted door with no key. First, she tried to open it, but that was a futile effort. Second, she tried to go around the door only to find a heavy, block wall stopping her in her tracks.

"What else can I do?" she asked herself.

When she finally came up with an idea, she snapped her fingers! Sarah realized that she could "conjure" up anything she needed, because it was a "dream" world, in a way, but at the same time, real memories. So, she "dreamed up" a couple of bobby pins to pick the lock. She knelt down, and began to work. It took a long time, but finally, she heard a "click", and turned the knob. She grinned thinking that if her friends knew she could pick locks, how it would shock them about their little pixie! Well, it worked, and she slowly pushed the door inward.

Cordone's memory was still very hazy, but with Sarah's help, he was finally able to push the haze away to an extent that Sarah was able to pick the lock on the door. He smiled as he realized their little pixie could pick locks. Wondering how she knew, he pushed that aside to ask her someday. They passed through until they stood together on the fourth landing looking at the scene unfolding below them. Cordone was a little boy of about four, and Sarah held his hand. He was crouching hoping that those on the main floor would not see him, yet both of them could hear everything. One thing she noticed, though, was that the waterfall was not running. That must mean the house either was still being built, or had just been finished.

"Do you know what is happening, Cordone? Who are these people?" she asked him.

"I don't know what's going on, except there was yelling. But, below us are my Father, Zoar, and my Mother, Marta. And, the tall Elf is called Ter'act, Johnson's mate."

It was really odd that Sarah heard him speak as an adult, but with a child's voice. If only Kaitlan could see him this way! He was an adorable little boy!

"Anyone else?" she wanted to know.

He shook his head, and then stopped.

"Well, Johnson is in the shadows to the left, I think. So, he has been at my family's house!" Cordone was furious with himself for not remembering!

"OK, Cordone. It's obvious that we won't be able to hear, or watch everything below us, so let's try something else."

Using her mind, she told Cordone that they should be on the main floor with Johnson and Zoar, and… they were on the main floor! It was a case of think it, and it happens.

Now, Sarah could see the faces that matched the voices, and she could see what was really happening right along with Cordone. She was truly amazed that she was able to do this as she felt the power flow through her. How the hell was she able to do this? Tara and Canaan had told her she would be developing powers, but they had never told her they would be anything like this!

Yet, it was what happened next that truly showed Sarah the power of the mind. Her mind. She found herself being able to push into Zoar's mind! How was that even possible with something that was so far in the past? Briefly, she wondered if it was because Cordone was his son. However, while she'd love to stop, and try to figure it out, she was wasting time they didn't have. Sarah shook her head to concentrate on what was happening. She found that she could also pull Cordone into his Father's mind so he, too, could see. Now, they were both able to see the entire scene! Holy shit!

"How?" Cordone whispered.

"I don't know, but we can't waste any more time," Sarah shrugged.

Cordone nodded in agreement. Both of them were quiet as they watched the past play before their eyes. What they heard was slightly different from what Cordone had told them earlier. Cordone's memory had left out some things.

"We listen only, Cordone. We cannot change the past."

"Shhh!" Cordone told her, and she gave him one nod, then settled back to listen and watch.

" 'Johnson, you go too far! The land is mine, not yours! I will not allow you to take it from me, or my family! And, most especially, I will *never allow* you to take it from my son! This is my family's land, and it is his inheritance!'

'You have no choice, Zoar! You agreed to the terms given to you when Ter'act built this house! You gave part of your land to me!'

'No, I did not agree to any of that! Ter'act only oversaw the building! Marta and I designed it, and the Elves agreed to build it. The Agreement was with the Elven Clans that once the house was built, the Elves would be given the right to use it on occasion, since its properties enhance the powers any supernatural being! Never did we make an agreement with you alone! And, I certainly did not *sign* anything over to Ter'act, or to you!'

'Then, I will take it, Zoar!' screamed Ter'act as only an Elf can do. 'This land is mine! I still cannot believe that my own people allowed your disgusting family of werewolves to own this land!'

What Cordone had not seen, or heard, was the rest of the argument. They both watched, and Cordone's anger and horror rose as he saw what happened through his Father's eyes.

Zoar noticed that Cordone was watching them from above, and his eyes were full of terror.

'My son does not need to see any of this, Ter'act!'

Ignoring Zoar's pleading, Ter'act forced Zoar to his knees using her Elven powers telling Johnson what she was going to do.

'I will take care of Zoar and Marta, and then, Cordone! I will kill all of them! Go get the little whelp!' she ordered.

Johnson started toward the lift.

'Cordone!' cried Zoar, obviously in tremendous pain. Without looking up, he yelled, 'Go to your room, son. Lock the door, and don't let anyone in! *RUN!*'

The idea that Sarah could see through the eyes of multiple people at once had to be a huge deal! This was far beyond anything she thought she could do! If it was like this for her, what about him?

Little Cordone started to turn, but didn't obey his Father. Why was it Sarah was not one bit surprised at this? Instead, he dropped to his knees to keep out of sight as his Father told him to do should he ever encounter something bad he might witness. And, then, no matter what to report it to Canaan as fast as he could. Little Cordone could still watch, but not as well as he would have been able to had he been standing. But he could hear, and knew that his parents were in danger. Cordone wanted so much to help, but he knew he would never have a chance against an adult, let alone an Elf. He was terrified for his parents, because they could never hold their own against Ter'act's powers. Worse yet? Neither could he!

Zoar felt his son's eyes on him. It killed him to know he had not obeyed him, and was still watching. He also knew that he and Marta, his mate, were dead. Never had he ever wanted his son to see death. But, he would watch his Father and Mother murdered. There was a reason that he told Little Cordone to report to Canaan. He did not have the strength against an Elf. As if he and Marta did! Silently, apologizing to his son, he turned his face to Ter'act.

'You will never get away with this, Ter'act. And, Johnson, I will hunt you down to the end of time! Do you understand me? And, if not me, my son will come after you! I'm glad that Cordone won't have to worry about Ter'act!'

'You will *not* touch my mate! Do *not* threaten my mate, Zoar! You will *not* win!'

'Keep thinking that, Johnson. I do not threaten anyone without cause.'

'You think that your measly threat means anything to me? It does not! You will not kill her!'

Zoar nodded in agreement.

'You are correct, Johnson. *I* am not going to kill her,' his eyes looked beyond Johnson.

Johnson's eyes widened in terror as he whirled around. Suddenly, a beautiful, silver wolf appeared from nowhere, and jumped onto Ter'act's back causing her to fall to the floor on her face. Marta's mouth dripped with blood. Ter'act tried to reach behind her to yank the wolf off of her back, but she couldn't. Then, the silver wolf made a huge mistake, and jumped forward. She leaned forward opening her mouth to grab Ter'act's throat. Marta wanted to see Ter'act's face as she broke her neck!

Instead, Ter'act reached up, grabbed Marta by her mouth, and threw her over her shoulder. She stood quickly before Marta could even stand up. Ter'act grabbed the wolf by the throat, and threw the wolf against the wall breaking Marta's back. She was dead. Ter'act breathed hard, then felt something thick and warm running down her back. She turned, and looked down. At her feet lay a large pool of blood and flesh that once covered the back of her throat. She grasped the back of her neck, but felt nothing there except the bones of her spine, which had almost been severed by Marta. Her eyes shot to Johnson in shock, then they rolled back into her eye sockets. Ter'act's head and neck fell forward onto her chest hanging by only a small amount of flesh still left on the right side of her neck.

Johnson roared in anger and pain while Zoar watched Marta with pride even as she lay dead. He knew that he would follow within days without Marta. Zoar would go down fighting, and join Marta in death. Even a minute without her was too long. The only thing he regretted was his son seeing it all happen, and leaving him alone. He knew that Canaan would take Cordone in, and keep him safe. And, that was enough to help him do what he had to do.

Sarah was horrified and nauseous as she watched all this unfold. She couldn't believe what a werewolf was capable of doing - what she would be capable of doing! She wanted to stop, to pull away from Cordone's memories, but she couldn't tear her eyes away. She knew if she did, she would miss seeing the truth, and that just was not an option. But, worse than that was that she could tell that Cordone, while having seen it all happen the first time, was more horrified than she was. Seeing what he did not remember unfold before his eyes, must be the most soul-wrenching thing he had ever seen in his life! Sarah could feel his desperation to know why. Unfortunately, they may never know the entire reason. So, as more and more bile rose in her throat, Sarah continued to watch while her heart broke for having to put Cordone through this!

Johnson's face registered shock as he saw his mate's head fall to the floor as the small bit of flesh tore from her neck. His face contorted with more anger and hatred watching as her body followed. He started to attack Zoar, but stopped as if someone had yanked him back. Instead, he issued a threat against the Clan.

'Everything is because of Dillon O'Hara, and your life is forfeit as of now. It will continue to his son, his son's sons, until all their line is dead! However, your line is ended today. Here and now!'

Both Sarah and Cordone frowned. Strange. It didn't sound like Johnson's voice. But, they saw no one else. They looked at each other wondering what any of this had to do with Dillon?

'Perhaps you take my life tonight. Perhaps it will not be you, but another. But, your time is limited, Johnson. Perhaps your life will be taken by my son, or by The White Wolf when you return to this land. It may even be taken by the one you serve, because of your blind following. Whatever way the Creator chooses, you will be ended forever! Your horror is only beginning. May the great Creator serve on you justice from now, and even after your death!'

Zoar phased quickly, and darted through the door avoiding the glass.

'Oh, but it *will* be me!' " screamed Johnson.

Johnson darted after him. Zoar could hear Johnson's feet bounding down the deck behind him only to stop abruptly. But, he could still hear running feet. It was a different sound unlike a human footfall. And, it certainly didn't sound like a werewolf! Zoar stopped, and whirled around to face this enemy only to register fear…pure, unadulterated fear at what was in front of him.

Sarah and Cordone watched Zoar breathe his last breath of life as he was sliced to pieces! They saw Johnson standing in the doorway looking out at them with a huge grin on his face. It wasn't Johnson? Johnson was not his killer? Then, who?

Both of them had a brief glance at what killed Zoar, and that is when Sarah pulled out of Zoar and little Cordone's mind, as well as Cordone. Sarah's immediate instinct was to yank her mind out of his without waiting, but she stopped from doing so. Pulling out slowly, and when she was safely out, Sarah yanked her hands away from Cordone, and started to scream and cry uncontrollably! Sam gathered her in his arms.

Cordone just stared unblinking at what he had seen, and then he broke down in to great sobs of pain. Kaitlan ran to his side, and pulled his head to her breast holding him as her mate's breakdown continued. She began to cry while seeing their pain echoing in both Sarah and Cordone's faces…hear it in their voices.

Cordone was in such pain. Why? Why had he not remember all that he had seen until now? Who had taken his memories away to keep him from seeing the truth? But, at the same time, he also realized that if he had remembered them, his life could have turned out much different! He had no doubt that he would have turned into a rogue werewolf from what he had just witnessed.

No one spoke for a very long time as they watched two of their own suffer horrendously.

Finally, Sarah slowed her crying, and Dan, very gently, asked her what she saw.

"I don't kn-know!" Sarah stuttered between sobs. "It was horrible! *HORRIBLE*! Oh, Creator, Sam! I've never seen anything like it!" she cried as her wails began again.

For a long time, there was silence except for Sara and Cordone's cries. When, their cries ceased, again, Cordone spoke in soft gulps.

"I-I thought they had died in the Vampire Wars," he whispered. "I don't understand? Why did I not remember this? I saw it, y-yet didn't remember? Why?"

Anita bent to hold Cordone's hands with tears streaming down her face.

"You were a little boy, Cordone. Sometimes, our minds see things that are so horrific, it shuts down to protect us. Your mind could not process the truth, therefore it put up a block to keep you from remembering. Whoever found you realized this, and took you into his care."

"I remember that Dillon took me in, and that's how Canaan and I came to be the best of friends." He looked at Kaitlan. "Kind of what you wanted to happen to Sarah, so you could be sisters. But, Dillon told me that they had been killed in the Vampire Wars. He lied to me!" He said as he looked back at Anita.

"Why, Anita? Why would he lie to me?"

"Easy, Cordone. When they found you and your parents' bodies, they must have realized you didn't remember at all. He kept you in the dark, because your own mind 'erased' it. Dillon must have figured it out, and played along. The alternative may have set your feet on another path that could have ended in your own hatred driving you to kill. Perhaps, like me, you would have turned rogue, and it is highly possible that not even Dan could have brought you back. We'll never really know, but that would be my biggest guess."

"Sarah. What did you see? Who killed Zoar?" Sam asked her.

"Not who, Sam. What! Zoar had no idea who killed him until he was already being sliced to pieces! It was…Oh, Creator! I can't describe what I saw! It was so horrible - and, so fast!"

Richard knelt by Sarah.

"Try your best, Sarah. We need to know, because if what you saw is still around, then we are truly in far more danger than we thought."

"And, Cordone? What did you see?" Cordone was silent, but Sarah nodded her head, and took a deep breath.

"I didn't see all of it. Just a glimpse. But, its eyes were," she shuddered at the memory. "its eyes were a burnt orange color. They were elongated. The face was very large - the size of a massive lion. And, it was long! Really, really long! It had no hair that I was able to see, but something like the scales of a leviathan, and its teeth were like razors. The mouth opened just before it killed Zoar. It reminded me of sharks' teeth. Yes. That's right! Sharks' teeth, but so much worse! Row upon row upon row of nothing but sharp, pointed, rotten, yellow, and black teeth!" Sarah really wanted to throw up again, but she was determined not to let that happen.

"I saw it, too," Cordone agreed. "It was huge! Monstrous!"

"Yes. You're right, Cordone. But, it was too close. I can't believe that I saw through your Father's eyes. How did this happen? He's been dead a long time."

Lynne dropped down next to Sarah.

"I don't know what exactly happened to you, Sarah. But, remember what Canaan and Tara told you. You were given powers to understand. Perhaps they were given to you to understand with not only your research, but also the power to see through not only the eyes of the living, but the dead. It is a powerful gift. Those kinds of powers are only given to one who is completely worthy of such powers."

"Yeah? Well, as cool as that sounds, it ain't!" Sarah complained loudly.

Kaitlan continued to hold her mate tightly against her breast as he broke down in tears all over again. His memory released the floodgates as they returned to him. It's so hard to watch people you love break down like that, but to watch a male Alpha do so, caused everyone's emotions to be so overwhelmed, and they all felt them.

Once again, their cries ended, and there was silence for a very long time.

It was Tim's voice over the intercom that shook everyone out of his or her own thoughts and sorrow. And, his cheerful voice was the last thing they wanted to hear.

"We will be landing in ten, everyone. Time to buckle up!"

~ 6 ~
Repeating Time

"OK. Anyone have any great ideas about what we're going to do if we find Johnson sacked out in Cordone's house?" Anita asked from the front seat of the black SUV that also carried Lynne, Richard, and Dan as well. "This whole thing has my tail twisted in knots!"

Dan looked at his mate in amusement, and laughed.

"Tail twisted into knots? Seriously, Anita? Wellll, on second thought, that might be a great thing to see! I so love your backside!"

Anita's face turned as red as a bog of raspberries! Everyone laughed so hard, the entire SUV shook, and Dan had a very hard time holding the vehicle on the road. It swerved from side to side, because he was laughing so hard at his mate. Luckily, they were driving down a road on Cordone's land, so he didn't have to worry about traffic!

Actually, the laughter broke the tension, and relaxed them. They all knew that whatever was going to happen was closer than ever, and just having a laugh was great.

In the other SUV, a green one, thanks to Kaitlan, things were more somber. Sam was holding Sarah tightly while Cordone had insisted on driving, much to Kaitlan's disapproval. She just didn't think her mate was alert enough to drive after what happened in the jet. They were behind the others as they wound their way up to the house. Seeing the SUV swerving ahead of them caused the four of them to look at each other in alarm. However, seconds later, Dan had the vehicle back on the road.

"What the hell was that all about?" Sam declared as

he looked at the SUV in front of them.

The other three just shrugged their shoulders.

"I'm sure we'll find out soon enough!" Sarah told him.

Kaitlan wondered if his beautiful home was going to look different to Cordone, now. Would it be traumatic to him? As usual, she forgot to shield her thoughts as Cordone answered her through their bond.

"I don't know how I feel, or how I will feel, mate. I still don't understand how I remembered zero to nothing about my parents being killed there!"

"Damn!" Kaitlan thought. When would she ever learn how to shield her thoughts? Cordone turned to look at the woman who was his life, and reached out his arm to slide her closer to him. When she was next to him, he felt much happier. Whole, and complete. She was his balance in life.

Kaitlan snuggled against him, and laid her head on his shoulder. She lowered her hand to stroke Cordone's very sensitive spot where the others couldn't see what she was doing. He jerked at her touch, but it was almost imperceptible to others.

"I love you, mate! I know. It's not the time, but I disagree. It is the time. It has to be. What's coming I just don't want to think about for awhile."

"Mate! You keep that up, and we won't make it out of the garage!" he laughed at her silently.

"Promises, promises!" Then, she remembered something. *"You know, I had this wonderful dream of you taking me in the back seat of that Rolls Royce Phantom II! I mean. It's just sitting there, not doing anything, right?"*

She felt him harden quickly under her hand at her description. And, grinned up at him.

"Really? In a car? Are you serious, Kaitlan? We are grownups, the parents of twins, and you want me to ravish you in one of my most prize possessions as if we

were horny teenagers? How would that look to our children?"

Kaitlan nodded her head slightly.

"Why not? I mean, it's not as if we got to do it before. And, our kids are babies, Cordone! Just how would they know?"

Cordone just turned to look at her. His eyes narrowed as his glowed into hers seeing hers glow right back at him.

"What? You don't want to be the horny teen who wants to have sex with his girlfriend in the back seat of a car? Who will take my body anywhere, and anyway, he wants? Because, I assure you, mate, I'm as horny as hell, and I have no intention of letting this last time we might have together go to waste!"

Cordone growled at her lightly.

"OK. If that's your dream, I guess it will happen!"

Kaitlan's head turned down, and she grinned. She felt heavy wetness pool in her core, and it increased with every mile they drove.

"Uh. Cordone?"

"Yes?"

"Are we there yet?" Kaitlan asked innocently.

He jerked as her hand groped him.

"About another five minutes," he said aloud to the rest of the group.

"DAMN!" Kaitlan thought to him with a mischievous wink. *"Just the thought of being naked with you pounding into my body in that classic car, well, I'm coming right now!"*

Cordone slipped his hand between her legs. Her jeans were soaked! His foot shoved down on the pedal. He couldn't get to his house fast enough, now! The SUV jerked forward as Cordone increased his speed!

In the meantime, Sam and Sarah were having their own private conversation.

"What if I'm not ready, Sam? What if I do something wrong? What if we do something wrong?"

"You won't, Tink! There is no one I have more confidence in than you, and the girls."

Sarah ducked her head laying it on his chest.

"Well, Hunkalicious! You know what? I could really use some of that wonderful mojo from Cujo when we get there!"

The last thing Sam had expected her to say was that, and he laughed outright. Trust his mate to come up with a name or a line from the many movies she had watched growing up, and Cujo from Stephen King was yet another! He hardened the minute she said Cujo. He made a subtle move so he could feel her breast with his hand.

"Cujo? I'm not a crazy dog, Tink!"

"Really? Well, you sure look like one when you're all furry, and most especially when you are horny! And, you know *how much I love furry stroking anywhere on my body, too! So, what's it going to be? Cujo, or not?"* she asked him, reaching down to "accidentally" brush against his hard cock with her hand.

Sam squeezed her tight against him grabbing her breast without worrying whether Cordone or Kaitlan could see. He just didn't care at that moment! She was *so* going to pay for that one!

"I'm ready, willing and able to pay for my mistakes with Cujo! Promise he'll do whatever? To have his way with me?" Sarah grinned up at him.

Sam sent her a picture of where he would take her, when, and most especially how.

Sarah's legs tightened as she felt wetness flow from her. It still surprised her that just a picture sent to her by Sam could give her an orgasm! How in the hell was he doing it? Even before they mated, he had been causing her to come at the most unbelievable times!

"This damn vehicle can't get to the house fast

enough for me, Tink!"

She slid her glowing eyes sideways to look up at him giving her that same devilish look she had given him that night when she had nicknamed him "Hunkalicious". Oh, man, thought Sam. I'm in trouble, now! Deliciously glorious trouble!

"You'd better believe it, Hunkalicious! And, don't lie! You LOVE it!"

"It's a good thing Kaitlan asked how far we have to go, because I don't know if I can even last those five minutes, Tink!"

The rest of the drive seemed to last *forever* to all the mates, because of their desires. Finally, the SUV's drove up to the house, and into the garage. They all exited the vehicles, stretched, and the men streaked through the house to make sure that Johnson was not there, before they proceeded to check the grounds. After a thorough search by the men without finding him, they were certain he wasn't in the house, nor was he anywhere within the vicinity of the house. It still didn't give them cause to relax, but it was a brief respite. They knew, though, that Johnson was *somewhere* nearby. The tracking on his phone seemed to be still indicating he wasn't moving. It was late, and he could be asleep. That might be possible. Now that they all knew what he had done, they were very certain that Johnson wouldn't try to take them on by himself. It tensed them up, but that seemed to satisfy them for the moment. Whatever was going down, it wasn't going to be tonight.

Everyone knew this might be the last time for them to be together as friends and lovers. All were determined to make the most of the time they had left. No doubt was in Kaitlan's mind that tomorrow was going to be the final showdown. It was becoming obvious that Zanack and Johnson were in league with some *thing*. From just the few things Sarah had described, it was horrific, and the same creature was also responsible for the death of Cordone's parents. Yet, what was Zanack's connection with them? That's something for which none of them had an answer.

The males met in Cordone's office talking strategy while the girls gathered together to discuss their fears.

Sitting with her feet in the pool, a tear slipped down her cheek as Kaitlan began to speak.

"The four of us know that tomorrow is going to be the final act with Zanack. Honestly, I have a very, very bad feeling about it."

"Yeah. So do I," Lynne said. "But, we are here to put a stop to him. It's apparent that this has been what our entire lives have been working toward."

Anita looked at Lynne.

"This whole thing has never made a bit of sense from the get-go. Nothing. Not since Kaitlan turned into the White Wolf. All those tests I put Lynne and Richard through as my guinea pigs, yet they lost the vampire gene just by mating with each other. The fact that Sarah is a werewolf, but the tests prove she isn't. The Wolfsbane, Sarah's death, and returning alive. Pick something! 'Time' has been skipping around. I agree with Sarah's description about the broken record. The music sounds right, then the needle skips, and you know you've missed something. You keep thinking the music will get back on track, but it never does. And, it continues to skip in random places. It drives you *absolutely insane*!"

Sarah thought about that a minute.

"You're right, Anita. Zanack fooled around with that record, or time in this case, and because the curse wasn't permanent, it's just been skipping around."

"Has anyone noticed, lately that we keep repeating ourselves?" Lynne asked while scratching her head.

Three sets of eyes darted to hers. Now, that she had said it, they realized it! Repetition was happening!

"And, it's getting worse. We repeat the same thing over and over. Maybe not in the same way, but always about the same things," Lynne said.

"Well, hell!"

Again, Sarah's mind started working quickly. She was determined not to repeat herself this time!

"Holy shit! We are repeating ourselves! Like the closer one gets to the final act, or the event, the more frequently things make no sense until it builds to the end. That's probably why we are finally noticing it. In other words, the reason your tests started making no sense is because we were almost at the end. Other things might have happened that didn't make sense, too, but they were few, and far between in the past. It would have been impossible to realize it. Like Entropy."

"OK. Pretend I don't know anything at all? What the fuck are you talking about?" asked Kaitlan.

"Oh. Right. Great! Something that isn't repeating! Well, entropy measures disorder within a closed system," Sarah started to explain looking at their glazed eyes.

"Hmmm. Let's see if I can explain it better. It is a way of measuring the loss of information in a transmitted message, and the second one is an inevitable deterioration of a society." Sarah looked at the same, glazed looks. "Put simply, it is what I said before. The loss of information was in the past, therefore, Anita, Lynne, and everyone else didn't notice them simply because the transmission of the message was slow to permeate the timeline. They didn't notice. However, the closer it gets we can see it, now. And, as it escalates, that loss of information is just like a skipped record, deteriorating rapidly. Time is skipping over certain parts. Put even simpler, everything will break down until it disappears altogether."

Kaitlan, Anita, and Lynne all dropped their mouths open. When she put it that way, it was sort of easier to understand. But, how did Sarah know this?

"Wait a minute. You mean as long as all this is going on, whether we do something or nothing is done about it, it is going to disappear anyway?" Kaitlan asked.

"Yep. It will. Well, at least this timeline. We could go to the end, and let this timeline take its course, but then there would be nothing left! Everything would cease to exist. It's a paradox of sorts."

"We all know you were given great knowledge, Sarah. But, this is just too far over our heads!" Kaitlan asked her.

Sarah shrugged.

"Well, being given knowledge doesn't exactly have to do with it. I already knew about some of this stuff. I had to do a bit of research years ago for one of our science writers. But, of course, they take liberty with the information."

"Wow! That's amazing!" Lynne exclaimed, and Anita nodded.

"So that's why no matter what I did, what tests I ran, it would never have made sense anyway. The results would always be different. Oh, crap! I'm repeating myself again!"

"Yep, and it's going to get worse. You repeated them. Just like we have been repeating ourselves off and on, and it's getting worse," Sarah said.

"Wouldn't that mean that because this timeline was altered into a timeline that wasn't supposed to ever happen, it was Zanack who pushed it into a different direction? Like in "Back to the Future"? Kaitlan asked.

"Well, that's as good a guess as anything. I mean, when Zanack cast the curse, it would have altered the timeline at the point in time where the curse was cast. If it had been permanent, the timeline would probably have been sent into a different direction than this one," Sarah answered.

Kaitlan hung her head to think. This whole thing was so confusing she couldn't even begin to figure it out. Maybe they needed to stop trying.

"Zanack just altered the timeline, right?"

They sat back, and thought about it. Richard had entered hearing the girls' discussion. Sarah was right. She had to be. That would explain why he buried the village. Unwittingly, he had been a party to the curse by acting as the Earth element in a way. He stepped up to Lynne to rub her stiff shoulders.

"You know. That just might be," he said.

"So, because he cast the curse, and you buried that village after-the-fact, it caused…" Sarah began.

"…the timeline to go in a different direction screwing it up," Kaitlan finished.

"That makes sense," Sam said entering with Cordone and Dan.

"So, what does it mean?" Sarah's mind was working hard and fast. "Now, we really are talking about something that no one can do. To recast it, he would have to make sure this timeline was replaced…"

"…and that would mean???" Dan asked.

Everyone stopped for a moment to look at each other.

Cordone said aloud the conclusion that everyone had reached together.

"He would have to go back in time. Or, aka Time Travel!!"

"SHIT!" Sam said.

"Wait! We are repeating ourselves again! We are talking time travel as if we haven't thought about it before!" Anita almost shouted.

"Ah, hell!" Lynne said. "This thing is really bugging the fuck out of me! Repeating, and rehashing the same thing over and over. That record is not just skipping, but it's as if we are running in place!

As if no one else heard her, they continued, because they couldn't stop themselves.

"How in the HELL is that going to happen? No one can time travel!"

"Unless………" Kaitlan said, and let it string out while she thought.

"Unless what, mate?" Cordone asked.

"Unless…. Richard, you are a wizard, right?"

He nodded. "Like I said, I'm not very good, though."

"What if, like the prophecy, there was also another scroll that told how to go back into time, and Zanack found it?" Kaitlan asked to really no one. "I mean, Richard told us that Odfrin was the most powerful wizard, ever." She looked up. "Is it possible that there is one?"

"Well, maybe not quite, Kaitlan," Richard answered. He noticed everyone's face shoot to his.

"What is that supposed to mean?" Sam asked him. Finally something that wasn't repeating!

"Well, Odfrin was the oldest, true. He was the most powerful in that time. However, there is an ancient story about a far more powerful line of wizards to have ever lived."

"Say what? And, you didn't think to tell us about that until now?" Cordone asked him.

"In truth, I hadn't given that a thought in years. It just never occurred to me."

"Yea! Something we haven't repeated! Wait! That's a repeat, right? Maybe they are the ones who wrote the prophecy?" ventured Anita. "Maybe there are many scrolls that they wrote? Maybe one having to do with Time Travel, even?"

All eyes turned to her. Why was it something so simple had to be so complicated?

"Hmmmm," Cordone mumbled. "Maybe. Possibly. No one in the werewolf communities could ever pinpoint who wrote that false prophecy, let alone the real one."

"True. And, the same goes for the vampires and elves as well. No one ever knew."

"OK. So, let's assume that these ancient wizards wrote it. That would preclude that they knew it was coming…" Dan started.

"…and the only way they could have known that was…" Lynne continued.

"…they either had knowledge of the future events of Zanack…" Sarah mumbled.

"…or they were able to travel in time," finished Kaitlan.

"Well, shit! Where can I go to get off this merry-go-round?" Anita complained. Her head was starting to pound.

"And, with the information that we gained from Cordone's memories, this land would enhance anything, or anyone, who came into contact with it who has magic of any kind! Wasn't that where you were going earlier, Kaitlan?" Dan asked her.

Kaitlan nodded. She guessed that was where she was going. Actually, no, she really didn't know. At least the repetition seemed to have stopped for the moment.

"I'd assume that one needed some type of heavy power to go into time." Ah, hell and damnation! She had thought it too soon!

Cordone nodded. "Time travel. Everything points to Zanack going back into time to make this one disappear," Cordone huffed. "So, that's it, isn't it? We will be going back in time using the power of the land. Damn the Elves to hell! The elves obviously knew about it!"

"Ali'on knew about the properties on this land? About time travel? And, he never said a damn thing?" Richard's voice continued to rise.

"Damn! I'm sick of repeating this shit!" Dan complained.

Cordone's eyes narrowed, and his anger became apparent.

"Then, why in the hell did they NOT tell us about it?"

A new voice entered their midst.

"Would you have told others about time travel knowing that it could have destroyed this event from taking place? Knowing it *must* take place?" Ali'on said in his soft voice.

Everyone jumped at the sudden appearance.

"What the fuck, Ali'on!" Richard had Ali'on around the throat in seconds.

Cordone, Sam, and Dan all converged on Richard trying to stop him.

"Explain yourself, Ali'on," Cordone demanded.

"Well, I will, if you'll remove your Neanderthal from choking me!"

At Cordone's nod, Richard dropped him suddenly, and Ali'on landed on his ass. Picking himself up, he made movements to brush off his silver pants, and then looked at them.

"Zanack fooled around with the timeline. And, yes. The ancient wizards - when they lived - did write the prophecy, and they did know of the future time. But, they did not travel. The most powerful wizard of all time was also a seer. It was he who saw what would happen. The consequences are dire. So bad, it scared even the wizards. They feared it so much, they were forbidden to use it. Unfortunately, instead of destroying the scroll, their arrogance would not let them, so they hid it within the Hall of Records. They never expected it to actually be found."

"And, they considered themselves smart? But, why not stop Zanack before he cast the curse? And, why the hell are we repeating ourselves?" Sarah asked.

"Sarah, you have knowledge. Think about it," Ali'on

told her.

Sarah thought for a moment. Ignoring, for the moment, the repetition, she realized, "Time is not stable, is it, Ali'on, if one can travel through it?" Seeing him nod his head, she continued, "If any of them had gone forward in time, they risked the same alteration of the timeline even trying to stop Zanack. And, if they altered it, then Zanack's curse could have altered it making the timeline worse. Or gone altogether. And, then, we might not be able to stop it when the time came."

"Yes," another, softer voice entered the conversation.

"Sandra!" exclaimed Kaitlan.

Joining Ali'on, she bowed to Kaitlan. "Alpha of the O'Hara Clan."

"What are you doing here?" Cordone demanded.

She walked to stand next to her mate. She was beautiful in a long silver gown that hugged her body like a second skin. It glittered, and danced with every movement. It was ethereal, and something Kaitlan had never seen. And, it clung so tightly to her body, it left nothing to the imagination!

"I'm here to assure you that Ali'on, nor any other Elf, had anything to do with the timeline that exists now."

"So, Ali'on! Do you know how we can get off this repetitious Ferris wheel?" Lynne complained again.

Ali'on looked at her, and shook his head.

"I do not. The closer the time comes for Zanack to recast it, the more we will repeat ourselves. Nothing can stop that. And, it could ruin us all. We are stuck on that wheel without a chance," he told her. "Zanack knows that if he misses the point in time, we'll be stuck in a time loop that we will never stop. That is the reason you must follow him back through time. It's the only way."

Sandra turned to Kaitlan.

"Kaitlan, the White Wolf Prophecy was written by

the ancient wizard known as Ma'rol'n. He was not just *a* wizard, but he was *the* most powerful wizard who ever lived. Odfrin was an infant compared to him. Ma'rol'n was so powerful that other wizards plotted to kill him. They wanted his power. And, one wizard can steal another's power *if* someone has enough power. But, Ma'rol'n knew what they were doing, and he 'disappeared' with the prophecy and the Scroll of Time."

""Well, it figures they'd call it a fucking 'Scroll of Time'. Wait. You mean we'll be stuck repeating things over and over forever? Fuck that!"

Nodding to Dan, she continued.

"The Scroll of Time was hidden within The Hall of Records by Ma'rol'n's decree. Ma'rol'n knew that someday, it would be found, so he charged the Elves to protect it giving them a spell until the time came to reveal it. It fell to the Elf Kings of the future for its protection. As was meant to be, we lifted the spell, and Zanack found it just days ago."

"Well, that's just great!" Sam said. "We have a total, fucking maniac running around who has access to the real prophecy, and a Scroll of Time. And, Johnson lured us back to Cordone's land to use the magical properties of it for the end of everything! And, to beat all that we are repeating ourselves!"

Everyone's eyes darted to Sam.

"What? I'm right, and you know it!" he barked.

"Oh, Sam! I love you, you brilliant man!" Sarah squealed, throwing her arms around her mate.

Ali'on picked up where Sandra had left off, and continued.

"Look. Nothing could have prevented this from coming. I'm here…we're here…to inform you that the Scroll of Time has been found by Zanack. And, with it, there is an incredible price that must be paid for using it. It is so dangerous, the supernatural world has never dared to use it. But, Zanack is evil. Worse? You know he has been in your midst this whole time.”

“There’s always a price for using magic, Ali’on,” Richard said. “I’ve paid it.”

Ali’on nodded.

“This price will be high. It will demand blood. A lot of blood. And, Zanack will lap it up! He will do whatever it takes to get him back to the original day of the original curse.”

Everyone jerked upon hearing his words.

“Exactly how much blood are we talking about?” Dan ventured.

“It will make the Maya who sacrificed, and cut out beating hearts, look like a child’s playground. No less than ten beings, and possibly more will be required to open the portal, close it, and recast the curse.”

Sarah made a gagging noise, and rushed out the back door followed by Kaitlan and Anita. Lynne was sick, too, but she was able to control it.

When the girls returned, Ali’on and Sandra were gone.

“Cordone? Where are they?” Kaitlan asked.

“They delivered what they had to deliver, and left. It’s up to us to stop Zanack. It always has been.

“But, they left us one last piece of information. If we succeed, the timeline will be reset, but no one knows what will be after it does.”

“REPEAT!” all four girls yelled! Might as well have some sort of fun.

“I agree,” Richard said shaking his head at their silly behavior. “But, we all know that we cannot let this timeline go forward.”

With nods of agreement, and the prospect of what was coming in their heads, it made their last moments together that much more important.

Dan grabbed Anita, and picked her up in his arms.

"I'm damn sick of repeating ourselves. And, if it's going to continue, I'd like to repeat it over and over by mating with my mate. So, if you will excuse us, we are going to have our last moments alone."

As they darted out, the other couples agreed. Silently, they all went their separate ways. Sarah to the poolroom. Lynne and Richard to the cabin they shared together after their mating, and Kaitlan out to the garage for her fantasy!

Leaving Cordone and Sam alone, they spoke one last time about what was coming. Somehow, both of them knew the outcome, and decided to let things take their course.

"We are dead, Sam," Cordone said quietly hoping the girls couldn't hear them.

"I know. It was easy enough to figure out what Ali'on meant about lots of blood. He will use our blood to open the portal. But, what of the girls?"

"I don't know, Sam, I just don't know."

"So, we prepare the girls?"

"No. It's best if we don't. They will need the anger that will come from our deaths. Otherwise, they may not win."

Sam nodded in agreement, and the two men went their separate ways. If this was the end, and with no idea what would happen, they were going to spend it one last time with their mates.

~ 7 ~
Love is the Great Equalizer ~~~ Kaitlan

Cordone may have thought she was kidding about sex inside his Royce Phantom II. Kaitlan wasn't kidding at all! She wanted sex in a car. Her other friends had indulged while she was in high school as well as college, and now, she wanted to do it!

Once she was inside the garage, Kaitlan stripped throwing her clothing onto the floor, and climbed into the backseat. If they were going to be killed, or just cease to exist tomorrow, she was going to make sure that she and Cordone had whatever fantasy they had ever wanted. She sent Cordone a visual of her lying on the back seat with her legs up, knees spread wide, so he could see her face peeking through them.

In the middle of the conversation that he and Sam had been having, he gasped. Sam looked at Cordone knowingly. He knew that gasp. They'd all had it at one time or another from their mates.

"That's it for now, Sam. I have to take care of my mate." Cordone told Sam.

"I couldn't agree with you more, Cordone. Me, too."

Both men headed in the directions of their mates. Cordone headed for the garage as fast as he could to spend the rest of the little time they had left together.

While she waited for Cordone to come to her, she thought about their children. Luckily, Odin had been good enough to take them, and the others along with Milon and Muriel over the Bifrost into Asgard for protection. Success might not mean they would ever have existed. Failure might not mean they would ever have existed. Either way it really didn't matter.   It was a strong possibility that they would not exist in the reset timeline. Kaitlan knew the other girls had been thinking the same thing, but they didn't want to voice it aloud. Everything depended upon them. Everything, even if it meant none of them were ever were born. Kaitlan decided she would push what was coming out of her mind. Otherwise, she wouldn't want to do anything except brood. She was not going to give Zanack the satisfaction of ruining this time with her mate. Therefore, she pushed Zanack, and what was coming to a special area of her mind, and temporarily locked the door.

Then, Kaitlan stretched out on the car's seat naked - and, felt totally decadent doing it! The seat was soft against her back, and she knew when Cordone took her, it would be wonderful! She'd always wanted to know how it felt when her friends had told her they made out in their boyfriend's cars, and now, she was going to have first-hand knowledge! It was the most erotic feeling she had ever had! She was so horny, she put her hands on her own breasts, gently brushing her knuckles over her nipples causing them to harden even more than they already were. Kaitlan pinched, and pulled her nipples moaning as she felt wetness begin to pour from her sex. Needing relief already, she used one hand to stroke and pull on one nipple. With her other hand, her fingers slipped to her wet sex, and using them, circled, pulled, and gently stroked her clit. She groaned with need as her body throbbed in unison with the soft touches.

A noise broke her concentration. Heavy footsteps approached the car. She knew those steps of her mate better than any other sound. He appeared at the car door stark naked, and his arousal was very, very apparent standing straight and pointing right at her! He'd just walked across the garage naked? OMG! That was just so *hot*! She couldn't wait for him to be inside of her!

"You just soooo turn me on being naked in the garage! This cat would really love to eat the canary!" she purred in a sexy voice staring at his hard cock while still stroking her sex.

Kaitlan watched his face intently as she let one finger slip inside her opening, sliding it in and out while he watched her. Each time she removed her fingers soaked with her liquid, he watched as more flowed out of her opening, and onto his expensive seat!

Cordone stood nude gazing at Kaitlan's naked body with her legs wide spread across his seat. His cock hardening more and more as he watched his sexy mate sprawled across the seat of one of his most prize cars masturbating herself!

"I couldn't wait, so I decided to start without you," Kaitlan said coyly to him in the sexiest voice she had.

Kaitlan pulled her finger out, and Cordone protested.

"No. Don't stop, Kaitlan. I want to watch you come by your own hand!"

Kaitlan jerked in total desire, and felt more creamy liquid flow from her! She looked into his eyes as she continued at his request. When Cordone grabbed his cock, and began to stroke it, she came to a dead stop. She felt completely wanton as she slipped three fingers into her entrance, thrusting them in and out of her body while she watch him pump his cock, and rub his own finger along his slit that was oozing with his creamy liquid. She licked her lips in hunger.

Both of them stroked and thrust harder and harder, until Kaitlan cried out with her orgasm. Cordone's balls were contracting hard, and he was about to explode. He slipped his leg into his car, and sat on the seat still pumping his cock harder and faster. Kaitlan watched her mate groan aloud, throwing his head backward as he felt the pressure of his balls push his hot, wet seed into his cock. His cock spewed wet seed onto the carpet of his car's floor as he called out Kaitlan's name! A large puddle of white semen pooled and grew larger with each shot of his seed.   Kaitlan felt another orgasm as she watched.

Then, he turned. His cock still hard, and with a wicked grin, he sprawled himself right on top of her pushing his hardened cock at the opening to her womb. He needed her to erase all the bad things that had happened to all of them over the past few hours, and what was to come. Cordone wanted her, and he wanted to give her the "ride" of her life on him in the most expensive "ride" he owned! To *HELL* with what they might do the upholstery. In fact, he wanted to see their "liquid love" flood onto the upholstery, staining it. If they lived through all of this, he planned to stain the seats repeatedly. He hardened more as he thought of what they would do inside it tonight! He could have it redone later, but as he said to himself…he probably wouldn't live, so it didn't make a damn bit of difference! Cordone wanted their smell to permeate everything inside of it! If they died tomorrow, and if this would be his last memory, he would gladly die happily!

"Oh, babe! My canary is ready for you! Are you ready for it?" he purred back to her as he stroked his penis against her entrance.

Kaitlan felt her body begin to orgasm, again, but he didn't wait. Cordone dove his cock inside her body just as she began to orgasm, grinning devilishly. She cried out his name, as her fingers scraped his biceps, arching her back while holding onto to him. His movements were fast, and furious. He emptied himself into her quickly. She moaned. Her mate's cock stayed large and continued moving inside her slowly this time. Cordone planned to drag this mating out for a very long time.

Kaitlan thought she would come unglued! He was glorious as he pumped into her body, again, fast and hard! It was such an amazing feeling, especially since she was already on her way to a fourth orgasm! He quickly spilled his hot seed inside of her, and their rapid movements rocked the car as their cries of passion echoed throughout the garage.

Cordone slid out of her, and sat up pulling her onto his lap to straddle him. Kaitlan held him to her as his head dipped to suckle her nipples, and knead her breasts. Tears ran down her face as she lowered herself onto his hardness, again, and her movements were slow, taking him inside of her as deep as possible. They gave to each other as they had on their bonding, lasting into the night. They knew that it would be their last time to be together. The future may meet with their deaths, but this would last beyond it.

His movements became rapid, and just as their orgasms climaxed, Cordone opened his mouth, and his canines descended to her neck. She screamed out his name as he bit her. Turning her head, her canines also were let loose, and she bit his neck. Their bodies rocked into each other hard and fast as they drank each other's blood, meeting thrust for thrust at the same time. It was the ultimate in sex between werewolves, and he spilled his seed into her, again, the heat of it exploding into her. The moment he stopped thrusting into her beautiful body, their teeth left their necks, and both howled. If only they might live! She so wanted to become pregnant again! Especially after this orgasm!

As if he was reading her mind, he flipped her over onto her back.

"Get on your knees!" he demanded panting with desire. "And, open the other door!"

She pushed the door open as he requested, and Kaitlan thrust her ass up into his face while laying her head on her forearms. She felt Cordone's mouth at her entrance, licking it slowly. His tongue dove into her entrance tasting her and drinking their love that was flowing from her. Kaitlan cried out as she begged for him to slam into her, but instead, he thrust three of his fingers inside of her. She groaned loudly as his tongue met her clit flipping it, until she came with his fingers thrusting in and out of her pussy fast and hard! Just as she came, he removed his fingers, and plunged his hot, aching cock into her slippery channel! He slammed into her so hard, he had to hold her hips still so she wouldn't fly out of the open door! Kaitlan begged for more and more, and Cordone held back nothing from her. He wanted her at his mercy, and his desires! He wanted total control of his mate. And, she loved it! His seed exploded inside of her again, and not giving her a second to think, he dragged her out of the car, pushed her naked breasts against the car, spread her legs with his knees, and plunged back inside of her from the back then stopped.

"Phase," he ordered in one word.

Kaitlan groaned aloud as they both phase at the same time, and the White Wolf whined in ecstasy when his huge wolf's cock plunged in and out of her faster, harder, and for the first time in his entire life, Cordone gave himself over to his wolf completely. He became nothing but the wolf, letting his wolf take total control. The wolf showed her how big he could really be. It was his fantasy. To let her feel his full size as his wolf took over. She gasped as she felt his cock lengthen, and expand! Turning her head, she looked into his eyes, and gasped. Cordone was not there! It was his wolf - free of restraint! Kaitlan turned back, closed her eyes, and gave her wolf the same freedom to which she howled with happiness. The White Wolf felt his paws on her ass, and she pushed backward meeting his thrusts. She wanted his seed. Wanted everything that he could give to her!

Cordone's wolf let itself go as he brought the two of them to climax! His wolf's seed flowed into her body, hot and wet, filling her deeply. She had been full of his seed before, but this was different. Since their wolves were in charge, everything was a different perspective. The male wolf could think of nothing but impregnating his mate, so he filled her full of his wolf's seed. He filled her so full that when he removed himself from her beautiful body, the garage floor was flooded immediately with a great quantity of juices as it flowed from her opening. Cordone licked her tasting their nectar's flood. Then, he nudged her to follow him, and ran to the garage door while her wolf's body was still dripping onto the floor. Cordone jumped on his hind legs, and pushed the button to open the door. Heedless of the fact it was thundering and lightning with rain coming, the two wolves, one snow white the other black, yin and yang, flew out the door into the night under the lightning of the night, and headed straight to their secret pool.

Cordone had already laid down the magic. When they phased back to human, Kaitlan gasped. It was so beautiful! Cordone had made a true paradise of love for them. It was even more beautiful than the night of their mating, if that were possible.

The pool was lined with candles - real ones this time. Cordone had figured if this was to be the end of everything, then he was going to do anything, and everything he wanted. He had laid quilts over all of the grass that was around the pool making sure that he could take Kaitlan at any time, anywhere. Pillows dotted the entire area along with several whipped cream cans, strawberries, chocolate syrup, caramel syrup, bananas, cheeses, and wine. A lot of wine. He had thought a bit ahead in case it rained, and had put up portable tents all around the pool, but leaving the pool uncovered. They could bathe, and swim in it all they wanted even if it rained. The entire place was completely soft, and very sexy.

Kaitlan turned to Cordone. "Oh, Cordone! It's so beautiful!"

"You really like it?" he asked as he came behind her, reaching around her body and cupping her breasts gently tickling her nipples. She turned in his arms brushing them against his chest. He growled as he felt them. She giggled, and brushed them gently against him, feeling his chest hair tickle her nipples into hardness.

"I do."

"Keep that thought."

Cordone scooped her up as they both felt the heavy raindrops begin to hit them, and quickly carried her under one of the tents, laying her down on the pillows.

Kaitlan pulled him down to her, and plastered her lips onto his. Cordone finally raised his head.

"So, my love. What do you want first on your beautiful, naked body? Whipped cream? Syrup? Fruit and cheese? Wine?"

She pulled him back down, and spread her legs letting him settle between them.

"You, my love. Only you," she whispered into the night.

~ 8 ~
Final Confessions of love ~~~ Sarah

Sarah had not totally stripped, but stopped undressing standing only in her panties just before she entered the pool to wait for Sam. Her mind was on overdrive. She was worried. No, not worried. Scared. No, not scared. OK. She was worried and scared! What if they didn't stop Zanack? What if…?

Sam silently walked up behind her, and reached around cupping her bare breasts his fingers gently brushing against her nipples. She turned her head to look up at him as she placed her hands on top of his. Creator! Even now, in their final moments, all she could think of was that Sam was unbelievably beautiful! She never got tired of looking at him! Her mate! His entire body was built like a steel building! His arms could rip someone's head off, but they could be so gentle when holding a baby, or caressing her body. Sam was gentle with her at all times. Well, except when his desire exploded for her. Then, she loved him not being gentle! However, she still had a problem, because she just couldn't figure out why he loved, and wanted her.

"Why do I love you? Why would I want you, Tink?" he paused his fingers letting them stay on her breasts. "What kind of a question is that?"

Oops. She'd let that one slip out. She shrugged, and then motioned with her hand across her body.

"Well, look at me? I'm not perfect, Sam! I'm short and not completely thin. Not in the way other girls are."

"Not perfect?" Sam growled. He jerked off his clothes by ripping them in anger.

Sarah's face turned up to her mate in shock when he growled at her. She'd never seen his anger directed at her. Sam's claws extended quickly, ripped off her panties in a violent motion, and jerked her into full contact with his cock grinding himself against her stomach leaving her in no doubt about his desire for her. Sarah almost melted as she felt an overwhelming desire to demand that he take her hard!

"Do not EVER say that to me, again, Sarah! Not to me, not in your mind, not in my vicinity, and not in secret!"

He stared down at her as if he was barely able to contain his desire. Oh, hell! Sam looked good enough to eat, and her womb decided she wanted to eat him! His voice became low, almost threatening, and yet, she wasn't afraid.

"Woman, *you are perfect*! You are the most beautiful, perfect woman I have ever seen. You still don't know the truth about how I feel? Why do you say this to me? Your mate? I never want to hear those words come from your mouth, again. Do you understand me? Do you really want to know the truth about how I feel about you? Do you really want to know what a total pervert I am? Because, I am going to tell you the truth whether or not you want to hear it! I have always felt about you this way, desired you, wanted to take you, and it did *not* start in my shower when you were seventeen, but when you were *five*!"

Sarah's mouth dropped! Five? Had she heard him right? He had never spoken to her like that before! She leaned her head against his chest trying to stop the shaking of her body against him as she heard his words. Wait! Five? That was when she first met him!

"But, you met me when I was five," she turned her head up to peek at him.

He growled at her in earnest, again, as he grabbed

her hair, and jerked her face upward into his glowing eyes! Sam wasn't being gentle at all. Sarah and her wolf loved it! She didn't want gentle!

Sam slammed her against the wall pushing his hard cock between her legs so that he could rub it along her wet entrance. He groaned as he felt how soaking wet she was! Nevertheless, he refused to enter her despite her pushing against him.

"Yes. Five! The day I met you! How perverted is that for your mate, Sarah?" Sam shut his eyes remembering. "Do you remember Kaitlan's seventh birthday party?"

OK. Sarah was lost. He jumped to that day? Why?

"Well, yes, of course I do? Why?" she asked almost fearing the answer.

Sarah was desperately trying to impale herself onto his cock, but he wouldn't let her. She growled in frustration, puzzled why he would bring that particular incident up right now, when all she wanted was for him to bury his cock deep inside of her!

The incident was burned into Sam's mind even if Sarah didn't remember. Would she look at him differently when he told her everything? Would she still love him? He knew one thing. He couldn't die without telling her. They say admission is good for one's soul. He just hoped it was true.

"Sarah, I can't lie any more. I'm tired of protecting you against the truth of things - especially me. You need to know, but you blocked it out."

Sarah was confused. Now, what truth? Hadn't she had enough of the "truth"?

"Sam, I don't think…." she began.

"Enough!" Sam growled at her.

Sam yanked her down to sit on his lap as he plopped his naked ass into a chair. His gut clenched, and bile rose in his throat as he began.

"Sarah, something happened that day that you don't remember," he paused seeing her frown. "We all went to the cabin by the lake owned by the company. Do you remember that part of it?"

Sarah just nodded not taking her eyes from his.

"You came for just a couple of hours, because you had refused to miss your best friend's birthday party. Your family had already had their vacation planned for that day."

"I know that, Sam. So?"

He closed his eyes, and then opened them to look into hers.

"That's not how it went, Sarah."

Again, she frowned at him, and waited.

"You had gone into the cabin to shower, and dress to get ready for your parents while I waited outside still in my swimming trunks." He sighed. "I have been guarding you since the day you walked into the publishing building when you were five. Even when you were adopted by the Collins, Canaan assigned me to guard you."

Sarah's mouth dropped open. He'd been guarding her all these years? How had she not known it?

"Seriously? But, why?" she asked in surprise.

"Uh-huh. A very good reason that only he may have known. He knew you were my mate, because my eyes glowed for you the minute I met you in the hallway for the first time."

Wait?

"What do you mean?"

Did she just hear right? Sam claimed her as his mate when she was five? Wow! That was such a damn turn-on!

"Yes. I claimed you at five years-old! Human years! What kind of pervert does that?"

Sarah reached up, and stroked his face.

"It makes you a werewolf who claimed his mate,

Sam. You were no pervert. Do you know how much of a crush I had on you all my life?"

He frowned at her. "I never understood that. Why would you crush on me?"

"Seriously?" she laughed. "Look at you, Sam!" Her eyes raked down his nude body stopping at his hard and pointy cock. "You are the most amazingly, hunkalicious man I have ever seen! I knew it then, and I still know it!"

"Really?"

"Really, but go ahead and finish what you wanted to tell me."

Sam cleared his throat.

"Anyway, I stood outside the door. No one was around. It was pretty quiet. And, then…I…I…."

His stomach rose into his mouth. How could he tell her what happened? After everything her Father had done to her, he was about to add charcoal lighter to an already massive fire.

"What Sam? What happened?" Sarah clutched her throat. What had happened to make him look like he was about to throw up?

"No one was around, because everyone was down at the lake. The thoughts I was having about you at that moment should have been censored, and I should have been thrown into jail!"

"What are you talking about?" Sarah asked, but she knew that he was talking about desire for her - at fourteen. She just wanted to make him say it! The thought made her grin.

"Come on, Sarah! You know what I was thinking about!" he said to her.

Sarah grinned wider.

"Nope. I don't, Sam. Well, maybe I do. I just want to hear you say it!"

"OK! I was thinking about marching through that door to pick you up, wrap your legs around me, just so that I could plunge this huge, massive cock attached to my body straight into your pussy! Satisfied?" he was really loud.

Sarah laughed aloud.

"Yes, I am - now. You are a werewolf, Sam. Sex works differently in your world - mine, now. And, I like it!"

He shook his head in confusion. Sam had just told her that he wanted to have sex with her at fourteen, but had to hold himself back. And, all she could say was sex worked differently in the world of the werewolf?

"OK. Now, that you got that out of your system, don't you feel better?" she brushed the tips of her nipples against his chest, and heard a satisfying groan from his throat. "Now, go on."

He looked at her. What a woman she was!

"OK. Where was I? Oh, right. My perverted secret desire. Well, then, I…heard you scream. I jerked the door open, and ran to the shower." He paused, again. "I found you on the floor of it, Sarah. But, that's not all. I found…I-I found…."

Sarah cupped his face.

"What did you find, Sam? Tell me. It's okay."

He looked up into her eyes. His eyes were glowing brighter than ever, but they were black as night! She pulled back in shock. He was more than angry. He was murderous! As long as she had known him, this was the first time she was actually scared! Not of him, but of what had him so terrified that it brought him to his knees.

"I found Milton on his knees between your legs with his fucking dick just about an inch from entering you pussy!" he ground out in anger.

Sarah not only gasped, she reeled backwards in shock. Sam caught her just as she almost fell onto the floor.

"Milton? Milton? He was…NO! That can't be! I-I

thought he liked me! H-he said he understood about my Father, and would n-never do anything like that to me!"

"Oh, he fucking liked you, alright. You were seconds away from being fucking raped by him!"

"Oh my God!" Sarah cried. Her Father, and Milton? Sam held her to him as she shook with shock. "How does that filth keep finding me? What is wrong with me?"

"Nothing is wrong with *you*. Sarah…fucking filth like that will always find good just to drag them down in the fucking muck and mire in which they fucking exist. You are innocent and beautiful, and fucking evil preys on it."

He kissed her throat, and mouth before he continued. Sarah melted under his touch. She never felt safer than when she was being held by Sam.

"My hand closed around his fucking throat, Sarah, and I yanked that fucking bastard to his feet! I turned him around to face me. When he looked at me, terror gripped his fucking face!"

"Sam. Your eyes?" Any time he used that many "fuckings" she knew he was truly murderous, and barely able to keep it contained.

"They were as you see them now. Glowing black. I was in a murderous rage! But, it was the glow that had him terrified."

"Wait. Your eyes glowed? Black? But, they glowed golden for me telling me I was your mate!"

"Yes. That's true. Golden when I claimed you as my mate when you were little. But, I had not claimed you publicly, Sarah. It's how I found out that Canaan saw my public claim to you. I claimed you, again, officially, that day when I almost fucking killed Milton for trying to rape you! That was what he saw, and that was why he was terrified of me. You know that when werewolves claim their mate, any male that so much as tries to touch their mate can turn into a true monster. No. Don't say anything else. I have to get this out without stopping, Sarah. I started to choke the life out of him. It would have been my right to do so as your mate. I wanted him dead! I wanted to watch the life drain from his eyes!"

Sam stopped for a moment, closed his eyes, and tried to gain his breath.

Sarah's shocked face dropped as he spoke, but he wasn't going to have that. He yanked her hair, again, to force her head back so that her eyes had to meet his. He wanted to see her reaction, to look into her eyes. He needed to watch her. Sarah gulped hard. His eyes got blacker if that were even possible. Sam needed her to see him at his worst - the part of him he had never let her see.

"He had passed out, and was on his way to the Creator! I didn't care. I wanted to fucking rip him to fucking pieces! He touched my mate! He fucking almost raped you. But, then, I heard you crying. It broke through my rage and hatred. How it happened, I don't know. You were curled into a ball crying hard. I threw him into the wall, and bent down to touch you. You flinched from my touch, and it just fueled my hatred against Milton more. I didn't have a clue about your fucking bastard of a father at that point. Your beauty, and kindness seemed to bring out the beast in me, along with other boys and men."

Sarah's hand was over her mouth as she listened to Sam admit his anger and hatred toward a fourteen year-old boy let alone admit he, too, had dark thoughts about her! But, the fact that he prevented her being raped, again, just made her love him that much more. And, secretly, the idea that he wanted her that much was a turn-on!

"It's okay, Sam," she tried to sooth him with her hand, but he yanked it from his face holding it tightly in his hand as he stretched it around her back pulling her tightly against him, again.

"No, it isn't, Sarah. I never wanted you to know my dark side."

Sarah just nodded, her love for him increasing by the second. She hadn't told him her secret about that day, yet, either. As he had spoken, everything came flooding back to her. *Everything.*

"I had to leave you for a few minutes to take that fucking bastard to Canaan to deal with, because I was going to fucking kill him. Maybe I was worse, in that moment, because I desired you. I desired to thrust into your body. I was not going to let another fuck you! I was the only one who would do it! You were mine!"

His hand relaxed on hers.

"When Canaan saw me carrying Milton still unconscious, and he saw my glowing eyes, he knew something terrible had happened. He took Milton, and gave him to Dan, then pulled me aside into the trees, and I told him what I had found. Then, he asked me if I was claiming you as my mate. I told him I was. He warned me about the dangers of a werewolf taking a human as mate, but if anyone understood, it was Canaan since he mated with Tara. He completely understood that implicitly. He asked me if Milton had seen my eyes glow, and I told him he did. Milton was a young werewolf, but he knew the signs of mating. Canaan finally asked if I wanted to exercise my right to kill Milton as your mate. I shook my head, because the way I was feeling right then, I would have easily dismembered him, and laughed about it. But, I didn't want you to know that I was a killer, Sarah. It's the only thing that saved his fucking life until the council sentenced him for termination. Canaan kept my claim secret from them."

Sarah's mouth had dropped open listening to Sam tell her all of it. She started to speak, and he held his hand up to silence her.

"There's more, Sam?"

"Yes. Canaan asked me to wait to claim you until you reached at least eighteen. I promised him. But, I couldn't keep that promise when I found you naked in my shower. It's a really good thing he never knew I took your virginity three years later."

Sarah silenced him for a moment with her fingers on his lips.

"You mean when *we* took each other - all night long, in your shower, your bed, on the walls…. I knew exactly what I was doing, and so did you."

He smiled, sat back in the chair, and pulled her back onto his lap. He was so hard, Sarah had no place to sit other than his cock. She didn't mind that at all. She was wet anyway.

"Go on, my love," she urged him as she turned to straddle his cock, earning a deep groan from her mate.

"I returned to find you still curled into the ball on the shower floor. You were shaking so hard with shock that I was literally scared to approach you. But, I did, anyway. Your eyes saw me, but didn't. When I said your name, you blinked, stood up fast, and cried out *my* name. You flew up, and into my arms sobbing so hard, I didn't know what to do except to hold you to me. I almost lost it, Sarah! You were naked and in my arms! I almost did the one thing I did not want to do. I wanted to take you then. My wolf wanted his mate. Then, and there. I had a horrendous time trying to pull him back. My cock was so hard, I was horrified that you might notice!"

"In other words, Sam, you saved me, and claimed me as your mate that day - again. Interesting coincidence that Milton tried to rape me in the shower, and then you took me in yours," Sarah stated with a smile.

"Hmph. I never thought of that. Your body was already the body of a woman at fourteen. When I felt your large, bare breasts pushing into my naked chest, I groaned in desire. I couldn't stop my erection from growing. You were my mate, and you were naked. I opened my mouth, ready to recite the mating words to you right then. But, then, reasoning reached my mind. I knew that I wanted you, but I feared that I would scare the hell out of you if you even noticed I was hard. But, I also saw your beautiful naked body, and your large breasts these delicate pink nipples, and those beautiful red curls where I bury myself every chance I get, now. They had already been burned into my eyes forever. Why do you think I take you as much as I can?"

He paused to wrap a finger in those same red curls exciting her further as his finger slipped onto her wet core. He absentmindedly circled her clit with his finger, putting increasing pressure on it as he fondled. Sarah started to groan, and then, it turned into a growl.

"I so wanted to take you away, and bury myself inside of you, to make you mine in that moment. It took everything in me not to do it. Don't you see, Sarah? I was actually no fucking better than Milton, or your Father. Less, even. I felt like a fucking pervert, because I wanted to fuck a fourteen year-old girl that had almost been raped!"

Sarah frowned for a moment taking it all in as she thought about it. She had an epiphany at that moment, and she asked him something he wasn't expecting.

"Sam? You were my guard, right? Did you kill my Father?"

He looked at her. No more lying.

"Yes. Canaan ordered me to do it, but didn't tell me who he was. He just gave me his name and that he raped one of our own. He didn't tell me that it was you, nor did he ever tell anyone else. Until Kaitlan told me, I had no idea. I should have told you before this that I found out about it. I'm sorry. I will understand if you hate me, now."

He buried his face into her neck. He couldn't look at her after that.

Sarah just held him tightly. Even though the memories began flooding back, she still had to open that door fully in her mind that she had locked so long ago. She was sure that behind it was where she had put the almost rape when she was fourteen. Probably because of her Father. Oh, whom was she kidding! Of course, that was the reason! But, she had to open the door. Dahll had told her that all three of the girls had to put emotions aside. If that door opened while she was in the battle with Zanack, it could jeopardize everything!

"Sam, I need a minute," Sarah told him, and walked to the edge of the pool.

"Of course." Sam watched his mate dive into the water. Had he just ruined everything?

Sarah dove to the bottom of the pool wrapping a bubble around her. She closed her eyes, and forced herself to see the door. It was locked, but that didn't stop her. She held out her hand demanding the key, and it appeared. She unlocked the door, and walked into the darkness beyond.

Thirty minutes! She'd been down there thirty, fucking, whole minutes! Sam just sat on the side of the pool staring at Sarah. He put his head in his hands in despair. What if he had ruined everything? A hard yank on his leg pulled him under the water. His mouth opened in surprised, and he swallowed a lot of water until he started to cough it up in the air bubble Sarah had extended around him. She patted his back, and kept apologizing.

"O-OK, Sarah. I'm fine. You just surprised me, that's all. Your strength is increasing."

She turned and smiled at him. Thank the Creator! She wasn't mad at him! He reached for her, but she stopped him by putting her hand on his chest.

"Wait, Sam. I need to tell you that the reason I came

down here was to remember all of it. Now, it's my turn for confession. Milton had hidden in the cabin. He'd been after me for at least two months! I really thought he liked me, and I told him of my Father's rape. But, then, I discovered he was nothing more than another piece of shit! When I wouldn't put out, he threatened me. Either I let him fuck me, or he would take it. I laughed in his face not realizing that he was really crazy. He wasn't invited to Kaitlan's party, for obvious reasons. He must have snuck in without anyone seeing him."

"Canaan knew?"

"Of course he did! Now, I realize why Canaan assigned you to protect me. I had gone straight to Canaan just as he had told me to if anyone ever threatened me again. And, then, Canaan called me into his home office the day before the party to tell me that Milton had disappeared. He took his threat to me very, very seriously! It had me scared, but he assured me that you would let nothing happen to me. And, of course, my secret crush let me trust you completely."

Sam began to circle his fingers gently along her right breast slowly working his way inward toward her nipple. He paused when Sarah continued, but didn't move his hand.

"We'll probably never know how he got there, or where he was hiding. I was in the shower, and just about finished when I heard a noise behind me. Milton was there with his filthy eyes looking at me. He came toward me, and I had nowhere to run. I was trapped just like when I was little with my father. But, I wasn't afraid to try to fight back this time. When I tried to get past him, he hit me, and I fell onto the floor. I watched him unzip his pants pushing them down and grabbing his dick. My Father's face merged with Milton. I wanted to throw up. He dropped to his knees, and that's when I kicked his balls. Hard. He rolled back as he grabbed them, and held them crying in pain and anger! I was almost up, but he attacked me again. I struggled with him until he sat on my legs, and held my hands in one of his own, while the other one kneaded my breasts. Then, his mouth lowered to suck my breasts - at least that's what I thought he was going to do, but he didn't. He hit me in the stomach - hard. That's when I started to curl up, but he yanked me straight again. I felt his cock touch my opening, and I moved hard sideways knocking him away from me. But, he came back fast. Of course, now I know that he was a werewolf. I had no chance against him. I never had a chance, and he knew it. That's when I screamed, and I barely remember seeing you come in, and yank Milton off me! I curled into a ball holding my stomach. I was in pain from his punch."

She looked up at him seeing his eyes glow black, yet again.

"First, just to get it out of our way forever, I'm glad that you were the one to terminate my father. He was a bastard, and he deserved it. I will say no more about him for the rest of my existence whether it lasts only three days, or forever. Second, when you came back to me, I was still out of it. But, then, I heard you call my name. Somehow, some way, I knew the voice was my salvation. I turned, and saw your glowing eyes, but it didn't register. All I wanted was for you to hold me. I don't know where I found the strength to lunge into your arms. When your arms went around me, and held me tight, I felt something hard in my stomach."

She grinned when she saw his blush. That was just so darned cute!

"I was hoping you hadn't noticed, Sarah," he said scratching his head in embarrassment.

"Me? Not notice this?" She reached for his cock, and cradled it in her hands. "You have to be *kidding*? Anyway, I buried my head in your chest, and, then, I smelled a scent coming from you. I'd never smelled anything like it before, but it calmed me down considerably. And, then, it was all I could do not to raise my head to kiss you. It was the same scent when we had sex the first time. It was so strong, I remember sniffing deeply. But, I remember something else, too."

"What, Sarah?" His breath was coming hard as she continued to stroke him, her fingers lingering at his tip spreading the clear liquid across it.

"I felt your naked chest against my breasts. As I said, I also felt something hard against my abdomen. It took me a minute, or two, but I realized what it was. I'd seen enough of them to know the feeling. But, Sam? I wasn't scared of yours. Other guys had tried to get me to take their dicks, and it *always* scared the hell out of me. But, not yours. I held on as long as I thought I could get away with it, because I wanted so much to feel my bare skin against yours. To feel your hardness against me. To feel my naked breasts against your chest. If you had claimed me, and had asked me to be your wife, or whatever, I would have gladly laid back down on the floor, and asked you to make love to me!"

Sam's eyes bugged out in shock.

"You don't know what you're saying, Sarah!"

She stroked his thick, soft steel of velvet. He flinched, and it just became harder in her hand.

"Oh, yes, Sam. That feeling never left me as I continued to grow up. I do know exactly what I'm saying. I wanted you so badly, I was wet for you that day the moment my breasts and curls touched you." She looked him in the eyes. "Don't tell me you didn't smell my arousal? You must have done so!"

Sam thought back on it. It dawned on him that he had smelled something, but he was so angry, it had bypassed him altogether!

"Shit!" he exclaimed.

"Ah, you do remember!" Sarah grinned wickedly,

raising one eyebrow. She wanted her mate. Now.

He looked at her.

"I do! Holy shit, Sarah! It was the mating scent! But, I would never have taken you then. You know that don't you?"

"Of course I do. You are an honorable man, Sam Knight," she told him.

She straddled him, and slid her wet sex up and down on his massive cock.

"But, honor be damned right now! I'll bet you that I could have seduced you that day. See? What I'm doing now is all it would have taken. Don't deny it."

Sam was ready to take her, now, and lifted her up just enough so he could plunge into her wet channel. Sarah gasped at how deep he got with just one thrust. It always surprised her how massive he was, and how she craved it thrusting inside her body.

"OK. I won't. But, in all honesty, yes. If you had laid your luscious ass on that floor, and spread your legs for me, I would have taken you, Sarah. You're right. I can't deny it. You would have been the youngest mate in our history!"

"And, your lifespan would have ended if Canaan had found out!"

"You know it! My ass would have been royally kicked down the road to the afterlife!"

Sarah stroked his face with her hands. She wiggled as she lifted off him, then sat down hard on him again.

"Maybe. But, I would have followed right after you!" she whispered to him.

Sam pushed his mate's beautiful red hair away from her lovely face, bringing her lips to his gently.

"I love you, Tink," he whispered back to her using his pet name for her. "With everything that is in me, with all that I have, and all that I am, I love you. No matter what happens, remember that above all else," Sam told her reverently. "You four must do whatever it takes to stop him. No matter what. Promise me?" he begged.

"And, I love you, Sam. With everything in me, all that I have, and all that I am, I love you. I will. And, I will never dishonor you. I promise!"

"Then, we will be together wherever we will go forever," he told her with tears in his eyes. They both knew, somehow, neither would survive.

"Always, Sam," she murmured against his lips. "Forever."

"Forever."

Sam took her hard. It was fast, it was desperate. He had loved her even when she was a minor. He had claimed her telling Canaan in secret when she was but fourteen. But, she was his. She had always been his, and he was hers, now. They'd gone through a hell of a lot together, and now, they would never talk about it again.

After their fierce love making, they both collapsed into the pool where they promised their love forever.

~ 9 ~

What if there won't be a future? ~~ Anita

Dan had disappeared. Anita had no idea where he was, and she was feeling desperate. Should she go get everyone, and interrupt everyone's last minutes, or should she just go look for him?

Pacing back and forth, she finally decided to go look for him by herself. Heading for the glass door, she breathed a sigh of relief when she saw Dan walking up the deck. She darted out to him.

"Oh, Dan! Where the hell have you been? I've been so worried!" she cried, plowing into his rock hard body, and throwing her arms around his neck.

He had smelled her incredible scent before he reached her. When Anita threw her arms around him, Dan put his arms around his mate burying his head into her neck sniffing deeply in memory. Yes! That was the scent he remembered from so long ago! He couldn't believe what he had discovered! More than that, how could he have ever forgotten? They have forgotten?

"I'm sorry, my beautiful Anita. I would never have worried you like this, but what I had to do took me a bit longer than I expected."

"What were you doing?" she asked him.

Putting her away from him, he could see the hurt in her eyes, and kissed her nose.

"Come with me? No questions?" he asked grabbing her hand.

"Where?" she questioned him. His eyes narrowed at her. "Oh. Right. No questions. Sorry."

He grinned at her wickedly, and proceeded to lead

her out into the night. Anita felt something in her stomach. Butterflies? No, that wasn't it. More like a dragon flapping in her stomach while shooting fire into her belly!

As they walked, they spoke about what was coming.

"Are you OK?" he asked her.

"Dan, I'm not going to lie to you. I am scared of what will happen. What if there is no future?"

"If there is no future, then we will at least be together where there are other tomorrows. Besides, all that matters is right now. The two of us." He turned to look at her. "Let's phase."

The two wolves ran out into the night together. Clouds were building, and one could hear thunder in the distance that would never come closer. Just like the first time they were there, rain began to fall as they reached their destination. Anita recognized where they were, and phased to her naked, human form along with Dan.

"Déjà vu! What are we doing here?" She was puzzled.

The trees were less full than they were the first time, since it was late fall, and a very soft glow was filtering through them. Dan weaved Anita through the small grove of trees to reach the protected outcropping where they had acknowledged they were mates. Anita looked up at him in question. Dan's arms went around Anita's waist, and he pulled her gently toward the glow.

As they exited the trees that surrounded the overhang, Anita's eyes widened in surprise.

Stunned, Anita saw their overhang glowing gently with candles that were set into several, small indentations resembling small shelves in the solid rock. Knowing the "shelves" were not there the first time, Anita realized that Dan must have carved them! She also knew that the interior of the cleft was deep enough that even a heavy rain could not touch anyone who was under it. The ground was covered with quite a few huge, thick quilts with the largest being forest green in the center. A bucket with champagne graced another, larger indentation with fruit and cheese. Above, hanging from the top of the overhang, a small candelier with ten candles was flickering happily putting an end to the darkness around them. Pillows piled high covered the back of the rock, and completed the full-on, romantic, and seductive scene that lay before her. No wonder Dan had been late! She slowly turned her head to meet his glowing, but devilish, eyes. She knew that something was going on, but she had no idea what it might be! A very sexy smile turned up on her lips.

"You did this for us? Is this why you were so late?" Anita felt a tightening between her legs. "Oh, Dan! It's beautiful! Thank you!"

"You're welcome. I will admit the candelier was a bit of a challenge! Our mating should have taken place where you and I first acknowledged it. But...," Dan hesitated.

"But, what?" Anita frowned.

"Unfortunately, where we first became mates is a lifetime ago, and we can't go back there. Well, I guess, technically, we could, but it's quite a bit further away and probably wouldn't look the same."

Anita's mouth dropped. What the hell did he mean?

"What the hell are you talking about, Dan? This overhang was where we realized that we were mates."

"Come," he said simply pulling her underneath just as a deluge poured down around them.

A small bowl of water was there for them to wash the dirt off of their feet and hands. Their phase into wolves did not mean that their feet and hands were not dirty from the mud while running. They were always dirty after a run. He bent to wash her feet, then his. After washing their hands, Dan slowly lowered Anita onto the pillows behind them, and Dan followed sitting next to her.

"You want to explain what you mean, Dan?"

Dan nodded, and put his arms behind his head leaning back onto the pillows.

"It's just so damned comfortable here," he thought to Anita as he stretched his glorious and tattooed naked body out on the quilt.

Anita couldn't argue with that, because she, too, stretched out while deliberately jutting her breasts forward just to get Dan's attention. And, it did - just as always!

"Well, it's been bugging me for a long time," he began. "I just couldn't figure out what it was."

Anita locked her arms around her knees, and waited.

"Remember how I wondered why I had a second chance at love after Miria? It should never have been possible, because we are only granted one life mate. I have puzzled over it for a long time, now, and I finally realized why just earlier today."

He stopped, and pulled her next to him. She shifted in order to press her breasts against his side so she could see his face.

"Why?" she whispered stroking his chest moving her fingers downward to his thick erection.

"Because, love of my life, I claimed you as my mate when we were fifteen."

Anita's fingers stopped their browsing, and her brows drew together in total confusion. What was he saying?

"You're not making sense, Dan! What do you mean?"

Dan grinned at her. He knew Anita didn't remember, either. But, he sure did, now, and his cock hardened and lengthened even more. Seeing Anita notice, too, her eyebrows rose higher in a silent question.

"Miria was never my mate. Could never have been

my mate, because I was already mated - to you."

"What? I really don't understand, Dan." Anita was so confused, now, she shook her head as if she had cobwebs in it while spiders wove twice as many more of their thin jewels of the night in her head.

"I know. I was confused, too. But, then, I remembered something." He stopped and looked at her. Her long hair was hanging loosely over her breasts just like he loved it, and he brushed it back across her shoulders. "Do you remember those last three days we were together at our 'secret' swimming hole?"

Well, of course! How could she forget that their parents, and Cordone, were away for four days, and Dan and Anita stayed home ostensibly to study. Oh, they'd studied, alright! And, they had a plan to "study" the moment their parents left. They would meet at their pool, strip, and skinny dip for three days straight. Both of them loved being naked as much as possible. She also remembered being terribly excited to be with Dan for three solid days - alone. It was a first for them. Anita also remembered that she spent a lot of the time staring at Dan when he wasn't looking at her. Looking at his strong, nude body. And, OK. So. She stared at his dick when he wasn't looking, too! She even remembered the two of them holding each other at night with their chests pressed against each other as they lay looking up at the stars, and waking up together spooning, swimming, and playing all day long.

"Being fifteen, well, we were curious, and in those days, twelve was considered adult."

"Yep, and twelve was an 'old maid' in most villages. A lot of girls were married, or at least mated at that age, and some had already had their first baby at ten, or even eleven."

"Right. Of course, by today's standards, that would be horrific and perverted. I wasn't aware, totally, of what constituted mating at the time. But, I did know how to do it, and what happened afterward. All I knew was that I wanted to spend all my time with you."

"Skinny dipping," she giggled.

"Oh, yes! We'd been doing it since we were pups."

"And, no one knew."

"Anita. What do you think your parents, and mine, would have done if they had caught us naked?"

Anita blinked. Her mouth turned into an "O" when she realized what he was saying.

"You and I would have been horsewhipped, punished, drawn and quartered, tar and feathered, and finally, forced to mate. That would not have been a bad ending!"

She nodded, but had to laugh. "I know. You're right."

"And, those three days we spent alone? Sleeping together, waking, playing, swimming, teasing, and most of all holding each other quite a bit - especially at night."

"I do remember. I still don't get what you're talking about."

"We played 'doctor', Anita. You remember that, too?"

She laughed.

"How could I forget that? We explored each other's bodies thoroughly. I don't think there was one part of them that we did not touch!"

"Yes. Touch. We touched every part of each other's bodies, Anita. Did you forget there was one way we 'touched' each other that neither of us want to acknowledge? Or remember?"

Anita's face went red when she did remember. She hadn't forgotten, but neither of them spoke of that one thing after it had happened. After that incredible three days, they never skinny-dipped with each other again.

"We loved stripping in front of each other. We

loved holding each other nude. Did you never ask *why* we loved to strip, and skinny dip at every opportunity?" Anita opened her mouth to deny what was obvious. "No. Anita. Don't deny this. Think about it. How did it make you feel when I stared at your body back then? You were already filled out nicely!"

She blushed again, but shook her head. Anita just didn't want to acknowledge the truth!

"Not really. I never really thought about it. But, you're asking how I felt when you stared at me back then?" Heat flooded her lower body as she thought about those times when she had caught him staring at her. While she didn't realize it at first back then, she couldn't deny it now. "Horny."

Dan roared with laughter as he pulled her closer to him. Creator! He loved her large breasts against him! They were soft, full, and her nipples were hard against him.

"And, that's how I felt, too. I was horny for your body. For you."

Her face showed complete mystification.

"What the hell are you getting at, Dan?" she asked him, again. She was very confused.

"We already admitted that we both 'looked', right?"

She nodded watching his eyes rake from her breasts down to her soft dark curls, and back to her eyes.

"Then, we 'touched' - everything."

She nodded again.

"Then, I took my mouth, and…"

Anita threw out her hand, and shook her head vehemently. She didn't want to remember.

Dan gently lowered her hand to his heart, and quietly said, "Anita. Only mates look and touch each other like we did."

The dawn of sudden awareness began to show on her face in the way of shock.

"A-are y-ou trying to tell me that we looked at each other's nude bodies, because we were…you think that we were…?" she squeaked out in a high pitched voice.

"Yes, I do."

"No! No way! Impossible! Where was the glow?"

"If I had that answer, I'd tell you. Best guess? Sarah's 'broken record' that skips around, because of the curse."

Anita's eyes drifted closed as she made the connection. Anger gripped her.

"So, you're saying that Zanack fooled around with our mating? I mean…if we were mates at fifteen, then Zanack *prevented* us from being together?"

Dan nodded.

"But, then, something happened between us that we have tried to forget all this time."

He sat up to cup both her voluptuous breasts in his hands gently massaging them, and rubbing his thumbs lightly over her nipples. He continued listening to her moan at his touch.

"That first night…"

"…we became lovers," Anita finished, gasping in desire as he continued to assault her nipples. Yep! That's what she had tried to forget.

"Yes. The first day of that three days, we did everything we had always wanted to do with each other," his eyes were sultry, and his voice husky as he finally spoke the words aloud. "We didn't just strip. We stripped each other, because we were curious."

"We wanted to know what it felt like to touch each other."

Dan leaned over, and licked her nipples - first one then the other. Her womb clinched hard.

"I wanted to feel you with my hands. Every square inch of you! Your breasts were mine…even then," he claimed quietly in awe, looking at her with desire in his eyes.

"I remember. You spent a lot of time looking at them," she giggled putting her hands over his to help him caress her breasts.

"And, you let me touch you intimately, kissing your nipples, and suckling gently. I remember my eyes slipped down to your curls, and knew what was there. I was more curious than I had ever been about a woman. The other boys talked all the time about how wet their girlfriends were for them, and how much fun it was to have sex! I wanted to know what it would feel like to hold you against my nude body. I wanted to know what it was like to plunge my dick into you!"

"And, I wanted to know what it felt like against a man's hard, naked body. Your naked body. I also remember spending a lot of that day seeing your cock harden and soften. When it was hard, I felt a strange feeling here."

Anita took his hand, and placed it between her legs so he could touch her wetness. His fingers plunged into her entrance, wetting them, then they began a slow and lazy circling of her clit. He felt Anita's sex shudder and throb at his touch.

"Then, our first night came, and we lay together looking at the sky. Naked. My fingers ached to feel your body. I gave up, and yanked you to me, our bodies touching each other fully."

"And, I felt your hardness against me when we kissed."

"I asked to look at you, to touch you."

"And, I you."

"Anita, we started exploring every single part of each other. We looked, touched, and explored our bodies with our hands and our mouths! Every square inch of each other! My cock hardened with every single second I touched your body. The taste of your nipples on my tongue was unbelievable. They were large, pink, and hard. Ripe."

"And, I felt wet between my legs. Hell. We both knew what we were doing."

"We did. I was hard for you. When I pulled your legs wide, and I saw your wetness with my eyes, I felt my balls fill for the first time in my life. I wanted to be deep inside of you. My friends and their girlfriends fooled around a lot. It was hard hearing them talk about sex when there was only one girl I wanted to fuck..." he kissed her quickly, then added, "...and that was you."

"I know. Even the girls talked. But, Dan, I didn't want any of those other guys. I..." her voice broke at the realization of what they had done. "...wanted only you."

"And, I wanted only you more than anything I had ever wanted, Anita. And, that's why when you rolled onto your back under the stars, I lowered my body onto yours, spread your legs, and pushed into your heat."

"And, once we started..."

"...well, we didn't stop for three, full days," Dan finished. "And that first night? Do you remember what happened? I didn't until earlier today."

Anita frowned trying to remember. She closed her eyes, and suddenly, the scene broke in front of her. As if a veil had been over her eyes, they flew open, and Dan saw them widen in shock as she remembered.

"We didn't say the words. We said nothing. But, in our ecstasy, as our first orgasms hit, I bit you, and you me. We blood bonded that night, Anita. That's why neither you, nor I, ever found a mate. I just fooled myself with Miria."

"We're mates!" she whispered in amazement.

"Anita, if I had just remembered our mating, nothing on this planet could have stopped me from claiming you as my mate."

"Fuck! Why did we forget?" Anita snorted.

"Again, I believe that 'skipped record' happened to us. That's why we forgot. But, we spent three solid days mating after that, and went well over the twenty-four hours. It sealed our mate bond forever."

"But, it doesn't make sense that we forgot!" she exclaimed, then slammed her hand over her mouth.

Dan laughed at her knowing she realized that was the final truth. It made no sense just like nothing else did.

"But, if we were mated, then, why make us mates again?"

"Uh, 'skipped record'."

Her mouth opened, then shut.

Dan's fingers began to gently brush over, and pull at her nipples watching them harden more. He licked his lips as he dipped his head, and let his tongue flip one of them. She jerked at the desire that fled through her body.

"So just how did you become so adept at seduction, Dan? I mean…those three days were incredible!"

"It's a secret among werewolf males that females have never been privy to know." His mouth turned up in a devilish manner. "Don't you know that we males are born with the ability to know how to seduce our mates? By fifteen, I knew all there was to know about seduction and making love," he smirked.

"Wait one doggone minute! I thought you just said you didn't know about mating?"

"I said I didn't know much about the mating process, not that I didn't know how to have sex! We males keep the secret from our females. Have you ever heard of one female that was not satisfied from being seduced by their mates - or even non-mates?"

She opened her mouth to say yes, then stopped. He was right.

"Wait! You knew what you were doing for those three days?"

He flipped her body so that it lay underneath him.

"Oh, baby! Yes!" and his mouth began to suckle her nipples causing her to moan in great desire.

"Dan. We've lost so much time."

Dan nodded, while thanking the Creator for the billionth time for being the one who was her mate as he suckled both of her breasts! She arched against his mouth demanding more!

"I-I guess you're right, Dan."

Her voice was breathless as her mate lavished his tongue and mouth on her nipples. He lifted his head, again to stare into her desire laden eyes.

"You know, Anita, when I woke up that day under here with my hard cock pressed against your luscious ass, I never knew that my day would end with the mate of my youth!" He squeezed her butt tightly.

Anita laughed stroking his hardness.

"I know. I will never forget your cock pushing against me. It took me a few minutes to figure out what that hardness was! And, then, I was truly embarrassed!"

"Seriously, though. I was never more shocked when I looked into your glowing eyes. It was even more shocking, because I'd just told you about Miria."

"Hmmmm. I wonder if, maybe, that might be a part of what Sarah was thinking."

"What do you mean?"

"Well, maybe that information was lost, somehow, just like our being mates? Not by you, but by this curse?"

Dan thought about that for a moment, and just for a split second, he thought, *"Weren't we just saying that a few minutes ago?",* and then lost his train of thought as Anita's gentle fingers began spreading the drops of semen that were leaking from the slit of his cock.

"Maybe you're right. Perhaps that piece of information got lost somewhere as well."

"Well, either way, I've never been so happy that my very best friend has been my mate since I was fifteen,

Dan. This beautiful place you prepared for us is perfect. Thank you for it."

"Me, too, my precious love, and you're welcome. Now, can we get down to coupling?" he grinned up at her.

She grinned back at him, and watched as he filled his hands with her breasts, again, squeezing them, and gently moving his fingers over her nipples causing them to harden even more than ever.

"Your breasts are so incredibly luscious, Anita!"

"Don't you mean huge?"

"Both. I used to envy the lucky bastard who would get to fondle and suck your tits! I guess I am that *lucky bastard* to have you as my mate with these beauties! They have always lured me - even at fifteen. I want to bury my head and lips in them forever!"

He leaned down to lick first one nipple, then the other, creating a firestorm within Anita.

"Well, I don't know," she said as he lifted his head in question.

She pushed his hands away, and put hers under them to lift them, and pushed them together creating a huge, deep valley. She looked down at them, and back up to Dan who couldn't keep his eyes off of them.

"I've always thought the girls were way too big. I even considered having a reduction. I wonder if I should have that done?"

She watched his expression with amusement. She knew how much Dan loved them, and she kneaded and fondled them for his eyes.

"Don't ever say that again! The 'girls' are perfect. You are perfect. In every way."

Her breasts were full, her nipples hard for his mouth and lips.

When he slipped over her body, she spread her legs wide. Just before he pushed into her, he continued to speak.

"Tits, we have always been mates. If our parents had known that we mated during the three days they were gone, well…."

"Riiigghht! That would really have gone over with my parents, let alone Cordone!"

He gave one thrust pushing his cock deep inside of her.

"What makes you think they could have done a damn thing about it, Anita? We spent hours on end alone. Naked. Sometimes late at night. Cordone knew we skinny-dipped! But, did he ever come around when we did?"

She thought a moment - not easy with Dan moving all the way out, and back into her again.

"No," she gasped

"Exactly. We could have been mates for years, before they ever found out if we had started at the age of six like everyone else - unless you had become pregnant, that is! Then, they would have known everything!"

Anita's finger patted her chin in thought.

"Like fifteen was any better?" A thought came to her. "And, don't tell me. You did everything you could to make sure I became preggers, right?"

He slammed deep into her as he released his seed.

"I did!"

"And, if I had gotten pregnant at fifteen?"

For once, Dan was deadly serious. "We were mates, Anita. A child - our child - would have been a blessing, and because I did mate you, they couldn't have said a damn word!"

They both laughed heartily at the thought. Dan had slipped from her, but was still laying over her.

Anita lay back on the pillows where her legs were still spread with his between them.

"Why green?"

Dan looked at her in surprise. "Huh?"

"I mean, why a forest green quilt?"

"Ah!" He leaned down to whisper in her ear. "Because, mate of my fifteen year-old body, white doesn't let me see our love on it when we blood bond, again, tonight."

Anita's womb jerked hard, and their liquid flooded from her body at his words.

"Good point. Now, show me," she demanded.

"Show you? What?"

"Seriously? We mated at fifteen, so show this amazing prowess of your knowledge to make love to me. And, show me just how you would have put our child inside of me!"

"Well, I already did that when we were fifteen, more than once, I might add. Not to mention I put Rachel inside your body, too! But, since you asked so nicely? My pleasure!" Dan replied as he flipped her over, and pushed her up on her knees.

~ 10 ~
A future that might never be

Lynne lay in Richard's arms after their love had reached a height that even they never realized it could. The night was black with lightning, thunder, and heavy rain. Richard got up, and walked out the door of the cabin to stand on the front porch followed by Lynne. With her long, white hair blowing in the wind, she joined him, and his arms went around her pulling her to him tightly. They both peered into the storm.

Lynne pulled his head down to kiss him.

"Eric?" she asked knowing he knew what she was about to say.

"It's bad, Linora. Maybe it's because of my long life? I don't know, but I can feel that time is beginning to unravel."

Richard turned to look at her eyebrows up in surprise. He knew she wasn't expecting what he just said.

"Huh? Are you telling me you can 'feel' time?" she whispered into the night.

"Yes. Zanack is about ready to open the time portal. His thoughts about opening it may very well be causing the ripple effect that I am feeling. All realms strictly forbid it. We are not allowed to change time. We cannot even try to change it! The closer we get to the final moment, the faster it will unravel."

"Well, you heard the conclusion we all decided earlier. He has to go back in time to recast the curse. But, I still don't understand how it is possible in the first place."

His head turned to the naked beauty by his side.

"How indeed," he kissed her lips gently. "Linora, I am so in love with you, I can't see straight! Tonight…just for tonight, we will forget everything, and spend what is probably our last night together before this comes to pass."

"I love you, Eric."

Richard turned and gathered his mate into his arms as his mouth increased its pressure. Both moaned low as their hands gently roamed each other's bodies.

Lynne pulled away first, and watched as her mate growled at her. She laughed, and ran out into the pouring rain. Lightening and thunder had wandered off into the distance, but the rain was still heavy, and she moaned as it poured down over her naked body. She turned to Richard who was standing in the doorway watching the water flood over her breasts, and drip off her nipples. He was jealous of the raindrops that lingered there. Lynne threw her hair back so that the rain could caress her body. It was erotic, and extremely sexy to her. Being an Elf, their symbiosis with nature was different. She wanted to wrap herself up in everything around her. She let the rain caress, and stimulate her body for her mate.

Richard could do nothing but stare at the beauty that stood before him in the rain. His mouth watered for her nipples, and her wet core. Everything else was pushed to the back of his mind.

Lynne wanted Richard to come to her, so she slowly slid her hands up her body until she cupped her small breasts. He watched with narrowed and desired ridden eyes. The rain allowed her thumbs to slide easily across her breasts as she caressed her own nipples. Parting her legs, one of her hands slipped lower to her curls where he watched her twine her fingers into the soft, white fur, then as they slipped between her legs to stroke her sex. She groaned loudly as she dove into her tight channel with two fingers. Her thumb circled her clit while juices flowed into her hands and down her legs.

Richard's cock was standing upright pointing directly at her. It needed release, too. Grabbing her eyes, he stared into them as he leisurely slid his hand along his hardened shaft walking toward Lynne one step at a time until he was just a foot away from her. His eyes dropped to her hands that were bringing her to ecstasy.

They stood where anyone could see them. Their excitement grew as they watched each other masturbate. Lynn couldn't stop the wetness from sliding down her legs, and Richard grew much harder. He licked his lips in anticipation of using his tongue on her clit that was drenched with her liquid. Richard's hand massaged his cock faster and faster, and Lynne's fingers plunged in and out of her channel, bringing her to her climax.

"Linora. This is the most erotic thing I have ever seen! I can't stop rubbing myself watching you," he gasped feeling his balls tighten.

"I am Elf, Eric. This is what I am; it is who I am. We are erotic beings, and we desire sex more than anything else. One of the things to heighten our sexual desire is to touch ourselves while our mates watch. I remember my Mother telling me. It brings both the males and females to climax," Lynne was breathless as she explained. "We have never discussed this aspect of our mating."

Richard's cock tightened, and Lynne could see he was about to release his semen onto the ground. She reached out, taking it into her own hands. She used a feather touch around the head, and she knelt down in front of him.

"No, Eric. Not on the ground, but in my mouth," she told him softly as she put her mouth over the sensitive head licking it. "The precious liquid fire that you make should never touch the ground. It should be placed inside my womb, on my body, or in my mouth - always.

Nowhere else. Let me show you another trick that Elven women can do."

Her tongue licked his shaft from the bottom upward, and then took it into her mouth. Lynne cupped her hand around his balls, squeezing gently as her mouth suckled the tip of his cock. Richard's eyes widened in surprise as he watched the tip of her tongue narrow! His engorged head broadened as she deliberately slid the narrow tongue into his slit!   Then, he felt her tongue lick him from the inside of his shaft!

"Fuck, Linora!" Richard gasped, causing him to rock back and forth as she slid her tongue in and out of the slit in his cock until he ordered, "Suck me, Linora! Now!"

Richard thrust his cock harder and faster as she slipped her mouth over his cock. He thrust repeatedly into her luscious, wet mouth. Lynne suckled him harder providing a slick friction for his shaft. Richard looked down at his mate, and his balls filled heavier and tightened. His cock contracted, and exploded his seed into Lynne's mouth. Her head thrown back, mouth open, he pumped his cock over it shooting every drop of his hot seed into it.

Lynne's eyes closed, her breasts jutting outward, as she let him fill her mouth so full, his semen dribbled out of the corners of her mouth, and slid down her already wet body.   Finally, she opened her eyes seeing his glowing with great desire. Without turning her eyes from his, she swallowed his seed.

Richard had never seen anything more sexy and beautiful as his mate's mouth filling with his liquid fire. She swallowed it. That did it. He narrowed his eyes, and yanked her body up to him.

"Now, Linora. We do it my way."

He picked her up, and her legs went around his waist as he crushed her lips with his.

Lynne laughed softly. "And, what is your way, my lord?"

"Get on your knees."

Lynne didn't think she could be wetter than she was in that moment. She was horribly wrong. She sank to the ground onto her knees, and Richard's hands lay on her hips using the water to slide them over her ass. They slipped further down, and his fingers gently skimmed her entrance pulling her wet folds apart so he could look at her. Pink and creamy, his mouth lowered as he licked her clit, and pushed four fingers into her channel.

Lynne cried out at his ministrations. She wanted…no she *needed* more.

"Please, Eric! Oh, please!" she begged him.

Richard stopped just long enough to answer her.

"Not just yet, Linora. I am watching the most beautiful ass in the world dripping with our juices. It's time to bring you to your orgasm the way you did to me."

Lynne jerked hard at his words. His fingers quickened inside her as they pulled in and out until she cried out with need. His mouth circled her clit putting just enough pressure on it to have her writhing side to side. This was what she needed. One with nature. She needed her mate to act the way animals acted in nature.

"Do you want me to behave as an animal does to his mate, Linora?" he breathed hard.

"Yes! Please, Eric?" she panted hard, and couldn't breathe.

"Then, I will give you what you wish."

Richard's mouth left her, and just when she was about to demand it back, in sudden surprise, she felt a very long, wet, soft tongue shove deeply into her channel!

"Eric…?" she began, and turned to see Richard's face combined with his wolf! His eyes glowing devilishly at her, his tongue slipped back into his mouth, then back out again as it licked her clit, and dove deep into her body. They were not compatible for sex in the two different forms, but Richard found a way to give to her everything she wanted, and needed! His wolf's tongue thrust into her deep and fast having desired nothing more than to mate with his Lynne, but could not figure out a way to do it until now. The wolf used his tongue, and his gentle nipping at her clit with his teeth made her scream his name out into the night. He phased back to himself, and she felt Richard's cock much, much bigger than he had ever been, inside of her!

A sudden, great amount of semen exploded into his mate's body with a force Richard had never felt. He and Lynne screamed out repeatedly as he and his wolf filled her full!

Lynne's legs lost purchase as she started to fall onto the ground. Richard caught her before she fell, lifted her into his arms, and carried her back into the cabin laying her on their palette. He lay down beside her.

"Eric!" she gasped in a whisper. "Y-your wolf! Its tongue! Your cock? How…?"

Richard stared down at her grinning like a Cheshire cat. His tongue scraped both her nipples, before he answered.

"Your tongue inside me caused me to partially phase."

Her head shot up. "What?"

"It's the first time in my life that I did not have control over my wolf (minus the time as a vampire)!"

Lynne was so weak, she could barely raise her head from the most amazing orgasm she had ever had.

"Oh, my beautiful Linora. You now know my deepest, darkest desire," he whispered against her lips. "To mate with you in wolf form. But, we know that can never happen. The only thing I can say is that my wolf was determined to find some way to mate with you. When I told you to get on your knees, it wasn't me. It was my wolf demanding it. He wanted to bring your desire for nature to come true. So, he took me over, and I partially phased. His tongue is so much longer than my human form, and if this is the only way he could mate with you in his wolf form, and you in your human form, then that was what he was determined to do."

"You mean he used his tongue to mate with me?" Lynne asked in surprise.

"Yes, but only partially. He wanted his mate, but he couldn't mate the normal way, so he chose to do it another!"

"And, you let him?" she asked.

"Why wouldn't I? He loves you as much as I do! But, when I phased back is when I realized something momentous happened to me. What did you feel inside of you?"

"You were - huge!" she told him holding his hardness in her hands while his fingers dipped underneath her. Her eyes met his. "You were harder, and much larger than ever before!"

"I don't know how, but my wolf's cock came forward. I had no control. I have never been that long, big, and hard in my existence!"

She stopped fondling him, and looked up into his eyes in shock.

"What are you saying...?" she began, and he finished.

"My wolf found a way to merge with me, and its cock mated you!"

"What does that mean, Eric?"

"It simply means that my wolf has found a way to mate with you on his own level." He stared at her, and his eyes narrowed as he finished in a whisper, "And, I gave myself up so he could do it!"

Her mouth dropped. His wolf mated her? She suddenly smiled big as she continued to stroke him.

"Hmmm. Can your wolf do it at will if he wants?"

"I don't know. Maybe?"

"He's wanted to mate me for a long time, right?"

Richard smirked. "He has," knowing exactly what she was about to say.

Lynne pulled herself up to whisper in his ear.

"Then, let your wolf take control, Eric! Let him out to do what he wants to do with his mate. Let him combine with you. It's only fair."

Richard threw back his head, and roared! How his wolf figured a way around the physical aspect was beyond him! But, he had no problem letting his wolf combine with him.

"As you wish, Linora, and he's asking me now! Are you willing to let him mate you with my body?"

In answer, Lynne got back on her knees, and looked back at him. Richard let his wolf combine with him, and together, they gave her everything she desired.

Hours … and Hours … and much, much Later ….

"If I have any energy left, Linora, we need to dress. It's time to go."

Richard's wolf was finally replete - and very lazy! They were all exhausted, but he still grinned at Lynne as he watched her stretch her nude body in total bliss.

"Very funny! You have more energy in that luscious and sexy body of yours than most supers have in just one of their atoms, Eric!" She stroked his chest lightly with her nail. "Besides, all three of us need to take a little nap after our monster sexathon!" she teased him.

"Sexathon? Monster? The *three* of us?" Richard asked with mock horror. "That's just so - well - *so fucking dirty,* Linora!" He pulled her up, kissed her hard on the lips, and then slapped her on the ass. His hand slid between her legs gripping her sex to pull her toward him. "I love it when you *talk dirty* to me! And, so does my wolf!" He nuzzled his mate between her breasts.

She grinned. "Well, after all, technically, we did have a three-way...."

Richard's mouth slammed into hers - not so much to silence her, but to agree. It was exciting knowing that three, different beings participated in an act of sex together. Yep. It was dirty!

"You know, you're right," he told her feeling his wolf bound back to full energy when he realized that his mate and his human were ready to let him have his way with his mate - again. "Let's give my wolf one more monster sexathon!"

Richard removed his hand from her sex that was dripping with their liquid. His wet fingers teased her hardened nipples. Linora stretched her naked body to its longest length jutting out her breasts. She groaned when Richard's hands began to caress their tips once again. She would never get enough of her god/human/wolf lover. Ever.

She pulled his head to her lips. "Oh, goodie! I so want to repeat our 'three-way', Eric!"

Laughing, Richard let his wolf join with him in human form, and all three were ready for one more monster sexathon!

~ 11 ~
"Be Prepared" is the Boy Scout Motto

The night was over, and it was time to end the waiting. Time for the final chapter in the book. Time for the epilogue. Time for the End - of everything.   If only…*if only time would just stand the hell still!*

Cordone needed everyone to meet in the main room in one hour's time to prepare whatever futile strategy they might have.

When they all arrived, they lounged on either the sofas or the chairs. Cordone gave the floor to Richard.

"You're on, Richard," Cordone said, and then sat down next to Kaitlan.

"As I was telling Linora earlier, I am beginning to feel the timeline changing. Whatever he is doing, it has begun. His thoughts, alone, are doing it. We have very little time, now, before this act is played out."

"Why can you feel it, and we can't?" asked Cordone.

"More than likely, it's because only certain people from other realms can actually feel these things, and the Asgardian people are one of them." He snorted. "As you know, I made my decision to stay on Earth eons ago. I didn't want, nor desire to rule Asgard much to my Father's anger. He threw me out of Asgard, because I was a loose canon. I desired, lived for, and loved nothing but war, and fighting. I cannot tell you the countless lives of other beings on other worlds I killed. To my undying shame, that is something I can never escape. However, when he banished me to Earth, I learned a great deal about a people who didn't want war. Forced into war after war when the majority of people in this world don't want a war, made me realize that I was stupid to want war. When I had learned my lesson after a very long time, and returned, I realized that Asgard was no longer my home. Only a place where I was born. I tried very hard to return to my previous life, but the truth was that I couldn't do it. I didn't want to do it. I had fallen in love with the beings of this world. Yes, even humans. I couldn't be what my Father wanted, and so, I defied him."

"You defied him, Richard? Why?" Kaitlan asked.

"Because I was his first born, he would not accept that I would not rule in his stead one day, Kaitlan. My family and friends watched me become more and more depressed as time went on, and I couldn't bear being away from Earth. It began to consume me to the point that I did not want to live any longer." He looked at the assembly. "As you know, killing us is almost impossible. We can be killed, but it would not be easy."

Nods were all around. They'd heard all this before.

"So, I finally went to Odin, and I asked him to please let me go back to Earth. I knew my happiness existed here somewhere," he reached for Lynne's hand. "He refused, and threatened that Earth would not be left unpunished if I returned. So, I left without his blessing. I took the only thing that belonged to me, and that was 'Thor's Hammer', as the humans loved to call it, promising myself I would never use its power. Yeah, well, it's one thing to make a vow - another to keep it. So, of course, time and again proved that I used it anyway. I visited Asgard numerous times, but still refused to return on a permanent basis. When Odfrin turned me into a werewolf using his abominable creations, it effectively eliminated any power that I did have with Mjölnir. I am lucky to be able to create lightning, but, as you all know, what started this whole, damn mess was when I buried the village in the dirt. Of course, I had no idea about the curse or that Odfrin was still alive living in another being. The curse was not permanent by the time I buried it, but just burying activated it. At least until Kaitlan became The White Wolf. I can only guess how angry Zanack must have been when he realized that it had not worked the way he though it had. Of course, I've told all of you this before, and damn it! I'm repeating myself!" Richard complained, yet he continued to repeat things as if he had to complete the story, and he couldn't stop.

"The 'new' Zanack disappeared, and I was left 'holding the bag', as it were. I stopped using my adopted name of Zanack, because I didn't want anyone confusing me with the other. For eons, or at least it seemed like it, I finally migrated to a large village near Norway, and after a while and many battles, they begged me to be their king. I became Eric, King of the Vikings. From that day forward, I vowed to protect Earth and humans along with all others."

Richard paused. An idea had been forming in his mind.

"I also have been wondering if Zanack had something to do with the Vampire Wars."

Both Cordone and Sam jumped up in shock, but Sam spoke first.

"What? Wait! That's not a repetition! That is new info!"

"Well, it's just in the last couple of hours that I had a thought running around in my mind. The more I think about it, the more I'm positive that Odfrin destroyed Zanack, and took his body since his was dying. Oh, damn! Not again!" He continued repeating while trying to expand his idea. "As we have talked about, he was almost like a parasite. Just like he created the rogue werewolves, I have to wonder if he was working another one of his spells to create another species, and it backfired into the rogue vampires."

Lynne gasped!

"Holy shit!" she exclaimed.

Cordone sat back, his thumb and forefinger rubbing his chin in thought. What if Zanack conjured up another spell? The Vampire Wars would be a direct consequence of Zanack.

"I actually believe you are on to something, Richard," Cordone told him. "If so, then what else did he do, I wonder?"

"Who knows?" Sam said. "Hell! He's been in our fucking way how many times, now?"

"Too many," Dan answered as if to himself. "Hmmm. Rogues. Interesting. I became adept at tracking down and terminating rogue werewolves, first, then rogue vampires."

Richard continued after nodding to Dan.

"Eventually, Cordone found him, and killed him. Or…" Richard paused in thought, "at least you killed someone who *claimed* to be Zanack. Maybe he was a decoy for the real one. Who knows? Anyway, time progressed, and the name Zanack just ceased to exist."

He turned to Lynne who was busy trying to wrap her mind around everything.

"If we're right about this, Lynne, then you were an indirect victim of the Vampire Wars, and if he did create the rogue vampires, my guilt has just gotten larger!" he hung his head, shaking it in shame.

Seeing Lynne open her mouth, he knew she was about to jump in with the old "is that why you mated with me out of pity" bit, he forestalled her.

"No, Linora. Don't even go there! You are my mate, and it has nothing to do with my guilt. Our mating was one of the few things I ever right did in my entire life."

She stood, and threw her arms around his neck. He held her to him tightly, and looked over her shoulder at everyone else. He started frowning. Something wasn't right.

"What, Eric?" Lynne asked him.

"Well, if it wasn't Zanack that Cordone and the others, killed, then that's why he's here now."

"Where are you going with this?" Cordone asked him. "I thought we had already established that we didn't kill him a few months ago."

"Crap!" Richard said.

"REPEAT!" all four girls said at the same time bumping fists in the air.

The men turned, and gaped at them.

"Really! This repetition shit is just getting ridiculous!" Dan griped as he agreed with the girls.

Everyone stared at him, and he looked at them.

"What? Just saying the girls are right!"

Shaking her head, Anita added her two cents worth.

"Geez. OK. Let's see if we can keep on track, and stay off the repeats, shall we?"

Kaitlan glared at her.

"Yeah. Let's all get right on that one!"

Anita shook her head.

"Well, let's roll with Richard's idea. What if he did turn vampires into rogues? Since Wolfsbane has been at the heart of all the poisonings, I'm thinking that he manufactured it in a totally different manner, poisoned some vampires, almost to the point of death. Slowly. More to the point of, well, zombification, I guess you would say."

"Now that you mention it, they did act more like zombies than vampires," Cordone mumbled. "Never did think of it that way."

"Yeah. I guess they did. Right up to eating their prey," Sam agreed. "Those of us who were in the Vampire Wars were all witness to their horrendous killing."

"Hmmm. But, they were also able to turn others into rogue vampires, and if so, then it would have had to effect them on the DNA level," Anita continued. Looking up at everyone, "That is a very good conclusion. So, we were right originally. He really was trying to get rid of supers! I just can't get over how none of us ever realized it before!"

"But…," Lynne asked the inevitable question.

"BUT…." Richard emphasized with a grin seeing Anita smile a little. "Cordone…what did you do with his body?"

"I knew it! I knew it! There just had to be a 'but' in there!" exclaimed Sarah.

Richard glared at her, and then grinned.

"BUT…" he repeated. "Where did you bury his body?"

Cordone, Dan, and Sam looked at each other with wide eyes. True. Cordone killed Zanack, personally. The three of them all saw it happen. All were present, but none of them had buried him. That was left to another group of weres.

"Uh, well, we, uh…we didn't bury him, Richard," Dan put forth. "I mean, the three of us didn't bury him!"

"Dan's right. We didn't!" agreed Sam in surprise. "This is what happens when one lives a long time. You have a tendency to forget some things. Or, it's Sarah's 'broken record' effect. We were all so glad that we'd finally gotten rid of him, it never occurred to us that it might not really *be* him!"

Sarah took Sam's hand.

"OK, so, where is his body? Cordone, Sam, Dan…who buried his body?" Sarah asked the men in the room.

The three men realized who had been charged with the burial. They looked around at each other in disbelief. Then, Cordone answered Sarah's question.

"Roland Turner."

The whole room was silent. You could have heard a pin drop even on the carpet! Kaitlan finally found her voice. She had always believed that you should let someone finish a story before interrupting. But, with all of this, well, she was in the middle of a triple GRRRR moment!

"Roland Turner?" she dared to breathe the name aloud. "Cordone, you told me that he had been with my family for eons? Why would you suspect him?"

Cordone nodded. "Actually, it comes down to two suspects - Turner and McClain. Roland has been with the O'Hara Clan since the first Clan leader, Rudolpho Canaan O'Hara, formed the Clan almost 6000 years ago."

"And, McClain?" Kaitlan asked.

"McClain joined the Clan about a thousand years later."

"Well, that's no help! Both Turner & McClain would certainly fit within the timeline, but still, the curse and burying the village happened before the O'Hara Clan was ever established. So, I fail to understand that line of reasoning." Richard interrupted.

"No one ever questioned who either of them were, or where they came from. Unlike the rest of the council members - even you, Richard - Turner & McClain are the only ones who were present from the beginning," Dan remembered.

"What about Caesar and Wayne?" asked Kaitlan.

"No. They are both fairly new, because Canaan appointed all of them," Sam said. "That clearly eliminates them, and that means that both Turner and McClain existed prior to the curse."

The group was silent while they thought about it. Was it possible?

Sarah voiced everyone's thoughts.

"So, you think that Roland Tanner is Zanack - uh, I

mean Odfrin? Oh, whatever! For the Creator's sake, I am so damned confused!"

Questions were coming right and left. But, there was only one, logical answer. Sarah rubbed her temples.

"As Richard said. Odfrin took Zanack's body and identity. Identity theft wasn't just in today's world," Sarah grinned trying to lighten the mood.

Everyone turned with frowns, and rolled their eyes at her.

"Identity theft, Sarah? Are you serious?" Sam laughed at her.

"Oh, come on, guys! It happened more frequently than you know in those days, too. It was really easy to do. Anyone could take anyone's identity. There was nothing to prove who anyone was, now, was there, Richard? Lynne? I mean…if someone wasn't from their neck of the woods, or dead, wouldn't it have been that easy?"

Lynne nodded. "Sarah, that actually makes sense. It really was easy for anyone to claim to be anyone. Maybe lining out an actual timeline might help us. It might keep us from repeating ourselves?"

"Good idea, Lynne," Sarah said, and began. "Alright. Timeline."

She held up her hand. Sarah stuck one finger up as she outlined the timeline.

"Before everything, scrolls were written by someone - both a fake and the real one - along with others. And, the fake one is found by someone within the werewolf community telling of a prophecy involving The White Wolf. Next,

    A) Richard was taught by Odfrin.
    B) Richard escaped, and didn't see him again."

"I was Eric back then, Sarah," Richard reminded

her.

"Richard, that's not helping!" Kaitlan frowned.

He just grinned at her.

"OK. Starting over for the how many umpteenth times? And, you, Richard," Sarah pointed at him when his mouth opened, "Shut the hell up!"

That just elicited a laugh from everyone.

"Geez! Moving on…and, starting - *again*!" she said pointedly looking at Richard. "Let's see…

A) Thor was banished to Earth
B) Thor went back to Asgard
C) Thor came back to Earth, and Odfrin brought him."

Sarah glared at Richard to make sure she was right so far. He nodded, grinned, but didn't speak.

"Next…

D) Thor took the name of Zanack
E) Zanack would not cooperate
F) Odfrin put him in prison for twenty years."

She just looked at Richard, again. Then, just to tease her, and to lighten the moment, he opened his mouth.

"Well, you see…." he laughed heartily when daggers shot out of her eyes. "Sorry, Sarah."

"I love you, Eric, but will you shut the hell up, and stop teasing Sarah?" Lynné told her mate with a huge grin, which took the sting out of her words.

"Ha, ha," Sarah's voice was dry. "Continuing on…

G) Odfrin decides to create a new race of beings with werewolves
H) Zanack, aka Richard, is bitten by those werewolves."

Waving her hand at Richard when he tried to correct her again was the last thing she needed right now, if she was going to keep on track.

"Richard! Yeah, yeah! I know! You were Eric! I don't give a flying flip right now, OK? I need to get this done, before I start repeating myself!"

Richard stared at her, and nodded once.

I) Zanack experiences his first turn, runs away

J) Zanack became Eric, King of Vikings

K) A 'new' Zanack, possibly Odfrin, appears

L) 'New' Zanack casts the curse gone wrong using only three Elementals

M) Eric buries the town that was destroyed by elemental powers, unknowingly

N) The curse takes partial effect

O) Odfrin, aka Zanack, disappears

P) Assumption: Zanack creates the rogue vampires using Wolfsbane

Q) The Vampire Wars begin

R) Cordone, Sam, and Dan kill who they think is Zanack

S) Turner is charged with burying the 'new' Zanack, aka unknown

T) Jump ahead, Tara killed by Wolfsbane, almost kills Kaitlan

U) Kaitlan becomes the White Wolf."

"Yep. Not bad, Sarah," Lynne said to her. She had been quickly taking down what Sarah said so they wouldn't forget, and repeat it. "But, can we get rid of the M, and change the 'M' to 'N', the 'N' to 'O', the 'O' to 'P', the 'P' to 'Q', and so on?"

Heads turned toward her with questioning frowns.

"Huh?" Kaitlan said.

"What? I mean, M is the thirteenth letter, and we all

know13 is bad luck! Especially for Elves!" she complained.

Anita stood up, and moved to stand behind Lynne, patting her on the head.

"Poor little Elf!" She looked at everyone with her doctor's deadpan expression. "It's obvious she's gone whack-a-doodle with stress!"

"What? I'm just saying we don't need any *more bad luck*!" Lynne crossed her arms, and sat back. "Hmph!"

Ignoring Lynne, and closing her eyes trying to keep from answering with another smart aleck remark, Sarah asked, "OK. Cordone, I get a little fuzzy here. Did I get that right? You killed Zanack before the Vampire Wars after?"

Cordone took a deep breath.

"Yes, you're right. It was after, but we had heard of the name Zanack before they started."

"Ah! Then, it's highly possible that Zanack could easily have decided to create another type of race like he tried to do with werewolves. He would have done this probably right after he took another body, and became Zanack, then created the vampire rogues."

Sarah looked around, then in a teeny tiny voice said, "Well, isn't it possible?"

Cordone wasn't so positive about anything, now.

"With Zanack, anything is possible, so, sure, why not? He could have actually manufactured the vampire rogues."

"Moving on for the moment. Zanack casts the curse." Sarah turned to Richard, "Richard, am I right about the curse being before the Wars?"

"Long before the Wars. The O'Hara Clan had not been established. And, an FYI? The Vampire Wars lasted well over ten years."

Sarah's eyebrows rose. "Well, that's the first time anyone has mentioned the Vampire Wars lasted ten years!

And, you buried the village before them?"

"Yes. Very long before them. You have the timeline right."

"Yeah. Right. OK. At least it's not a repeat. So, that means that obviously the curse came sometime before Richard buried the village," Sarah suggested. "Prior to 6000 years ago."

Raised eyebrows, and stunned looks met hers.

"That might be about right, but we are still working on assumptions. Taking it in chronological order seems to be putting everything in perspective," Richard said.

"So, let's assume more, then. Zanack created the vampire rogues, and does seem to suggest the same MO."

Nods.

"OK. After the wars, Richard hightails it home, meets 12 year-old, Elf/Vampire Lynne who was created by the rogues. Richard becomes a vampire/werewolf/Asgardian, and he takes her to his own city that was not in Norway?" She looked at Richard who nodded, again, "And then, establishes her as his daughter and princess." She paused to turn to Cordone. "Now, Cordone. Sometime during the years after the Wars, you killed Zanack, and Roland took the responsibility of burying him, right?"

He nodded once.

"And, that was before you met Richard?" Another nod. "Then, finally, Richard and Lynne came upon Canaan and Sam fighting what was left of the rogue vampires, and killed the rest of them. Richard and Lynne find their city in ruins with just a few survivors. They gather them up, and return to the O'Hara Clan taking the name of Richard O'Malley."

"And, yet, Zanack resurfaces only recently."

Kaitlan pointed out, "You mean like Odfrin just disappeared, Zanack just reappeared, again."

That started everyone thinking.

"Yes."

"The next significant thing that happened came when my Mother was killed by Wolfsbane," Kaitlan whispered.

"And, no one put it together, because it was the first time in thousands of years that it had been used to kill," Lynne finished a thought she'd been having.

"Yeah - since the Elves and Ali'on's Father," Anita offered. "At least as far as we know."

"Fast forward. Kaitlan is born, transforms into The White Wolf, and mates Cordone. And, the curse begins to unravel…"

"…causing the timeline to unravel…" Dan added.

"…and the curse is broken, because of Kaitlan," Sam finished.

"So, now we have a timeline of what happened from day one."

"It's your fault, Kaitlan!" Dan quipped to her, and she just grinned widely.

Cordone rose, and walked to the windows looking out on his land, then turned with his hands behind his back. One hand came up to run through his hair.

"Added to that, my house…this house…was built by the Elves in a contract with my Father and Mother. Long before the Vampire Wars, Johnson and Ter'act are in desperate need to get their hands on my land. Ter'act kills my Mother, my Mother kills Ter'act, Johnson is there for someone else, apparently, and finally, my Father is killed by some horrible monster that bears no resemblance to anything on this Earth. "

Kaitlan jumped in with her thoughts. She new there were a few more pieces to the puzzle.

"OK. That begs another question. Who else was with Roland the day they buried Zanack?"

"Let's see…," Cordone said, then felt his stomach drop out from under him as he remembered. "Shit!

McClain, Johnson, and Tim," Cordone said flatly, his stomach curling in knots.

They had their answer!

"Fuck!" Sam said loudly. "You're right!"

"Dammit to fucking hell!" Dan was right behind Sam.

"So Roland, McClain, Tim, and Johnson buried Zanack, but from what Richard has said, the power of the wizard, Odfrin, was more powerful than anything, or anyone, right?"

Richard nodded.

"OK, then.   It is not uncommon in myths and legends, that a wizard, creature, or even parasite can transfer their conscience to another body when a body they are inhabiting dies, right? It's not a myth? Not to mention they have power over other minds?"

Kaitlan's fingers snapped.

"Like in the movies we see! They transfer their powers to the nearest body available when the body they are in dies. So, it is conceivable that either the real Zanack was dying, or at least dead, because Cordone killed him. Maybe the human body could not contain Odfrin? Maybe he *needed* a much stronger one - like one that was supernatural? So, he survived the host just long enough to jump."

Cordone turned to Richard. "Would Odfrin have that kind of power?"

Richard nodded. "In spades."

"But, why?" Anita asked the major question that had been bugging her all this time. "What would he hope to gain? What was his reason for invoking the curse in the first place? It's obvious he was trying to hurt all the beings on this planet! But, even more so, Canaan and the Clan, which was so much later, and there just doesn't seem to be a connection to them. Why?"

Richard's head jerked up.   No.   It couldn't be.

Surely, he had not been than angry? Angry enough to hurt the people of this planet? Suddenly, he slapped his head as realization came to him. How in the hell had he not seen this? It was all his fault!! All of it!

He turned to everyone with haunted eyes.

"Me."

"Excuse me? Who, love?" asked Lynne gently.

"Remember, Odin sent me with Odfrin. Did Odin know the power of Odfrin? What he could do? To punish me, he sent me to Earth only to let Odfrin do whatever he wanted to this planet? To me? Is that possible? Would he have done this on purpose?" His eyes narrowed as anger began to grow quickly. "Did he set this monster loose on the Earth? And, if he did, what did he hope to gain?"

Dan jumped in with his idea.

"Why not, Richard? He was angry at your war mongering. He sent you here with Odfrin to straighten out your attitude. So, when you returned, you didn't want war any more unless forced upon you, but you don't want the throne, now. You angered him more by coming back."

"But, he was so happy when he met Richard, Jr. Would he still be angry?" Lynne said.

Anita finally decided it was time to speak.

"Maybe he changed his tune?"

"If he did, it makes no sense for him to unleash his anger through a powerful wizard like Odfrin, let alone on Earth where his grandson lives. No. He wouldn't. I think we can discount that theory," Kaitlan said.

Sarah stood up, and began to pace.

"Kaitlan is right. And, Anita asked a great question. If his soul, spirit, or whatever was too strong for a human's, then…?"

"What, Sarah?" Sam asked.

Kaitlan knew. She and Sarah stared at each other in shock.

"Then, he did need a super's body," Kaitlan

answered. "Only a super's body would have the strength to hold his essence for a much, much longer period. Which means only one thing…"

"And that would be - what?" Dan asked.

"Cordone, it was Zanack you killed, but maybe the parasite really wasn't dead. Parasites can usually survive a short time before they have to have another body on which to feed," Anita said. "It's what Kaitlan and Sarah said earlier…aaand I'm repeating myself, again!"

Anita's words stunned everyone. This was just not going in a good direction.

"Yep. You are. But, at least it waited a bit!" Cordone said. "If that's so, Anita, then, perhaps you're right, and his body was not completely dead. Odfrin jumped into the nearest available body - a person who was burying him."

"And, that's another repeat, but at least it was followed by something new. Anyway, it is highly possible. That would not be unusual in those days," Lynne said. "Many people, unfortunately, were buried alive. That has to be when he jumped - straight into Roland. And worse than that, Johnson and Tim were witnesses, which means they are involved with Zanack. They have to be."

"Richard, could he have been able to control their minds?" Sarah turned back to Richard.

"I have no doubt, Sarah. If he, indeed, took over Roland's body, then his powers would be increased greatly. His powers are only as strong as the body in which he inhabits. Gaining a super's body would let him take advantage of the enhanced powers by a super, and being on Cordone's land would increase it several times."

"But, do you really believe that your own Father would do this to you? To the planet? Just because he was angry with you? If Odin is a 'god' then isn't he still ruling Asgard?"

Richard nodded his head. "My Father is able to do more than just throw around lightening. He actually has the ability to create a changeling. Odin can pour powers into it. Not all, of course, but some."

"A Changeling? So, now, you're saying that Odfrin was a changeling? Oh, goody! *Another* new thing for us to worry about!" Dan said out loud. Everyone looked at him. "What? Just sayin'!"

"Oh, Dan! You've been around the girls way too long!" Cordone snickered earning an "evil" look from Dan.

"No, Dan. I'm not saying that. At least not technically. A changeling has no independent thought. It only carries out instructions for what it has been told. But my Father has many things available to him. He uses them for many different reasons. As a general rule, it's for observation only. He has to create one out of a being native to their own world that is dead, and it would have been from one of the five original races on Earth. But, like I said. It is incapable of independent thought. It's not sentient. So, I am going to scratch that as well. My Father has done so many manipulative things that I automatically accuse him for making my life hell when anything goes wrong, but this is not one of them." Richard shook his head. "No. Kaitlan is right. Odin had nothing to do with any of this. As angry as he was at me, he would never take it out on the inhabitants of this planet. But, I never thought….I mean, it never occurred to me that he could……" Richard's voice trailed. Then, it appeared he made a decision. "No. My Father had nothing to do with this. It's not his style."

His spirit rested when he realized his Father had nothing to do with anything. Richard began his standard pacing that everyone was becoming familiar with while he thought.

"So, when the hell is this repeating thing going to

stop?" Dan asked, then held up his hand. "Never mind. I know the answer. It isn't."

Richard was still pacing.

"No. We're missing something. The more I'm thinking about it the more…."

"What, Richard?" Cordone asked him.

"Not a parasite," Richard mumbled.

"Huh?" asked Anita and Sarah together.

"Not a parasite…a being…." he mumbled again.

"A being? What the hell are you mumbling about?" Sam asked.

Richard continued his pacing, but it became frantic.

~ 12 ~
The Nivurian

While Richard was mumbling and pacing back and forth, Kaitlan was thinking of something else.

"We need to address the "thing" that Cordone and Sarah saw kill Zoar."

She turned to Cordone.

"I know you two skipped over a total description, because you didn't see all of it, and even with Sarah's mind manipulation thingy, it's not clear. Is there anything else that you could tell us about that creature? It's obvious that whatever it is - was - is very important to all of this. At least it's something new to figure out, and won't be a repeat."

Cordone and Sarah looked at each other, and then shook their heads.

"It happened so fast," Sarah told Kaitlan. "I'm not sure that I can."

"Sarah's right, Kaitlan. It was fast. Too fast."

"No…not a parasite. Something else. This feels familiar. Not a parasite." Richard muttered.

"Eric?" Lynne asked.

"OK. Let's approach it from a different angle. Can the two of you mesh again, and try to slow down what you each saw? Perhaps what one of you saw, the other saw something else?" Kaitlan asked them.

"Hmmm. Good idea. I hadn't thought of that. What do you think, Sarah?"

"Well, I guess I could do that Mind Manipulation thing, again, but it's still dangerous."

"I've seen Nico do amazing things in the past with

161

it, so I wonder if Mind Manipulation can be 'altered' to do other things."

"Weeellll, I suppose I could try," Sarah didn't sound very confident in this new power. "You want to try?"

"Sure. May as well. If there's nothing there, it won't hurt, but if there is something there, it could help."

"OK, let's do it."

Cordone stood up, and sat in front of Sarah with his back to her.

"Remember. Relaxing is the only way to do this safely."

"I remember."

"The rest of you? Go find something to do. This could take a while," Sarah suggested.

Kaitlan and Sam poured themselves a cup of coffee, and walked outside to sit on the deck. While Lynne called the office, Anita and Dan phased for a run. Richard remained in close proximity to Cordone and Sarah.

"Let's do this."

"WAIT!" Richard yelled.

Cordone and Sarah turned to him.

"I need you both to pay attention to me before you do this. Try to concentrate on as much detail as possible. It could be…. No. I need you to see if you can see its color, its size, how many teeth it had, and if it is covered with large scales."

"Say what?" Cordone asked.

"Humor me. This is truly important," Richard was almost begging, and his eyes were full of terror.

"Well, sure. Of course. We will, Richard, but…?"

"No questions, please. Not until you come out of it."

Both Cordone and Sarah nodded, and placing her hands, once again on his temples, she felt Cordone relax immediately, and was able to push into his mind faster this time. She weaved around his memories only stopping when she reached the moment that Zoar was ripped to shreds. Now what should she do? She paused for a minute, then got and idea.

"Cordone? I need you to use your mind's power, and join with mine."

"How?"

"I am at the memory in your mind. I need you to take my hands inside your mind, and both of us must concentrate on that moment as hard as possible. Like we did when we first merged, and I held your hand while you were a little boy."

"Done."

Cordone reached for Sarah's "mind hands", and took them in his. Sarah felt the merge begin, and she let her body relax completely while allowing their minds to become one. It was very intimate, and very dangerous.

"I'm going to check on them, Sam."

"Want another cup?" Sam asked.

"Sure. I'll get them," Kaitlan answered mindlessly.

Kaitlan silently traipsed through the glass door, and saw her mate and her bestie completely oblivious to anything around them - even more so than they had been on the plane. She said nothing, and tiptoed quietly to the kitchen passing Richard who was, again, pacing and muttering to himself. She picked up the pot of coffee, and carried three mugs out to the deck.

"Well?" Sam asked as Kaitlan handed the hot cup of coffee to him.

Kaitlan sat down and took a sip.

"Honestly? I don't know, but I think that nothing could disturb them right now. Nothing. It's as if they are not even here. To tell the truth, it's kinda scary to watch," she told him taking another sip.

"Well, it's probably more so for them." Sam took another sip. "I've seen Nico do Mind Manipulation several times, and it never ceases to amaze me what he can glean from it. He's the master, but Sarah? I'm not too sure. Perhaps the 'powers that be' have given her a special, fast learning curve?"

"We can only hope," Kaitlan told him.

Sam nodded his head in agreement.

"Are they done, yet?" Richard asked as he stepped onto the deck.

"You know this takes time, Richard. For heaven's sake! Grab a chair. I poured you a cup of coffee. It's right there."

Richard fell into the chair, and tipped the cup as he drained it in one gulp while Kaitlan and Sam just stared at him. He slammed the cup back down, breaking it. Mumbling an apology, he stood up, and began to pace, again. Kaitlan and Sam just looked at each other.

Finally, Cordone and Sarah were merged. They watched Zoar die quickly. That didn't help.

"Sarah, let's take this down to slow motion if you can?"

"Great idea. Slo-mo. Are you ready?"

"Yep."

Together, they were able to slow the scene totally down, and the next thing they knew, Cordone and Sarah were panting hard as she disconnected from his mind. They stared at each other in horror.

"Fuck!" Sarah said aloud.

"Damn!" Cordone agreed with her.

After catching their breaths, they went outside to the deck, and sat down. And, for a very good reason. Sarah and Cordone were drenched in sweat. Their skin was red as if they had been burned.

"What the fuck happened to you two?" Richard asked, finally stopping his pacing when they arrived.

"What did you see? Did it work?" Anita asked.

Cordone held up his hand, and everyone was silent.

"It worked," Cordone said silently. "Too well."

"Why do you look as if you have been burned?" Sam asked them concerned for the delicate skin on his mate.

"Easy. Because we were," Cordone said.

After everyone had gotten cups of coffee, and hot chocolate for Sarah, they all held their breaths waiting for them to speak. Their skin had begun to "tan".

"What did it look like?" Kaitlan asked her mate gently.

"It took a while, but when our minds merged, we were able to slow the scene down after about three tries."

"And?" pushed Richard.

Cordone looked at Sarah.

"We've never seen anything like it! Whatever it is, we know for certain, now, that it doesn't belong on this planet!"

"But, how is that possible?" Kaitlan asked.

"I'm here, aren't I?" Richard had to point out to them.

"Point taken."

"OK. Let me rephrase Kaitlan's question," Anita said. "Is it possible that this creature has something to do with all of this? Describe it to us."

Cordone and Sarah looked at each other.

"Describe it?" Sarah asked.

"Uh, yes. That's why you went back into his mind!" Sam told her.

"You want to go first?" Sarah asked.

"Sure." Cordone leaned back in his chair, taking a sip of coffee. "Somehow, we managed to slow it all down, but what we saw...? And, Richard, we paid attention to the things you asked us to look for. Let me see if I can describe the part I saw."

His eyes glazed over as he recalled it.

"OK. It's skin, well not skin, but large scales, were a 'putrid' gray with a purple cast that reminded me of mother of pearl, I guess," he closed his eyes to bring up the visual. "No. Not purple. A subtle, fluorescent orange. Yes. That's right. It wasn't mother of pearl. Fluorescent."

He looked at Sara who nodded agreement.

"OK. Let's see…it stood on two legs, but its arms were very long."

"Yes. And, he had clawed hands," Sarah agreed.

"Right. We've already told you about its teeth earlier. Like Sarah said, they resembled sharks' teeth, and its eyes were definitely a burnt orange, and elongated. But, unlike other animals, the eyes were in the front of its huge lion sized face instead of the sides."

Richard held his breath. No! Fuck, no! It's not possible!

"And, the teeth were almost worse than sharks' teeth. There were several rows of them. They were rotten, yellow, and black but extremely sharp! And his breath smelled like death! As if it ate rotten meat. He had saliva of some kind drooling from the corners of his mouth." Sarah almost gagged at the memory.

"You mean you could even smell his breath? Ewwwww!" Anita and Lynne both said at the same time.

"Yeah. Tell us about it," Cordone said.

"Go on," Kaitlan urged.

"Well, let's see. Its face was long with a pointed snout," Sarah told them.

"Yes. And, it had the scales you asked about, Richard. The strangest scales I've ever seen. Maybe a Leviathan. I don't really know. It was preternaturally fast, and very, very tall."

"Maybe about seven feet, Cordone?"

"More like seven and a half feet, Sarah."

As they continued to describe it, no one noticed that

Richard's face was contorting into horror.

"Its feet were huge, and only had three toes. Unlike the hands, which were claws, and had six fingers, I guess you could say. Really don't know what they were."

"That's right. They were as sharp as the sharks' teeth!"

"No hair. No eyebrows," Sarah said.

"And, that's about it, I guess," Cordone said. "It's the best description we can give."

"Yeah. What he said," Sarah told everyone.

"OK. That's just about the most horrible sounding creature I've ever heard of!" Lynne said with disgust.

"Yeah. And, it's making me sick!" Anita spouted.

"Well, if you ask me…" Dan started.

"No one asked you!" Anita quipped. Then, "I'm sorry, Dan. I didn't mean to snap."

"That's alright, Anita. I totally understand," he told her. Perching on the arm of her chair, he placed an arm around her.

Lynne finally realized that Richard wasn't saying anything, and that was just very unusual not to mention strange. She turned to see him, and almost collapsed when she saw he had fallen to his knees pounding his fists on his head.

"Eric! What's wrong, mate?" She knelt in front of him, while everyone else looked shocked at his face.

"I can't believe it!"

"Believe what?" Lynne asked him.

"It's not possible! It can't be! It's a myth! Not real…not real!"

"What, Eric? What?" she asked him, again.

"No! Not possible!" he kept saying over and over.

"Lynne! Let me," Cordone said.

He pulled Richard up, and slapped his face - hard.

"Get a hold of yourself, man! What the hell is wrong with you?"

Richard's eyes narrowed, and he began to shake as if he was going to phase, before he realized where he was, and he stopped in mid-phase. His claws were out, and fur was partially on his wolf snout. He shook himself, and returned to his human form.

"Sorry, Cordone. Thank you for slapping me. I'm having a very hard time with the description you just gave."

"Why?"

"Because, what you have just described is a creature of myth!"

"Huh? What are you talking about?"

"The Nivurians, Cordone. What you have described is a Nivurian! They are extinct!"

"How do you know?"

"Because, they were supposedly destroyed a very, long time ago - further back than Odin, his Father, and his Father's Father."

"Well, I guess, apparently, they aren't," Kaitlan said aloud what everyone else was thinking.

After everyone was able to "get their act together", according to Kaitlan, they all just sat around in silence waiting for Richard to speak. He was having a very hard time talking at all.

"Come on, Richard. Tell us what we are up against! It has to be bad for you to act like this!" Dan said to him.

Finally, Richard, taking a gulping breath, spoke.

"You have no idea!"

It was so bad, Richard was still trying not to believe that they were still around.

"It's unbelievable. I'm having a very hard time believing any were left!"

"Tell us, Richard. We can't know what to fight if we don't know what we are fighting." Cordone pulled out his Alpha powers, and Richard was forced to submit to him.

"As you say, Alpha. Well, it was long before I was

ever born. I remember, because my Father told me about it as part of the history of our people. It was a horrible looking creature! Just as you described. I have only heard of their existence, and only one sketch remains in Odin's library. In fact, no one even speaks of them any more!"

"How long ago?" asked Anita.

"You've heard of the ancient wars in mythology and legend?"

Everyone nodded.

"Well, this creature goes back much, much further," Richard stopped pacing, and sat down. "The supers and humans were not the first beings to occupy Earth."

Gasps were heard all around.

"Once, long ago, before humans, supernaturals, and even wizards, there was a race that populated Earth called the Nivurians. They actually resembled a reptile, but with big differences. And, they were very, very intelligent which made them even more dangerous. It is said that one of them wanted to rule Earth so badly that he made a pact with the Evil One. Even his kind would never have contemplated being on the Evil One's radar. And believe me that is saying a lot! The price that would have to be paid was so horrific, it was unthinkable. Even the worst of the worst would never have done it. But, he was so evil, he made that pact, and in consequence, he was given mighty powers, but with limitations."

"Evil One? What are you saying, Richard?" Lynne said in horror. She knew it was bad. Really, really bad from the expression on her mate's face. "Are you…are you saying…?"

He stopped, and looked at everyone while he nodded.

"Let me put it this way. When Grimm wrote his book of facts, his creatures would look like pure angels next to this Nivurian! This story would read like a terrible tale - without the fairies! It was always used to scare

Asgardian children, but no one took it seriously, because for us, it was just an old myth."

"Wait! Grimm was telling *real* stories?" Sarah asked in shock.

The others turned to look at her in surprise at her question.

"Never mind. I'm good. Reflex question," she told them.

"And, the price that must be paid?" Anita spewed out the question.

Everyone, then, looked at her.

"Seriously? Did you *really* just paraphrase a quote out of Pirates of the Caribbean? Now?"

"What?" she looked around. "Oh, right. What Sarah said. Reflex."

They turned back to Richard.

"I'm just not sure I should repeat it."

Even just thinking about it made Richard sick as he felt the bile rise into his throat!

"You may as well tell us," Cordone told him.

Richard looked at Cordone, then nodded.

"You asked for it!"

Several pairs of eyes turned to Richard.

"The price of this pact was that he must devour a living being once a day, drinking its blood and eating its flesh."

"Oh! I think I'm..." Lynne began, which was quickly followed by Anita.

"...going to be sick!" as Anita finished the sentence.

Ignoring the two women, Richard continued.

"It gets worse. The Nivurians not only ate their prey live, but they hoarded, and ate the rotted remains."

Gags and dry heaves hit the girls while the men felt the contents of their stomachs threatening to embarrass them in front of their mates.

"Yeah. I know. Me, too. Well, as time went on, he

progressed into something more evil with no bounds whatsoever. It is said that he began to eat his own children, and then went after any creature that he desired. Even his own species was not ignored. They were terrified of him as well. He ate whatever being he wanted for his needs. His powers remained unchecked until the Fair Ones came to fight the Asgardians. That's what the humans called the Frost Giants. As I said. No other beings in the realm gave a thought, or a care to the beings that were on the Earth. When the battle raged, others in the realms joined, only to discover the horror of the Nivurian race. It took all races to destroy them. The Asgards, and others, joined together to draw the Nivurians into a frozen valley, and the Frost Giants simply froze the asses of the entire species. The rest of the races destroyed all of them after they were frozen."

"But, not him?"

"According to the myths, they froze him as well! Even my own Father would never have believed it could happen today. Unlike other creatures in our realms, these were pure evil. My Father would never deliberately set out to destroy a whole race, but these creatures? If he knew about their existence, he would have followed his ancestor in getting rid of them! They fed off one another, and they even fed off the warriors. But, if the one who harbored the Evil One survived, then we are in a hell of a lot more trouble than we thought! It was one of the few times all of the realms were united."

"They were that bad?" Kaitlan's voice was soft.

"Yes. It is said that they dumped his frozen body on another planet far colder than even the Frost Giants could stand. And, let's face it. Sometimes we all make really stupid decisions that always seem to come back to bite us in the ass!"

Everyone nodded at that one. It was true.

"Would he have had the power to take another

body?" Sarah asked.

"I never thought about it, but in this case, no."

"There's more, right?" Anita asked.

Richard looked at Anita.

"Isn't there always?" he answered. "This Nivurian had one power given to him by the Evil One - the power to mask his true self - with those he kills."

"So, let's see if I have this right. The Nivurian isn't a parasite, but the Evil One is? This is getting so damned complicated! No wonder we couldn't figure it all out!" Anita said. When everyone turned to her, she said, "Yeah, yeah. I know. No wonder nothing made any sense. Yada, yada, yada…moving on. What we are dealing with is an ancient, disgusting being whose race was killed out by the other realms, but just not one of them. Because of his deal with the Evil One, he was given powers of such magnitude that instead of jumping from body to body, he masks himself with those he kills?"

"Not just one of those he kills, Anita. Anyone he kills."

"B-but are y-you s-saying that…t-that would mean t-that…! Oh, fuck! He can take on different forms to our eyes with however many people he killed? Is that what you are telling us, Richard? Multiple faces?" Kaitlan's eyes bugged out of her head.

"I am definitely going to say a big fat yes to that one, Kaitlan."

"Well, crap!"

"Instead of taking other bodies, are we now, actually saying, that it is this creature?" Cordone asked.

"I believe so," Richard stated.

"But, wait a minute! If that Nivurian who was dumped on the frozen planet…" Lynne started.

"…was obviously not the same Nivurian," Anita finished.

Richard darted his eyes at Anita.

"Not the same Nivu…?"

"What are you saying?" Sam asked Anita and Lynne.

They looked at each other, and shrugged. For whatever reason, the both of them had come to the same conclusion.

"If the Evil One in the Nivurian is that smart, then, I - I mean we - have to ask, why would he allow himself to be frozen and dumped on some frozen planet?" Anita's mind was working fast.

"Yeah. I agree with Anita. Would it not be out of the realm (pun intended of course) of belief that he used another Nivurian while he masked himself as a warrior he might have killed in battle?"

"Makes a lot of sense," Cordone said.

Everyone looked at him in shock. This made sense when nothing else did? He continued.

"What? It does, doesn't it? He could have masked himself as anyone he killed," Cordone mumbled.

Richard just stared at them, then added, "Even an Asgardian."

Sam was shaking his head. Unbelievable. This entire time, they were wrong - at least about whom Zanack was.

"Then, he would have killed others, masked himself over and over working his way back to Earth. But having to do it slowly in order to hide his true nature. He was biding his time until the next elementals were born."

"*IF* I'm right," said Richard. "Thousands upon thousands of years he waited, killed, and took other's identity."

"Well, shit!" Sarah said. "He IS an identity thief!"

Everyone turned to look at Sarah. She had been right all along! Just not the way they had all surmised! Sara felt useless - and dumb! She was supposed to have had all this massive power of the mind. So, why could she not have seen this? Kaitlan was watching her, and knew exactly what she was thinking.

"Sarah, it's not your fault. You were given knowledge to figure things out, and you did. The only difference was that none of us had all the info. Your skipped record. Now, we do."

"But, how could I not understand what he really was?"

"Perhaps we weren't supposed to figure it out until the end?" Anita suggested. Feeling eyes that bored into the back of her head, she continued, "Whatever. It doesn't matter who, or what, Zanack is - I mean was - I mean is. Oh, hell, forget it. I don't think that was the point. No matter what he is, the important thing is that we cannot allow him to recast the curse."

"It ends here. It ends with us. And, it ends now." Lynne threw in the last thought.

Zanack grinned listening to them. His powers were amplified now that he stood on Cordone's land just as they had deduced. And, that included his hearing. He was a good five miles from the house, but he could hear them as well as if he stood right next to them! It seems that the little female that he almost killed had figured most of it out, and the rest of them put two and two together. And, Richard was right, too. They all were right - to a point, but not completely. The truth was that he was Nivurian, and their real names were so complicated, no one outside Nivuria could ever have pronounced them! He was the one who made the deal with the Evil One, and who helped him mask who he was for eons. He was the only one of his kind left. When Zanack discovered that the Evil One let him mask his real form, he had taken the form of an ordinary Asgardian fighter during the purge of his people. As much as it infuriated him, he did not let it get to him. He had managed to help keep one Nivurian alive, and helped deliver her to the army, and they froze her instead of him. She had tried to tell them that he was there, but they wouldn't listen. After dumping her on some forsaken frozen world, he remained on Asgard masked as that dead, ordinary fighter for thousands of years just waiting for an opportunity. But, the Asgardians were just too good at seeing beyond what was, and he had to wait. That came when he met Odfrin quite by accident. A wizard on Asgard was not something that Asgard wanted, but they still had some of them. They had come from a burned-out world that was destroyed by some stupid comet, or something. Anyway, it provided the opportunity. He followed the wizard, and before Odfrin knew what was happening, killed him. Then, the Evil One allowed him to absorb Odfrin's wizard powers, and then, he masked himself as Odfrin. He burned Odfrin's body, effectively getting rid of any evidence. No one had missed the fighter, of course, so Zanack carried on as the great wizard with no one the wiser.

His chance to get back to Earth came when Odin threw Thor to Earth, which was now occupied, by humans, werewolves, vampires, and even elves. But, he was master of Nivuria, and had no intention of allowing the filth that infected his beloved Nivuria to live. But, then, he decided he could raise them like cattle for his own personal sexual pleasure and food since the two were a constant desire of the Nivurian race. But, he needed to thin out the herd in order to take possession of the planet..

So, he had an idea to make a hybrid being using werewolves. He had Thor in an underground prison for twenty years, before his idea was ready. Then, he captured some real werewolves that roamed the woods. After many years, his experiments were finally a success.

Even though it took him and the Evil One a long time of hit and miss, he was able to create the rogue werewolves - those without thought - to serve him.

That's when he decided that if Thor could be bitten, and turned, his powers would cease to be as strong, but having him at his command as the strongest of all the rogue werewolves was too tempting. So, he tied him to a great oak tree, and let the rogues have at him! He remembered the excitement as he watched them tear Thor to pieces, then watched as his body changed, and knitted back together. What happened, though, was not what Zanack had planned. He wanted Thor to be rogue; to serve him only. But instead, the rogues had actually created a new, werewolf who was completely cognizant of who, and what he was! Thor who was now Zanack, managed to get away after his first change! Zanack couldn't believe it! In addition to everything, he had not figured on Dan Wheeler. His ability was uncanny, and he destroyed all of Odfrin's werewolf rogues. And, that had set his feet upon another path. He needed another army. A stronger army. One that could defeat werewolves. Unless he defeated them, his entire plan to take over Earth would go up in smoke.

Before he completed a new hybrid, he decided to create a curse - one that would allow him to reign free, He knew about the White Wolf Prophecy, but not that the scroll was fake. He easily read the curse, and found the four elementals all within the same village. Before he could cast the curse, however, the Earth elemental was spirited away by someone. He didn't know who it had been, and he still didn't. But, he took a chance on the curse anyway. And, it failed. Zanack didn't realize it until he discovered that Thor had been the one to bury the dead village, and only after the White Wolf was born. Once he realized that it was still a failure, he knew that the world he had desired would not happen.

His next course after the curse was to create the vampire rogues. They were far more dangerous since they couldn't be killed unless their heads were removed. His Nivurian body could not be penetrated by the vampire fangs, so it was easy for him to kidnap them. He used the same experiments, creating the rogue vampires. But, again, as with all nefarious experiments, something went wrong - or, in this case, right. They became vampires with a lust for not just blood, but flesh. They lost the ability to think, and could only obey orders. Zanack turned them loose, and let them do their worst.

But, it didn't take long for the werewolves to be joined by the vampire nation, and the Elves who found a way to defeat the vampire rogues. Once the supers joined together, his plans were in the toilet yet again! This angered him greatly. But, what they didn't know was that he was one of the werewolves. He had let the werewolf rogues bite him as well, and by tearing off four of his huge scales, he let the rogues bite him just as he had done with Thor. He surmised that because he was from another world that it was the reason that he did not turn rogue. And, he was right. He didn't turn rogue, either. He became a trusted werewolf council member of the O'Hara Clan. From then till now, he bided his time. Just waiting for what he always waited for - his opportunity. Now, it was here.

Zanack was standing on the bluff waiting for Johnson and Mu to join him. His mind continued with the past as he waited.

Years went by, and Zanack's thirst and hunger for blood and live flesh grew to desperate proportions. He craved it far more than any of his vampire rogues. That led him to remember Canaan's theft of Zanack's mate! It's the one thing they didn't know. Tara. His mate. Canaan had shown up at the orphanage five minutes after Zanack had left Tara. Tara had been taken with him, and

Canaan was thrilled! But, she was his! He planned to take her when Canaan butted his ass into it, and fooled her into being his mate!

Zanack had almost lost it when he discovered Tara was pregnant by Canaan! It should have been him! But, no! Canaan had fucked her, and she was carrying his child! He had to do something at that point. To get back at Canaan. So, he worked up an ancient Elven potion, and spell that would kill not only Tara, but the fucking seed growing inside her belly! And he succeeded in killing Tara and her baby! Except that somehow, and he didn't know how, the spawn of Canaan and Tara had lived! How the hell had she survived? He never understood how the Wolfsbane potion had not worked its way into Kaitlan! She was born dead, but then, a few minutes later, she gained her life back!

Now, Zanack's time was close. He was ready to spill blood. Part of the curse called for the blood of all four women for the curse plus the blood of four other sacrifices to open the Time Portal. Death and blood were his bread and butter. Killing them to get what he wanted gave him a high! Just his thoughts, alone, were causing the timelines to change.

"Is it time?" Johnson asked quietly on his cell where he had been hiding in the house while Zanack shielded him from the others.

"Yes. Are you ready to do what I need you to do?"

"I am."

"Good. Get your ass down here. When Mu arrives, he will join us. It was by my design, so far, that all has occurred. I do not want to attack them inside the house. It is warded against all forms of fighting since I killed Zoar."

Zanack's hoodie covered his face. But, his power to mask was becoming weaker, and he couldn't keep it up much longer. He was too weak from fasting without the food that he needed. As the ages progressed, and combined with his pernicious and depraved eating habits, it became harder and harder to maintain his powers, requiring him to eat more and more flesh and blood. But, the fast was definitely making it more difficult to maintain his "werewolf" persona. In fact, he could barely do so, now. But, he couldn't wait until he could be in his real form after all these years.

This same depravity only made him more determined to raise humans, and other supernaturals, for his own palate once he had recast the curse. The time was coming fast when he would be able to satisfy his lust for flesh, blood, and sex! Not necessarily in that order. He did so love to pound into his women with his massive dick inside of them. The terror in the women's eyes when he shed his pants, and his gorgeous (although the women called it hideous) huge cock out giving them a good view, before he fucked them, just fed his lust. It was such that it had tiny spikes on it that ripped through a human, vampire, elf, or even werewolf female's soft channel as he took her over and over again.

The women of his species were built to take the spikes except for a time when a male was in the burn of "Gre'ta'lac". Oh, he could retract them if he desired. But, he didn't. The screams only spurred him on before he watched them bleed out in front of him, drinking their blood, and then feasting on their flesh. The men, on the other hand, just got a good look as he proudly pranced in front of them. He pitied their manhood. Their smooth cocks were weak compared to his. He loved to bite them off, chew them, and then use his spiked tail to slice the males in half. He didn't care for a male's blood, much, but he knew he would have to keep them so he could breed more females into his new world.

One of these days, though, he would retract his spines, and force one of the females to bear his child.

Then, after the child ripped itself from her body using its claws, they would both feast upon her blood and flesh. His child would be glorious! Maybe he'd just use one of the Elementals for that purpose. But, which one? Kaitlan was mouthy, and Canaan's daughter was not worthy of him any longer. She was too slippery, and got away from him to easily. His true "mate" had been Tara. His original plan was to take her, kill Canaan, take the Clan, and breed with her so she would have many children. He would heal her between each birth until she was hideous to him. Then, he would kill her. But, as usual, there was always an O'Hara who bested him. He hated them! Hated the Clan. He only wanted it so he could use it to establish his rule over the Earth. Anita was the bane of his existence as, time and again, he had to sneak into the infirmary, and alter tests on the forced checkups required by Clan law. Lynne? YUCK! No way was he going to fuck an Elf, and then have a fucking Elf feed his child from inside her! That left the woman whose child he had murdered. The woman he had killed, but who came back to life after seven days. Yes! She was extremely special. She had beaten death. Sarah would do just fine for his child. Her body was small and delicate, and watching his seed take root inside her filled him with a lust he had never known. After the curse was completed, he'd take her, lay her in the blood of her own family, and fuck her implanting his seed inside her. He licked his lips with the thought. He would have no trouble listening to her scream, and begging him to stop as she felt him bury himself deep in her body with his glorious manhood! And, when he came inside of her, she would feel his burning seed spill inside her womb. It would feel as if her womb was on fire. The idea of watching her suffer through five, endless months of excruciating pain while his child grew inside of her belly, spurred him faster. His dick was huge, now. He wanted this over, so he could fulfill his destiny!!!

Footsteps were heard behind him, and Zanack turned as his last cohort arrived.

"Took you long enough, Tim!" Zanack said to him.

"And?"

"So? When are they coming?" Johnson asked.

"Patience. They will be here soon enough. We will claim them, and kill them. Let them have one more time with each other."

"Sarah. You are our keeper of knowledge. Do you know where they are?" asked Cordone.

Sarah closed her eyes, and she could see. Cordone's land was magnifying her powers. All of their powers were magnified, now.

"Yes. They wait at the bluff. It is there he will open the Time Portal which will transfer us all back to the original time. However, I don't think he can return us to the exact place, though. Only the general area."

There was more, but how could she tell them their fate?

"OK." Cordone said. "It's time. We will be heading to the bluff in a few minutes where Zanack, or Roland, will be. And, remember who our enemy really is - Roland. You girls *must* go through the Time Portal in order to defeat him. He *must* go back to the original time. It's the only way to stop him. And, remember, Kaitlan. The last Earth element was kidnapped. We don't know by whom, nor do we know why. Whoever did it was on purpose. You must be careful."

Kaitlan nodded.

"I will."

"But…." Sarah started. She had to tell them.

"What, Sarah?" Sam demanded of his mate.

"I don't know how to say this, but you may as well

know all of what I do know."

She looked up at everyone with tears.

"Our mates will be sacrificed tonight. And, Cordone is right. It will be bloody."

Her voice broke, and she grabbed Sam to hold him tightly. Horror appeared on everyone's face. Except for Richard.

"She's probably right. There is always a cost to be paid for evil and magic. And, that cost is usually in blood. But, to open a portal through time, blood, and lots of it, will be required. And, I think, now, there must be a fifth element."

"A what?" Sarah said in shock.

"Kaitlan is the fourth element, but The White Wolf is the fifth."

He turned to Kaitlan.

"Kaitlan, you must be prepared to take what is needed when the time comes."

"What's that supposed to mean?" she asked him. "Take what?"

Richard shook his head. "I really don't know. I only know that tonight, I will die along with the rest of the mates. But, I do know this. You and The White Wolf must merge into one being, and you *must take* the powers needed to rid this world of Zanack. It will require one death, Kaitlan - at your hands."

"NO!" Kaitlan yelled.

But, Sarah had more to say.

"Kaitlan, it's not just our mates who must die. All of us will be asked to give up something to complete the prophecy, and that means that the girls will also be sacrificed as well on the other side of the portal. You have to be ready to take that which you have been given, merge into the fifth element, and then take from us what is needed to put an end to Zanack forever."

"What the hell does that all that mean?" Kaitlan

demanded, again.

"I have absolutely no idea, dearest friend. I only know that we three girls will have to give up our lives, so that you can complete what has always been your destiny. It was a destiny sent to all of us by the Creator. Death is our price to pay for defeating Zanack, and restoring the timeline."

"Eric, can he even kill you?" Lynne asked him.

"I'm only hard to kill, Linora. It's not impossible. If he takes my head, or my heart, yes."

"Oh, God!" cried Lynne as Richard wrapped his arms around his mate.

The girls held their mates tightly crying openly. The men were saddened by what was to happen. That they would not be able to protect their mates. That they would see things they never wanted them to see. But, all of them would die.

All the mates kissed with their last kiss. It was over. Their lives were over, but their love would be forever in the next life. They had faith that the Creator knew what He was doing, and accepted it.

"Whatever is needed to open the portal, we will give to Zanack. Oh, and one last thing." Richard turned to Kaitlan. "Be warned. Dahll warned you. The massive power that you will wield can corrupt your soul and your mind. If you give in to it, you will be lost. Beware of this. And, if by some miracle you succeed, and our Creator allows it, time will be reset. The timeline will return to its original direction, but it will be different. It could be better, or worse. It could be the same, similar, or different. Any one of us may, or may never have been born. Everything is on your shoulders, now. Be ready, and you must not cry, or lament our deaths, girls. To do so would be to weaken your powers. We will see you in the next life!" Richard instructed.

"Let's go," Cordone said, and took Kaitlan's hand to

lead her out of the house.

Without looking back, each couple held the hands of their mates, and proceeded to their final destiny. Death was certain. Time was not.

Kaitlan thought about what Richard had said. Could she really do this? She had to be prepared to phase into her human incarnation of the White Wolf, or everything would be for naught. And, worse? She may very well be the cause of her friends' deaths, the destruction of her own soul as well as the destruction of the world. How the hell could she kill?

~ 13 ~
**Quoting the brilliance of others to learn
from our mistakes is a waste of time.**

It is said that time is relative. However, it is only relative to where you happen to be at the moment.

Eight, brave souls of sacrifice walked slowly toward the bluff. They had a very bad feeling about it. Most if not all of them would be dead in minutes. They all knew it.

Three hooded figures stood at the bluff watching their approach. The hood was just for theatrics.

Kaitlan looked up at Cordone. He was scared as was she, but this was what their lives had been heading toward.

Finally, they reached the bluff, and stood. Waiting.

"Well, well, well. I see everyone found their way?" Turner sneered. His voice was raspy, because he was fighting changing before he was ready.

Two others came up to them with handcuffs of silver with what looked like Celtic markings on the circlets.

Cordone's eyes narrowed. Who? Who was the other traitor? He knew Roland and Johnson, but the third?

The figure removed his hood.

"Tim?" Cordone gasped.

Tim was in cahoots with Zanack?

"Yeah. It's me. Fooled ya, didn't I!" Tim gloated, and laughed. "Besides, he pays better!"

Zanack's hand came up, and slapped the back of Tim's head.

"Hey! What was that for?" Tim asked, rubbing the back of his head. "That really hurt!"

"That's for being a total idiot." Zanack said.

Cordone had a ghost of a smile. *Hmmmm. Seems there isn't joy in demon land."*

Kaitlan laughed out loud. In a split second, Zanack's foul, putrid, rotted, and decaying teeth were in her face. Kaitlan wanted to throw up at the smell.

"Watch your fucking, little mouth, you bitch!" He grabbed her chin. "Your White Wolf is powerless in this place. I could break you in an instant!"

Kaitlan held her breath. She wasn't going to back down no matter what he said.

"Ewwwww!" She pinched her nose to make sure he got the message. "Honestly, Zanack! Don't you EVER brush your teeth? Go to a dentist? You smell like a garbage dump on a 115 degree day!"

The mates heard snickers all around.

Zanack yanked her hair back hard kicking her legs backward causing her to fall on her knees. Cordone tried to retaliate, but stopped immediately.

"Don't even try it, Cordone. I could snap her neck like a toothpick, but you know better than to interfere with fate!" He waved his hand, and hog-tied all of them in an instant. Then, Zanack turned back to Kaitlan. "You are a fucking bitch, Kaitlan O'Hara. Just like your Father was a fucking bastard. Your Mom, though? I still dream of her naked body under me, and fucking her!"

He lowered his mouth to her ear.

"You should have been my child, Kaitlan, not that bastard of a werewolf!"

Kaitlan was trying to jerk her hair out of his hands, but she couldn't move as he wrapped his arm tighter around her neck.

"Your precious mate can't save you. Want to know why I hate Canaan so much? Because your Mother was mine! My mate! MINE! I wanted to plunge my hot and huge cock inside of her. To take her, and implant my seed in her body!"

Kaitlan's stomach rolled with his words. She felt bile rise in her throat as she listened to the vile depravity flood out of his mouth. But, that didn't make her weak. On the contrary, her wolf was just about to emerge if he didn't let go of her, now.

"Your wolf cannot emerge in this place, so you may as well stop trying!" He glanced at the other girls. "I have placed a spell on the eight of you. None of you can do a damn thing right now! No wolves, no Elven powers, nothing. This place is sacred!"

He turned back to Kaitlan to gloat further.

"So, now, shall I tell you how much I desired Tara? How much I wanted to bury my massive dick inside her? To take her over and over and over? How much I wanted to rub her body against my scales as I took her? I wanted to see her blood flow as my scales cut her tits, and the rest of her body! To see the fear in her eyes when she felt my burning, hot seed implant into her? To watch her pain as my seed grew within her womb for five months until our child clawed its way out of her? She was MINE! Not Canaan's! MINE! He took her. He ravished her, and he put *you* in her! He ruined her! That's why I killed her! I killed her personally. And, you should have died, too!"

Kaitlan wouldn't keep her mouth shut, but Cordone was positive she was doing something else with Zanack at this moment. But, what, he couldn't figure out at the moment.

Kaitlan's anger grew by the second as Zanack spoke to her. He was vile. Evil incarnate! If a Nivurian was as evil as Richard had told them, then the Evil One combined with the Nivurian was far worse. Her wolf was at the surface, and she knew she could unleash her when she wanted. Zanack could not stop it, but she decided to let him "think" he had stopped her. They all needed some answers, so she said the first thing that came into her head.

"Yours? You think my Mother would come near your filth? You think too much of yourself, Zanack. It's no wonder that the other realms destroyed your entire race letting *humans and supers* replace you, and your whole fucking race!" Kaitlan sneered, and she spat in his face.

She had done it! She had made him really mad. He pulled his arm back, and backhanded her right across the face. Several of his spikes sliced into her cheek. It hurt like hell, but there was no way that Kaitlan was going to give him the satisfaction of letting him see her pain. Instead, she spit out some of the blood that had dripped into her mouth, and turned her face back to face him.

"Oh, my dear Kaitlan. Of course, she would have come to me. As if she would have had a choice. I am far more powerful than you know. She would have not only come to me, but spread her legs whenever I told her to do so! I wanted to take her in front of her whole Clan, and let her mate watch me!"

Kaitlan's eyes narrowed dangerously. Cordone stared at his bloodied mate's face. He couldn't protect her, but he didn't think she would want him to anyway. The more angry she became, the more the White Wolf would enjoy her vengeance, so he kept quiet. He didn't have much of a choice. Zanack had spelled the four of them on their knees, and they couldn't move at all.

"Oh, really?" Kaitlan's mouth turned up in a menacingly evil grin." Why, Zanack…*if* that were so, then *why* couldn't *you* take her away from my Father?"

"How dare you speak to me that way?" Zanack screamed. "I'll teach you to…."

Kaitlan completely ignored his warning.

"I'll tell you why you couldn't take her away from my Father - her *mate* - you fucking son of a bitch! Because, you are a nothing but a prick! And, yes…pun intended! You are a flawed piece of shit called a

Nivurian! A fucking bastard perpetuated by his own, self-aggrandized vision of himself! You have no power whatsoever! You never have! Your shell is not even real! It's only a glamour receptacle for the piece of shit that you are! Your desire to kill this world will fail, and we will bring you down! Do you think, for one moment, the Creator will let you live to mess up his creations? Seriously? You must think that you are the most fucking, great son of a bitch jackass to have ever been on this planet! You think it's about *YOU*? About what *YOU* want? Well, it 'ain't'! You don't belong here! You don't belong *anywhere*! Your damn, fucking whole race was destroyed by the realms, because of the filth that you are! As for the part of your anatomy you are so fond of, well, you can bet that I will burn it off your body slowly, painfully! And, more than that, you will suffer as you have never suffered!"

Zanack was quiet a moment as his eyes dangerously narrowed.

"Bullshit, White Wolf! You have no power. It was all a ruse. It's a lie. It always was! You so much as come near my dick, and I'll shove my spiked hand and arm up your cunt, and watch you bleed out!"

"Well, what do you know? I got under your thick putrid scales, and into the skin below! So, what's the matter, Zanack?   You think *you're* in charge?" she sneered. "You make the same mistake as all evil does by thinking you're in charge!" Kaitlan sneered even more. "You think that you are indestructible? Well, I got news for you! You aren't! A Nivurian who struck a deal with the Evil One is all you are, and then, you are nothing but his vessel! You murdered Roland, and used your glamour to pretend you were him. Don't you know that evil always loses? Trust me when I tell you that the EO deceived you. What did he promise you?   Rule of Earth?   Money? Plenty of food? If you think you have escaped from his retribution, you are lying to yourself! You were played by the EO, and I will destroy you, and send him back to the hell-hole he crawled out of!" Kaitlan finished quietly, which made her all the more terrifying to those around her - even her own mate.

Zanack's fury drove him to pull her hair forward, and slammed her face into the ground. Hard. Then, he backed up. She raised her head, which was covered with dirt along with more blood from the impact. Zanack licked his lips as he started forward. Fresh blood always turned him on! He came to a sudden stop when she continued to speak.

"Is that all you have, Zanack? You think slamming my face into the ground will stop me? It won't. I am the White Wolf, and I will make sure that you will suffer all the fires from the hell that I will bring down upon your head!"

"Why you fucking, bi…." Zanack grabbed her head, again, and stopped when Tim put his hand on Zanack's arm.

"Stop acting like a bloody moron, Zanack! We are running out of time! Just open the damned portal, and let's get on with it!"

Zanack stopped his advance. If he so much as took a drop of blood, now, everything he had worked for would have been for naught.

He stepped back, and jerked his arm out of Tim's hand.

"Yes. You're right."

He slowly removed a dagger of such beauty, it awed everyone there. It was pure gold with many rare gemstones beset into the handle. The Gem on the top of the hilt was red - and the size of a small fist.

Zanack laughed maniacally when he saw their eyes widen.

"Where in the hell did you get that?" Cordone

demanded.

"What? This little ole' thing? Come, come, Cordone. Where I got it from is superfluous, of course. But, just in case you don't know its purpose is, well, it is a special…,"

"I know what the hell it is! Where the hell did you get it?"

Zanack continued as if Cordone hadn't spoken, "…ceremonial dagger for blood sacrifices used long ago throughout the ages. Most recently, the Mayans. It is ancient, and as with all things magical, there is always a high price to be paid in using it." Zanack turned the blade over and over, then raked it back and forth over his hand, his eyes glinting in its glow. He continued to speak as if in a trance. "It let me sacrifice countless humans and supers. Allowed me to easily cut the beating hearts out of their writhing and terrified bodies."

He stopped, and looked up. "And, unfortunately for you four, bastard males, well, I will thoroughly enjoy slitting your throats! A little bloodletting, as it were. Actually, a *lot* of blood-letting!"

He waved the dagger in the mens' faces. Shackling the four werewolves even tighter, he threw their faces down to the ground. The girls wanted to stop him, and tried to move forward, but they couldn't move, because Zanack used his magic to root them where they stood. Quite literally, their feet were captured by roots from underneath the soil! None of the mates were able to move a muscle, and the girls watched in horror at what he was going to do!

"Oh, and Kaitlan? Don't even think about asking the Earth to help you. This piece of ground was consecrated to the EO, as you call him, long ago for just this purpose. So, if you do, I guarantee all four will die instantly!"

"Liar! You need us on the other side, so you are not going to kill us."

His mouth turned up in a sneer.

"What makes you think I mean you girls? You're an idiot, Kaitlan! Now, if you don't mind, I have to open the Portal of Time. We have a date with destiny!"

"A date? Methinks thou dost not know what the word means. We know you are going to kill our mates to open the portal, Zanack? Is that the best you can do?" Sarah uttered.

Zanack took a deep breath to keep from strangling both Kaitlan and Sarah, and turned to face the bluff. Turning his hands upward, he sliced both of his palms with the tip of the dagger. A thick, mustard yellow blood poured from his wounds covering the dagger. He placed the blade across both hands in a form of offering, and recited an incantation as his blood dripped onto the ground.

*"By the realms of time and space, my demand to
hear my case.
Open the Portal of Time released, the curse once
bound, now is ceased.
A sacrifice of four to you, with their blood both
pure and true,
Raise the barrier of all time, so I may take what is
rightfully mine!"*

"Who thinks up these spells anyway?" Anita muttered under her breath. Lynne, Sarah, and Kaitlan turned their heads to stare at her.

"What the hell, Anita?"

Anita just shrugged.

Zanack turned to the four men who were bound. There were four channels that had been dug into the Earth, and these led to a larger, basin also dug into the ground next to the bluff. Zanack's yellow blood poured into the main dirt basin. And, it didn't take any imagination why it was there. He wished he had the time to make them suffer slow deaths while their mates looked on, but he just didn't have it. Raising the blood-covered dagger, Zanack struck with precision. Slicing Dan's throat over the channel in front of him, Zanack yanked his head back, tearing the flesh he had not cut, and allowed his blood to gush into the channel. The thick blood slowly made its way to the basin. In seconds, Dan's head was laying beside his body. Zanack was fast. He followed with Richard's throat, Sam's throat, and finally, Cordone's throat. Each mate's blood flooded into their own channels mixing into the basin. Zanack threw back his head, and laughed. He was clearly mad.

Silent screams tore out of the women's mouths, but none would allow a sound to escape, and give Zanack the satisfaction. Watching their blood empty, the girls looked upon their mates' headless bodies. Tears flowed down their cheeks quietly. They knew that the rule was that a mate couldn't live long without the other, but there was something that they did not know. And, now, Zanack happily told them.

"You think that because your mates are dead that you will follow after them soon? Not so, my beauties, not so!"

Eight, tear-stained eyes stared at Zanack with hatred behind them.

"You cannot die! None of you!" He guffawed at their stunned faces. "No. You will never die. Why do you think I need the Elementals? They are immortal once transformed! Their power is great, because of their immortality. They are the only beings that will permit me to cast the curse! You fools! You will not die - at least until I'm ready to split your heads from your bodies, and spill your blood! If you were left alone, you would live forever. Your mates will be in the hereafter, but you will never gain entrance. Not sure where you do go, but you will not follow your mates! Did your "Creator" not explain this? No? I didn't think so! As happy as that makes me, I want the death and destruction that I will unleash on this world after I recast the curse into permanence. And, you will give your lives for me! This is the Elemental's fate, your destiny, and your curse!"

He looked at them, and with a slow, evil smile, he pushed the hood back from his head, and they could see the Nivurian standing before them. Sarah and Cordone had underestimated what they had seen! Dear Creator! What the hell was that thing? Horror gripped the four women. Kaitlan and Lynne's eyes were blazing with hatred and revenge. Sarah and Anita were growling with furor at the monster before them.

"Your days are over, Zanack," Anita hissed through her teeth. She had never been filled with such hatred as she was now.

Lynne's low growl echoed Anita.

"You are dead, Zanack."

Sarah turned to Kaitlan.

"Kaitlan. Promise us that you will make this bastard suffer for every single tear that we have shed." She turned to look at Zanack. "Your end is near, Zanack. I know you feel it with every breath you take. Your destruction will come from the White Wolf. You will be torn to pieces slowly with great glee from a vision that will so terrify you, you will piss in fear as you gaze upon her. What you will face will be more powerful than any wizard, or 'god', that has ever lived. You. Zanack," she pointed at him, breaking his spell as she stood. "You will know true fear as you are slowly dissected by the vengeance that will be brought upon you as you have brought upon others throughout the ages! Neither you nor the EO will be able to fight The White Wolf. She will be far more terrifying than anything you have ever seen, and she will use every ounce of her hatred to fuel her strength combined with ours. And, then…then, you will beg for death while you cannot move! You will feel every painful cut as she slices your body to pieces - slowly. You will suffer as you have made others suffer! She will return to you the pain of all your victims, and she will laugh in your face as she does so. You will not win."

Sarah's chest was breathing hard as she finished the prophecy given to her by the Creator.

"You need not fear, Sarah. I promise to make him suffer a slow, and agonizing death!" Kaitlan promised. "I guarantee you, and the others that he will not live, nor will he recast the curse. You have my word!"

Zanack, threw back his head, and roared with laughter.

"You are magnificent, Sarah Knight! Kaitlan, it is too bad that your words are without merit. Yet, you still do not understand, do you? It's *hatred and fear* that drive my needs! I devour these for breakfast, lunch, dinner, and snacks! The more hatred and fear I can absorb, the stronger I become! You will never touch me, Kaitlan, nor any of the rest of you, because I feel the hate and fear coming from your Elemental bodies. Those are the most powerful of all powers! It feeds me. I am Nivurian! Never forget that!"

He turned to the blood that was at the edge of the bluff. A gentle wind began to blow expanding in intensity. When it became a gale force, Zanack was ready to finish the sacrifice to open the Portal of Time. He walked unsteadily against the wind to each girl with a horrific grin on his face. Using the dagger, he cut the middle finger of each girl, allowing three drops of blood from each to drip into a small ramekin he held in his hands. Taking the small bowl, he tossed it into the large gale-force whirlwind, and immediately a vortex appeared vertically in front of them at the bluff. Shock assailed the girls as they saw a portal expand to a huge size for them to pass through. They could all feel the pull as the wind tried to suck them into the portal.

Zanack called to Tim.

"Go," he ordered, and Tim leaped into the portal, and disappeared.

"Tim went first so that he could make sure you all could not run from me. Now, step into it!" He ordered the girls pointing the dagger at them.

All four knew that this was it. It was time. They did as he asked. Each girl leaped through the portal, and disappeared.

Kaitlan was the last to go, and she turned to him.

"Remember Sarah's words, Nivurian. I will use whatever it takes - even the lives of my friends - to rid the Earth of you. Mark my words carefully."

Before Zanack could say anything, Kaitlan did not leap, but walked into the portal.

Zanack shook with anger as he watched her disappear. When, Johnson made a move to step through the portal, Zanack stopped him. Johnson turned in surprise.

"Tim will need me," he said. "He can't handle all four alone."

"No, Johnson. He won't."

Zanack swung the dagger into Johnson's gut, and yanked it upward to his throat leaving the dagger inside of

Johnson.   The shock in Johnson's eyes was one of disbelief. He tried to speak, but instead, he gurgled blood.

"I needed six, male sacrifices, you fool! You are number five - you are needed to close the portal on this side so no other can follow, and Tim on the other to close it. You have fulfilled your purpose."

As the portal's vortex shimmered, Zanack grabbed Johnson's body, leaped into the vortex first, then he let Johnson's body go just as they passed the opening. Johnson was always an idiot, and he let himself believe that if he joined him, Zanack would bring his wife back to him. What a gullible idiot! Only proving, once and for all, that all the races were far too stupid to take care of themselves. And, you just can't fix stupid!

The Portal of Time shut, leaving blood and death behind.

~ 14 ~
"The best laid plans of mice and men often go awry." ~
Robert Burns

Yep. Burns had it right! One may plan and plot evil, but there is always...*always* a catch - somewhere. This catch was far more insidious. So much so that not even Zanack knew what that catch was. The spell only warned of it, but did not explain it

One by one, each girl stumbled out of the portal gasping for air. It was as if they had stepped into a vacuum, and even though it had been mere seconds, it felt like hours. They fell on the ground just trying to catch their breaths!

Tim was standing on the other side with a pistol. He waved the gun at them "Silver bullets. Didn't think Zanack trusted you, did you?" Tim laughed.

His mind was one foot in the here and now, and another thinking that he just couldn't wait to taste the wenches on this side of the portal. They should be even more available in this time period, and more willing to fuck!

Lynne gathered her breath.

"And, you think he trusts you, oh ye of little brain cells!"

Tim backhanded her across the mouth, causing her mouth to bleed.

Lynne just laughed.

"You think *that* is going to make me whine, or shut up? After everything I have been through? You are nothing but a little prick who has no idea who, or what he is dealing with. He will kill you."

"No he won't. He needs me." Tim answered sounding just a bit wary.

Where was Johnson? He hadn't stepped through yet, and neither had Kaitlan!

"If you really think that," Sara added, "You *are* more stupid than you look!"

Anita began to tend to Lynne's mouth, but Lynne shook her head, and brushed Anita's hand away.

"I'm OK, Anita. Don't waste your time. Zanack will be here in a minute."

Anita nodded when she felt a sudden heat rise inside of her. She turned to the other girls.

"You feel that?"

They all nodded. They felt the heat and the power of their elements here more than at home. Elementals were used in a time before technology. With that technology removed, they could feel their powers so much more.

Tim continued looking toward the portal. Where was the fourth elemental, he wondered, again? She still hadn't come through it. He pointed the gun at the girls, his hand slowly squeezing the trigger.

"Where's Kaitlan?" he demanded.

Lynne moved with Elven speed, which Tim couldn't see, and her hands were around his throat in a split second, holding him high. The other girls surrounded him.

"Good question, you little fuck. Where is she?" Lynne demanded.

She had no mercy left in her, and when he was dead, she'd dance on his grave!

"How sh-should I know?" he gasped. "Did he even send her through?"

"ENOUGH!" Lynne yelled. "But, you are quite right. Zanack won't be killing you."

With Tim's last breath, he realized that Lynne was a full-blooded Elf, and true terror gripped him.

Lynne's anger was such that she broke his neck easily, and dropped him onto the ground. She slapped her hands together up and down, ridding her of the feeling of the little prick!

"We need to get away from here as fast as we can!" Sarah said.

The girls turned to run to the forest that was just up ahead when suddenly they felt something wrap around them, and jerked them back to where they had been.

"Going somewhere…are we?" sneered Zanack.

Zanack rooted them to the spot as he had done on the other side of the portal. He looked down at Tim's lifeless body.

"What? You killed my trusted servant?" He laughed heartily. "That's OK. You just did me a favor, and saved me time. He was such a prick! His blood is still fresh and warm, though, and I'm extremely hungry. I needed his blood to close the portal on this side."

He bent down to Tim, and with his sharp teeth sliced through his artery in a heartbeat, and he drank deeply while the girls watched in horror. He looked up at them with his face covered with Tim's blood. He left enough blood needed to close the vortex, and threw his bloody body at the portal. Tim's body disintegrated instantly, and it was closed.

Finally, he was free! He could be what he was, and it was a huge relief! He grinned as the three girls all fell backward onto the ground at the full and nauseating sight of Zanack. Seeing the girls puzzled expressions.

"It's a one-way portal," he shrugged.

"So, that's a Nivurian?" Anita squeaked.

He was straight out of hell! His head was elongated, and the skin tight to his skull. His eyes were slanted and pure black. The old term of "Don't shoot until you see the whites of their eyes", certainly didn't apply with him! There were no whites in his eyes. He had no nose. His lips were very thin and black as night, and his teeth! Like that of a shark! Rows upon rows, with no less than four rows of sharp, pointed teeth blackened and yellowed with decay! No wonder he could eat his prey so easily! They could tear through anything in an instant without a problem. His hands were claws. His skin was charcoal gray with an orange cast, and he was covered in scales that sported sharp spikes barely half an inch long. He had a huge, five-foot tail covered with even more spikes on it. He was horrible looking. He smelled worse than death. He smelled putrid. Rancid. As if he was rotting from the inside out.

"Ick! Kaitlan! You were so right! I sure wouldn't want to be the prick's dentist!" Sarah quipped earning another spiky hand slap.

Despite Sarah's bloody face that had begun to heal, she just grinned back at Zanack.

"I told those two idiots that I only needed the blood of four, male sacrifices to open it. I just didn't tell them I needed two more to close it at either end!" he laughed, then looked around.

The iron stench of Tim's blood covered his face, and his clothing. The girls were sickened by the smell. Nevertheless, he loved it. He walked closer so they could smell it on him, savoring the smell of disgust from the girls who gagged and vomited. Lynne deliberately spewed her vomit onto him. He just grinned, and scooped it into his mouth. Not a bad snack!

Zanack continued looking around him. He was back!

"Good. I was hoping we'd exit close to the original curse. We have a couple of days walk ahead of us. But, no need for you to worry your pretty little heads about what will happen to you."

Lynne and the girls looked at each other, and started to laugh. He had yet to notice that Kaitlan was not present, and that just made them laugh harder. Well, let's face it. They watched their mates murdered, jumped through a time portal, and were now in the hands of a mad man…uh, Nivurian.

Zanack growled at the women, and looked around to see what was so funny. Wait! Only three? Where was the bitch? He came up to Anita, grabbed her hair, and jerked her head up right into his. She could smell his breath with each breath.

"YUCK! You stink!" she gagged.

"Yeah? Well, get used to it! Where's the mouthy bitch?" he demanded.

Anita just grinned at him trying to hold her breath against the stench of blood dripping from his teeth and face.

He shook her hard snapping her head back.

"I will ask only one more time: where the hell is Canaan's little bitch!"

Still Anita said nothing. The snap had made her head hurt. She refused to answer him.

"Stop!" cried Sarah. "Please, stop! She doesn't know! Neither do we! She didn't come through after us!"

Zanack dropped Anita on her butt to turn toward - Sarah. She would be the one. He had made the decision before he stepped through that she would be the woman who would bear his child. He walked over to her, and caressed her jaw, his spikes gouging cuts into it.

"Don't lie to me, Sarah. Where is she?"

"Oh, hell! She didn't come through with us! Isn't that obvious you fucking idiot?"

Zanack's fury was unleashed in that instant. He drew back, and slammed his fist into her stomach. She couldn't move since she was rooted to the ground, and the pain was excruciating. It was just a good thing she was a werewolf, because if she had been a human, Sarah was positive she would have internal bleeding. He had retracted his spikes, apparently, because she was not bleeding.

Zanack turned back around, and pushed Sarah to the ground, then turned to look at the area. He was beyond rage! NO! This was *not* happening again! The Earth Elemental had been taken from him? Again?

"Fuck! Fuck! Fuck! This cannot be happening! Not again! Who the fuck took her?"

Closing his eyes, Zanack tried to gain control of himself. He breathed deeply, and opened his eyes. No! Not this time! She would not escape him this time! This time he *would* find her! No one was going to stand in his way this time! But, where to look?

Chuckles from the women around him brought him back to the present…or the past.

"Seriously? This is just too funny! Poor 'wittle' Zanack being thwarted, yet, again! How hilarious!" Lynne sneered at him.

"Yep, Zanack! It is just poetic justice that the Earth Elemental was snatched - again! I mean, really! Can't you figure out that somebody up there is not going to let you cast the curse? Poor little jackass just can't get his act together, can he!" Anita laughed earning hearty giggles from the other girls.

"You are already set to your destruction, Zanack. Since Kaitlan isn't here, your desire to recast the curse is set for failure once more!" Sarah giggled.

He darted to them. Since they couldn't move unless he touched them, they were still stuck.

"OK. Don't think that will deter me! I *will* find that little bitch! In the meantime, I think I'll have a bit of fun!"

He turned to Sarah, stroked her face a second time, and then, let his fingers slide down her throat, cupping her breast. Sarah uselessly jerked back in horror and pain as she felt his spikes cutting shallow slices into her flesh along her throat. He grabbed her breasts, and squeezed them tightly, retracting his spikes.

"Oh, don't worry, Sarah. I don't want these beauties marked! I plan on feasting on them soon - in more ways than one!" he groaned as he felt his excitement speed toward his groin.

Sarah tried to wiggle out of his grasp, but it was completely useless. She was being humiliated not to mention she was about to throw up, because his hands were on her.

Zanack's eyes closed, and he moaned feeling his cock harden even more from the touch of her breasts. Oh, yes! He was right! Her body was going to be wonderful for him to impregnate her. Maybe he should do it now? His orange eyes began to glow, but he reigned in his lust. No. Not yet. He needed to gain control, and although he was horny as hell, well, work came first. He decided to give her, at least, a look at what she had to look forward to when the others were dead.

"Yes, Sarah!" he whispered into her ear, panting in excitement. "You will feel my dick inside you soon! Here. Let me show you what I know you are anxious to feel inside of you!"

Sarah's eyes widened, but fear was far down on her list of sick.

He unzipped his pants, and pulled his huge, spiked manhood out to show her. He wiggled it at her watching as she and the girls gagged.

"When everyone else is dead, and I have indulged in a feast, you will get this inside of you. Don't worry. I promise it's just for you. I will retract my spikes so my dick won't cut your cunt to pieces! I cannot wait to feel it inside you! Feeling you tighten around it, milking it for my burning seed to flow into your womb!" Zanack's excitement was growing. "And, it will be plenty big enough for you! I promise! Women love my dick inside them! I can do things that no human male can do to a woman! And, I plan on fucking you over and over without stopping until your womb is filled with my child! It will be entirely for my own pleasure!"

"*LEAVE HER ALONE, YOU FUCKING BASTARD*!" screamed Lynne, terrified for her friend. He was going to rape her with that - that horrible thing covered in spines?

As he had gained in sexual excitement, he began masturbating himself in front of them turning his eyes up to Sarah's which were closed. He was furious! Sarah should be looking at him as he shot his seed out onto the ground!

"I'm doing this for you! Look at my cock, Sarah! I said *LOOK AT IT*!" he screamed.

Sarah refused to open her eyes. He backhanded her across the face, but kept her head bent. She wouldn't give him the satisfaction of looking at him.

He flipped his cock at her. Its tip had some sort of orang-ish ooze coming from its tip. He grinned. Zanack yanked her head up causing her eyes to open automatically, and forced her to look at his pride and joy!

"Sarah, I have decided that after everyone's dead, and my curse enacted, you will be the recipient of the first, human woman to receive my gift to you. My hot, burning blood-seed will flow into your beautiful body, and you will bear my child."

The horror on Sarah's face was unmistakable, along with bile. She tried to keep her vomit back, but failed. Miserably. She vomited the contents of her stomach out all over Zanack, and then, she continued to dry heave. All the while, Zanack's hands caressed her hair as he spoke.

"Don't worry, my dear. As I said before…I would normally leave my cock's spikes so that I can fuck. It's the way of our species to give us the most in our orgasms. But, to impregnate you, I will retract them. I won't be able to get as much release as normal, but I'll sacrifice for our child." He tilted his head as his hand continued to rub his cock. "Yes! Women, even human women, absolutely love my dick, and I give them such great pleasure when I pound into their cunts watching blood flow out of them. They scream in ecstasy as I spill my blood-seed into them. But, no. I will not do this to you. See? I can retract my spines, and you will only feel my normal scales inside your cunt. Humans have such a way with words! Then, I will plant my burning seed inside you, and watch your belly grow until our child tears its way out of that beautiful body of yours. Then, we will feast on your blood and flesh together while you are alive!"

And, then, he pumped his cock hard feeling his orgasm reach its peak.

"Yes!" Zanack cried as he spilled himself onto the ground over and over until he was empty. It sizzled on the ground killing the grass, and burning it to black. He hadn't been kidding that his seed would burn! Sarah was sick to her stomach more than before! He planned on putting that burning goo into her body?

Sarah began to spew vomit all over him!

Zanack quickly shoved his dick back into his pants, and zipped them up. Then, he grabbed her cheeks, and spit on her. Sarah gagged again, and threw up more on his face.

Finally, she looked at him, and in a voice of hatred so strong, she answered him while wiping her mouth of her vomit.

"You will *never* take me, and over your dead, and mutilated body, you will *never* plant your mutant spawn within me! You *will* regret touching me. That, I promise you!" Sarah had never been so angry.

Zanack just shrugged. "Fine. You know, maybe I'll just do it now, and let your friends watch us."

He turned to them, as he yanked Sarah's pants down

along with her panties. Sarah began to panic watching him pull his green, spiked cock out again, and put its tip on her leg. The green ooze began to burn her skin leaving a blackened spot! She screamed, and he slapped her face hard causing her lip to bleed.

"Oh, my lovely mate! Your pregnancy is going to be extremely painful for five months, Sarah. He will burn your insides up as he grows. I'll look forward to watching him torture you from the inside out!"

He pushed his cock back into his pants, and, again, zipped them, but left hers down.

"I want to get a good look at your ass. It really turns me on! I don't have time to fuck you, now. I'll do that after I have enacted the curse. First, though, I have to find the Earth Elemental. That little bitch is the key to this!"

His eyes traveled down to Sarah's red curls at her apex. His mouth watered for it. He sighed dismissing his thoughts for the moment.

"I will find her, then, we will get busy. I don't have a lot of time before I have to begin. And, when I'm finished, Sarah, I'll be back for your pussy!"

He laughed maniacally - just like the evil villains on TV, books, or in movies except this was real life, and it was far worse than those were! The girls were left lying in the dirt while he whirled, and took off at more than super-speed.

"*Oh, GOD*!!!" Sarah cried. "I'll die before I let that bastard put his hands on me, or that - that 'thing' inside of me!!!"

"Never gonna happen, Sarah!" Lynne sounded so confident, but deep down? Not so much.

Sarah glared at Lynne.

"Anyone ever tell you 'never say never'? We always seem to quote the brilliance of others to learn from our mistakes, and that's just a copout, because it's a waste of time! Never always comes!"

"You're making up quotes in the middle of this?" Lynne asked in shock.

"Yeah? Well, it just came to me, so back off!" Sarah cried even harder.

"Kaitlan will never let that happen to you, Sarah!" Anita tried to comfort her.

Sarah was beyond comfort. She was beyond angry, and beyond rational. Her body shuddered in the cool air that hit her bare ass, but it wasn't entirely due to the cold. Not by a long shot!

~ 15 ~
Out of the Fire, and into the Frying Pan

Kaitlan groaned. She didn't want to open her eyes at all. All she wanted was to stay in the blessed darkness. Nevertheless, her eyes opened automatically anyway. It really *was* dark! She could smell the Earth surrounding her. The same smell she remembered when she was on that bluff on the planet where Dahll had forced her to jump!   More than that, she could *feel* the Earth's vegetation calling out to her. Wanting to help her. Right now, though, she needed to know what was happening. She looked around, again. Her eyes were slowly adjusting to the dark, so it was a bit easier to see. Where was she? Where were the girls? Did she even enter the time portal? OK, she did remember falling through the vacuum, and that she couldn't breathe at all. Something - or someone - had her taking a detour. Where was she? Hell! Her whole world had fallen apart, and she wanted to cry. Let's see. What was the last thing she did remember? Oh, right! Their mates were dead, and the Nivurian had dug a trench to the end of the bluff letting their blood flow to create the portal! She had to make sure she destroyed Zanack, and then wondered if it was possible. Could the timeline be changed? Would everyone still be alive in the new time? Or, would some live in a different timeline, while others lived in others? Not necessarily with her, but at least Cordone and the others would live. Kaitlan just didn't have the answer. Damn! She wished that Dahll were around when she needed him!

They were still alive, though. Here. Now. And, in the past. Just not anywhere near here - wherever "here" was! She sat up, and noticed that she was in a bare room of massive stones with one massive door being the only way out of this place. She heard a noise outside that door, and watched it begin to open slowly with narrowing eyes. She stood up shakily, and brushed the dirt off her clothing. Yep! Another shocker was definitely coming. She just knew it! The person who stepped through it left Kaitlan stunned and speechless!

"Close your mouth, Kaitlan. You look like a fish!" The man grinned at her. "I'm glad you finally made it. I've been waiting for you for quite some time."

Her mouth dropped when she saw him! She *was* speechless. How? When? Where? How? She opened her mouth, closed it, opened it, closed it, and finally she tried to speak.

"Speechless, Kaitlan? Wow! Never thought I'd ever live to see that one!" Laughter followed. "I know you're full of questions, and I'll try to answer them. But first, let's get you something to eat. Even though it's only temporary, time travel still has a bad habit of not only zapping your strength, but leaving your muscles weak as well. It's OK. You're among friends. Zanack will not be allowed to get his hands on you. We must make sure he fails, and that is why we, well, 'we' sort of 'hijacked' you just as we did the first Earth Elemental!"

Kaitlan stood on wobbly legs, and tried to move them. He was right. Her muscles were not working very well. She put one foot in front of the other, and soon she was walking out the door. Nervously laughing, was she really paraphrasing a song from "Santa Claus is Coming to Town"? Kaitlan laughed aloud! She really *must* be tired! Once out of the claustrophobic room, Kaitlan stood with her feet apart and fists on her hips observing the white hair, the lavender eyes, the height, and the ring of the man who stood before her. He seemed much younger! Wait! How did he know her when she had not been born yet? Had not even met him?

She breathed one word quietly.

"Ali'on."

Smiling, Ali'on held his hand out to her, and shaking his head, took it. He led her away from - well, where had she been? That's when she remembered. Her friends were in real danger, and the worry came flooding back from her mind.

"Was that a dungeon? Or is this all a dream?" she asked.

"No. It's not a dungeon," Ali'on snickered. "Placing you in the Earth Room allowed your body to rejuvenate. The portal, as I said, weakens you. But, by ripping you out of it, can very well cause your muscles to atrophy."

"Well, that doesn't sound good! But what about the girls? How? I mean, where? I mean when? I mean how could you possibly know me? We haven't even met yet!" she stuttered. Gah! She just wasn't making any sense out of this senseless situation. So, what else was new?

Ali'on smiled at her.

"Don't worry. The girls are fine for the moment. They are weak, tired, and Zanack has them immobile, but still all right. I promise. Even Zanack was weakened by the portal as well as lack of food."

Why was it that didn't make her feel better? Kaitlan wasn't going to feel better. This was war, and she was the end.   Looking around her, she realized that she was standing in a massive underground cavern! So large she could only see the walls, but beyond, just darkness! She looked at Ali'on as he was asking a silent question by frowning. What she didn't know.

"This way, Kaitlan." Ali'on's extremely long legs started to walk so fast, Kaitlan had to jog just to catch up with him. But, when he realized it, he slowed his walking to her pace.

Ali'on led her through the cavern that was lined with

silver columns on either side of her. So tall were they that she could not see the tops of them above her. There was no doubt that she was in a massive cave system. On and on she followed him down corridor after corridor of the great cavern lined with those silver columns. As she walked, she began to realize that the smooth columns had carvings on them. She wanted to stay, and look at them to study them, but Ali'on kept on going, and she knew if she didn't keep up with him, she'd be lost. Maybe later? Perhaps it was their history carved into them like stones in ancient cities. Well, not so ancient, now, if she was in the time when they were built. Maybe not all, but some of them? She shook her head. Hour after hour of walking in mostly darkness with an Elf who wasn't prone to talk, was messing with her head.

"That's enough, Kaitlan! Pay attention to the Elf!" Did she say that, or did he?

Finally, they reached a massive double door, and it opened slowly inward with a wave of Ali'on's hand. He stepped inside, and stood aside for her to enter.

Kaitlan entered an incredible room! It was still a cavern, and while it wasn't on the scale where she had just been, it was still huge. It looked familiar, somehow, but she just couldn't put her finger on it right now.

How in the hell would she ever describe this place to anyone else? It was almost unbelievable!

Her eyes turned, first, to the walls. They glittered - everywhere - in the firelight from the candeliers, which hung from the ceiling, and torches that perched on the same, silver columns. It was as if there were diamonds imbedded into the walls, and caressed by large veins of silver flowing and connecting the diamonds through the rock! Could those be real? She squinted. *Real diamonds and silver?* Her eyes strayed toward the same columns she had seen as she followed Ali'on. Unlike the columns in the cavern, she was able to see the tops of the silver columns in this room. These were not the same type of columns. Kaitlan remembered some research on columns that she had done for a writer when she was about fifteen. Because they had smooth shafts on the "hallway" columns, then they were most probably Tuscan. In this room, though, these were Doric columns which are a bit more elaborate, similar to Tuscan, but with fluted shafts. Whether they were actually needed, or only used as decoration wasn't that big a deal to her. She looked down at the floor - black as obsidian, and yet so clear, you could see below into the depths, as if you were looking through a pair of sunglasses. Light and water flowed beneath her feet from what appeared to be an underground lake, or maybe even an ocean. Even though it was far below them, it could be seen easily. Abundant waterfalls were everywhere! She could see levels upon levels of diamond, clear walkways as far as she could see, which crisscrossed above the ocean while Elves crossed them as they went about their daily activities. The cavern was illuminated by a huge light above her that appeared to shine like the sun, and which lit everything below her feet to the ocean. She squinted trying to figure out why things didn't look right! She had seen the same light in her dreams, or visions, if that's what you want to call them. And, women? They were everywhere! But, Ali'on and Sandra had distinctly told them that there were few women left due to Wolfsbane poisoning that killed them in the distant past. Yet, women were in abundance, so Ali'on and Sandra had lied!

"Focus, Kaitlan. Focus!" she said to herself.

Kaitlan looked up seeing two crystal thrones at the end of the room on a dais. These were about the only things that actually made sense to her! It fit Ali'on. To her right was a long, low, clear table surrounded by pillows piled high. They must eat sitting on them. Well, it was not that unusual, considering some cultures preferred to eat this way. She found it quite charming, actually.

From the end of the room, a beautiful woman of oriental heritage, rushed to them, and bowed her head to Ali'on. Her name, however, was definitely not Oriental. It was, by and large, strange, yet beautiful.

"My Lord."

"Please, will you bring Miss O'Hara - oh, excuse me, Kaitlan - Mrs. Valon, some food and drink, Li'nwha'a?"

"It is my pleasure, my Lord." Li'nwha'a bowed her head, again, rushing off to gather the food.

"Where am I, Ali'on," Kaitlan asked.

"Please, let's sit," he motioned to the table.

As she approached, she realized that the table appeared to be carved out of solid crystal.

Kaitlan sat down, and looked around. She didn't realize what he had said, because another thought had occurred to her as she looked at the table. Crystals were gorgeous, but this was more brilliant than a crystal. A light shown upward through it giving it an ethereal quality.

"Is this table? I mean…is this a-a diamond?" she squeaked.

Ali'on grinned. "Yes, it is, Kaitlan. Hand-carved out of a solid diamond. Diamonds in this time period are not rare, nor are their size."

Kaitlan's mouth dropped open. Her hand reached out to stroke the smoothness of the diamond table! This was just one of those things that was not possible, yet, here it was! How did they carve it?

Then, Li'nwha'a shuffled forward, placing a bowl filled with a huge variety of fruit, some of which Kaitlan had never seen. There were also cheeses, fizzy water with lemon, and something that looked like flatbread. After thanking Li'nwha'a for the food, Kaitlan reached for one of the pieces of fruit she didn't recognize, and tasted it.

Her eyebrows went up! It was red, and lusciously delicious!

"What is this?" she asked eagerly taking another bite of it.

"Once, it was called 'The Forbidden Fruit'."

Kaitlan almost choked, and she looked up.

"You mean like in the Bible?"

"Yes."

"And, you just let me eat it??" she squealed dropping it onto the table as if it burned her hand. " Are you nuts?"

What would it do to her?

Ali'on couldn't help but laugh at her.

"It's OK. It's just a variety of the fruit. The original tree was hidden long ago. No one can find it, now. The trees are but a poor copy from one seed that was kept from it. The powers that came from the tree no longer exist in their offspring."

"Well, I can't say I blame the Creator for that!" Kaitlan answered picking it back up, and eating the last few bites.

She continued to help herself to the other food before her. She was hungry! While there were meats on the table, most were fruits and vegetables. As she felt her strength return with the delicious food, she had to comment.

"This place, Ali'on? The columns? It sure looks like Moria in the Lord of the Rings: Fellowship of the Ring!"

"Well, actually, there is a legend that Tolkien was brought here, before he wrote his books. An Elven writer wanted him to tell the story of Middle Earth to the humans, and other supers. Unfortunately, though, he chose to write it as a fictional story, embellishing it quite a bit. Essentially, while not totally, it's fairly accurate. But, he left out the parts about the diamonds and silver on purpose."

Kaitlan's mouth dropped open in shock. A large "O" rounded her mouth.

"So, the end of the books, in "Return of the King"? Are the Undying Lands, well, I mean, are they…"

"Atlantis? Well, of course!" Ali'on laughed heartily, the sound vibrating the room around them.

Again, Kaitlan's mouth gaped at him. Shit! She sooo did not see that coming!

"What about…?" she began to ask as more questions flooded her mind.

"Kaitlan, let it go. We have more pressing problems. We just don't have time for questions that, quite frankly, you really don't need to know."

"Killjoy," Kaitlan muttered picking up something that looked like a Kiwi, but was the purple color of a beet. She bit into it. Nope. Tasted nothing like a beet! Whatever it was, she wasn't going to ask, again

"Fruits and vegetables come from the Earth whether under the ground, on a vine above ground, or a tree towering over the Earth. It is no wonder that you prefer them. These will give you strength for the battle you must fight."

She nodded. But, then, her mate, the other mates, and the girls flew into her mind, and she was suddenly full. They weren't eating. Probably being tortured, and here she sat in a beautiful, mythical place at a table carved from one, solid diamond. What kind of person was she?

"The girls, Ali'on?" she asked him sitting back on the plush pillows, and about to throw up everything she just ate.

"Zanack has them Kaitlan, and he plans on doing something to Sarah we must stop!"

Kaitlan's eyes got big, and she felt a horrible clinch in her stomach. Creator! What did he have planned for her little pixie friend?

"What?" She was afraid to ask, but couldn't stop her damn mouth from asking it! Less was more!

"After he tries to kill you and the other girls, he plans on making her suffer by bearing his spawn of evil."

Suddenly, the food she had just eaten was coming back up. Her hand flew to her mouth.

"Where?" she begged quickly.

He pointed to a door opposite them, and Kaitlan made a beeline straight for it where she quickly found their version of a commode carved into the obsidian floor. She threw up everything she had just eaten, and then some. Another Elf came into her with some items to cleanse her mouth, and some cool cloths. Kaitlan nodded her thanks, and leaned over a diamond sink to clean her mouth as best as she could. If she hadn't been so miserable, she would have noticed the bathroom was incredible.

Afterwards, she wobbled back to the table. She didn't think she could eat anything, but Ali'on insisted. She had to have the nutrition in order to fight. No way! She just couldn't eat another bite! However, she picked up a particularly delicious looking apple anyway, and bit into it, and then downed some of the fizzy water. It immediately made her sick, again. Ali'on pushed a glass filled with an opaque brown liquid.

"It will settle your stomach,"

"You have antacids here?" she asked downing the glass fast.

Ali'on roared with laughter, yet, again.

"No fizz, Kaitlan. It's a concoction of minerals ground by our wizard for just such a purpose. It's not used very often, as you can imagine, but I'm glad we had it for you," he paused a moment. "Better?"

Kaitlan was shocked. The drink did settle her stomach immediately, and she nodded her head. She began to eat once again.

A raven-haired beauty with a small strand of white at the crown of her head, entered the room, and Ali'on reached out to her, pulling her onto his lap. She smiled, kissed him, and then turned to Kaitlan.

"Hello, Kaitlan."

Kaitlan looked at her with a frown. There was something familiar about her. Her eyes bugged out as she recognized her!

"OMG! Sandra? Is that you?" Kaitlan whispered.

"Yes. It is I, Kaitlan. This is how I looked in the past, or the present you could say, before I became full Elf. I know you know that human women, over time, become pureblooded elves. We never told Anita after she discovered human women could mate with elves. There was a lot of mating!" She grinned at Kaitlan who grinned back at him. "Of course, it took a long time for the Elves to procreate. Ali'on and I only mated about a year ago. When I became part of the Elven community, Ali'on explained it to me. It's a secret that we selfishly guarded. As you can see, my hair already has a bit of silver-white in it, and I am already changing. The change begins, and ends within only five years. In four years, I will look as you beheld me in the council room."

Kaitlan's mouth dropped. "Not two hundred years like you told us?"

Sandra shook her head, and smiled. "This is our biggest secret, Kaitlan. We dared not tell you the truth, before you came here."

"So you see, Kaitlan, why I did not want to tell the MC about it."

Kaitlan's mind was struggling to process the information, but she nodded her head. That was something very, very simple to understand. Well, it was about the only thing that was simple in her life at the moment.

"Kaitlan," Ali'on interrupted her thoughts. "You are

the White Wolf. We only know that Ma'rol'n, the great wizard, wrote the original prophecy, but we were charged with forging the other."

Kaitlan gasped, and Ali'on continued with his story.

"The original was hidden until it was time for Sarah and Sam to find it. We forged the false scroll leaving out the most important lines. It is the one found long ago by the Werewolf community. Hiding the original worked for thousands of years, but Zanack was far more cunning than we thought."

Sandra and Ali'on stood causing Kaitlan to stand as well.

"There is more Kaitlan, and it is for only you to see. No other. Come."

"It's amazing how many things I see coming that I wouldn't have only a few hours ago! So, why should something else I don't know about be a shocker? This is just peachy keen dandy," Kaitlan complained. She had never been a complainer until now. She was getting tired of having more and more information poured into her brain without complete answers!

Sighing, Kaitlan followed Ali'on and Sandra down an obsidian staircase, which was to the right of the table that she had not noticed when entering the room. It took her under the floor of the King's throne room, and she found herself spiraling downward until she stepped foot on the first landing that was below her feet.

"Kaitlan. You are about to enter a place that no other being knows about, and I was ordered by Ma'rol'n to guard it with my life long, long ago."

"Ma'rol'n, huh? Figures! You act as if I should know him," Kaitlan said as if in a trance.

"Don't you?" Ali'on watched as Kaitlan shook her head. "Well, yes. You should. It is part of your heritage.

"Too bad. I don't, and I'm guessing that you won't tell me, right?"

A smile lit his face.

"I will see you later, Kaitlan, for only you and I are allowed to go beyond these doors."

"OK," Kaitlan said.

Sandra gave her a kiss on the cheek, and then scurried away to her business at hand.

Before they entered the doors, Ali'on showed her the intricate carvings on the doors

"Our history is on these doors," Ali'on explained.

She peered at them more carefully.

"As Elves, we once lived in the Woodlands. Communing with nature is our highest joy."

"Above ground," Kaitlan said.

"Yes. This is where my Father showed no intelligence with his own mate. Do you see this Elf?" he asked her as he pointed to a figure at the top.

She nodded. "Yes."

"While his name was never known - or it was deliberately obliterated from our records - this was the Elf who desired my Mother so much, he was willing to destroy all female Elves, and proceeded to do so on a massive scale. This carving shows the grief that our world suffered, and was the reason we migrated down below."

Kaitlan saw huge piles of female Elves in a common grave with flames licking their dead bodies. She felt her breath hitch as she saw other females thin with illness dropping as they died, and being placed into the ever-burning grave.

"Oh, Ali'on! I never imagined anything like this! How long did this go on?" Tears were running down her cheeks. She could never imagine what the males must have felt as they watched the bodies of their mates, mothers, sisters, and the other females burn.

"Some say the Grave of Fires continued for over one thousand years, since it takes a long time to burn our bodies. No one really remembers how long. It was the darkest time in our history, Kaitlan.”

He pointed to a small boy Elf.

“You,” she guessed.

“Very good! Yes. When my Mother was gone, my Father lost his mind. You know what they say about hindsight, and her death drove him mad.” He closed his eyes as he remembered. “He went insane, and began to kill the Elven males.”

“He went ‘rogue’, you mean?” she said.

“Well, yes. I guess that is a good description of it. He wanted so desperately to rid the world of the Elves that I…” Ali’on stopped. Tears adorned his eyes.

“What?” Kaitlan asked him. “Ali’on, what?”

“Here,” he pointed at the same young Elf standing over a male Elf’s body, his dagger dripping with the blood of the male he had just killed.

She caught on immediately, and gasped! Ali’on killed his own Father! She turned horrified eyes on him.

“I suffer every day knowing that I killed him!” Ali’on told her.

She wanted to ease his pain, but he had no choice, but to kill his Father. Even Kaitlan knew it! She put her hand on his shoulder.

“Don’t do this to yourself, Ali’on. You had no choice. Just like Dan never had a choice in putting down rogues. He, too, suffered with the faces of friends and even relatives, but even so, there was never a choice. Your Father went rogue. You had to do it. And, you know, as well as I, he would still have died anyway - either by someone else’s hand, or by his own. He would not have lived either way.”

“But, he was my Father,” Ali’on told her. She heard his voice break with anger, sadness, and regret.

“Of course, that’s true. But, did it ever occur to *you* that your Father chose *you* to take his life? Had he lived, the suffering he would have endured would have been excruciating."

Ali'on's eyes darted to Kaitlan. He blinked a couple of times at her. Could Kaitlan be right? Could his Father have deliberately goaded him, because he desired death?

"I-I never thought of it that way," he told her quietly.

"From what I see on these walls, Ali'on, he would have wanted you to take his life, and put him out of his misery, because he was still partially coherent. Perhaps he wanted *you* to take his life - before he hurt others; before he was no longer an Elf; but a creature of destruction. I've seen the powers that Elves have thanks to Lynne, and I also know I've not even seen the worst of them. What would have happened to your people had he been allowed to fully turn?"

Ali'on leaned against the doors crossing his arms over his massive chest as he considered her words. He had never been able to forgive the pain within himself at taking his Father's life. But, now, he remembered his Father's last words to him, before Ali'on had run his dagger into his Father's heart.

"Please...Ali'on...please, save...!" his Father had ordered while a purple foam gushed from his mouth.

But, Ali'on thought he had meant for Ali'on to save himself! It never occurred to him that his Father meant save their *people* from *him*! His Father had grabbed his arm, and stared into his son's eyes. They were pleading with him just before Ali'on saw his eyes turned from silver to black instantly, and his Father was gone. Whatever was in the physical body was not his Father, and that was when he ran his dagger into his Father's heart twisting it to make sure he could not come back from the dead. Only an Elven dagger can kill, or behead, an Elf. Kaitlan's words echoed in his ears as Ali'on's mind returned to the present.   For the first time, in thousands of years, he finally felt at peace. All because of The White Wolf. Ali'on had no doubt about it, now. His Father had forced his hand. Forced Ali'on to kill him. To save their people from the death that would surely follow by his Father.

"Thank you," Ali'on told her. "You have healed a part of me that I never believed would heal."

He took her hand, and placed it on his forehead while his other hand covered his heart, and bowed his head to her in gratitude. It was an ancient symbol of thanks for the Elves, and one he had never used until now.

"I pledge to you the help of the Elves whenever you may need us should we all survive after Zanack, Kaitlan. You will have our gratitude, our hearts, and our swords when needed."

OK. This was really weird. What was she supposed to do, now? Closing her eyes, she let instinct take over. She took his hand to her forehead, and bowed to him.

"I accept such an honorable gift, Ali'on. Thank you."

He lifted his head, and if there was ever a happiness and light in one's face, it was Ali'on. His face lit as if someone turned on a flood light, and he smiled at her.

"No. It is I who owe you everything, my Lady Wolf. Please, follow me."

Opening the great doors with a wave of his hand, they entered, and the doors closed automatically behind them. Then, he led her down another corridor across the ancient ocean below. She stopped. She just had to look at it, and ask.

"Is that an ocean below us?" She just had to know.

"It is."

"How…?"

"It is one of the Creator's 'holding tanks' for the 'waters of the deep'. The ones that were released in the first Earth Age. They are released when the great Creator decides they are needed. Once they flood the surface, they retreat back to their original place to be held until, or if, needed again."

"Atlantis?" she asked.

"No doubt," he answered. "About ten-thousand, or so years ago - I mean from your time - it was a …. You know what? Never mind. It obviously hasn't happened yet," he told her sheepishly. "Too much knowledge of what is to come can be dangerous."

Kaitlan could understand that very well. So, she continued to follow him across the crystal walkway over the underground ocean.

"How big is it?" she asked him. She was curious, of course.

"Probably about as big as the oceans above ground," he answered

Ah, well, that explained why the Earth could be entirely flooded. Jury was still out whether, or not, this was Noah's flood as well, but she highly suspected it. She had also had a secret belief that the great land where Noah lived just might be Atlantis. The descriptions from Plato and the Bible seemed to fit seamlessly.

"Well, that's big!" was all she replied.

Ali'on nodded agreement, and continued on to a set of secondary doors on the other side of the vast cavern. They, too, were carved out of the same obsidian stone on which she walked. Ali'on, again, with a wave of his hand plus adding something like a chant, opened and walked through them into what appeared to be a smaller antechamber, however, little else could be seen. That was until Ali'on lit up the chamber with the same amazing white light which resembled sunlight, but didn't.

She gasped when she saw what was in front of her eyes! A massive, hand-carved, metallic-like wall stood before them. And, it was beautiful!

"Is this real?" she said in a whisper as if she had

stepped into a sacred place.

"Truly."

"What are these carvings about? They don't resemble Earth," she asked him.

"I do not know, Kaitlan. Best guess? They show a time long before us - the time of the wizards."

Kaitlan approached the wall, and stared at the carvings. Ali'on had to be right, because the wall showed no recognizable - well, anything! It didn't even look like the Earth she knew! She studied the wall intensely, and shrugged her shoulders turning to Ali'on.

"I don't recognize anything on this wall, Ali'on. The landscape bears no resemblance to anything I have ever seen."

Ali'on agreed.

"That's how I look at it as well. I have spent eons in front of these doors trying to understand the carvings, but never getting anywhere. Wherever this is, I'm going out on a limb and say that what we are looking at is the home world of the wizards."

She turned to him in shock.

"What?"

"It's the only explanation for it. I've been looking at this wall off and on for thousands of years, and it's the only conclusion. It's my belief that the wizards came from another world, or realm, and it's been so long, the only thing left for posterity are the carvings on this silver wall. However, I do not know what is on the other side of it, and have no idea how to get to it."

"Wait. Inside? There's an inside?"

"I believe so. It is heavily warded - obviously by the great Ma'rol'n - and not even the elves can break through it. And, if we can't, no one can. But, he gave us one specific order." He turned to her questioning look. "Whatever is behind this wall is for The White Wolf only. And, that is you!"

"But, why? I'm not a wizard, so what's the deal?"

All Ali'on could do was shrug.

"Even I have no idea, but I will leave you alone, so that you can figure out how to open it."

"But…," Kaitlan began only to realize Ali'on was already gone. Geez! He was fast!

She breathed out in a huff, and turned back to the wall. There was no visible opening anywhere on it. She used her powerful werewolf eyes, and still … nothing.

"I am going to channel my inner Sarah! OK. Let's review, Kaitlan. Ali'on said that the wall was warded against all, but The White Wolf. So, what? Should she turn into a wolf? The instant she thought it, she tossed it out. No. That would be ridiculous! Come on, Kaitlan! Get your head in the game!"

Closing her eyes, and praying for strength, she stepped up to look at the wall, again.

~ 16 ~
A couple of hours later…

Damn it! Still nothing! Kaitlan couldn't figure out the fucking wall, and turned to plop back down on the floor, her head in her hands. She was this far from crying - meaning her thumb and forefinger together without a space between them! So, the tears came.

"Right! Sure! I'm supposed to be this big, badass wolf that is going to put Zanack down! But, I can't figure out the riddle on this damn wall!"

Suddenly, Kaitlan raised her head.

"A riddle? That's what I'm missing! Just like the White Wolf Prophecy, this-is-a-riddle!"

That's when she saw it. Out of the corner of her right eye, she saw something very small - on the wall. Grinning at her bad attempt at rhyming, Kaitlan jumped up, and moved closer. Yes! There *was* something there! Her werewolf eyes began to focus on that one spot.

"OH!" she squealed jumping up and down like a little kid!

There! There it was! A tiny wolf face hidden behind some rocks with his head barely up, and it looked as if it was biding its time as it watched the activity of the wizards standing in front of the rocks. Its eyes? Wait. Oh, my Creator! They were green - just like hers! Two, tiny, glittering imbedded emerald eyes were staring at her! Wait a minute! She knew she wasn't that unobservant! A second ago, that wolf was looking at the wizards on the wall! Now, she could see its chest and neck above the rock, its eyes looking straight at her. What the hell?

She felt a pull - a strong one. The eyes beckoned to her, and she had no choice. Kaitlan moved her fingers to hover over the little wolf. In a second's decision, Kaitlan pushed the wolf's face. Nothing happened.

She waited. Nothing continued to happen, but the tiny wolf's eyes glowed brighter than before she pushed it. There has to be a common denominator! Sliding down with her back against the wall, Kaitlan sat on her butt. She rubbed her head.

"Come on, Kaitlan! Channel your inner Sarah, again! What are you missing?"

Shaking her head, she raised her eyes to the top of the cavern.

"Come on, Ma'rol'n! What the fuck did you use on this damn wall to get it to open? Why the hell would you make this so hard on the White Wolf? Really? Didn't you have something better to do than to try and piss me off?"

And, there she sat. No answer. Waiting for some idea, *some thing* to come to her. She was just so damn tired. She decided to close her eyes - for just a couple of minutes. That's all. Just a couple of minutes.

"DAMN, DAMN, DAMN!" Zanack swore aloud. "This is impossible! Where the hell is that fucking bitch?"

He'd made sure the girls couldn't move at all, and then he had left to search for Kaitlan for the last several hours. She had to be in the general area! But, she wasn't. Not a sign that she ever even came through the portal! But, she had to have come through it! He slammed his fist down on a huge boulder breaking it into three pieces. This was impossible! He'd planned it down to the nth detail! This couldn't be happening! Not again! He stomped down through the woods with anger. He really thought he'd had everything set in stone, this time! Obviously not! Who in the hell stole the first Earth Element had also stolen Kaitlan! Who? Who was doing it to him a second time, and why?

Zanack was angry. Very, very angry! Sarah, Anita, and Lynne's faces appeared in front of him! If he was going to suffer like this, then so would they! A few well delivered swipes with his spikes, and they would burn! Their werewolf anatomy would allow them to heal fast, but not for a couple of hours! And, they would suffer as if they were in the fires of fe'na'lac'im! No human word could suffice to describe the burning from the poison on a Nivurian's spikes. They would writhe on the ground while their insides burned. They would desire death. But, on second thought,…he'd wait by fucking Sarah, and let the other girls watch her face smile with ecstasy as he pounded into her!

His cock had been far more active lately, and it hardened with just the visual of his dick thrusting inside Sarah's body! What was wrong with him? He couldn't concentrate! Nothing would take his mind off of her, and he didn't have time for this! Shit! No wonder he was having trouble concentrating on finding Kaitlan! Zanack cried out, and had to stop walking when he realized he was in the throes of Gre'ta'lac! It happened when a Nivurian went too long without sex! He hadn't had this feeling in a very long time, and he needed to be sated. Zanack felt the green ooze of his cum flow heavily from his cock onto his pants. He was too far away to relieve himself inside of Sarah. Damn! Zanack frowned as he looked down watching the heavy wetness spread burning the cloth to ashes. What the hell was he doing wearing clothes, anyway? He didn't need them! Not any more, now that his true identity was revealed. He extended his massively sharp claws, ripping his clothing to shreds flinging them onto the ground, and then, sank to his knees. Feeling his balls tighten in his excitement was overwhelming him, and he had to find something to satisfy his dick, now! If he didn't, he wouldn't be able to fuck Sarah without killing her!

Just before he grabbed hold of his cock, he retracted his spines, and began to masturbate with both of his hands - fast and hard, but he couldn't rub it hard enough! This was a side effect of the Gre'ta'lac. He needed a Nivurian female, but that was impossible. A super, or even a human female could not stand up to the physical aspect of their females. He'd rip them to part in seconds, and wouldn't be able to come! He needed something as hard as a rock! A log was lying on the ground near him, and he scooted to it. A small hole was in it, and he pushed his cock into it pumping into it as hard as he possibly could watching as the hole grew with each thrust, before it was too large to help him. He stood up panting in pain from his balls! He stumbled around for a while till he found a rock with a small hole in it, and he shoved his cock into it. It was perfect! He had to "drill" his cock into it over and over, enlarging it until he was able to push into the hole so the rock could grip it tightly. Laughing at a sudden thought, he pumped his "cock in a rock", and that took another hour, before he could feel himself coming! Finally! By now, he was literally humping the rock like an animal!

"YES! YES!" he screamed.

Semen shot out of him into the rock's hole as he pumped. When he was almost satisfied, he pulled out of the hole feeling his semen shoot the last fluid from his shaft flooding the outside of the rock heavily.

Finishing his orgasm with his hands, he continued to scream for another thirty minutes with each spurt until he was completely sated. Zanack collapsed onto the ground panting hard. Zanack managed a look at what was left of the rock, but the pounding of his dick had torn it to pieces, and the rest had turned to ash with his semen. And, now, he was very tired! The Gre'ta'lac was the most powerful, sexual excitement the males of this species could experience. Many times, the Nivurian females would be killed during it - loving every second of the male's dick as they died! It was the most erotic desire any female could have, and they would be revered in death for dying during it! If they could be killed during it, how much more so could a mere werewolf stand? He'd have killed her before he had even shoved his dick into her a second time! And, unfortunately for him, he would have had no choice but to continue pounding into her until his release. She would resemble the log that quickly burned to ash. It exhausted even the strongest of the males. He had to rest. To sleep for many hours.

He had to cast the curse, but first things first. Zanack curled into a ball on the ground still feeling his semen pour from his body - and it would be flowing from him for several more hours. He knew he wouldn't be able to fuck Sarah, now. It made him angry that it would hours before his dick would be up again. But, at the same time, the warmth of his semen was coating his entire lower body relaxing him, as it should. Zanack knew he would be covered in it when he awoke, but that was the way of the Gre'ta'lac. He would find Kaitlan, but until then, he would take a short nap. Sarah's luscious body with those huge tits would just have to wait! Even after he awoke, it would take them two, damn days to get to the location of the first curse. He was especially depleted, now, as he was after he had consumed full quantities of food. His fasting caused him to feel weak. In most curses, one had to have a lot of strength to cast them. In this one, though, he had to be almost empty of all food - a penance to be paid for casting the curse. As his eyes began to close, just the thought of Sarah's naked ass was enticing! Zanack looked at his dick. Nothing. Limp as a baby Nivurian! As much as he didn't want to do it, that meant he'd have to pull her pants back up, because he sure as hell couldn't let his fabulous sex organ get in the way of everything else! He looked down at it. Even small as it was after his massive orgasm, it was beautiful!

He fingered it gently remembering how the Nivurian race thought of little else but sex and food, before they were wiped out. Their females were designed to take their spiked cocks unlike all other species he had ever encountered! He felt the revenge swell against the Creator. It was His fault that he had no female! His anger grew against Canaan for taking his woman, and against Tara for daring to have a child by Canaan! And, that meant his anger against Kaitlan was worse than ever! He would find her!

Unfortunately, Zanack couldn't stop the sleep that overwhelmed him, and he slid into darkness.

Kaitlan moaned, and rubbed her neck. She opened her eyes realizing that she had fallen asleep! What the hell? OK. She was tired, yes, but her besties were being held by Zanack! She couldn't believe that she had fallen asleep!

She wondered why no one spoke to her, as always seemed to happen while she slept? Did she forget? She searched in her mind. Nope. She had nothing! So, what? Was she supposed to solve this "riddle" without help?

She rubbed her eyes, slapped her legs, and stood up. OK, then. This is it.

"I either solve this, now, or we'll all go down!" Her eyes narrowed as she stared at the wall. "What am I missing?"

The common denominator. What was the common denominator? What is the same in the wall and her?

She glared at the silver wall. Well, let's see. The little wolf on the wall had emerald eyes, right? She knew that the little wolf had something to do with opening the wall. OK. What's next? She was stumped. Seriously? Why would a wizard deliberately stop the very person he wanted to enter? That just didn't make sense. She huffed, and shook her head. Damn! This was ridiculous! She looked back up.

Again, she huffed. Now, if *she* had planned it, well, she would have just put some sort of DNA in the locks. And, only a descendent could open it! Yep. That's what she would do, but then, he'd have to be a very powerful wizard by even knowing what DNA was! But, even then, she would have to be a descendent, which she wasn't.

"OK. Again. What's the commonality in all of this? Green eyes. Werewolf. Strange world. No trees. Stone circles. Wizards." She pursed her mouth while staring and thinking.

Her eyes darted back to the wolf. She frowned. Something had to be there, but wh….

"Wolf has emerald eyes, right? Right. My eyes are green, right? Right. But, what's the connection with the third denominator? She started at the left of the wall, squinted, and didn't miss any part of the magnificent carving. It *was* a strange world. It looked as if it was mostly stone. No vegetation at all. Bare. The landscape looked blackened as if their world had been burned up. Nope. Nothing. She shook her head, and raised her eyes upward into a roll then stopped.

"What is that?" She saw something totally out of place.

A very tiny tree sat on a rolling hill at the top of the wall. A tree? In the middle of a burned out world without vegetation? She shook her head. That's when it hit her.

"Well, hells bells!" she squeaked. "I'm 'Mother Nature', right? Trees are vegetation. And, what color is vegetation? Well, it can be anything, Kaitlan. But, the majority of vegetation is - what color? Wait for it! Green! That's it, my girl! That's the common denominator! The tree is symbolizing 'Mother Nature'! My *elemental* sign!"

She was able to touch the wolf easily enough, but she needed a ladder, or even a chair to stand on to reach the tree. She turned, and noticed an overstuffed chair behind her she had missed. She hoped it wouldn't be heavy as she went around, and pushed it up to the side with the tree. Oh, right. Easy. Werewolf!

"Now what? Kaitlan," she asked herself, again, "if you were a wizard, and wanted to make sure something stayed shut forever, how would you go about it?"

Kaitlan looked at the wall again. OK, on the left, the wolf was peeking out from the rocks, whereas the Wizards were inside of a stone circle.

"Hmmm. Stone circle." She cocked her head. "Like Stonehenge? Or, maybe something like it?" she thought. "OK, little wolf. Let's try you one more time, shall we?"

Kaitlan touched the wolf's head. Nothing. She touched it again, and was about to pull her hand back, again, when she felt the tiny wolf move. Her finger tried moving it up and down. It definitely was loose, but that didn't do anything. Then, she pushed it to the left, then the right. The little wolf came out from behind the rocks gleaming snow white! The wall began to shimmer a bit, and a loud noise hit her ears. In fact, it had begun to shake, and even under her feet, the floor moved and shifted. In seconds, she saw the wall split down the center! Jumping back in shock, Kaitlan covered her ears. Three locks appeared in front of her, and the shaking stopped. The top lock was a waterfall that was actually flowing water! Kaitlan reached out and touched the water lock, watching it split down the center, and both sides flipped back. Now that it was open, would the rest follow? She waited for a minute. Nothing.

"Well, that's just annoying!" Kaitlan's frustration was growing.

It was similar to a computer, which has so many protections on it, the only way to get through it was to know something about computers. Computers, she knew about. Great, magical, silver walls, which turned into doors, she didn't!

Kaitlan paced back and forth. Now, what? If it were a computer, she knew she could get through the security. She shook her head. Her feet hurt, her head hurt, and everything else hurt. If she hadn't been on a time schedule, she might enjoy working through it, but she just didn't have the time. She decided to climb onto the chair, and had to stretch her smaller stature to touch the tree. It didn't work - again?

"Fuck!" she exclaimed.

She just didn't have a clue, so, she stepped off the chair, and gave the wall a massive kick. Stupid is a stupid does, and she hurt her foot.

"OW!" she yelled, jumping around holding her foot until she stumbled backward, falling into the chair.

Taking off her shoe, she began rubbing her poor little hurt foot. Well, that was really, really stupid!

"Yeah. And, I deserved everything I got, too! Either that, or the wizards really used a lot of cuss words!" she snorted to herself.

Kaitlan looked up at the middle lock while she rubbed her foot. OK. So it had nothing to do with green, damn it! She had been positive! And, then....

She was The White Wolf. She was also the Earth Elemental. She began to realize that the three locks were Elementals! Why in the hell didn't she notice it when she pushed the lock that looked like a waterfall?

"The wolf must have been the first lock! And, the water was the second lock! Chalk it up to exhaustion."

She jumped up, and stared at the center lock.

"Well, obviously! Air. Air is the next Elemental!"

But, how was she going to open the air lock? Air lock? She'd been reading way too much science fiction! She rolled her head upward when she realized the simplicity of the combination. The lock looked like a tornado! She stepped forward. On instinct gently blew on the middle lock, then stepped back. In seconds, the tiny tornado whirled counterclockwise, and she felt the wind from it. In seconds, the middle lock was completely destroyed, and flipped back.

"OK. I got it! The last lock is fire!" Kaitlan studied the lock. It was a scene much like what was on the wall, but with vegetation. It was a very small scene. There was vegetation everywhere, but it was being consumed by fire. Why did it look so familiar? She stared at it for a minute, then she looked closer. She saw what appeared to be a comet or something about to crash. It must have been a lush, and green place at one time, but the comet must have struck it, and the wizards' world had been destroyed by fire! That explained why there was nothing around the wizards but rocks and dirt, and why everything was blackened. That was it! It wasn't necessarily fire, but heat! Given enough heat, a fire could result. She needed heat! But, what could she use? She didn't have anything with her. She stared at her hands, and shrugged. What about the heat from her hands? Well, there was only one way to find out. Kaitlan rubbed her hands together creating friction until they felt warm. Gently, she placed both hands on the final lock. She felt the heat from her hands being extracted into the lock, actually leaving her hands cold but the lock extremely hot.

"Ouch!" Kaitlan squealed, and she jerked her hands

away from the lock.

It was as if she had put her hand into a flame, and left it there. She looked at her hands sure that they were red. Turning them over and back, her eyes widened when there was no sign whatsoever of any burn! She heard a sizzle as the lock turned red, glowing as if it was on fire! It burned its way through the lock, and the lock flipped to either side. She waited for it to open. Several minutes passed, and…nothing.

"Oh, *come on*!" Kaitlan whined. "This is absolutely ridiculous! Open, already! OK. Open sez me!"

The noise that followed her demand sounded as if the entire world was about to come apart! The obsidian floor lurched so hard, she fell and sprawled flat on her face! Every attempt to get up failed! So, she just lay there waiting for the apocalypse to end everything. Kaitlan had no idea that she was the only person experiencing the upheaval.

Then…silence. She raised her head half-afraid that the floor would jerk again if she so much as moved. She stood carefully, and looked at the wall, which was no longer a wall, but double doors. She stood silently just watching. A tiny slit appeared followed by a brilliant green light, which burst out, and the doors slowly opened inward. The massive solid silver doors continued their travel revealing nothing, but a brilliant green light, so bright that she was blinded. Even closing her eyes against it did not help.

After what seemed like years to Kaitlan, the doors made a loud noise as they locked into position. The light began to fade. Opening first one eye, and then the other, she beheld a massive, oval room that beckoned her to come. Raising her eyes, she scanned the room, and walked slowly forward into a pure, silver-lined room. She stopped just inside the doors, and gaped. The room was almost as massive as the throne room she had left.

Kaitlan had no idea what to think. All she knew was that she had never seen any place as beautiful as this. It was almost spiritual. No. It was spiritual. She couldn't make a sound. It was almost ethereal in design. She walked to the center, stopped, and turned slowly observing everything that was around her. Another light was shining down on her from above, causing her to raise her eyes to the ceiling. A beautiful stained glass ceiling met her eyes. It was so beautiful, she was frozen at its sight as a familiar voice spoke to her.

"It is beautiful, isn't it?" Ali'on said with quiet awe while lingering just outside the doorway.

She turned to look at him. His eyes widened. Her green eyes were glowing brighter than ever before. He backed away with deep respect, and bowed. Then, he continued.

"This room holds all the answers for you. It holds who you are. Use your wolf's eyes to see it, for in that will you find the truth. It is not only the history of the Earth, but it also your inheritance. Remember who you are, who you always have been. Remember your mate, your children, your friends, and family. Remember this world. In that will you see all that you need to know. All of this was only ever meant for you, and was only held by us until this day. The ancient wizards knew it would come, and it was our place to protect it until you came. We are forbidden to enter. Only you can see the truth in it, Kaitlan. Only you."

Ali'on turned to leave, and then, Kaitlan heard the locks turn, and the doors began to close.

Kaitlan wasn't even afraid when she saw that she was locked in, but she did try to open the doors. A half-hearted attempt, mind you, but nothing budged. She sighed as she backed up, turned, and looked at the room, again.

It was beautiful! It was oval, and looked like solid

silver, but she backtracked on the description. It glowed as if it was a…!

"Holy shit! It's a diamond! I'm inside a gigantic diamond!" Her mouth dropped in shock.

She was surrounded by a diamond laced with silver lines running through it. It glowed just like the moon! The only light came from the stained glass window above. It looked so familiar to her, but she had no idea why.

She felt her wolf asking to be released. Why, she didn't know, but something told her the White Wolf needed to be released, so, she allowed her to do so. Kaitlan allowed her wolf to change into her human incarnation, or as her children liked to say, a "furry, live stufftie". She was overwhelmed with sadness. Her parents, children, her mate, her friends' mates - all gone. While she piddled in this room, her best friends were in Zanack's hands. Everything that had happened. Everyone taken from her. And, all due to Zanack. Tears streamed down her furry cheeks when a massive pain in her stomach grabbed her.

"Ow!" she screamed, and heard her voice echo in the room.

Dropping to the floor in great pain, it reminded her of her first change, but this was far, far worse. Kaitlan curled up on the floor writhing as the pain increased. Now, it was all over her body! And, increasing. She knew, instinctively, that something was happening to her. And, she felt - Power. She could feel it flooding her body through the severe pain turning her into someone, or something, entirely different. The power…great power…surged through her body. Through her pain, she could see the silver swirling inside the diamond, heading straight for her from different directions. She lifted up as much as she could, and realized that her clothing was completely gone! The silver reached her, and began to flow into her body. Wherever her skin and fur touched the floor, the silver flowed into her body, and she felt it infuse her with some ancient power. She was truly terrified, she was naked and she was alone.

All she knew, for what seemed like forever, was pain. Excruciating pain. She wasn't sure that she could hold the power. Maybe her blood was too diluted to absorb it? Maybe it had made a mistake? Kaitlan held up one arm, and saw that her skin had turned to silver. As it continued to swirl inside of her, she saw the silver threads move in the directions of both her head and heart! When the first silver thread reached her heart, she gasped as she grabbed her chest - just before she collapsed in such excruciating pain. As it reached her head, Kaitlan grabbed her head. Kaitlan knew that she was dead. In answer, she screamed so loud, the diamond walls vibrated.

Two Hours Later…

Kaitlan realized that she had lost all track of time as she awoke. This was really getting out of hand! This passing out, pain, and everything else! However, at least the pain was gone as she lay on the cold, hard, diamond floor. She was exhausted, and turned onto her back to look at the stained glass ceiling. The first thing she noticed was that all the silver was gone. No silver threaded through the ceiling, walls, and floor. Her wolf was gone, and she lay nude. No wonder! The silver threads were undulating in her, now, extremely pale skin. Good grief! She looked more like a vampire! Lowering her arms, she found that her wolf's eyes had become clearer than ever in her entire life! She could see things - details. What she saw took her breath away with its beauty!

Above her, a five-pointed star surrounded a circle, and within that star were the four lower points between each other. Three circles were inside the center of the star. Then, she lost her breath! Is that…is that her Father's face within one of the circles? In another circle, a face appeared to be her Mother. And finally, the face of a beautiful white wolf was in the center circle. But, it wasn't her wolf. It was different. This white wolf had two coal black rings above her eyes, and a third one on its back. Rings? What the hell? Was this something that even the Elves didn't know? If it wasn't her, then who was it? What the hell was happening?

Concentrating on focusing her eyes, she was able to pull the picture to her eyes clearly. At the top of each point was a picture of each of the original five races of the Earth - werewolves, vampires, elves, humans - and the wizards, which disappeared. Following the line of the points of the stars down to the four lower points, she saw a picture of four elemental women! Their faces stared down at her, and they were - Anita, Sarah, Lynne, and herself? Kaitlan looked again. Their pictures...centered in a black ring. Her ring was glittering silver. It was obvious; now, that the white wolf with the three black rings represented her three best friends.

Pain slammed into her, again - twice as painful as before! She was curling up into a ball as the pain racked her body. *A* change was coming. But, what was she *be*coming? A light appeared within the room. Its intensity increased until it was shining brighter than the sun. She closed her eyes against it! It was just as painful as the physical pain she was feeling! Kaitlan felt a sudden burning. The light was burning her skin. Oh, Creator! The pain was killing her! She had no idea how long it lasted, but when the pain subsided, so did the light. And, Kaitlan lay there for a long time worrying if she would have more pain. At least she didn't pass out this time, but after a while, she knew whatever was happening had ended. Finally, she tried to sit up, and her hands went to the back of her neck to rub it. She could still feel the burn in her skin, and she winced as she traced the burns. Her fingers stopped in shock. There were three raised areas on it! She traced them! Damn! There were three rings on the back of her neck! Next, Kaitlan saw that her eyes were far sharper than they had been the last time the pain had subsided. In fact, all of her senses were multiplied a hundred fold including her anger, and her love. She felt an odd power circulating inside of her - a power she could not deny. An ancient power that was unbelievably incredible pulsed through her veins!

Another loud noise rumbled under the floor. Jumping up quickly, she backed away as the shaking became harder, and that was when Kaitlan began realizing that she had been laying in the exact center of the room. The floor was as plain as the ceiling was ornate, except for the same three, black rings beneath her feet. The rings interlocked each other. Kaitlan stepped away from them quickly as the shaking increased. A small door about six inches square slid open in the center where the rings overlapped each other. A green crystalline structure began to rise. Yeah. Of course, it was, and it was an emerald pedestal! What *wasn't* a real jewel around her? It stood about waist high when it stopped rising, and that same bright light shone again, except this time, it was pinpointed on the structure. Kaitlan looked at the light, then took a couple of hesitant steps forward - smack dab into a solid, invisible wall, and was thrown back against the room's diamond walls right on her ass - again. She was spending way too much time falling on her ass!

"Ouch! Geez! Couldn't you have just warned me?" Kaitlan complained to the pedestal while standing, and rubbing her backside!

The light disappeared leaving only the small emerald pedestal.

"OK. I get it. Don't approach until the light goes away, right?"

The light blinked once at her. Her mouth dropped,

and then closed. Kaitlan looked around, again, and took a cautious step forward, then another, and another until she reached the center structure. She checked carefully to see if the barrier was still there. It wasn't. Guess she was right about waiting till the light disappeared. A beautiful and intricate designed ring was lying on top of the emerald pedestal. Kaitlan took a closer look at its beauty. Never had she ever seen another like it! The center stone was an emerald about twice as large as the other stones. The band was entirely pure silver, or maybe even platinum, and intricately carved with the three circles on either side of the top of the band intertwined with vines. This ring was similar to the other supers' rings, but was also vastly different. A fire-red ruby, a London Blue sapphire, and a pure white diamond surrounded the single, larger emerald in the middle.

Carefully, she held her hand over the ring, and looked around. She was thinking about Indiana Jones. Should she offset it with something? Was it a trap? Or, was this a test for her? A test of faith, perhaps? Kaitlan really, really hoped it was the latter. She reached out, and took the ring off the structure. The ground shook again, and the structure lowered back from wherever it had been.

She studied the ring with her clarified eyes. The stones were so beautiful! Kaitlan decided to try it on, and slid it onto her right ring hand. It fit as if it were made just for her.

"Why the four colors?" she puzzled.

Another great pain on her finger under the ring yanked her to the floor. Oh, shit! She just knew it was a trap! She tried to take it off, but couldn't. Pain increased dramatically, and she was rolling all over the bottom of the floor. The pain was so severe that she screamed and screamed. And, then, mercifully, she blacked out.

~ 17 ~
Again with the Afterlife?

"Kaitlan? Kaitlan?" a gentle, soft voice called. "Wake up, sweetheart."

Drifting…No reality.
No pain.
No sound.
Nothing.
Is this Peace at last?

Drifting…No time.
No sight.
No touch.
Nothing.
Is this Peace at last?

Drifting…No space.
No feelings.
No life.
Nothing.
Is this Peace at last?

Drifting…No beginning…drifting…No end.
No heart.
No love.
Nothing.
Is this Peace…Is this Peace…Peace at last?

"Kaitlan!" the voice was stronger this time.

Shit! She just knew it was just too good to last! Peace. Kaitlan didn't answer the annoying voice, but put her hands on her ears.

"Kaitlan! I am your Alpha! I command you to wake up!"

Well, hell! She had no choice, now. Her eyes barely fluttered open, so she could answer.

"Go the fuck away!" she said to the voice, turned over, and closed her eyes, again.

"For the Creator's sake, Kaitlan! Open your damn eyes!"

Damn! Trying to hold back the tears that threatened to fall, she muttered to the cosmos.

"What is it about the afterlife? And, how come it's a hell of a lot more active than the mortal world? Shit! Why the hell are you always calling me, anyway? Can't you guys just go mind-fuck someone else for a change? Leave me the fuck alone! I'm tired, and I don't want to know a damn thing!"

A single tear slowly cascaded down her right cheek.

But, her Alpha had ordered her to open her eyes, and she had to obey. Kaitlan slowly opened them, and turned over only to look up into an ancient sky where the stars were shining brighter than anything she had ever seen in her life! The four moons of ruby, sapphire, white, and emerald glowing above her like gorgeous, giant jewels reminded her of the ring that she had placed on her fing…wait! Four moons? Jeweled moons? She shot up in one motion shaking her head. Then, she closed her eyes, and opened them, again. No! She wasn't imagining things! There *were* four moons overhead! Looking around, she saw that she was on a rolling hill. Rolling, green hills stretched as far as the eyes could see in all directions. It was dark, yet it was so light, she could see - well, everything!

Her eyes darted back to the sky. The four moons were close. Very, very close. They graduated in size with the smallest one closest to her. Each was larger, and brighter than the next. In fact…if she walked to the top of that rolling hill under the closest moon, she just knew she could step right onto it! Nevertheless, even their bright light could not disguise the beauty of the stars. Wherever she was, she definitely was not on Earth.   *"OK.   That was the most idiotic thing I have ever thought in my life! Not on Earth? Indeed! Ya think, Kaitlan?"* she sneered at herself.

"Kaitlan?" a softer voice called to her. She looked around, and saw nothing. Then, again, "Kaitlan?"

Kaitlan wobbled as she stood, and turned to look behind her. Several figures were walking - well, more like floating - over the rolling hill framed by the smaller moon. They all looked familiar, but her eyes were not letting her mind process who she was seeing.

As they approached, her wolf eyes took over. She gasped in shock. Was she dead then? Seeing things?

"Cordone!" she breathed in sheer joy.

"Wait!" he yelled in her mind.

But, she was not going to stop! Running toward him, she tried to throw her body onto him, but only succeeding in passing right through his body - and finding herself sprawled behind him with her face in the soft grass and dirt!

Kaitlan sat up, sputtering, and wiping the dirt out of her face, mouth, nose, and eyes. She stood up, and looked at Cordone in surprise. Was he? Wait! Zanack beheaded their mates! This couldn't be real.

"C-Cordone?" she whispered not believing her own eyes.

"It's me, Kaitlan," he told her with a huge smile.

"I-I don't understand. Am I dead? Why didn't I go through with the other girls? What happened? Why am I here? And, where the fuck am I?" she asked him with hope in her voice. She was just so damned tired of everything.

"Oh, you did. But, well…we just sort of 'stepped

in', and well…kind of 're-routed' your destination."

"Huh? 'We'? Who are 'we'?"

"All of us, Kaitlan, and with the help of Ali'on."

Kaitlan slowly turned, and saw several people gathered around her. Sam, Dan, and Richard were there as well as her Mother and Father. Cordone joined them. Kaitlan was really confused, now. All of the people she loved stood before her. That's when she realized where she was. Was this where her parents had brought her the first time? No. It couldn't be. There were trees before, and now there were none. She certainly didn't remember the moons. This place did look like the one that Sarah had described to her when she came back from the dead. It had been the day after, and Sarah wanted her to know how beautiful her parents were to her. Even though she did mention the four moons, she never said that they were in the colors of jewels. She slowly walked toward them, brushing off her sheer white robe and rubbing her temples.

"OK. Seriously?" She raised her head, and spread her arms outward. "What is it with the white clothing? I mean, really! Look at me! Grass stains and dirt! Why don't you just change the clothes to green?" Kaitlan huffed. "So, why the hell am I here this time?" she asked when she stopped in front of them. "You do know that this whole afterlife stuff is getting old pretty fast!"

A chuckle came from the group, and her Father stepped toward her.

"Still have your sense of humor. That will always stand you in good stead no matter what, Kaitlan," her Father said. "And, no, Kaitlan. You are not dead."

"Yeah. Sure, Dad. You just keep reminding me of that, OK? Really? Our mates are dead, obviously," she waved her hand toward the four men. "My best friends are being held by that maniac, Zanack, who really isn't Zanack, but a Nivurian from another world, and the

Creator only knows what he is doing to them! And, you yank me away from them? Why? Come on! Give me a break, will you? Let me go back to them! I have work to do. I have to take care of Zanack, so I can finally die!"

Canaan waved his hand, and an entire living room appeared in the grass around her - all white, of course.

"Come, Kaitlan. Sit with us."

"Sit?" she said in complete surprise. "You want me to sit? How can I sit knowing what is happening with my friends?"

Her Mother came over to her, and touched her arm. Kaitlan jerked. Wait! She could touch her Mother, but not her own mate? Why?

"Because, your mates have not yet ascended to the high plains of the Creator. Once they have ascended, then they will have a corporeal body when necessary like your Father and I do." Tara explained. "Now, come on. Sit down. We have much to discuss, and an even shorter time to discuss them."

Oh, great! There was going to be more talking, when all she wanted to do was kill Zanack.

"Talk. Right. Great. Here's your hat, what's your hurry, huh? And, by the way…what is it with all this white anyway? Damn it! I have a headache the size of Mt. Rushmore! Ah, hell! It's white, too!" she muttered, and then asked, "What is all this about? What life-altering shocker are you going to throw at me this time?" she asked them as she plopped into an overstuffed, white chair with her head in her hands. "Oh, and I'm having a really, really GRRRR moment, so all of you had better beware!"

Kaitlan was fed up! Fed up with this whole mess! Fed up with Zanack. No. She hated his guts, and wanted to kill him so badly, she could taste it! Her wolf demanded she enact revenge for her mate, her friends, her Mother and Father, and her children! She wanted it over.

Finished. Done. Then, maybe someone would bless her with darkness. Because, that's what she desired, now. Darkness. Oblivion. No existence. Nada. Never to know anything at all.

"Here, my love. Drink this. It will help you," Cordone said as he set a small glass down filled with a dark blue liquid. She looked up at the man to whom she had given her heart, her loyalty, and her body. Creator! He was still glorious! Was it wrong to be horny for him even after he was dead?

Cordone spoke to her through their minds.

"No, it isn't wrong. I'm horny for you, too, and because we are mates, only we can hear each other's thoughts."

"Oh, Cordone! I'm so wet for you right now. How in the hell can this be?"

"I don't know, but if I were mortal again, nothing would keep me from diving into your gorgeous body!"

She sighed as she picked up the drink, and downed it in one gulp. It was surprisingly delicious, cool, and her headache disappeared entirely in an instant!

"Wow! That's amazing! My head doesn't hurt any more!" she exclaimed. "What's in it?"

"That doesn't matter, Kaitlan. We need to get down to brass tacks," her Father said.

Kaitlan looked at him with her mouth open. Brass tacks? Who the hell talks like that any more?

"Oh. Sure. Brass tacks. Right," she repeated. Her head began to droop as her exhaustion caught up with her. "OK, Dad. Let's have it."

He nodded, and looked up to the men.

"It is time for you to ascend, boys," he told them.

"What? NO!" cried Kaitlan. "You can't take him away, Daddy! You can't!"

Cordone came over, and knelt in front of her.

"Please, Kaitlan. You must let me go. Us go. We

only stayed long enough to say goodbye, and to ask you to tell the girls goodbye from their mates. And, worse is that Canaan and Tara broke the rules to let us stay. Unless I go, you can't become what you were meant to be. You have a destiny above all other destinies, and while I was a part of that destiny, I am but a distraction, now. Kaitlan, you cannot afford to be distracted. You must concentrate all your power, and strength into getting rid of Zanack. Do you understand, my love?"

Kaitlan's tears were rolling down her face. She was crying hard. Silently, but hard. Her face turned up to his.

Cordone's heart was breaking for his mate! She was his love, his life, and there wasn't a damn thing he could do to help her! He didn't want to leave her alone in this, but it was beyond his ability to be with her. He wished he could hold her one, last time.

Suddenly, a brilliant light surrounded Cordone, and everyone's mouth dropped open as all watched in amazement! Cordone's body began to solidify, and his body rose in the air! Kaitlan leaned back in surprise, her tears drying instantly as she watched her mate become ethereal!   In moments, Cordone floated back to the ground to reach for Kaitlan, and pull her to him, holding her tightly.

"I-I don't understand, Cordone?"

He smiled down at her, then looked up to see everyone's stunned face, and smiled.

"I have more than ascended," he told them all.

His light surrounded all of them, now. Cordone had become something more. Something so ethereal…so…so beautiful! And, then, Kaitlan gaped as she realized what she beheld in her arms.

"Y-you're a-an angel?" she breathed reverently watching as thirty-five foot wings of coal black woven with silver extended from his back!

"Yes, Kaitlan. I am," he held her tightly, again.

"Now, my love, it is time for you to become what you were always meant to be. Just as, apparently, I was always meant to be an angel - at least in this timeline."

Kaitlan backed away from him, and stood staring at Cordone. He was a real angel! Her mate! OMG! She had an insane desire to bow to him, and from the looks of the others, they felt the same way!

"Now, my love, it is time for us to discuss things. You need to know all of it, before you are returned."

She just nodded.

Cordone turned to the other men, nodded, and they just - "poofed" into thin air! Then, he turned to Tara and Canaan, both of whom had their heads bowed. Should she do the same thing?

"No, Kaitlan. And, you do not need to bow, Canaan…Tara. I am not the Creator. I am only his servant just as you are."

Their heads rose.

"Good. I leave her in your hands," Cordone said. He turned to Kaitlan. "Listen to them, Kaitlan. They have everything that you need to know to 'become'."

Cordone kissed her lips gently, and his tingled against hers! It was more than a kiss. It was as if he merged his essence with hers. When she opened her eyes, Cordone was gone, but the tingle from his lips remained.

She looked at her Mom and Dad in a daze, and they, too, had the very same, dazed look on their faces! Then, as if whatever happened to Cordone began to fade, Kaitlan began to cry.

Meanwhile…

Sarah, Anita, and Lynne were lying on the ground where Zanack had left them. Sarah's teeth were chattering. With half her body bare to the elements, she was going to freeze to death. She could already feel it.

Worry gripped Anita and Lynne when Anita remembered, and would have slapped her forehead if her hands were free.

"Sarah, can't you turn yourself into water to get out of the shackles?"

Sarah didn't answer. She was too far-gone, so Anita looked at Lynne.

"Lynne! Sarah is in la-la land! Can you start a fire for her?" she asked. "Can you burn through our shackles?"

Lynne turned her head, and glared at her. Why the hell didn't she think of that! She immediately drew on her elemental power, and let her body not only warm Sarah, but also she discovered that her fire broke the spell that Zanack had placed upon them, and it burned through the shackles that Zanack had placed around her wrists!

"Use your elements, girls! It breaks Zanack's spell!"

Sarah awoke, and was warmed up enough to change to water, while Anita turned into a gentle wind. The spell was broken the minute they released their elements. As they changed back, Sarah pulled up her pants. But, it didn't stop her from shaking remembering Zanack's plan for her.

"Now, where do we go?" Sarah asked.

"I don't know, but one thing is for damn sure," Lynne said to them. "We are definitely not staying here!"

The girls picked a direction, and ran. But, they didn't know that they were running the wrong way!

~ 18 ~
The Final Visit

Kaitlan's head was hurting - again. Everything that her parents had just told her was completely, and utterly, unbelievable! Was it all true? It was just not possible! Had she just heard her Mother right?

"You have to be joking, Mom!"

"Why would I joke about something like that, Kaitlan?"

"But…but that's completely, totally, and utterly ridiculous!" she squealed using every unbelievable word to describe it.

"Why? I told you. You are more than just the White Wolf."

Kaitlan jumped up, and started pacing back and forth in front of the white sofa where her Mom and Dad were sitting. They were so calm! How in the fuck could they be this calm after what they had just told her? In addition, and just to make it worse, her Mom told her - again!

"Kaitlan, you come from a long line of incredibly powerful wizards."

Kaitlan was still stunned even after hearing it for the fifth time! Well, maybe not the fifth. More like the third, but that didn't make it any better!

"Yeah. What kind of idiocy is this?"

"Kaitlan! Sit down!" her Father ordered.

"Damn you, Dad! Will you stop pulling your Alpha mojo on me!" she yelled, but obeyed him immediately, because she had no choice.

"That's much better. Now. Calm the hell down,

Kaitlan! You are who you are, and nothing can change that fact! Not your whining, griping, stomping, or GRRRRRing!" her Mother said to her with amusement in her voice.

Kaitlan dropped her head into her hands. Could things get any more ridiculous - or more terrifying? Now, she had to contend with the fact that she was a wizard on top of everything else? She shook her head, and threw it back onto the back of the sofa, shutting her eyes against the white - everything. For once, her Mom and Dad weren't talking to her, and she had a minute to think.

Finally, her Dad spoke.

"Yes, you are a wizard. Your body accepted all the silver quickening."

She sighed. With her eyes still closed, she asked, "And, if I had not been able to accept them?"

"If you were not the White Wolf, you would have died," her Mom answered before her Father could.

"Wow! Well, I could have made book on that answer!" Kaitlan said to herself.

Her Mother continued.

"Kaitlan, Wizards were the fifth race on the Earth. What Richard did not know is that the race was destroyed by a young and angry Odin while his Father, Borr, was still King of Asgard." Kaitlan's head jerked upright in shock. "However, that's an entirely different story that we won't go into right now. Unfortunately, he destroyed not only the bad wizards, but the good ones as well. The ring recognized your lineage. I did not know until I died what my heritage was, but, you are the last descendent of one of the most powerful wizards to have ever lived. His name was Ma'rol'n."

This is just impossible! Who opened up the curtain of another reality, and worse, forced her into it?

"Huh? You mean the same Ma'rol'n that Richard was talking about? The same that Ali'on told me who wrote the original prophecy?" Kaitlan breathed quietly.

"Yes. Ma'rol'n and the other wizards were from another world, as you discovered on the wall. The name of that world is impossible to pronounce, and not important to the story. But, their world was virtually destroyed by a cosmic event, and they had to find a new home."

"Is that why their world looked as if it had been destroyed by fire?" Kaitlan asked. "That's why their world was barren, right?"

"Yes. Nevertheless, to get to Earth, they had to pass through the other realms of Yggdrasil. Unfortunately, Borr did not want them in any of the nine realms, and sent his young son, Odin, to stop them. Odin was very successful in destroying most of them, but not all. The Evil One desired entrance into this universe, and tried to make a deal with Ma'rol'n - the same deal he offered to Zanack. Even though he tried to get around it, the Great Creator had prevented the Evil One from ever making deals with wizards. The power he would wield would be too horrendous to consider. Instead, he came up with a new idea. If he couldn't get into this universe by dealing with Ma'rol'n, then he needed a new plan. And, he did. While he was forbidden to make deals with wizards, he was not prevented from making deals with other beings. He needed a war for distraction. So, he plotted to get the nine realms to wage war against an evil race that lived on Earth before other beings existed. That race was just what he had been looking for to get into this universe. They were blood thirsty and sex-driven - two of his favorite evils. Their bodies were indestructible, and he knew that he could make a deal with one of them. In order to do this he offered another deal to a young warrior from Asgard, named Esoryn. Esoryn wanted revenge against the wizards who had killed his wife."

"Why?" Kaitlan asked.

"Well, the why isn't even important, but since you asked, he had married her, secretly, when the first of the wizards originally tried to enter the realms. Unknown to Odin's great Grandfather, some of them got away with staying, and they renounced their wizardry to hide the truth. Like all who seek power, she was drunk with the idea of being the only one on Asgard. And, the other wizards killed her to stop her from killing them."

"Ah! I almost see why they were not wanted in Asgard. Sounds like a lot of them were psychopaths."

"I agree with you. Anyway, to continue, the Evil One promised Esoryn that if he would merge with the Evil One, he would give him the powers of a wizard so he could defeat them. He found a way around the rules, but, then, the Evil One was never one to follow the laws."

"Well, duh!" Kaitlan quipped.

"Kaitlan," her Mother said.

"Sorry. Go-head, go-head," she flipped her hand quickly at her Dad who frowned at her. She smirked.

"After the Evil One merged with Esoryn, the two were at war within the same body. Once Esoryn realized he'd been tricked into merging, he was bound by the Evil One who took over his persona. Then, he mingled with the Asgard warriors for many years, finally becoming one. He was able to use a simple glamour spell, so no one ever realized that Esoryn was in their midst. His next move was to cause the war against Nivuria, or Earth, to happen, and of course, the entire race was destroyed. The war against the Nivurians proceeded as he had planned, and he observed which Nivurian was the strongest. Once he found him, he approached him in his real form without the glamour. The Nivurian, noting that his race was going to be eradicated, greedily accepted the Evil One's proposition, and the Evil One told him to kill Esoryn. And, then the Evil One merged with the Nivurian.

Immediately afterward, before he could throw up the glamour or take over the Nivurian, Odin's great-Grandfather attacked the last group of Nivurians, and killed them. The Evil One had a bit more power, because of the Nivurian's indestructible body."

"So, what does that mean?"

"Well, it appears that the Evil One was able to cloak the Nivurian with glamour, and could do so with anyone that the Nivurian killed. In this case, Esoryn."

"Are you telling me that he could not only cloak himself with Esoryn as well as every person, or whatever, he killed afterward including Odfrin, Zanack, and even Turner?"

Her Dad shrugged. "He could choose which one he wanted to use, yes."

"That's just so damn wrong on all levels!" Kaitlan gasped.

"Agreed. Moving on, Odin's great-Grandfather only knew that one of them survived. A female. Now, for whatever reason, he regretted having wiped them all out, but he wanted to be reminded why he would never again kill off an entire race of beings. So, the female Nivurian was frozen, and was taken to one of the coldest planets known in the galaxy, and there, he left her as a reminder - frozen forever. Never did he realize that there was another within his own warriors."

"Big mistake," Kaitlan muttered.

"Obviously. But, the Evil One had underestimated his new body and the fact that this race was ruled entirely by emotions. Everything was magnified thousands of times. The Evil One could not take its body over entirely, because they had been merged a short time, and the Nivurian's strength of will and emotions were overwhelming to him. At the same time, knowing that his race was extinct, the Nivurian combined with the Evil One's cunning, used his deadly skills to find his next victim. They were limited at that point, but still powerful. It took a while during the war, but the Nivurian consented to let the Evil One use glamour, and he simply joined with the Asgard warriors as Esoryn, and left with them. Sarah and Anita were partially correct. The Evil One was a parasite, but the Nivurian was a full-blown predator. Where most parasites cannot live without the host, this merging was not quite the same. It elicited a far more dangerous type of parasite and predator - one that could kill any other living being, and use glamour of any they killed as much as they wanted, and no one would be the wiser."

"We were right, but wrong, too," Kaitlan said.

"Yes, you were. They have been bound for thousands of years, and eventually became part of each other. Both not knowing where one begins and the other ends. They are truly symbiotic. One cannot live without the other. When the opportunity presented itself, they killed Odfrin, and the Evil One allowed Odfrin's power to flow into them. With his glamour, the Nivurian finally found its way back to Earth thanks to Odin. As you see, it was thousands and thousands of years later. This went on throughout the reigns of Odin's great-Grandfather, his Grandfather, his Father, him, and now, today. No one knew that another Nivurian had survived the war, and everyone thought the race was destroyed. What the Nivurian did not know was that the bargain made by Esoryn with the Evil One, would corrupt him more with each merging. His hunger was already great for blood and flesh. So, the Nivurian begged a secondary deal with the Evil One. He promised to serve him if he would give him great power to take over the Earth - to let him breed humans for his hunger. The Evil One agreed, and gave him more power than before. There was, however, a price to pay for his deal. Just as Esoryn agreed to his deal to destroy those who had killed his wife so, too, was the deal with the Nivurian and the Evil One. The price was that his life would be ruled by insatiable hunger for flesh and blood. The Nivurian accepted, and from that point forward, with each subsequent merging, his hunger became unquenchable. If there were two of the most dangerous creatures in the realms, no one could ever have come up with Zanack in their wildest dreams!"

Kaitlan's eyes popped out while she felt her stomach needing to empty its contents.

Tara nodded, and continued.

"The Evil One had desired an escape from his own prison, and sought to steal the Nivurian's body, but, this time, the Evil One tricked himself, because the Nivurian would not give up his body. At least not immediately. When the Nivurian thought it over, he realized that by merging his body with the Evil One, he would become the most dangerous, and deadly creature ever. So, the Nivurian agreed. But, he did not understand the Evil One's power, and he lost the fight while the Evil One took on the Nivurian's gluttony for blood and flesh. The two fell into madness. Even the Evil One didn't realize, at first, that he was trapped in the Nivurian's body. When he did, he blamed it all on the Great Creator. He never could realize that the Creator gives free-will to all."

"Even to the Evil One? Then, how…?" Kaitlan was horrified. "Why would he give him free-will?"

"The Creator wants those who would love and be loyal to him despite the bad times, Kaitlan. Only they can be trusted in his service."

"Whoa! Is that why we think of the Evil One in terms of a reptile?" Kaitlan said absentmindedly. No one answered, but she wasn't expecting one anyway. Then, "And, this Ma'rol'n?"

"He had more power than any wizard that ever lived, because was an angel, Kaitlan. A white angel. His Earthly persona could transform into a white wolf,"

Canaan injected.

Kaitlan's mouth gaped open. Was there ever going to be a non-shocker ending of surprises? Nope.

"Yes," Tara nodded. "He also had the amazing gift to see the future, and he pushed the white wolf, along with his powers, through his two descendents until it was given to you. That same power flowed through me, but I was not the one to receive the White Wolf inheritance. He used me as a catalyst to make sure I met Canaan. It was Ma'rol'n who wrote the original prophecy."

"Ah," Kaitlan was snarky, now. "Well, Ali'on told me that, and it sure explains things. It's one of the things that we just didn't know - like everything else!"

Kaitlan stopped talking when a though occurred to her. Why the hell did that name, Ma'rol'n, sound so damned familiar? It was on the tip of her tongue, but her mind just couldn't grab hold of it.

"Why does Ma'rol'n sound familiar, Mom?"

"I am not at liberty to tell you, Kaitlan. It is for you to understand."

"Well, that figures! That was so not helpful! Thank you very much!"

"Concentrate, Kaitlan. You are the White Wolf and a werewolf. You are part white angel, part human, part Elf, and the holder of the wizard's power."

Kaitlan breathed deeply, and closed her eyes.

"Okay. Let's see. Maybe if I sound out his name it might help?" She began to speak his name. "Ma'rol'n. Ma'rol'n. M-a-r-ln, Marlin? No. That's Nemo's Dad," she giggled. "Oh, hell! Whoever heard of a wizard by the name of…."

Her eyes widened in shock as she stared at her Mom and Dad who were smiling widely at her.

"Oh, Creator!" Kaitlan gasped, then squeaked. "Not - Merlin. Merlin? *The Merlin*? As in *King Arthur's Merlin*? *He is my ancestor?"*

Canaan answered her.

"Yes, daughter. *The Merlin*. Arthur and the Round Table. Swords and swashbuckling. He hid himself when the wizards were wiped out by the purge. Even Odfrin didn't know Ma'ro'ln was still alive. But, *Merlin's* secret was that he was a white angel. No other wizard ever knew it. The combined strength of the wizard and white angel was quite formidable, and very hard to kill. By the time Arthur was around, the time of the Wizards had been gone thousands of years."

"Oh. Is he still alive? Merlin, I mean?" Kaitlan had to ask. Everyone else seemed to be! "I mean...does anyone ever really die around here?"

"No, he isn't. When he met his mate in the 1940's, she presented him with a daughter. He decided it was time to rid himself of his powers, but he had to become human. So, Merlin gave them to his daughter without her knowledge. She never knew who her Father was, and they were dormant. Merlin and his mate, Felicia, lived to the age of sixty. Like all supers, when his mate died, he followed. She was my Mother, and you and I are his daughter's descendents."

"Holy shit!" Kaitlan said aloud. "But, I don't feel any power other than the White Wolf and the Earth element, Mom!"

"I have to admit that becoming an elemental was not figured into the equation, but the Creator deemed it to be. I'm supposing that you will be able to draw on the power from Merlin when it is time, Kaitlan. The white light within that room should awaken the latent wizard powers within you," her Father explained. "The ring was meant for you. It's your heritage. The amplification of the Wizard's power." Canaan looked down at his own ring, turning it around on his finger. "Just like my ring is my inheritance, so is yours."

She held out her hand with the ring, and like her

Dad, turned it around on her finger. The jewels, the circles meant something. In seconds, she knew what the jewel colors represented - the Elementals!

"OK. Where's the remote control so I can just rewind this crazy show, and start all over again," she muttered. "What is this? Some sort of LOTR thing as in 'One ring to rule them all'? What kind of alternate reality have I stepped into? For Creator's sa…."

"Kaitlan! Shut up, and listen. We are out of time!" Tara ordered.

"Huh? Uh, can do," she told her Mom. Wow! Her Mom really was an Alpha female!

"Good. Now, listen carefully. Do not take off the ring. No doubt it was Merlin's magic that kept it hidden. No one in our family knew where it was, or even that it existed in the first place. Since I am dead, I have learned a great many things, and this secret was so secret, I was placed in an orphanage to prevent me from ever knowing. Now, I know why. It was so that I could become Canaan's mate, so that you could be born for this moment." She took her daughter's hand, and held it tightly.

Kaitlan's mouth straight-lined.

"So, let me see if I understand all of this right." She took a deep breath, and continued. "OK. So. You want me to put on the ring of Merlin that has some type of wizard power - the same ring that put you in an orphanage, then hidden, but you never even knew existed until after you died, and now, I'm in the past where I have never been, and have no idea where I am, but I was led to the vault where Merlin not only left the ring, but sealed the room with his own wizardy mojo until I came along, and now, a crazy creature is running around who masqueraded as a werewolf named Roland Turner, for Creator knows how long, who really wasn't a werewolf, but really is, who originally was on Earth, but doesn't belong on Earth, who is really the Evil One, and is a type of parasite taking bodies wherever, who is imbedded into a sycophantic, hard to kill, thing that eats flesh and blood who can pretend to be whoever he kills, and who is holding my friends, doing Creator knows what to them, and is threatening to destroy the timeline in his favor, who killed our mates, shoved us through a time portal, aka wormhole, to carry out his curse that went wrong in the first place, and desires blood and flesh to eat, and the destruction of Earth, and, in the midst of all this, we are supposed to stop him, and I'm supposed to turn into my White Wolf using my elemental powers combined with my wizard powers that I don't have yet, and I also have to join with my friends' powers in order to stop this creature?" Kaitlan stopped, and began to pant heavily.

Tara's mouth pursed, and her eyebrows went up as if she was looking for patience. Then, she looked back at Kaitlan with a tiny smile.

"Yep. Pretty much!"

Kaitlan's mouth just dropped. She was beginning to hyperventilate, because she hadn't taken a breath during her tirade! After a few minutes, Kaitlan just fell on the sofa exhausted. She was beyond words.

"You done, now?" Canaan asked his daughter with a grin. Her rant was almost comical, and even though he tried not to laugh, he couldn't help it.

"I'm not really sure, Dad." She sat up, and held up a finger. "Yes, more. Wait for it! No, lost it. Got it back," she muttered. She looked into her Dad's eyes. "Nope. Done."

"Very funny. Let's get serious for another minute, and then, you will be sent back to your body."

"Oh, great! I just *can't* wait!" Kaitlan rubbed her temples feeling her headache return.

"Now, Kaitlan. You need to know that the ring holds the symbol of all five elements."

"Yeah. Already got that," Kaitlan snarled.

"Good! The four elements, and the power of Merlin. The triple rings signify his powers. You have been imbued with his power, and you will always carry it. If you win against Zanack, the ring will disappear back into the void, and the power will be submerged within you. Even in another timeline, you will not know it is there until needed again." Canaan continued. "Kaitlan, there will always be those who think that they can mess around with nature and the Creator. And, it never fails that they always screw it all to hell. When this happens, a correction must be made, and it is your line, Kaitlan - your Mother's line, that has been charged with that correction."

Kaitlan's eyes widened.

"My children?"

Tara and Canaan looked at each other. Tara had a tear run down her face as she looked back at her daughter.

"If you succeed, my darling, things will change."

"You mean they may never have existed, don't you?"

"Yes, it's possible, but truth be known, we don't know what will happen." Canaan said with sadness.

Somehow, hearing everything else that they said, this one thing made it seem very real right now.

"How can I get along without them, Mother? How?"

Kaitlan was crying in earnest now. Her Mother wrapped her arms around Kaitlan.

"Shhh. It's OK. Please, Kaitlan. You cannot allow this filth to take your friends no matter what you want to do. If it remains as it is, Sarah's life will be in agony. Zanack plans to implant his seed inside of her! She will die a horrible death, and the world will be lost to evil incarnate. Anita and Lynne's lives are already forfeited. Nothing can change this. You are the only one who can change it all. The power you wield within that ring is the power to affect a time shift. To change time itself. Our line is called upon to do it. The Creator commands it. You can't say no, Kaitlan, or it will destroy your soul forever."

Kaitlan gulped. "How do I use it?"

"I only know that it has to do with the elemental forces of nature. They will be channeled inside you when you take the powers of your friends, and then, the power of the ring will take you over, and you will become the White Wolf Wizard - the descendent of Merlin. Once that has happened, nothing can stop you from tearing him apart. In fact, you will be able to unmake his very essence if you so desire."

Tara stepped away from Kaitlan.

"Use your mind, Kaitlan. You have already connected with the ring. That was the pain and the light you felt when you held it. Merlin's power is held within that ring, his spells are within the silver that your body now harbors, and guarded by the elves until this time. You will be merged with all of these powers through the rest of this time, and the next."

"How can I go on when my heart aches with this pain of loss?" she cried.

"By doing that which is commanded. Save your friends, save the world from Zanack's power. Stop him, Kaitlan. Use everything you have. You are the one, Kaitlan. You are the only wizard to ever combine four of the races and a white angel in one person."

Kaitlan stopped crying. "What do you mean?"

"Merlin deliberately manipulated his line to bring about The White Wolf with the impossible. I was mostly human when I became pregnant with you."

Kaitlan's heart shriveled into sadness. How would she go on with out her love or her children.

"And, you do it by believing in the faith of our love, and those who love you, my darling."

A voice came to her. She looked up. Cordone stood there. She ran to hold him, but he stopped her with one hand.

"I have ascended to the next existence of life. An, angel, but more. The Creator sent me to you to tell you that He needs you to complete this task. It is His direct request."

Kaitlan's eyes were as big as saucers.

"The Creator? S-sent you t-to ask me to finish this?"

"Yes, my love. Please. Do not let what will happen to our world happen. I must leave you, now. Know that I will always love you. It extends beyond time and space, and I will always be with you. I love you, my darling."

He was gone as fast as he was there.

"One last thing, Kaitlan," her Father said.

"What?"

"You must be prepared to make the hardest decision you will ever make in your life."

"What kind of decision, Daddy?"

"To take that which is not yours through death, for without it, you cannot win."

"What the hell does that mean?" Kaitlan asked, but he did not answer.

"Do you understand, now, Kaitlan?"

She shook her head. That last made no sense to her. But, the Creator had appointed her this task, and she would complete it. Talk about trust and faith being tested! Her heart was heavy with sorrow, but she could not let the monster hurt Sarah, or the others. And, certainly not her world.

"Yes. I guess I'm ready," she took a very deep breath.

"Know we love you, and we are always watching over you."

Tara handed Kaitlan a glass of the blue liquid, again,

and she greedily gulped it down. Too bad, she didn't ask what was in it, because it affected her very differently than before. She was dizzy within seconds.

"Ohhhhh! Why are I'se so dizza?" She sounded as if she was drunk!

"It's time, Kaitlan. We will not see you again in this timeline," her Dad told her, as he placed a kiss onto her forehead.

"We love you sweetie," her Mom said, but she was having a very hard time wading through a fog of voices. She kept trying to keep her eyes open, but she just couldn't do it.

As she began to feel herself crossing space and time once again, she though she heard her Mother say, "The ring, Kaitlan…the ring…the ring…."

Kaitlan wanted to tell someone to stop that ring ringing in her head, and to answer the damn phone, but she just couldn't get the words out of her mouth. She plunged into the depths of the abyss.

Kaitlan groaned as she slowly opened her eyes. Looking around, she realized that she was back in the silver room. No. She probably hadn't even left it! Her hand went to her head. Did it really happen, she wondered. She slowly sat up, and knew there was no doubt in her mind that everything she had just seen was real, and her pain was totally gone. She looked at her hand. Where was her ring? Looking around, it apparently had slipped off her finger, but she had no idea how, but it was on the floor beside her while the four jewels glowed with a brilliant energy!

She reached out taking the ring, and slipped it onto her right ring finger, again. The jewels glowed even brighter, and suddenly, she knew, now, what she had to do. As she walked out of the room, her mind was flooded with the past, the present, who she was, her people, her legacy, and more importantly, the ancient spells of the wizards that she realized had been embedded into her brain. They wrapped around her brain like the tendrils of a jellyfish. There were just so many of them, and she realized they could never be removed - ever! Not in this timeline. Not in the next. With great sadness of heart, Kaitlan turned, and without a word, she stood, opened the door with a wave of her hand, walked out, and without looking back, closed the door, again with a wave of her hand - not even surprised that she could. The room had been created by her ancestor, Merlin, and had been given into the Elven hands for protection for just this day. The doors slammed shut behind her, and reverted to the wall once again.

Ali'on and Sandra had been waiting for her to return. Kaitlan raised her eyes to them, and they both took a step back. They saw tremendous power flowing in those eyes - the same power that was coursing through Kaitlan's body. Her eyes were glowing with a brilliant green with flecks that reminded them of stars within them.

Kaitlan knew that only with a wave of her hand, she could eliminate them. With a thought, she could destroy them. And, they saw it in her eyes. It was strange to Kaitlan as she realized that they were terrified of her. It's a good thing she saw it, because if it could terrify the Elves, then hopefully, the same would happen with Zanack.

Kaitlan smiled when they bowed to her.

"Oh, come on, guys! Stop with the bowing, will you? I'm the same person. Don't be afraid of me, guys. Seriously. I know why I am here, now. I know what I was chosen to do. I will do as The Creator has asked me, and I will not fail him. I know what I have to do, but honestly, I don't know how I'm going to do it, and not suffer with my decisions. I only know that I will become something entirely different than who I really am. I'm sorry, but I must go. I need the Earth surrounding me, now."

With one final look at them, "I will not fail the Creator. This, I promise you."

Ali'on and Sandra started to bow to her, again, when she shook her head, and they stopped. She might be the most powerful being in any realm at the moment, but she believed all were equal.

She smiled sadly at them, and with a nod, disappeared.

Ali'on and Sandra looked at each other.

"What do you think, Ali'on?" Sandra asked her mate.

Ali'on shook his head.

"I don't know what to think. All we can do is pray that she does not choose the path of evil."

"You mean she could *still* choose it?" Sandra asked in terror.

"With the power that is coursing through her veins, the temptation to embrace it will confront her, and it will be almost impossible to resist it. If she doesn't, she will become more evil than anyone that has ever been."

Sandra put her hand up to her hair. His words scared her badly. He looked up, and saw that her hair had become almost full white in a matter of seconds. Just because she was in Kaitlan's presence, she was on the verge of becoming full Elf earlier than they ever expected. Stoking her hair, he pulled Sandra tightly to him.

"We all have choice, my dear. The Creator has always given us free choice. It is her decision. Pray to the Creator that she makes the right one."

For the first time in his long life, Ali'on was truly frightened. Would she make the right decision? Would there be a future? It bothered him greatly that he had no answer.

On Asgard, Dahll looked into the void, and saw Kaitlan's powers. Still, he could see no future. All that was in the universe was black. Empty. No life at all. As if everything had decided to suddenly shut down. Suns and Moons, galaxies and even black holes ceased to exist. There was no space; no time; nothing. Kaitlan was about to become the most dangerous being to have ever existed. He wanted to believe that she would not choose the path of evil, but the powers coursing through her, now, would tempt the strongest soul in existence. But, the soul of a young woman? How could he believe that she could resist it? Would she make the right decision? Would there be a future? It bothered him greatly that he had no answer.

"Tara, don't be afraid. She will be able to resist. Her heart is pure and good. Nothing is stronger," Canaan said.

"I'm not afraid. Not really, Canaan. I'm only afraid that she might be tempted, and that could be her end."

"I do not believe that will happen, Tara," Cordone appeared to them. "She is strong. I have complete faith in her."

"Perhaps, Cordone. But, we can't be sure, can we?" Canaan said.

In sadness, even Cordone had to shake his head. Would she make the right decision? Would there be a future? It bothered all three of them greatly that they had no answer.

~ 19 ~
Free to Choose

Kaitlan sat in a cave - somewhere. Well, honestly, she didn't know if it was a cave. All she knew was that she hadn't cared where she went just as long as she had her element surrounding her. She needed its power to flow into her. She also asked the Earth (she would never demand from it) if it would remove the remains of the being which she was about to annihilate. The Earth would do as she had asked, because it, also, knew the danger of Zanack. Through her connection, the Earth showed her what he really was as her newfound power presented the story through a vision. She apologized to the Earth as she threw up on it. The Earth immediately swallowed it up so she would not smell it. A small opening appeared, and a trickle of fresh water flowed from it. She drank, and spit out the taste left behind, then gulped the water greedily.

Finally, Kaitlan took a very deep breath.

"I will ask you for this favor when I am ready."

She dried her eyes, and prayed that her heart would harden. It was the only way to take the powers of her friends.

"Where is the bitch?"

Zanack had caught up to the three women after almost two days, and he had bound them once again. He looked at Sarah. He was too angry to take her right now, and that pissed him off even more! The girls had managed to scoot together, and he eyed them as he stomped toward them

"Well? Where is she?"

"We really don't know. She just did not come through the portal with us," Anita said.

She had never been so disgusted in her life. Just looking at this filth made her want to gag.

Zanack walked over to Anita, and yanked her hair back causing her to yelp in pain as he ripped a hunk of it from her scalp.

"If you are lying to me…."

"And, why would we lie to you? Besides, whoever took the Earth elemental away from you the first time, obviously took her away again. In addition, and quite frankly, we are damn fucking grateful that someone took her out of the picture. So, you will either just have to give it up, or cast another, weak curse that will never be permanent, or we'll just all have to go through this again! That is your curse, Zanack!" Lynne yelled at him.

He threw Anita's face on the ground hard. She came up sputtering with blood and dirt coming from her mouth and nose. She spit it out of her mouth.

"Zanack."

Zanack froze in place when he heard Kaitlan's voice behind him. He turned, and there stood Kaitlan. In an instant, he had her bound. He slithered to her, swishing is massive, spiked tail back and forth, and yanked her hair back as hard as he could. But, Kaitlan made no sound. He didn't know that he could no longer hurt her.

"Where have you been, you bitch!"

He backhanded her twice, then picked her up, and threw her against a tree. He had no idea that she let him tie her up, and that she could erase his puny spells easily. But, she played along.

Kaitlan slowly stood up. Her face was sliced down the left side of her face from her left eye down to her neck, and blood was flowing freely. A small branch protruded from her stomach, and blood was gushing onto the ground. Anita, Sarah, and Lynne gasped in shock as they watched their friend losing a lot of blood. Yet, despite her wounds, they were in shock as she stood up, and walked forward with the branch sticking out of her. Kaitlan cocked her neck from side to side, and then proceeded to pull the branch from her body! Anger grabbed her, but he would be no more in a few minutes. He just didn't know it. Kaitlan turned to look at the girls, and gave them a sad wink. They knew it was time, and they were ready.

"Where I have been is not important, Zanack," she told him quietly as she walked toward him tossing the bloodied branch away. "It is where you will be going that should be important to you."

Zanack's eyes widened as her clothing and wounds healed! But, his anger was too far-gone.

"It is if *I* say it will be, you fucking bitch! I'm ready to cast the curse!" He walked over to Lynne, and Kaitlan stopped. "Now, here's how this is going to work. You, Kaitlan, do not move."

He waved his hand, and a small, round bowl-shaped indentation appeared in the soil at his feet. In his hand, he held the same, jeweled dagger that he had used to kill their mates.

"In turn, and to make absolutely sure that this time the curse will hold, I will slit their throats from ear to ear, and their blood will flow into the small crater. They will die, naturally. Well, all but the woman who will bear my child that is."

Kaitlan had stopped walking, and resumed again.

He leaned down, yanked Sarah's hair, and pressed his mouth to hers. Sarah thought she was going to be sick. When his mouth left, she gathered the saliva he had dumped in her mouth along with her own, and spit it into his face. Kicking her in the side twice, caused her to slump over in pain. Kaitlan did not she react in any way, but continued advancing toward him.

"*STOP*, Kaitlan O'Hara."

Kaitlan halted once, again, but not because he told her to stop.

"I'll be merciful, and let you say goodbye to each other. You have two minutes."

He walked away.

"Kaitlan, where were you?" whispered Lynne gazing with awe into her brilliant green eyes.

Kaitlan shook her head. Her eyes began to fill with tears.

"Irrelevant. I have to ask something of all of you."

"What?" Anita was apprehensive noting Kaitlan's lack of emotion.

"I must ask you to let me take your elemental powers to merge with mine. None of you were ever meant to help me destroy Zanack. It was always my charge. All three of you held that power until I was meant to take it from you."

Silent tears began to slide down her cheeks. No emotion, Anita thought? She was wrong when she saw Kaitlan's tears. Anita knew what Kaitlan was about to say was something she couldn't believe, and she would ever have said. Sarah looked at her, and nodded, as she understood.

"You have to kill us to receive the powers, don't you?" she teared up.

"No. Not you Lynne, nor you Anita. It was ordained that you will die by his hand. I cannot stop that, nor should I want to do so. But, Sarah, I was ordained to kill you in order to take your elemental power. But, I refuse to take them without your permission. All of you."

"It's going to hurt," Lynne stated the obvious.

"Yes."

"Then, take my fire, before I die from loss of blood. You have my permission."

"Take mine, too, Kaitlan, before I also die from loss of blood. I refuse to give him the satisfaction of the use of my element. I would rather die by your hand than his bloodletting."

Kaitlan nodded once to each of them. Then, Sarah looked at Kaitlan with tears.

"Please, Kaitlan," she whispered desperately. "He will not kill me. Don't let me live to be a receptacle for his spawn! I would rather feel pain for a few moments, and die by your hand, than have his seed inside of me! Please?"

Kaitlan looked at her. Finally! She felt her heart harden. If it did not harden, she could never do what she had to do.

"So be it, Sarah."

"Kaitlan," Lynne whispered one last time. "What happens when you have killed Zanack?"

Kaitlan bowed her head, and then raised it. All three girls looked at each other. This was not the Kaitlan they knew. They could feel great power emanating from her. It overwhelmed, and frightened them.

"Then, after I have destroyed Zanack, I shall join you in death," she told them.

"So touching! So…sad," he interrupted with a huge smile on his face, before his smile died away. "That's enough! It's time for the curse to be recast."

Walking behind Lynne, he yanked her head back and put the jeweled dagger to her neck.

Then, he raised his eyes to the sky, and began to cast the curse.

Of flesh and blood, these elements bound,
Of Fire and Air; of Water and Earth.
I call, to thee, with souls unbound,
This curse of evil all time to bare.

On knee I bend, for all time,
Give back to me what should be mine.
Forever alter time and space,
I cast this curse within its place.

The blood of Fire is first to spill,
With blood of Air, and Water still.
With sacrifice of blood to Earth,
A second chance to prove my worth.
The final blood I offer thee,
At last, will Earth forever be.
Give all power to me in sign,
To return, forever, what is mine.

For evil, finally, to rule this Earth,
A new one begins, my proof of worth.
I cast this curse unto its core,
To last, I vow, forever more!

A sudden hush fell over the Earth. No sound at all was heard, except Zanack's voice as it roared into the sky. The Earth began to shake, and the clouds above began to gather above them. Lightning and thunder began to rage.

"First, the blood of fire, I spill!"

He dragged Lynne the short distance to the impression into the Earth, held her over it, and without hesitation, he sliced her throat open. Blood spurted from the deep, open gash, and Lynne's blood gushed into the well. Finishing severing her head, he picked her body up, and threw Lynne into the same tree where he had thrown Kaitlan as if Lynne's body was trash. It didn't occur to him to wonder why Kaitlan was so still and silent. They heard the sound of bones breaking as Lynne hit the tree.

Kaitlan closed her eyes, and let her powers flow through her. Unknown by Zanack, she kept Lynne alive long enough to absorb Lynne's fire element into her body. She saw her red stone absorb the power. When it had all passed into the ring, she allowed Lynne to die.

Next, Zanack dragged Anita to the well, and quickly slit her throat spilling her blood into it.

"Next, the blood of Air is due!"

Anita's head was also taken from her body, and her headless body was carelessly tossed into the same tree, her broken body landing on top of Lynne.

As with Lynne, Kaitlan kept her alive just long enough to draw in Anita's power of Air into her ring, watching it glow while Anita breathed her final breath.

Kaitlan fought against the tears that were threatening her concentration. It was one thing to draw the power when they were already dead, but entirely different to draw it from her living friends, even if they were already dead. Sarah's pain would be horrific, even if it were only to last about ten seconds before she died. It gave her no comfort.

Still, Kaitlan's power was invisible to Zanack, and he did not question why she didn't move.

"Ah, Sarah! My love. Mother of my child to be. I will not take much from you. Just enough to add to the mix!"

He grabbed her wrist, and made a small incision. Blood poured forth from it as he held her hand over the well.   Then, his long, yellow tongue licked over the wound sealing it. He leaned into her ear.

"The blood of water I do add," he chanted. "Your, frail, human body was not made for my dick, but I promise to retract my spines! I cannot wait until I mount you with it, and implant my burning seed into you!" he whispered to her, his tongue sticking in her ear. "I have been dreaming of fucking you for a long time!"

She gagged, and threw up on him - again. He backhanded her so hard she flew ten feet in the air, and landed hard as her back landed on a large rock. They all heard a crack, and a scream.

When Sarah landed, she knew her back was broken, and cried, "KAITLAN! DO IT NOW!"

Kaitlan nodded, and allowed Sarah's head to slam backward into the rock, knocking her out, and began to drain her of her elemental power. Sarah's body, unlike the other girls, willingly gave up her power to Kaitlan without a fight. The elemental power of water flowed into her ring, and with the final element, the blue ring glowed. All four elements, now, existed within her power, it was incredible!

Kaitlan turned her eyes to his. Her ring held all the elemental powers, now.   She heard Sarah's body convulse behind her flopping in horrible pain. With complete lack of emotions, she turned back to Zanack, and gave him an evil grin, but Sarah was already brain dead, so only her body was reacting of its own accord. Kaitlan decided, at the last second, there had to be away of taking the power without worrying about Sarah feeling pain. It worked. And, Zanack thought *he* was evil?

Zanack ran over to Sarah when she took her last breath. He stared in disbelief! No! Then, he turned to look at Kaitlan. She was looking at them without so much an ounce of feeling in her eyes.

"YOU FUCKING BITCH!! WHAT THE HELL DID YOU DO TO HER!!!!" he screamed at Kaitlan.

Kaitlan felt the massive power of all four stones

suddenly release into her body mixing inside of her. It was overwhelming, and she could feel madness as they mixed. Her feelings and emotions were draining from her leaving her mad with the desire to kill Zanack.

"Why should you care, Zanack? And, why do you think I care whether they are dead? Is there some reason I should care?" she asked, her voice like steel.

"I'm going to kill you! You're always in the way! If it hadn't been for the fact that the scroll was flawed in the first place, I would never have had to do this a second time!   Who wrote the forged scroll, Kaitlan? The Wolfsbane I used to get rid of you, did not work. And, if I had not learned the truth if I had succeeded the first time, we would not be here now! Your blood will enact the curse, and by the Evil One! I will carve your body up slowly, relishing as your blood drains!   Your Father begged for his life, and you will do the same!"

"Liar," her voice was deadly.

"What did you just say to me?" he asked in surprise.

"Lie. My Father never begged you. Please, do not insult my intelligence."

She cocked her head at him, and he saw something in her eyes that suddenly made him wary. He shook it off as imagination.

"Believe what you wish. I was there. I know."

"I know one thing, Zanack."

Kaitlan's eyes became a steel gray as she looked at him.

"And, what is that?"

"You will die in about three minutes. So, how about getting on with it. Maybe I can make it shorter just to spare you the pain I intend to inflict upon you."

Kaitlan's voice was so quiet, Zanack had to strain to hear her words.

He slapped her face so hard, she bit the inside of her cheek. Blood welled in her mouth, but it only made her stronger. She spit it in his face. He took his finger, wiped the blood off his face, and then licked it.

"Your taste is really revolting, Kaitlan," he complained as he spit it out.

It was the worst tasting blood he had ever eaten! What the hell was that taste? His stomach began to roll.

Kaitlan laughed maniacally, and Zanack took a hesitant step backward.

"Ah, Zanack. Do you not know the taste of poison? My blood holds a deadly poison I made just for you. The White Wolf is in charge, Zanack."

His eyes met hers. He saw no deception in them. He proceeded to spit the blood from his mouth trying to expel it. Kaitlan sneered as she saw that he believed her. His clawed leg flipped up, and kicked her in the face. Her body didn't flinch, move, nor did she make a sound. His eyebrows drew up as his mouth dropped open when she raised her head.

"The poison was designed to enter your body immediately. No amount of spitting, or anything else, will get rid of the poison, Zanack. You will feel it very soon, and you will beg for death. Two minutes," said Kaitlan as she counted down to his death.

"*STOP IT*! Stop counting!" he screeched.

"One minute, fifty seconds. Come on, Zanack! Slit my throat! What are you waiting for?" She stuck out her middle finger, palm up, and wiggled it. "You know you're dying to slit it."

Zanack watched as her face turned a pasty white. An evil grin rose as her mouth tilted upward into an expression that would have terrified anyone. She felt drunk with the incredibly massive power as it continued to flow through her body. All the elementals power. Merlin's power was released from the ring into her body. All the powers of the White Wolf combined within her in seconds! Suddenly, Kaitlan could "see" everything. She knew the universe, and all its secrets. The power surged, and Kaitlan knew she could destroy worlds with just a word! She could see everything. Understand everything! She knew everything that Merlin had known, and then some. It was a euphoric feeling, and she even forgot about her mate, her children, her friends. She was beyond pain, sadness, or despair. *She was pure power!* Her mouth turned up in a hideous grin as her body began to morph into part White Wolf, part wizard, and all the elemental powers. Because Kaitlan was so high on the power, she felt a darkness invade her body giving her even more power! A dark power that she gladly embraced!

She forgot everything as she seethed with vengeance and rage against Zanack. She remembered Dahll's warning not to allow the evil consume her, but the anger and hatred had built to such a high, she wanted to keep it! Why shouldn't she keep it? It was *hers*! She wanted to rule this world of little people! She craved the power!

But, before she claimed her rightful place on the throne of Earth, she would deliver the final deathblow with pure hatred, and she watched as her poison took effect. It would flow through his body slowly. He would suffer an extremely slow death from both the poison and her vengeance. And, she would cheer and dance as she killed him! The evil she felt welling up inside of her body was escalating. If this is how Turner felt, she knew why he loved the evil power so much! She was floating on a high with the power of the four elements, the power of the White Wolf, and the power of the most powerful wizard that had ever lived. Turner was nothing but a magician compared to her! She licked her lips with anticipation, and prepared to deliver her judgment! Hers! She would have revenge in the most horrific death she could imagine for Zanack, and she would have no mercy! And, then, she would claim her rightful place.

"You asked for it, Bitch! Poison or no, your throat I

will slit slowly. I want to see you bleed out in front of me!”

Kaitlan allowed Zanack to drag her over to the well of blood - right past her friends' lifeless bodies. He raised his dagger to slit her throat. Nothing happened. He tried again. And, yet again. Nothing! No mark! No blood!

“What the fuck?” he yelled.

Kaitlan's laugh was frighteningly evil. Her eyes turned bright red. Merlin had not just been a wizard and white angel. But, what her Mom and Dad didn't know, and she had just realized, was that Merlin also had vampire blood within him! She truly was the product of all five races on Earth! It remained in the ring he had left for her. She pulled all of that power into her body combining with her powers, and those of all the races - Wizard, Vampire, Elf, Werewolf, and human - each racing into her veins warring with each other for dominance, and for the moment, vampire was winning.

“Your time is up, Zanack. Now, you die,” she warned as she felt her fangs lengthen. Kaitlan easily bit into his neck - even through his leviathan scales releasing pure poison into his body!

Zanack struggled against her, yet he couldn't get away from her. But, the dagger was still in his hand, and he stabbed Kaitlan through the heart! The ancient dagger broke into two pieces, and the broken blade fell to the ground while the hilt was still in his hand.

Her eyes were glowing red when she released him. Zanack staggered away from her holding his neck. Taking his hand away, he saw a lot of blood flowing from her bite. Kaitlan was laughing! At him! His stomach wrenched, suddenly, followed by a stabbing pain, which was so intense, he looked down to see what had caused it. Everywhere he had tried to stab Kaitlan, his own, blood flowed from identical places on his own body. Then, he felt a burn in his blood that began to increase. He dropped the hilt of the knife to grab his neck.

"What the fuck did you do to me?" he screamed.

His eyes showed fear for the first time as he watched Kaitlan's body begin to glow with the same brilliant red light that echoed in her eyes. She stood up, and loomed over him. She seemed taller, somehow.

"I am The White Wolf, Zanack. Did you think I was a myth? The White Wolf was born to kill you."

Her glow increased, and he watched the air around her begin to whirl.

She pulled on the human power, and the Air Element lifted her from the ground. She cried out for retribution and vengeance. She was far from justice having rejected it from her human side. She began to phase to a werewolf, and it merged with the other four races and the elemental powers. Kaitlan was angry from all the blood and flesh that had been spilled by Zanack over the thousands of years! This fueled all of her powers, and they began to merge together into unlimited power!

Zanack took several steps backward. He registered shock at the vision of the "god" that was transforming in front of him, for that was the only word that could describe her! Despite the terrible pain he felt from his knife wounds, and even as his insides were being seared with her poison, he watched as Kaitlan's eyes became wild with untamed and unlimited power! Even as scared as he was, he couldn't help but feel the jealousy rise within him. That should be him! That power should be his! And, yet, this filth had been endowed with powers beyond her possible comprehension. He also knew that it could easily turn her more evil than he was! Maybe he could make a deal with her to gain the power! Her evil side just might let him!

"Kaitlan! Hear me! I make you a deal. You let the Evil One merge with your body, and together, the two of us can rule this world, and countless others! I know you want this! I feel it! What say you?"

She didn't answer, but held her hands at her side then raised them slowly upward. Her body began to grow larger and larger with each second until she became three times the size of her normal self. She drew in the Fire Element as it exploded around her, surrounding her with a strange yellow-red light! Everything around her now had a reddish tint to it. She opened her eyes, and they not only glowed with blood, but blood ran down her face! Her clothing changed to blood red, which blew out behind her with the winds that she created. She was transforming into something horrifying, and even Zanack had the smarts to become terrified beyond anything he had ever felt, and turned to run!

Kaitlan, now full of a power that only a god should have, released the elements. First, deep inside her eyes, the pigment turned blue. Her arms raised again, and allowed the water to flow upward from the fountains of the deep. The water surrounded Zanack, but did not touch him. It rose to washed away the blood and flesh of her friends, cleansing the Earth, and the Earth took her friends into her depths. Then, she used the water to form a dome over Zanack and herself - hidden from any who might dare to come near, but making sure no one would be harmed. No one could enter - or in Zanack's case - exit.

He sank to his knees in pain and fear as he gazed up into her face. He had never been so terrified! What was she? He had never seen anything like it, not even the Evil One!

"Who am I, Zanack? Have you not yet guessed? I am The White Wolf. My Mother was from a line that goes back to the most powerful wizard to ever live. Ma'rol'n was his name. I am everything than you can imagine! I AM power glorified!"

He gasped when he heard the name. Ma'rol'n? No! That was no possible! He was dead! Zanack began to cower in fear when he realized that even the Evil One did not doubt it. Not now. She floated toward him, and lowered herself just out of his reach.

"I am your judge. Your jury. And, your executioner. You have been found guilty of horrible atrocities for thousands upon thousands of years, and you have corrupted Wizard Law - Lon McClain!"

There was no fucking way she could have known.

"How did you know?" McClain gasped. "I made sure you would suspect Roland!"

"Helloooo! Wizard!" She tapped her head at the same time. "You think to fool me? You cannot! But, you can be sure that it is I who will send you to your death. It will be slow, and merciless! I am all-powerful! The Earth will cower before me, and I will let my vengeance flow upon you! You will be sent back to the depths of Hell, and this land cleansed of your evil! And, then, I will rule unobstructed by all!"

He put his hand over his head as her glow built to a brilliant light, and even though he closed his eyes against it, he could still see it. He began to shake in terror!

Kaitlan's body trembled with power. She could feel the explosion that was inevitable within her. It grew to an almost painful proportion. And, with one point of her finger, she began with fire as she slowly began to burn McClain's hideous body. She made every moment of the fire his tormenting pain. The Elements were meant to combine with the poison she fed to him, making the agony one thousand times worse! She let the power flow from her as she burned each of his fingers separately turning them to ash. His screaming made her giddy with pleasure, and she laughed.

"What? Not enough, Zanack. Hmmm. Let's see. What's next?"

One forearm at a time, she seared to ash. Amid his screams, she laughed as she watched each piece of flesh burn and fall on the ground. Next, came the rest of his arms. She came much closer to him. She sniffed.

"Your scales and flesh burn, Lon McClain! The scent is beyond intoxicating to me! If only you could know the pleasure with which it consumes me!   I understand, now, how you felt when you ate flesh and blood! You have had the pleasure from your feeding and brutality! Now, it is my turn! Yes! Scream louder! It invigorates me!   More! More! I need more pain and screams from you! What do you not need? Ah. You don't need your tail, do you?"

McClain's eyes widened in terror, his body already wracked with horrific pain from what she had already done to him. He never knew he could have such pain in this body! It was impossible to hurt it! But, Kaitlan's vengeance was proving him wrong for the first time. He felt his tail burned to a crisp, but she left it attached so he could truly feel the pain. But, it was the next thing that terrified him more than ever. His eyes widened as she told him his cock was next. He tried to run, but she stopped him with a wave of her hand calling up the roots within the Earth to hold him fast. Her finger sent a small stream of fire to his cock. She used slow motion as it burned slowly. She reveled in happiness as he screamed. She licked her lips for the pleasure she felt! Over ten minutes, she burned his cock off of him slowly. Then, his balls were burned off of his body. It gave her intense satisfaction as she watched the offending organs turn to ash.   She laughed as he screamed.   The louder he screamed, the more she laughed.

"How do you like that? You who have tortured how many women with your filthy body. With that filthy cock? And, I wager, men as well! I know I'm right, aren't I? Children? Animals? What else? Well, you won't get a chance to fuck ever again, now, will you?" she asked as she roared with laughter. "Hmmm, let's see? Ah, eyes!"

She burned them out of their sockets in seconds. Zanack's feet followed by his legs came next, and she watched with glee when his torso fell to the ground rolling around in the dirt.

And, then…she stopped laughing. The horror of what she was doing grabbed her true heart, and her eyes returned to their green. She had been right! Dahll had warned her! But, she never understood, until now, the power that Dahll had meant! No one should ever command this type of power. She looked at Zanack on the ground, and called the roots away. He couldn't get away, now. The power she commanded was not for her! She wasn't evil, and she refused to be so!

One last burst of fire, and McClain was ash - gone forever. She had destroyed the last of the Nivurians. The last of a race. And, she also used the last of her power to bind the Evil One back to his realm of pain. Kaitlan did not want the power, and she had to get rid of it. All of it! She was numb as she scattered Zanack's ashes to the four winds using the power of air throwing his ashes into the water dome.

No! She would not become like Zanack or the Evil One! With the destruction of Zanack, she knew what she had to do. She could not live with this, or with what she had done and thought. Her arms lifted upward as she looked at the dome of water above her. Kaitlan knew the dome of water would keep anyone around the area from the danger she represented. Then, she allowed the power that was inside of her to explode around her. It left her body in that one burst of power as if several nuclear bombs exploded! Her entire world of family and friends were gone. Everything was gone. The water dome collapsed, sending the water into the air as if a waterfall flowed upward instead of down, and then, released it, letting it flood the landscape washing all McClain's evil away.

Kaitlan dropped to the ground. She was very weak, but had just enough strength to raise her head to watch the Earth swallow the water and his ashes into its depths. She would not live when all were gone. It was better for her to die, than to retain the horrible power that had flowed within her body. Dahll had been right. To start down that path would be her end. He had known. He'd been there. Now, so had she. She didn't want life, she didn't want to live any longer, because she knew that if she did, she would be unable to stay alive, and not wield that power. It was impossible for her not to be addicted to it! To release the rest of the power would be her death sentence, and she had never wanted anything more than death at that moment. To join with her mate, her children, and her friends in the afterlife was all that she wanted.

She felt the surge of power rising inside her, again, and so, with the last strength she had, she put her hands on the ground, and the White Wolf channeled all the power that she still had within her body into the depths of the Earth. The ground glowed with the power as it dispersed throughout the entire planet, cleansing it, and its inhabitants of the evil curse enacted by Zanack so long ago. Sinking into black, Kaitlan fell into the merciful arms of death.

~ Time has no meaning in death   ~

~ 20 ~
~ Epilogue? ~
Not Quite Yet

"Kaitlan?"

It was her Mother calling her - again. Oh, hell! At least she thought she was hearing her voice. She thought her parents had said she wouldn't be hearing from them again! Nevertheless, Kaitlan refused to open her eyes. She was so damned tired! Had they all not done everything asked of them? Was it too much to leave them alone? To let them sleep in the peaceful arms of death? Seriously?

"Kaitlan! Wake up!" Tara's voice demanded.

Kaitlan struggled to open her eyes, and finally managed to crack them open just a bit. The light was brilliant to her. Almost blinding. Her hands flew up to her eyes to try to block it out, but it didn't work.

"Fuck it, Mom! Why can't the afterlife leave me the hell alone?" Kaitlan complained under her breath. "I thought you said I wouldn't see you again in this timeline?"

Kaitlan was almost too damned tired to stand up, because her legs were so shaky. So fucking, damned tired! Wait. She already said that, didn't she? Whatever power she had in her body had seriously depleted her entire being. Told to walk into the light when one dies, she refused do so when she saw it! She wanted nothing but darkness. Black, blessed darkness where she knew nothing at all! Why could they just not leave her alone in that dark? She hated everything and everyone who prevented her from descending into that darkness. Not after everything she had done! She did not deserve to be in His presence. She had not just killed, Zanack, which is the only thing she did not regret, but her friends, she did! She was a murderer!

Stumbling to her feet, her Mother swept her up into her arms.

"My darling! You have completed your destiny! We are both so proud of you!" Tara enfolded her daughter into her arms, and kissed her on the forehead several times.

Tears formed on Kaitlan's cheeks. She was angry and hurt.

"What are you saying? I failed! It's obvious that Earth is gone, or I would be in a different timeline!" She motioned around her. "Where is it? Tell me *WHERE* is Earth, Mother? It's not here, is it? It's not up there! It's *gone*! What right do you have to be 'proud' of me? Just what the fuck does that mean in the face of the death of my mate, my children, and my friends, Mother? What does it mean in the face of the death of the Earth? What does it mean that I took my own friends' lives? As I took their elements within me even as I watched their lifeless - *headless* - bodies fall into broken bodies? The evil that I have within me, I cannot accept. I hold it within me; I won't let it take me over, and do unconscionable things that I would never have done otherwise? And, worse? I loved it, Mom! Every fucking, damn single second of it! I enjoyed killing! It gave me a feeling of incredible power knowing I had the power of life and death over everything, everyone! I wanted to rule the Earth! I would have let no one stop me! Do you understand me, Mother? *I. LOVED. KILLING!* And, even after I renounced the evil, it still is inside me. What difference does it make within the grand scope of life and death if I stay inert and unknowing? Everything - *E V E R Y T H I N G* I have ever loved is gone. Why would I want to live? Why would I believe I would deserve life after death after what

I have done? I do not deserve to cross into the light, and I will not!! All I want right now is blessed darkness. To know nothing!" she cried. "What was it all for? Why?"

She knew she wasn't supposed to ask, but she had to ask. Kaitlan broke away from her Mother, to shake her fists at the sky.

"Why, Creator? What was the purpose of allowing happiness? To take it from us? To replace it with such evil! To make me a killer? Please, I beg of you, tell me why!" Kaitlan dropped onto her knees crying in great gulps and sobs.

Tara laughed gently lifting her daughter up, and wrapping her arms around her daughter, again, holding her tightly to her breast.

"Oh, Kaitlan, my daughter. Nothing is ever final - even death!"

Kaitlan looked up with tearstained eyes, and disgust as she heard her Mother laugh! Laugh at her! Shit!

"Oh, you have to be kidding me! Is that really what you are telling me? Death is but the next step over those rolling hills into "a far green country" like in Lord of the Rings? Seriously? Is that all you have to tell me? Bullshit, Mom!   I call bullshit on that! Keep telling yourself that. Keep telling me that it exists. But, don't expect me to ever believe you!" Kaitlan was devastated. "What a bunch of fucking bullshit! What part of all of this do you not get, Mother! That I *KILLED* my best friends? My mate? Their mates? All our children? I killed them! And, why? Just to gain power to kill Zanack? I'm a killer, Mother!" she repeated screaming as tears flowed down her cheeks.

Tara grabbed Kaitlan, again, and rocked her daughter back and forth letting her cry it all out while making soothing noises.

"My darling, it is not you who killed them. That was Zanack, and his monstrous desires. When confronted by one evil, sometimes, one must fight evil with evil, and yes, sometimes we must do what we have to do in order to fight. There are times when we have no other alternative. This was one of those times. Therefore, Kaitlan, it was a decision of the lesser of two evils, which was chosen. No matter how we feel, in any war - and Zanack had declared war on the Creator and His creations - sacrifices have to be made. You made that sacrifice, and so did your friends. They all knew what was at stake. They all, willingly, gave over what was needed in order to make sure that Zanack was destroyed. And, you know this is the truth."

"Oh, come on, Mother!" Kaitlan pulled away furiously wiping her hands across her eyes. "You mean 'the end justifies the means'? Is that your answer to me?" Kaitlan complained. "That's not an answer! Nor will that excuse my acts!"

Kaitlan was being destroyed inside. Everything was being destroyed that made her a good, caring, werewolf. She began to feel very little inside. Only the darkness of the power that was consuming her in whole! She knew she was close to losing her own essence of life, and she just couldn't bring herself to cry about it!

"No, Kaitlan. More like the 'means justify the acts to an end', actually. But, without doing what you had to do, the world you know would be destroyed, and Zanack would have brought about a world of horror. He screwed up the timeline, and that had to be set right. Or, reset it, I guess. You have completed the task our Creator has asked. He knew it would be hard, but now, your reward will be greater than you will ever know. You have healed the timeline and the Earth. That was your destiny. And, your powers will always be at your command henceforth. Why do you think the Creator gave you these powers? Do you think he would give them to someone unworthy? The darkness within is a false feeling, Kaitlan. It isn't real!"

Henceforth? Who the hell even uses words like henceforth? But, it didn't matter! She did not want those powers! All she wanted was peace in nothing.

"*NO*! I don't want them! Never, ever! I am not worthy of anything that powerful! No one is except the Creator! Look, Mom, can I just go back to the darkness, now? Please? The blessed darkness of death? I just don't want to live any longer - in any universe!" Kaitlan begged.

Tara held Kaitlan one last time letting her daughter cry with the loss of everything she loved. It broke her heart.

Tara started laughing, and Kaitlan pulled away staring at her Mother in stunned silence.

"What the hell, Mom? How can you laugh at this? Are you crazy? I want the darkness. It's all I long for in death!"

"Darkness, Kaitlan? Death? Oh, my beautiful, smart, and brave daughter! You truly are the most amazing werewolf that has ever been! Your Father and I are so proud of you," she told her.

"Fuck it, Mom! Go away! Just leave me dead!" Kaitlan told her Mother.

"Seriously, Kaitlan? Remember? If you succeeded, the timeline would be changed. If you didn't, we would all cease to exist. Think about it. Just what makes you think that you are dead?"

Tara smiled as she saw the stunned look on Kaitlan's face as she thought about her Mother's words. It was just so funny!

Kaitlan's face showed extreme confusion at her Mother's words. What did she mean she wasn't dead? A pulsing light appeared, and she shielded her eyes from the brightness, closing her eyes. That didn't work at all. The white was burned on her eyes, and then, she plunged back into blackness. Blessed blackness. Eternal blackness. Yes, she could live with this!

"Michael?"
"Yes, Great Creator?"
"She succeeded, Michael. Take Gabriel and Dahll.
Reset the Timeline"
"Oh, and Michael?"
"Yes?"
"Make some interesting changes for my children."
"Any particular changes, Creator?"
"Nah. Just use your imagination."
"It will be as you command."

~ 21 ~
**I keep saying…Time is Relative, but only to where you
are at the moment! ~ LK Kelley**

"KAITLAN SENECA O'HARA! Get your ass in here now!"

Kaitlan groaned. Geez! Her Dad has been buggy lately! What *was* his damn problem? Of course, why would he use the intercom when the entire building could probably hear him without it!

"KAITLAN!" yelled her Father, again.

Sighing, Kaitlan had realized she was staring out her office window. She pressed the intercom button.

"Dad, you do know I could have been in the bathroom, right?"

"And?" he asked impatiently.

"Whatever," Kaitlan walked out of her office.

No answer, but she wasn't really expecting one. She got up, and proceeded to his office stopping on at the break room to get a large cappuccino, before she went to see him.

Canaan was on the phone as she walked into his office, and he waved her to sit.

"Yes, yes, of course! I will send someone right away. Right. Talk to you later!" he hung up the phone, and then turned to Kaitlan.

"Kaitlan, I'm sending you to our biggest writer to work with him personally. You will edit as he writes his next book in real time. Go home, pack, and you fly out this afternoon at…" he flipped the intercom button, "Jenny, what the hell time is that flight?" he bellowed.

"3 p.m., Canaan," Jenny told him.

297

"Right. Thanks…" and continued without a break, "…at 3 pm, to go to Denver, and then to Valon's home in the Rocky Mountains. Damn! We need a second jet!" He pushed the button again. "Jenny, contact Mathias, and tell him I want another jet!"

"Immediately, oh great one!" Jenny sneered.

If she had been in a better mood, Kaitlan would have laughed at Jenny, but she just wasn't!

"Oh, shit, Dad! Are you out of your frickin' mind?" Kaitlan had no desire to go anywhere near that arrogant bastard! "Seriously? How could you promise him without asking me first? For the Creator's sake! I turn twenty-seven tomorrow, and I will change to my wolf! How the fuck can you send me away on my birthday? On the eve of my wolf?"

For years, she had dreamed of the day she would change. Every werewolf got a huge party afterward! Instead, she was going to be buried - alive - at that bastard's house?

"Kaitlan! Watch your language!" Canaan yelled. "I am your Alpha, and you *will* do as I say! Do you understand me?"

Ah, hell! He was pulling the Alpha crap? She was stunned, because her Father never used it, especially with her!

"One of these days, your mouth is going to get you in a hell of a lot of trouble, Kaitlan! Anyway, when it does, don't come whining to me! Now. Let's go over what you are to do."

After his "orders", Kaitlan stomped out of her Father's office slamming the door behind her, completely missing her Dad's huge grin and chuckle following her. After she slammed the door, he broke out in silent laughter. Thank the Creator she had broken her engagement with Steve! If she hadn't, Canaan knew he would have forced to break them up, anyway! One way or another, both Cordone and Kaitlan would mate tonight! He was so damned tired of the two of them arguing all the time! They could mate first…then argue!

Kaitlan slinked down the hallway as slow as possible. She was in a damn, foul mood, and everyone who saw her in the hall either ducked into an office, or plastered themselves as close to the hall wall as they could, and tried to stay out of her way!

Her ex-fiancé, Steve, was a bastard! She had found him in bed three weeks ago with his little whore of a student! Then, he tried to explain it away as "This didn't mean a thing to me, babe!"

Then, the little tart in his bed sat up nude with her big tits bouncing all around, and snorted!

"Right, Steve. Our fucking has meant nothing! We only do it every single day, and sometimes twice!"

Steve whirled around on her.

"Get the hell out of my apartment, bitch!"

The girl had snorted, again, but she slid out of bed, and sauntered around the room naked picking up her clothes. She slammed the bathroom door so she could take a shower and dress. That had been enough to make Kaitlan see red! She was so lucky she found out in time! He wasn't her mate, but she hadn't found hers like most other werewolves! And, really…how sad was it that she was ready to settle for such a son-of-a-bitch? She'd thrown her 2-carat diamond ring at him, and left with him following her barely covered with a towel. She flipped him the bird, got into her red SUV, and left.

Her sister, Sarah, along with her other besties, Anita, and Lynne, had found their mates, and had been mated for years! All three of them!

Sam had taken Sarah as his mate when he and Sarah had discovered she was pregnant just before she turned eighteen. Their Dad seemed mad, but it was a false anger, and he relented quickly knowing that they were going to mate anyway. Their mating party had been a huge blowout, and everyone had celebrated over, and beyond, their tolerance for booze! After the twins were born, Sarah insisted on becoming a werewolf, and since only mates were allowed to turn mates, Sam had turned her. No one had any idea how Sarah and Sam would feel after her turn, but they were sickeningly, but ecstatically happy.

Second, Lynne and Richard mated barely two months later. Richard and his Father had a "falling out" long ago. He had been bitten by rogue weres, and turned, leading him to destroy all of them. Because of the anger against his Father, he had remained on Earth as its protector for thousands of years. The huge discovery that he was really Thor, Prince of Asgard, and heir to the throne, surprised them all! He had taken Lynne with him when Odin, his Father and King, had decided to step down. Thor was named King at a huge ceremony where all her friends had attended, and they watched as Lynne became his queen. Apparently, the Asgardians absolutely loved her! They admired a warrior, and they didn't seem to care she was Elf.

And, then, if that wasn't enough, her third bestie, Anita, had been mated to Dan Wheeler since they were only fifteen! That was thousands of years ago! When Cordone Valon, Anita's brother, had found out, he had hit the ceiling - big time! But, there was nothing he could do. It was already done, and in a short time, he discovered that Dan was a brilliant interrogator. Canaan's Father installed him within his security force. Now, Dan headed their security.

They all had found their mates! And, where did that leave her?

"Alone! That's where!" she muttered under her breath continuing to stomp down the hallway.

She was about to enter the elevator to go to the

secret floor where she could scream without anyone hearing her, when two, little voices called her name, followed by tiny little feet pounding quickly from the other end of the hall.

"Aunt Kait! Aunt Kait!"

She turned just in time to see Sarah and Sam's little, twin urchins rushing to her as fast as they could. They were her salvation every time she began to feel sorry for herself. She loved her little niece and nephew! Kaitlan bent down as they ran into her arms knocking her onto her back, crawling on top of her!

"Sam! Michael! Ooooh! I could just eat you two up!" she giggled as she grabbed the squiggly little monsters, and gave them both a big sloppy kiss, which caused the kids to wipe their faces.

"Ewww, Aunt Kait!" Mike said while Samantha just laughed.

Both little children had their Mother's red hair. They were just too adorable for words! They giggled as Kaitlan nuzzled their little necks. She stood up, and saw Sarah and Sam sauntering down the hallway holding hands just like they were newlyweds even though they had mated almost nine years ago. The twins were four in wolf years - eight in human years.

"Letting the little monsters out early, today, are we?" grinned Kaitlan as she struggled to her feet, and grabbed the children's hands.

Sarah laughed as they stopped in front of them.

"Monsters? They are terrors on feet!" Sam exclaimed, but his eyes told her he was proud of his two little offsprings.

"Mommy! Can we stay with Aunt Kait tonight? Plleeaazz?" begged Samantha Knight.

"Oh, I'm so sorry, squirt! I have to go out of town this afternoon on business."

Two little faces fell at Kaitlan's words. Her heart

broke in two, so she squatted down to look into their eyes.

"Tell you two what. When I get back, you can stay all weekend with me, and we'll go to the zoo, gorge on lots of pizza and ice cream. How's that sound?"

"Goodie!!! Love you Auntie Kait," they both said at the same time.

Then, the kids spied Jenny, and took off like rockets attacking Jenny.

Sarah laughed and Sam lazily followed his two progeny. There was never a man so proud of his kids - unless you counted Dan and Anita's little girl, Rachel, and Lynne and Richard's little son, Richard Jr, who would be heir to the throne of Asgard - sometime in the next few thousand years. Thanks to the Bifrost Bridge, they all popped back and forth to see each other often, and the kids played together as often as they could.

"Kaitlan, you spoil the little freaks!" Sarah laughed.

"Yep. And, then I'm sending them straight back to you so you can be the bad guys!" she laughed with her sister.

The girls hugged. Kaitlan led her into a small office that was empty, so they could have a heart to heart before she left. She really was on a set time schedule, and she knew her Father would at least let her talk to her sister before she left.

"I just have about thirty minutes before Dad sends me to that horrendous Cordone! And, not only on my birthday, but the day I finally phase!"

Sarah shook her head. She studied Kaitlan's face. Cordone and she had never met, but their arguments over the phone were legendary! Kaitlan couldn't see it, but Sarah was laughing hard inside! Oh, she was right on target to push Kaitlan even harder.

"Well, my wolf gets to come out, too! I'm so excited! Mom and Dad offered to keep the little urchins, so that Sam can take me to the woods! I'm excited to try sex in our wolf forms! Sam's been talking about it for the last year, he's so excited!" She stopped, and then asked as Kaitlan's words sank in. "Wait! What? When did Dad decide that you are going to go to Valon's house? And, what do you mean you're leaving today? We've had all your birthday celebrations planned for months!" Sarah wailed, while her brain told her that she should get an Oscar for her performance!

Despite her anger, Kaitlan was rolling with laughter by the time Sarah had finished! Trust Sarah to babble like a hyena! That was what everyone loved about her! Not to mention she was a whiz at research. She could find anything for anyone at any time. It was as if she had some sort of instinct where to look, and knowledge just stuck in her head. And, well, while the main office of Seneca Publishing was in St. Louis, Missouri, the Hall of Records lay beneath the secondary location of the Seneca Publishing House in Denver, Colorado, and was her favorite place to play since Sam and Sarah had moved to Colorado leaving Kaitlan stuck with her Dad!

"I know. Why would he do this to me, now?" Kaitlan huffed as she threw herself on a sofa in the vacant office.

Sarah sat back, and put her hands in her lap. She had a sneaking suspicion as to why their Dad had decided to send her there. She really hoped he was right. Her internal radar was working overtime right now. And, that led her to realize, now, why Dad had told her to put the party on hold. Really! Did Dad think she didn't know what he was up to? Her mind came back to Kaitlan's rant.

"…and, it sucks big time!"

"I just wish you could find your mate, Kaitlan! Nothing is more wonderful than being with him!" Sarah sighed in contentment.

Sarah was ecstatically happy, and Kaitlan was so

happy for her. Luckily, when she was little, Kaitlan had told her Dad that Sarah was being abused by her Father, and he stepped in just in time to stop her Father from raping her. Kaitlan still shuddered when she thought about it. Sarah's Mom had run off, and left Sarah to face the no good son-of-a-bitch. Sarah became her sister as soon as the guardianship, and eventually adoption, came through. They had so much fun growing up as sisters, and told each other everything. However, when they became teens, Kaitlan wished there were sometimes they didn't tell each other everything, especially about and incident a couple of weeks before she turned eighteen (she was human, of course). She had finally told Kaitlan her deepest, most secret of secrets. She had to do it, because she had found out she was pregnant just two weeks before her eighteenth birthday. And, she knew that her Dad was going to have a fit!

Kaitlan had always known - and so had everyone else - that Sarah had a crush on Sam while she was growing up. Sarah had told her that she and Sam had realized that they were mates a month after her seventeenth birthday, and they'd been together ever since. Kaitlan had received way too much information on how they discovered they were mates, but Sarah was far too happy to notice Kaitlan's shock upon finding out that she and Sam had produced a baby! Anita's research had allowed her to figure out the reason Sarah became pregnant was because Sarah was human, and even though humans were compatible will all supers, it surprised Kaitlan when Sarah had told her. It was very, very rare that a human and super mated, but Sarah was a special case. While Sarah babbled, Kaitlan's mind wandered back to the day when Sarah had told her everything! And, really? She wished she didn't know!

Sarah had told Kaitlan what happened that night with Sam, she had gotten just a tad too explicit. One thing about werewolves, sex was not taboo to them! Sam actually lived in the building, and his apartment had been an entire floor that Canaan had given to him. He had outfitted it beautifully!

Sam left on business for a solid week, and everyone knew it. They just didn't know when he would return, but no one expected him back in less than a week. Kaitlan was off on a date with her ex, Steve, and Sarah had not quite finished her work, since she was Canaan's private secretary at the time. Jenny had taken over after Sarah quit to take care of her children.

It was late, Sarah was tired, and she was to meet some girlfriends for dinner after work. So, she decided to use Sam's shower, since he was out of town. He had offered it to the girls whenever he was out of town if they needed it.

However, that night, Sam had come home early, and neither heard the other. Sarah had turned on the ambient lighting that was extremely soft, and stayed in the shower for a long time. When she turned off the shower, and stepped out of it, she came to a dead halt! Sam was naked having removed his clothing preparing for his shower, and then bed. Sarah watched as he ran his fingers through his hair. He was exhausted, and couldn't wait to crash. His eyes met Sarah's in the mirror, and turning around, she tried to reach for her towel to throw around her body. Both froze where they stood when she saw turn.

It had been impossible to take their eyes off of each other as well as their nude bodies. With boldness, Sam's eyes traveled from her rose-tipped breasts to her curls at the apex of her thighs. Sarah had been stunned at what she saw, and her face turned red as a beet. It was the first time she had ever seen a naked man. Well, apart from the internet and magazines, anyway. Her eyes automatically dropped. He was glorious, and his cock hardened as she watched. It was huge making her red face even redder, but her core was oozing with her juices! The red blushing against her red hair just increased the way he deliberately looked over her body. She grabbed the towel, and held it to her just a little too late. Having had a crush on him for years, she tried to cover herself quickly. But, this went way beyond a crush. Sarah never knew she could have these incredibly intense feelings for a man! But, she suffered them none-the-less, especially when it was a few months until she turned eighteen. She suddenly felt like a grown woman, and her body had betrayed her. Sam could smell her arousal as he closed his eyes, and she saw him sniff. It appeared Sam was not a total gentleman, now, as he always had been with her before. Not with her arousal and her nude body standing in front of him. He lost his cool, and his head, when he saw his mate naked.

Long story short, Sam had walked up to her, and without waiting, pulled her towel away. He gathered her to him pressing his body against hers, grinding his cock into her, and then kissed her - hard! Both of them forgot where they were. They had forgotten everything - even her age. He immediately, and officially, claimed her as his mate. Afterward, the two of them spent the rest of the night making love in his shower and bed. Sam had known it was wrong, but he was so in love with Sarah, that he had claimed her in front of Canaan when she was but five. But, he was tired, and he couldn't resist her when he saw her naked.

Canaan blustered as he knew a Father would do, but he was very happy when Canaan had laughed, and approved their mating. But asked him to wait until she was at least eighteen to mate her. Sam was a bit ashamed of himself, but Sarah had told Kaitlan it was the most wonderful night of her life. They had spent the next four months having sex as much as possible until the urchins were born.

Even so, Canaan knew how passionate Sam was

about her, and how much Sarah was drawn to him. He also remembered that he had taken Tara as his mate when she was just seventeen, and doubted that Sam and Sarah would make it beyond her eighteenth birthday before he mated her. Canaan, apparently, was right. Discovering she was pregnant two weeks before her eighteenth birthday had been a great happiness for both of them.

And, finally, her eighteenth birthday came. Sam and Sarah were planning their mating the day she turned eighteen, and Sarah couldn't wait! She and Sam were ready to start their family.

Kaitlan had secretly been just a bit jealous! OK. So, she was very jealous! She was very happy for her sister, but she wished she had someone who would look at her the way Sam looked at Sarah.

"Oh, Kaitlan?" Sarah interrupted Kaitlan's musings.

"Hmmm?" Kaitlan mumbled absentmindedly.

"I'm pregnant," Sarah grinned at her.

Kaitlan's mouth dropped. Then, she squealed, and ran to throw her arms around her sister.

"Really? I'm going to be an Auntie again? WOOHOO!" she yelled.

"Just kidding! You were so far off somewhere that you weren't answering me! Had to say *something* to knock you out of wherever you were!" Sarah laughed at her.

"You're not?" Kaitlan asked, a bit disappointed.

Sarah shook her head, and added with a mischievous grin, "Well, at least not yet!"

Sam chose to walk in at that moment.

"So, the little birdies told me that you're taking a trip to Cordone's place," Sam chuckled.

"Thanks a bunch," Kaitlan was sarcastic. "I really needed the reminder, Sam! And, about that little birdie? He's in a hell of a lot of trouble! Well, I have to go slay my own damn monster by the name of Cordone Valon.

Grrrrrrr! That man makes me so angry I could spit! I don't think I have ever been as angry at my Dad as I am right now! I've not had a Grrrrrrr moment in a while!"

She hugged the laughing Sam and Sarah, and walked to her office to gather what she needed to take with her, such as her computer, iPad, and a few other things. She got into the elevator, and left the building stopping to pack at her apartment before she went to the airport.

Sam loped to Sarah who was looking out the window watching as Kaitlan got into an SUV. He pulled her tightly into his side, and felt his mate chuckle. Sam had told her, years before, that she was mate to Cordone. Well, actually, he had told her the second time he had her in his bed. Kaitlan, though, was in complete ignorance, and Cordone was too stubborn to return. But, that time was over, now, and she wouldn't be ignorant for long.

"Just wait until Kaitlan finds what I did to her clothes!"

Sam turned to her.

"And, just *what* did you do, Kaitlan?" Sam asked her warily.

Sarah just grinned at him.

"Never you mind, Hunkalicious! But, don't you think it's time for us to get to be an aunt and uncle?"

"Uh-huh! Not going to tell me, huh?"

Sarah grinned at him again. Sam sighed. His mate was always up to no good! Oh, well, she'd tell him whenever.

"Well, while we are waiting to hear the good news, how about you and I go for another round?"

He laughed at her false outrage as his lips crashed down on hers. Sarah was breathless as Sam pulled back, and looked into her glowing blue eyes. With the promise of later shining from his eyes, the two of them walked down the hall to find their own little devils.

~ 22 ~

If a Rocky Mountain won't come to St Louis…

Canaan peered out of his office window watching his daughter walk to his private SUV grinning like the Cheshire Cat in "Alice and Wonderland". He heard his office door shut behind him, but didn't turn. He knew who it was. Arms reached around his waist, and he placed his hands over hers.

"So? You think we did this the right way?" he asked as he pulled her to snuggle into his side.

Her eyes watched with happiness as the SUV, with their daughter inside, pulled away from the curb.

"If Sam hadn't finally broken down, and told us what had happened when Cordone delivered Kaitlan, we would have never known. I'm so grateful to Sam. Well, the magnet and steel, you know. If one won't come to the other, then it's time to get downright dirty!" she laughed as her mate kissed her on the forehead. "Honestly, I thought we would never be able to get those two together!"

"Neither did I! That man is as stubborn as a mule! When he left, I had no idea it was to keep as far away from Kaitlan as he could!" He turned to kiss Tara who was having a hard time not laughing at him. "You know, I thought I had seen something the day that you delivered Kaitlan, but Cordone hid it so fast, I couldn't be sure that I had seen his glowing eyes. He would have been miserable waiting here for her to grow up, but then again, he has hidden away in that damn cave of a house for far too long. I needed to force the issue. I know my daughter, and I know what she needs. And, we should have our very first grandchild joining us in about four months!"

Tara was laughing up at her mate. He turned to her, and continued.

"I know how I might have felt if it had been me. I have to ask you. Why did you wait so long to do something about the two of them, Canaan?"

Canaan smiled a goofy smile, sighed, and then looked down at the love of his life! She was every bit as beautiful as the day he mated with her all those years ago. His mate. His life. The Mother of his child. He suddenly wanted her desperately. Their daughter was leaving them for her mate as was normal. More than anything his wolf wanted to give her another child right now. In fact, he wanted a great many more as their lives continued. Of course, not all at once, but that was beside the point. He had been thinking about it when he was holding Tara in his arms after they made love the night before. He looked into her eyes, and realized that he was not at all opposed to the idea, either! Would she want another child? So many children were running around within the Clan, it was truly a blessing. Mates were in abundance for his people, and many children were born with each mating! His Clan was growing rapidly, and he knew that he would have to make a decision to split it, soon. An Alpha was only as good as his Clan, but size was also a concern. When a Clan became too large, it was the duty of the Alpha to choose a new Alpha and offer the Clan a choice. He also knew that almost half his Clan really would love to relocate in Colorado. Of course, the obvious choice was his second, Cordone. Even though he had not been around for years, Canaan had never replaced his Second. Cordone would become Alpha to the Valon Clan, and he would let his weres choose to stay with him in Missouri, or join the new Alpha. While he was saddened about it, he knew that even he didn't have the resources to protect all of his werewolves. And, Tara had been pushing him to do it anyway, because she wanted more time with him, and *that* was enough for him to act. With everyone happy, life was almost about perfect. Now, he wanted her to have his child. He took her in his arms, and kissed her with a passion taking Tara's breath away. Her eyes glowed with the same beautiful green as their daughter's eyes.

"I need you, mate," he murmured against her lips grinding his hard length against her.

"As I do you," she whispered pushing back against him.

He started to strip her, but she stopped him. He frowned.

"What's wrong?"

"Don't you think that you should let me lock the door first? And, second, I heard your thoughts just now about another child. And, my answer is yes," she murmured against his lips.

Tara left his embrace, and quickly locked his office door. He rolled his eyes. He couldn't think of anything he could hide from Tara. When she returned, his arms folded around her, and he gave her that goofy grin, again. She so loved that grin!

"Are you really *sure* you want to do this all over again, Canaan?" she teased.

Canaan's mouth was nibbling at her neck. He could smell her heavy arousal. Sliding his hand downward, he unzipped and unbuttoned her jeans so that he could slip his hands into them to twist his fingers in her curls and to dip his fingers into her wetness. She wore no panties, and hadn't in years at his request. She also wore no bra. Again at his request. He wanted nothing to impede his fingers to cup, knead, and suckle her nipples when he wanted them. Tara moaned as she felt his fingers plunge inside of her, and his thumb circling her clit. That sound was so enticing he almost wasn't listening. He was craving to sink his fangs into her neck while he slammed his hard cock inside of her tight, wet heat. His wolf desired to impregnate its female.

He nodded at her silent question, but didn't raise his lips from his nibbling.

"Yes. It might be a boy this time, you know. How about you? Will you mind your belly swelling with our child, again?" He lifted his head to look at her. "You were so damn beautiful and horny when you carried Kaitlan."

She laughed, and threw her arms around his neck putting her lips to his ear.

"Yes. I would, but I think it's a bit late for that."

Canaan's head jerked back at her words. His eyes stared into hers in confusion.

"What are you talking about?" he asked her.

"Well, you can have your overly, horny mate as much as you want for the next four months, since your desire is already growing inside of me, my love. Why don't we just have a lot of fun?"

Canaan pushed Tara away from him in shock.

"You're not…I mean…are you…I mean…am I going to be a… I mean…Tara?" Canaan stumbled with his words.

Tara laughed the beautiful laugh that had first drawn him to her. She adored it when she could make him stutter, and lose his Alpha's control where he couldn't talk!

"Well, let's see if I can answer all of that. Uh, Yes. Yes. Oh, and yes, Daddy!" she laughed against his lips.

Canaan howled with the knowledge that his mate was pregnant. The entire Publishing House heard his howl, and smiles were everywhere within it. There was no other howl like it! That was the sound of their Alpha's happiness with the knowledge that Tara was pregnant!

And, Canaan and Tara? Well, let's just say that for

the next four months, Canaan and Tara were filled with a whirlwind of happiness and a 'whole lot of loving'!

Once on board the commercial jet, Kaitlan plopped down into one of the first class seats. It figures. She was stuck between a man who wouldn't shut up, and a woman who kept shoving Kaitlan's elbow off the arm of the seat. And, to make it worse, a little kid behind her kept kicking her seat, and thrusting her forward constantly! She gritted her teeth trying to hold onto her temper against these morons! And, where was that kid's Mom? She was encouraging him!

On top of that, she was so damned steamed at her Father for sending her to work with Cordone her fangs began to descend. She seriously considered biting all three of the jackasses next to her, and behind her.

Cordone and Kaitlan were long known to have a steamy relationship over the phone even though they had never met each other. Sarah used to joke that they were having phone, sexual foreplay earning a growl from Kaitlan, whose eyes narrowed giving Sarah the "shut the hell up" look! Kaitlan knew that Cordone had delivered her, which just made her anger grow every time she thought of his jackass attitude. She just knew he thought he was "all that". Just recently, he had been voted the best-looking man, and author, in the world. Little did all those groaning, panting, drooling idiot females know that Cordone Valon was nothing but an arrogant bastard! And, she couldn't tell them! He was their best-selling author, and knew it would be a PR nightmare of the worst type.

"Arrogant son-of-a-bitch," Kaitlan said under her breath earning a shocked look from the man next to her.

She huffed, but didn't apologize. Why should she?

Finally, one of the worst plane rides ever in the history of mankind was over as the jet landed at DIA. Never again, she vowed as she stomped to the shuttles that ran underneath the terminals, which transport passengers to the main terminal. She was still steaming when she pushed her way among a horde of passengers up the escalators, and headed for the baggage claim. Kaitlan stood tapping her toe as she waited for the carousel to start moving. Taking their own sweet time about getting the luggage unloaded, the first luggage popped out of the opening, sliding down onto the carousel followed by others one at a time.

Her first luggage appeared early, but her second one was one of the last ones up.

"Figures," she muttered. "After a day like this, what else should I expect?"

Kaitlan piggybacked her carry on over one of the larger luggage handles, and rolled them behind her to the car rental desk. Renting a SUV to drive to Valon's home was quicker than anything else was, today. Naturally, she noted that the vehicle was black. Figures. She couldn't catch a break. Why couldn't she just get a red one? How ridiculous was this that she would be obsessing about a color of a SUV? Her Father insisted on only black ones. At home, she had a red SUV just to defy her Mom and Dad. For the first time today, she grinned as she tooled the SUV out of the rental lot onto Pena Boulevard for the long, four-hour trip to Cordone's house. When she reached I70, she had to pay attention to the traffic going through Denver's monstrously heavy traffic, but once past it, she was able to relax. She would turn North at Silverthorne, making her way deep into the Rocky Mountains where there were no towns closer than fifty miles.

"'Forget Never Never Land'," Kaitlan said aloud.

"I'm driving into 'Nowhere land'!"

She'd heard about the house, and seen photos of it through the years. Everyone who had been to his house that was carved into a mountain had been amazed and awed by it. She grudgingly admitted that photos made it looked unbelievable. Her Mom and Dad had told her about it, although it had been years since they had been to see Cordone. Hearing so much about his house for so many years, she was looking forward to seeing it. It intrigued her, and even her parents said the house was unbelievably beautiful as well as everyone else who had been there. Even Sarah and Sam. Everyone and his aunt had seen it, except Kaitlan.   The idea of an indoor, natural waterfall was almost too much to miss! Elves had carved it for Cordone's parents thousands of years earlier. When they moved to Italy, they deeded it over to their son.

"Whoopee," Kaitlan wiggled her finger upward in a circular motion, because the only thing to mar it would be Valon!

After four hours of driving, and a couple of stops in between to use the restroom, buy some water and a Cliff Bar, which always gave her a boost of energy, Kaitlan finally turned onto the very long drive that wove upward high into the higher mountains to Cordone Valon's house. When the house first appeared, her werewolf eyes widened, and her foot hit the brake coming to a full stop throwing her forward. How long she gawked at the house, she didn't know. The huge wall of windows that had barely glinted off and on from the sun was the only sign that something not natural was there.

"Holy cow! It really is carved into the side of a mountain!" she thought. Then, *"Why the hell would anyone want to live out here where there is nothing?"*

And, yet, she had to admit that the house looked as if it belonged there! No doubt that was the intention. If you hadn't been looking for it, you probably wouldn't have known it was even there. And, because of its design, even air traffic could never see it! She noticed that the clouds were gathering quickly, and she stepped on the gas to hightail before the unpredictable, Rocky Mountain weather hit. One minute it could be eighty degrees, and the next a blizzard. And, right now, it looked like a blizzard was the winner. After all, it was April.

Darkness had descended by the time she reached the house, and already, the blizzard was making it difficult to see. Luckily, as a werewolf, their eyes could penetrate blizzard conditions, but she wouldn't want to get stuck out here for long. Even that could change in seconds. The drive was much longer than she had thought it would be due to the conditions, but finally she pulled up to the front of the house - or the back. Kaitlan wasn't sure.

Kaitlan parked the SUV under a rock overhang protecting the door. The wind was blowing snow into it, so she quickly unloaded her bags. An intercom to the right of the door was imbedded into the stone, and she pushed the button as her father instructed.

"Yes?" came a deep sexy voice.

Whoa! It was so sexy, her breath and heart increased! Just his voice could give her an orgasm if she listened to it long enough!

"Uh…hello? I'm Kaitlan O'Hara here to see Cordone Valon?"

"Ah. Good. It's about time," she heard a click as the door unlocked. "Come on in. There are stairs to the right of the entry, or you can use the elevator to the left. Your room is the Green room on the fifth floor. It's the center room on the platform. I know you might like to freshen up. Dinner will be served on the main floor at seven thirty. Please, make yourself at home, and if you like, you can take a nap. I'll make sure your car is put into the garage."

How can just a voice - through an intercom - cause her core to become wet? And, he said the word "nap" in such a caressing tone - as if he would join her! Creator! Help her get through this! It certainly wasn't what she expected, and she was angry with herself for the sexual feelings flooding over her body.

Gritting her teeth, Kaitlan walked into the foyer, which appeared to come out onto the third platform. She heard it long before she saw it. The massive waterfall. Her Father had told her that the Elves had not wanted to divert it, or get rid of it, since they were the original conservationists, and refused to mess with anything in nature. So, instead, they carved the house around it!

Kaitlan couldn't resist the draw. She had to see it! Her feet carried her toward the sound, which became louder with each step, and then…she halted in stunned silence. OMG! Her eyes bugged out. The waterfall was massive! Above her were two, crystalline platforms, but they didn't hold the draw that the falls did, so she continued to walk toward them. A crystalline bridge was in the center, and she walked to the middle.

To her right she could see where the water exited the mountain about fourteen feet across! She looked over the edge to see them plunge to a large pool beneath her feet. That's when she realized that the crystalline bridge was repeated in the two platforms below!

She could see everything without impeding the view! It was as if she stood on air with the falls below her, and there was no need to look over the crystalline rail. All she had to do was look down! Kaitlan had no idea how long she stood there with her mouth open! How did the Elves carve all of this? She knew they had incredible powers, but this was the first time she had ever seen an example of that power!

Kaitlan finally shook herself out of the mesmerizing view. Standing around was not getting her anywhere. She so wanted to take a shower, and a short nap! Kaitlan turned to walk back to the stairs and the elevator. Take the stairs in deed! Was he a moron? She had baggage! Well, truth was, she was a werewolf, so she didn't have to roll her two suitcases behind her, but it would be a bit easier. Taking the elevator to the fifth floor, she stopped at the center room. The door automatically opened. She walked two feet inside, and then gasped in shock at the opulence of green marble everywhere. In the center was a huge bed covered in a green duvet with lots of red and white pillows on it. She continued further into the bathroom, and gaped at the sunken tub as well as the elevated shower that drained into the tub by way of two rock steps! This was going to be a haven after her daily work with a Mr. Arrogant!

But, she couldn't wait to try out the shower. Kaitlan rooted around in her carry-on suitcase for her toiletries. She was tired from all the traveling. Tonight would be her first turn at midnight, so she picked something easy to take off before she changed. The idea of being naked out in nature was a strange feeling. On one hand, she was sexually excited about it, while on the other, she was actually embarrassed! But, nudity for a werewolf was one of those cosmic oopsies! Closing the bathroom door, she noticed a big, thick, Kelly green robe. If this was the "green room", she wondered what the other room colors were.

The shower was more incredible than she had ever had! Eight feet by twelve feet carved out of solid stone, a green marble floor allowed her to sit down to let the water run over her tired body. The showerheads were everywhere, and the control was intricate. She finally stepped out, donned the robe, and opened her luggage to take out a pair of jeans, and a green t-shirt that she had packed.

Kaitlan's eyes popped out of her head. What the

fuck? Panicking, she rooted around in each luggage, again! Where were her clothes? She knew she had put jeans, t-shirts, bras, panties, and sleepwear in it! What the hell? She threw what she did find back into the luggage, and flopped onto the bed. All that was in it was sexy lingerie! No bras and no panties either! How...no who switched her clothes?

"Sarah!" she yelled furiously. It had to be! Only Sarah would have had the nerve to put this shit in her luggage! Sarah was a nymphomaniac! She always had been. She never wore panties, or bras. She had told Kaitlan that she wanted to have orgasms during the day! Only she would sneak into Kaitlan's apartment, and do this to her! Why the hell did she do it, though? Kaitlan didn't know what to do. She couldn't wear the robe for however long she would be there. She rooted around again, and found a little green, shorty gown number that matched her eyes - with little left to the imagination! But it covered more than the other things she found. The top was sheer, but no panties. Sarah had been trying to convince her not to wear them, but Kaitlan just didn't like not wearing them. It made her feel vulnerable!

Sighing, Kaitlan looked at the clock, and saw that her time was almost up. So much for a nap! There was no reason to put the sexy nighty on, so she threw the green robe back on. She quickly thought up a lie. She would tell Valon that her suitcase had been a mix up, and she would have to go into the nearest town the next day to buy some clothes. That meant driving to the nearest town fifty miles away! However, what option did she have? And, she'd tell him she was going to go even if he didn't like it!

Taking the elevator to the main level, she stepped out of it. She felt embarrassed to be meeting him in a bathrobe, but she just had no choice. She had washed out her underwear, and hung it up before going down to the main level.

Stepping out of the elevator, she saw that the main level was a fully open plan except for two doors on either side of the falls. To her left, was a massive bar made of solid mahogany complete with matching stools. Also, to her left, and behind her was a chef's dream kitchen. It was monstrously large. Larger than anything she had ever seen in her life. Even her own parents' home was nothing like this! No less than six ovens were present, two massive refrigerators, and the cabinets were also solid mahogany with black marble tops interspersed with gold veining. Kaitlan just shook her head. It was beautiful. What woman wouldn't want this to be her home, even if the location was in "nowhere land" as far as she was concerned.

Kaitlan walked into the main part of the room pulling her robe tightly around her. She wouldn't have to worry about her clothes for her first phase. Question was…how was she going to manage to go out into the woods, and shed her clothing while Cordone Valon was around?

To her right was the natural pool into which the waterfall flowed. There were two doors on either side of it, and she was just too curious. She walked over opening the one on the left, and saw to her shock a gigantic, naturally carved stone swimming pool that was obviously fed by the waterfall that flowed from the pool outside of the poolroom. She was dumbfounded.

Not deterred, she tried the door on the right. Her mouth dropped completely this time. It was a massive garage! The man collected cars? Lots of cars! Including the Rolls Royce Phantom II? Her favorite? He had to be wealthier than her own Father!

Her heart was beating hard with excitement as she closed the door. She'd always had a secret desire for sex in a car like her other friends bragged about. But, she had never found anyone who suited her. Steve, included.

In the center of the room, and down a couple of stairs, was a sunken oval area, and in the center, a huge fire pit with a gigantic hood over it, which resembled a horn that reached all the way to the roof of the room. There were tan and brown leather sofas and chairs surrounding the pit. To the right, another door led to a room that looked like a media room with a huge flat screen TV, and at least ten chairs in stadium seating!

"Last, but not least…," Kaitlan muttered.

The monstrous glass wall looked out upon a view that froze her in place. It was so beautiful, she couldn't take her eyes off of it. It had a complete view of everything outside. It was as if you were living outside. She wondered what it would be like when her turn happened, because she couldn't think of a more beautiful setting to let her wolf run free for its first time! Her eyes moved to one spot of the massive glass on the right, and she realized it was a door, which led outside onto a giant, multi-leveled redwood deck! It had to be at least six levels as it wound it's way down to the ground.

Watching Kaitlan stare out the window, Cordone stared at Kaitlan from his office watching her reaction to his home. She was here! After twenty-seven years! He couldn't resist it when Canaan had demanded that he send Kaitlan to him despite Cordone's arguing against it. What was he thinking? Cordone had delivered Kaitlan while Anita had been away. Before Kaitlan had been cleaned, and even though Canaan was there, Cordone took one look into her beautiful, tiny, glowing green eyes, and claimed her as his mate. He remembered how he had felt dirty, and a total pervert. He couldn't look into the eyes of his Alpha after that, so he had resigned as his Second, and had come to his ancestral home. For the last twenty-seven years, he had literally suffered through what he had done. That was the entire reason he had started writing books.   While he wrote, he could get away from his memories.   Barely a handful of weres in the past had claimed a baby as their mate, but he was the first to claim a newborn!   He never told anyone, except his friend, Dan. Dan hadn't judged him, but he had kept asking him why he didn't go back, and claim her.   Cordone never gave him an answer.

Canaan had insisted he send Kaitlan despite Cordone's protests. He knew better than to argue with his Alpha, but he did so anyway! He could not have her here, and not claim her. Because Canaan was still Cordone's Alpha, he just had no choice once Canaan had made his decision.

Now, she was here. He had wondered what to wear when he saw her. Did it really matter? She was his mate. Period. How would he feel seeing her? If she accepted him as her mate, he knew, without a doubt, he wouldn't need clothing long, and neither would she. So, he put on a pair of silky, clinging black boxers, and nothing else. He wanted nothing in the way of his manhood expanding, and nothing that barred her seeing his desire for her. He wanted to get excited, now, but in truth, he was more scared than anything that had ever happened to him before - including her birth. And, that kept him small.

Canaan had been trying to get him to return as his Second over the last five years, but he continually refused. His shame at what he had done just wouldn't let him. He was trying to keep his honor. But, Cordone just didn't understand why in the world Canaan sent Kaitlan to him the day of her twenty-seventh birthday, and the night of her change. That was completely was anathema to him. He'd have to deal with that as well!

He was shaking a bit, and decided to wait for about ten minutes. He prayed that it would be her home soon, and more than hoping that she would be carrying his child before this night was over, and before her first phase. He could only pray that it would happen that way.

Cordone walked out of his room, leaned over the railing, and saw her walking around the main floor. His breath caught. His wolf eyes could see that she was more beautiful than he had even dreamed even standing there with a long, fluffy robe! More than any of her photos. It hadn't been a mistake all those years ago! Did he feel better about it? No. He would still have felt the same. But, the woman who was here was not a baby. She was a full-grown woman, and as sexy as hell!

Kaitlan continued to stand at the windows gazing at the beauty. It was so gorgeous, she hoped the arrogant bastard wouldn't disturb her any time soon. Maybe he'd go to bed, and see her in the morning?

"Beautiful, isn't it?" asked that same deep, sexy, and soft voice behind her.

Shit! No such luck, apparently. Kaitlan slowly turned around to give him a piece of her mind for sneaking up behind her, then froze in place as her eyes met his!

Cordone Tristan Valon stood before her. He was much, much better looking in real life than any photos she had ever seen of him! She stopped dead in her tracks as her eyes met the dark ones of the most gorgeous man she had ever seen in her life! *The man standing in front of her was the one who had delivered her?* This man? Oh, yes! He was *all* man! His looks, his scent, and his eyes declared it! She continued to stare at him for what seemed like minutes. She could drown in those eyes. And, as far as his body went? Kaitlan's cheeks grew red when she lowered her eyes.

Oh, crap! He was practically naked! His bare chest showed his rock hard abs. His arms were big, and each arm was probably larger than her waist! She knew he could crush her with them, but how she'd love to feel them around her! Eight packs? Do they even exist? He was dressed only in solid, clingy, black silk shorts that left nothing to the imagination, and she could easily see the outline of his smaller manhood hanging down. She licked her lips in nervousness. Her stomach did flips, and her heart stuttered. He was gorgeous! He was sexy with a capital *SEXY*! Now, she knew what Sarah had meant when she had been confronted with Sam's body. If Cordone put the moves on her, she knew that she wouldn't have a chance in hell of resisting him! But, then again, she honestly wouldn't want to resist!

Cordone stepped closer to Kaitlan with…glowing black eyes. She sucked in her breath, and gasped.

~ 23 ~
From the End, A Beginning

"Hello, Kaitlan. It's been a very long time," he smiled down at her.

Oh, Creator! That smile? His eyes bore into hers with a desire she couldn't mistake, and it certainly shook her to her core. He reached out his hand to shake hers. She put her shaky hand into it. The touch of his skin on hers sent a massive surge that felt a bit like electricity into her body stopping her breath. Desire exploded for him, and wetness pooled between her thighs. Her eyes flew back to his in shock, while only one word came to her heart and mind. And, into her very soul!

"Mate?" she whispered in shock, and froze at the slow smile that swept across Cordone Valon's lips.

Cordone Valon. The arrogant bastard with whom she fought over the years was her mate? The man she hated more than life itself was her mate? Shit! The man who she had loathed for how long? She couldn't remember how long she had hated him. Maybe her body was betraying her? But, no. Of course, it wasn't, and she couldn't deny it! Without question, Cordone Valon was her mate.

Their eyes locked as epic desire crashed into both of them. Werewolves mated for life, and it was instant. Nothing could prevent it from happening. That's why werewolves were driven to mate immediately, and produce their first child. It was inborn within them, and it was something that they could never deny. Like all others, Kaitlan and Cordone felt the mating bond, and they were powerless to deny it. Hell! Kaitlan didn't want to deny it!

Quietly, Cordone claimed her.

"I claim you as my mate, Kaitlan Seneca O'Hara, just as I did the day I delivered you," Cordone Valon whispered to her dipping his head to hers and crushing her mouth with his.

Cordone growled as he finally took his mate after all these years. She tasted so good! Their mating had to be now. He could not keep his desire from her long.

Kaitlan collapsed under his kiss. She was his. Forever. He was her mate for all time. She felt the desire rise in her more than she could possibly have ever felt. His kiss drugged her beyond measure. A desire as old as time itself welled within her. She needed him like she needed to breathe. Knew she had to mate with him, now. And, he felt it, too. The evidence grinding against her stomach was the proof. The desire for him to give her their first child rose like a flower opening to the sun at the first of spring.

Kaitlan groaned in ecstasy as his kiss continued to drug her deeper, the pool of wetness flowing heavily from her core. Wearing nothing underneath her robe, she wanted him to rip it off her, and let him take her right then, and there! And, it had better be fast and hard, too!

Chimes on the clock sounded. It was ten o'clock. He had prepared the place of their mating at his private pool where no one else had ever been but himself before she arrived. There were only two hours left before her first change, and he couldn't wait until after her phase. He needed to mate with her, make love to her, and then, they would phase and run together. But, above all, he couldn't wait to finally mate with her in their wolf forms.

"Come," he said as he lifted his lips from her.

Kaitlan pulled back a bit, but he took her hand, leading her out the glass door, and into the night. The stars were twinkling above, but with no moon.

"Tell me how you chose me," she asked him in a breathless gasp as he led her out the back door, down the deck, and out into the darkened woods.

"The night your Mother went into labor, Anita wasn't there. I was the only one around with the experience to deliver babies. I had done it many times over the years. My Mother was a mid-wife."

She nodded, but she'd rather his mouth crush hers again. However, she needed to know everything, so as they walked side by side holding hands, she listened to that sexy voice she was going to be listening to for the rest of her life!

"Anyway, Tara went into labor, and I delivered you. When you slid into my hands, Kaitlan, our eyes met instantly. Your beautiful, tiny, green eyes glowed as they met mine, and mine glowed as they met yours." He stopped walking, and turned to her lifting her chin. "I had never seen such beautiful eyes in my life, my love."

As if he couldn't wait, he kissed her, again, and then they proceeded to continue on their way. Kaitlan was breathless, but she felt this conversation was one of the most important that they would ever have, so she asked the main question that was in her mind.

"Then, why, Cordone? Why did you wait? Why did you not claim me when I was old enough?"

"Because, I was your Father's second, Kaitlan. His trust in me was unconditional, and mine to him. I couldn't believe that I had claimed you as my mate before he had even held you once! I feel as if I would have betrayed him. And, honestly? I felt like a pervert! I had to leave, or risk my best friend's disgust."

"A pervert?" she exclaimed, but her voice was full of laughter.

He stopped once more, and cupped her face in his hands.

"If I had stayed, Kaitlan. You would never have

gotten beyond nine years old, but more probably eight, because that would be just as long as I could take. I would have thrust my cock into you, and claimed you as my mate!”

Kaitlan's eyes widened, and he watched as a slow, sexy, knowing grin spread across her face. Her hand touched his bare chest, and she let her fingers brush over his nipples, which hardened immediately. He jerked at the feeling, and she glanced down to see his cock pushing the black, silky material outward. Her eyes met his again, as she let her hand cup his cock. Her eyes were full of mischief. Creator! He had never been harder!

“Enough!” he told her as he grabbed her hand.

He quickly led her through a stone archway that led to his private pool. Kaitlan stumbled along with him, her heart was beating a mile a minute. This was it! She was going to be mated in minutes! And, following, he would plant his seed within her body impregnating her! Her sex flooded with her desire, and she kept her thighs together as best she could to keep the wetness from flowing down her legs knowing that it was a futile attempt!

When he stopped, she looked around her as he let her hand go. This place was so beautiful! Candles were everywhere emitting a golden glow in the night, but lighting up the entire area. A huge, white quilt lay to the right of the pool piled high with white pillows. A bucket of ice holding champagne, and a platter of cheeses, chocolates, along with whipped cream, and other various goodies just waiting to be devoured by two lovers.

Turning her to him, she slowly untied the belt on her robe.

“I've waited so long for this moment, Kaitlan,” he said softly looking at her as she removed the robe, allowing it to pool around her feet.

He gasped as he looked at what she wore. Nothing, absolutely nothing! She stood naked before him. Her beautiful pink tips topped her buxom white breasts. As his eyes traveled down her, he saw tight abs, and blonde curls at her apex hiding her sex from him. Cordone closed his eyes, and sniffed. Her arousal smelled so good to him! He just hoped he could wait.

Kaitlan couldn't believe she stood naked in front of him without so much as an embarrassed thought. She wanted him to see her. She looked down at his silky shorts, and his hard-on was apparent as it lifted the material outward. She licked her lips, not in embarrassment, but for wanting him inside of her.

He cupped her face so his eyes could gaze into her beautiful green ones.

"You opened your eyes the second you slipped from your Mother into my hands, Kaitlan. I knew, at that moment, you were my mate. I love you."

She brushed his cheek with her hand when suddenly, a light bulb went off over her head, and made her laugh at the mental picture of it.

"Daddy forced me to come here," she stated, as if thinking to herself.

Cordone caught on to her meaning in an instant!

"And, he forced me to allow you to come here."

They stared at each other. Cordone grabbed his mate, and pulled her tightly to his chest grinding his hardness against her while pressing her full breasts to his bare chest.

"He knew," he said with certainty.

"He did," Kaitlan smiled back at him.

"Fuck it all! All that time I wasted since you were at least eight, Kaitlan! I would have mated you then! Hell! He's been trying to get me to return to St. Louis for years!" Cordone shook his head at his best friend! "No wonder he has been so adamant about my coming back!"

Both laughed as they realized what Canaan had been trying to do for a very long time! To bring his second and daughter together, because he knew they were mates!

"You know Sam and Sarah were mates, and they spent a lot of time in his bedroom together when she was eight. Did you also know that she was pregnant before her ninth birthday? And, Daddy was never shocked, or surprised. Nothing gave him greater pleasure than when Sam and Sarah were mated! Daddy should be on TV, he is so good at acting!"

"What? They did what? Holy Hell! I didn't know that!" His mind went back to the birth of Sam and Sarah's first child. "But, now that I think about it, I received the notice that their babies did come in three and a half months instead of four?"

Kaitlan nodded.

"Kaitlan, if I don't mate with you soon, I won't be able to hold back taking you before we do, and you will be pregnant before we are mated!"

Kaitlan blushed beautifully! He grinned a most mischievous and devilish smile as he reached for her.

"Come to think of it, I wouldn't mind your body ripe with our child before we mate. Wanna give it a go?" he teased.

Her face was priceless as she gave him a mock horror look. Just for a second, her eyebrows waggled at him, and he thought she was going to take him up on his proposition!! Then, she looked at him wickedly.

"Sure! Why not!" Her hand went to her belly, rubbing it, then she looked up at him from under her eyelashes. "If that is what you want to do, you aren't going to get an argument out of me! I'm right with you!"

He laughed as she had meant him to do.

"My wolf desires his mate, Kaitlan." Cordone whispered against her lips. "Now."

She shyly put her hand in his. He wanted to mate her in this beautiful place. She couldn't think of a more beautiful one. The cool air washed over her heated body, and she felt a definite temperature rise, which was the signal that she had begun the change. Those who had mated just before their change also had a libido the size of a planet! Wetness poured out of her, and she looked down feeling it run down her legs. Cordone followed her eyes, and his wolf growled. The wolf within her began to grow with desire to run, but more so for her mate.

"I don't like to use real candles for obvious reasons, but the Luminara candles are perfect."

She nodded. Having real flames in the wilderness was a real danger. But, it was beautiful, none-the-less. She turned to look at him. Her body was hot - very, very hot. Not just because of the change, either. She was very glad of the cooling air surrounding them.

Nudity was definitely not a big deal with werewolves, except when they found their mates. All Werewolves were taught from day one that the mate bond was always done naked, because of the extreme desire for sex at the end of the mating. The desire to impregnate the female overrode every other feeling. Once done, it was impossible to stop the consummation period of twenty-four hours. The first child of mates would be conceived during this time to ensure the werewolf community continued. It was inborn, and could not be changed. To deny the twenty-four hours would cause great harm, and the mating bond would never work. Both mates would turn rogue, and perish. Quite literally, they would die, or have to be destroyed by Dan.

Kaitlan's wolf was crying out for its mate, and her womb was throbbing hard to be filled with Cordone's seed, and their first child.

Cordone watched as her body quivered during his careful inventory of her when his eyes lingered on her breasts as well as what lay below! Her blush made him smile, she was so beautiful! Quickly, Cordone took his shorts off, and watched as she looked at his cock's desire for her. Closing his eyes, again, he sniffed. The wetness running down her legs had increased, and smelling her arousal for him was erotic to him and his wolf. His cock grew larger, harder as he watched her eyes linger on his manhood making his wolf swell with pride. As if he couldn't wait another moment, he picked her up, and gently laid her on the white quilt. Lying down beside her, he brushed her hair out of her face while at the same time letting his gaze lower to her breasts and her curls. Cordone could not believe this beautiful woman was his mate! His! The area between his legs filled and hardened with all the love he had for her, and it was becoming extremely painful. His wolf needed to spill that love inside of his mate. But, the ritual came first, and he had to tell his wolf it had to wait, and his wolf was not, in the least, happy! He noticed that her breath caught as she looked at the beauty of his arousal. Watching Kaitlan close her eyes, and sniff, he also knew she could smell his arousal as well.

Kaitlan's breath was almost non-existent. She could smell the delicious aroma of his arousal, and knew he could smell hers! Heavy wetness flowed from her body between her legs, and down her thighs as she continued to look at his hard-on growing longer and harder by the second!

"You are so beautiful, Kaitlan. I never thought this day would come."

Cordone stroked the face of the woman he loved so much knowing that he always wanted to see that face when he went to bed at night, and awoke the next day.

Kaitlan took his hand, and placed it at her breast covering it with her own. He felt the hardened tip press against his palm, and had to force his hand to be still without stroking it.

"And, you are beautiful, too, Cordone. Mate me. Fill my womb with our child," she whispered in a sexy, husky voice. She didn't even recognize it as hers!

The mating words were softly spoken in the silent of the night surrounded by the waterfalls gently pouring over the rocks into the pool, light from above in the guise of stars, the candles' fire, and a gentle cooling breeze.

Kaitlan gently pushed him to his back leaning over him pressing her breasts and hardened nipples to his chest. She rested her arm on his massive chest, and her eyes were heavy with desire and love. Her body gently shaking as her life was about to change forever.

"Cordone Tristan Valon. I claim you as my mate, now, and forever. I know, now, that when I looked into your beautiful black, glowing eyes on the day you delivered me, you were mine…my mate. You were my mate at the beginning of my life even before I was conceived. Our love will grow as time passes, but it will never stop growing. The heart expands with as much love as it can hold. I love you."

She paused looking into his eyes for his response. His eyes narrowed, and a single tear slipped out of one of them down his cheek. She licked the tear gently from his cheek.

"Cordone, my mate, my love, my life, and my joy. I am in love with you so much, my heart hurts. Will you accept me as your mate?"

Cordone had never thought to hear words like that spoken to him. He had been so alone for so long, but, now, his heart was filled with a brilliant light of happiness. His best friend's daughter was his mate, conceived just for him.

"Kaitlan Seneca O'Hara, I accept you for my mate from this point forward. You are my heart, my love, and my life. I love you."

Kaitlan lowered her lips to his taking her kiss of mating. Cordone turned his neck to her. She lowered her lips to his pulse, and kissed it gently letting her fangs descend, piercing his pulse, and drinking his surprisingly spicy and sweet liquid of life. Raising her head again, she licked the wounds as she left her mark and scent on Cordone for all time.

Cordone turned his head back to her with glowing eyes, and looked into the glowing green eyes of his mate. She lowered her mouth to his, and took her final kiss of mating.

Kaitlan was still shaking with the desire that was gripping her womb, and rolled onto her back giving Cordone full access to her body.

Cordone leaned over her, pressing his chest to her breasts feeling their hardened tips push into him.

"Kaitlan Seneca O'Hara Valon, I claim you as my mate. I have waited so long for this moment to make you mine. I no longer am shamed, and realize that I wasted so much time between us. I should have mated you when you were eight! But, we have long lives ahead of us, and I promise to make up for my stupidity. You are everything to me, and you are my love, my life, my world. Conceived just for each other. I have never been as happy as I am at this moment. Will you, Kaitlan, accept me for your mate?"

Kaitlan thought her heart would burst with the happiness that consumed it! Could a heart hold this much happiness? She was willing to risk it.

"Cordone Tristan Valon, I accept you as my mate, my lover, my love, my life, and my world," she told him softly.

Cordone took her mouth in his kiss of mating, and kissed her a bit longer than he needed. But, when she turned her neck to him, his wolf was eager to mark Kaitlan as his for all time. Cordone slowly lowered his lips to her pulse, kissing it. His fangs descended, and he lowered them to her neck, piercing her skin taking a small amount of her blood to swallow. It was spicy and sweet.

He growled as he drank from her, and Kaitlan felt his chest pressing even harder to her breasts as he did. Her hand came up to press his head closer to her. Then, he raised his head, and licked the only wound that would never heal. It was his mark, his scent forever. Lowering his mouth, he took his final kiss of mating, and she turned her face back to his.

"Now, Cordone!" she cried to him.

He lifted himself over her spreading her legs with his as he lowered his mouth to hers. His hard cock gently touched her wet entrance. Holding his cock, he worked it around her opening, and swirled it over her engorged clit. Kaitlan lifted her hips nudging him. Demanding he enter her. Cordone's hips drew back, and in one huge thrust, his cock plunged into her the moment his lips touched hers. Her arms went around his neck as she wrapped her legs around his waist allowing him full access into her womb. Using them, she drew his body closer so she could take him deeper into her sheath. The need for Cordone to place his seed within her overwhelmed his human senses, and he lost all reason and thought. His wolf combined with him, and his cock grew longer and harder. Deeper, harder, longer, thrusting into his mate over and over caused him even more pain than before. Her tight channel squeezed his cock harder and harder, and he didn't think he could hold back. In seconds, he felt Kaitlan's orgasm begin to hit her as she squeezed his cock harder, and his balls contracted as he felt his semen flood inside his cock, and then it was released into Kaitlan's womb with a tremendous force! Designed to impregnate his mate the first time, Cordone continued to expel more semen than he ever thought he could make!

Kaitlan was ecstatic as she felt Cordone's hot, wet semen flow through her channel into her womb! Her muscles continued to contract around him, milking him for every single drop of seed that was inside of him! She yelled his name as she continued to come with him. His seed coated the inside of her womb, and in that instant, Kaitlan knew he had planted their child within her. The thought caused her to orgasm again. With all his seed spilled into her womb, he was still hard. The last thing he wanted to do was to leave her depths. He felt his balls begin to fill again, and he began to thrust harder into her body. They continued to orgasm, and the two lovers were entwined for a very long time.

Cordone and Kaitlan howled as, together, their orgasms were released.

"I love you," Cordone declared as he cried out to his mate.

"I love you! I'm yours, Cordone. For all time."

~ 24 ~
Power is given to those who deserve it

Four months passed by quickly, and Anita delivered Tara and Canaan's baby boy, Tyler, before she had to leave for another award ceremony. Truth be told, Anita was getting really tired of the awards, but Dan kept her grounded especially when she would stomp around griping about having to go out of town, again, while Dan just laughed.

However, with Anita out of town, Cordone was called upon to deliver Sam and Sarah's newest twins, Lily and Thomas. Lily was not only the spitting image of her mother with her red curly hair and bright blue eyes, but Thomas looked just like his Father with his golden eyes. Their brother and sister only huffed when they saw them. They just didn't understand what all the fuss was about while the adults around them thought they were just hilarious!

It had been a very, very busy, but satisfying week for Cordone. But, nothing…absolutely nothing could have prepared him for his own children when they decided to make their entry into the world two weeks early - and Anita was still not back!

"Push, Kaitlan," Cordone growled at her.

Kaitlan could see his head between her raised legs ready to catch their child. He looked at her, again.

"Kaitlan, *push!*" he ordered her, again.

Sarah was lifting her up by her shoulders so that she could push, but that was just not enough for Kaitlan!

"I am pushing, you jackass!" she grunted back at him.

"Language," he said.

"Shut the hell up, Cordone! I'll say any damn thing I want to right now!"

Sarah couldn't help but laugh. Just two weeks earlier, she'd been right where Kaitlan was, and had said all kinds of things to her mate and Cordone.

"Sarah, shut it!" Kaitlan growled.

Sarah just laughed harder.

"No freakin' way! You couldn't get enough of laughing at me when I was where you are two weeks ago. Do you *really* think I'm going to shut up?"

Kaitlan screamed after that as her son slipped from her body into her mate's hands.

Cordone just stared at him. Their son was in his hands. Bald at the moment, he had been conceived in their wolf forms. Canaan was Cordone's duplicate, except with Cordone's black eyes! Then, Cordone sucked in a breath when he realized that his own wolf's eyes stared back at him!

"*Cordone*!" Kaitlan squealed. "A little help here!"

Kaitlan was panting, and grunting with another contraction. Sam was standing guard at the door.

"Sam?" he asked holding Canaan out to him.

Sam darted forward taking Canaan from Cordone so that he could deliver his second child.

"Agggghhhhh!" cried Kaitlan as she bore down, and her Father caught her as she slipped from her Mother.

Kaitlan slumped back onto the delivery table breathing hard with sweat pouring down her face and body. Sarah bathed her sweaty face with a cool cloth.

"Cordone? Please?" Kaitlan had just enough breath to ask him as she reached out her arms.

Cordone had been busy staring into the beautiful face of his daughter, Tara. Her black hair was in tiny, bloody ringlets, but she had the green eyes of her mother.

"So beautiful," Cordone whispered.

He looked up at Kaitlan holding out her arms. Standing, he walked over to her, and laid their daughter in them. Tears of joy ran down her face as, in an instant, she forgot the pain as she gazed into her daughter's eyes - green eyes. Gently, Kaitlan kissed Tara's tiny little head, and then looked at Cordone who had one tear running down his cheek.

"You're so beautiful, Tara," she whispered brushing a tiny curl off her forehead.

Cordone thought of the amazing gifts of life his mate had just given to him! How appropriate was it that the Creator of the Cosmic Universe allowed him to not only deliver his mate so long ago, but now, his own children! How often does that happen? He figured the odds were off the charts.

Hearing a tiny mewling sound, both of them turned to see Sarah carrying their son to them.

"He is so adorable!" Sarah told them. "Wouldn't it be an amazing thing if, someday, your son and our daughter would mate? Or your daughter and our son?"

Kaitlan nodded silently. She couldn't stop looking at the precious gift lying in her arms.

Sarah kissed Canaan on his tiny head laying Canaan in Cordone's arms, and then she took Tara to other room to clean up the tiny little girl.

Kaitlan was choked up with the sight of their son in Cordone's arms. Cordone laid Canaan in Kaitlan's arms, and she turned her face up to Cordone whose lips immediately met hers.

"Thank you for these two, beautiful gifts, Kaitlan," he told her with a smile.

"Uh…just in case you didn't know it, you were there, you know," Kaitlan laughed at him. "Both ways!"

Cordone snickered as Sam opened the door letting Sarah into the room. She brought Tara back into the room placing Tara in Cordone's arms. Then, she and Sam discreetly left the new family alone, and headed for their own brood.

"I love you, Kaitlan," Cordone kissed her again.

"I love you, too. And, thank you for these two incredible miracles, my love," Kaitlan whispered to him.

Two weeks later, Canaan, with Tara's support, had finally made the difficult decision about the Clan right after the birth of Canaan and Tara. He knew that the Clan had become so large, Canaan didn't feel that he could do his best for all of his people. In addition to that, Tara had been begging him for months to split the Clan into two, separate Clans, and appoint a new Alpha. Canaan had seen the wisdom in Tara's request, and he was ready to make the announcement. Canaan knew he should have split the Clan long ago, but everything kept getting in the way. But, it would make his life easier, and it would be a shared responsibility. Tara was saddened by the fact that some would probably leave their Clan, but she was also very happy at whom he had chosen to be Alpha of the new Clan. As if no one would figure out whom the new Alpha would be.

There was only one choice for Alpha for the new Clan. With Tara standing next to him, her head held high in support, Canaan decided to announce the changes on their own, internet television program. Clan members who were close enough to attend the meeting, came in person to watch.

Canaan began the meeting that was being streamed over the internet to all in the Clan wherever they might be. Everyone was excited about this momentous decision that had not been made in their entire history!

"As you all know, the O'Hara Clan has been blessed by the great Creator with many children, and it has increased a thousand fold over the last three hundred years. Werewolves have always preferred to live in smaller Clans for a reason. It is easier for your Alphas to take care of you, and provide individual attention when necessary. Our Clan has reached a size that makes it difficult to take care of everyone."

The silence was deafening.

"So, in a decision that has never been made in our history, I have decided to divide the O'Hara Clan, and I am announcing a brand new Alpha. This is a momentous occasion for werewolves, and one that will please most of you, I'm sure."

Canaan nodded to Cordone who walked into view of everyone. He put his hand on Cordone's shoulder.

"Although my Second, or Beta in the old ways, has not been living with our Clan for many years, he still has helped me in decisions that affected all of us. I never replaced him, and for good reason. He was far too valuable a Second, and a friend. He gave his counsel to me for many years, and I have appreciated it. Most of the decisions I have made were discussed with Cordone, before they were finalized."

Cordone's eyes held those of his Alpha. He knew what was coming, and still, he couldn't believe it!

"This is how it will work. Because this is unprecedented, we've had to come up with some sort of new rules. They are good rules, and we believe, fair. I am, officially and as of now, immediately, announcing the newest Alpha is - Cordone Tristan Valon."

The applause within the room was deafening as everyone yelled and laughed with joy. Canaan held up his hands for quiet.

"OK. Quiet down, people," he waited until they did, then continued. "The Valon Clan will consist of the west to mid-America splitting America down the middle. My Clan will be from Missouri in the mid section of America to the East Coast. Cordone's will be from Missouri to the

West Coast with his headquarters in Colorado. All those already living in these areas will be a part of one of the clans, and that takes care of quite a few of the O'Hara Clan members immediately. But, we have decided to change this as well. We want to give all of you a choice of which you would like to join. So, everyone in the O'Hara Clan may choose which Clan they wish to be a part of from the East to the West Coast of America. Of course, those who choose to be in the O'Hara Clan or the Valon Clan will be required to move into the area of that Clan. Cordone?"

"Thank you, Canaan. First, I am honored that I have been selected as Alpha for the new Clan. I will endeavor to do everything for the Valon Clan to the best of my ability having been taught by the best Alpha ever to have lived."

Cordone turned to Canaan, and clapped. Everyone followed him with lots of whoops, shouts, and cheers of "long live Canaan" and "long live Cordone"! When they wound down, Cordone continued.

"Everyone who chooses the Valon Clan will be welcome, and I vow, this day, to promise to become an Alpha you can be proud of and to follow in the footsteps of Canaan O'Hara."

More whoops and cheers, yet again, followed. As they calmed down, Cordone held out his hand, and Kaitlan walked to his side with a huge smile.

"As you know, this is my mate, Kaitlan Seneca O'Hara Valon. We would have brought the babies with us, but they just wouldn't wake up for the celebrations!" he laughed, and so did everyone else. "My mate is, of course, the daughter of Canaan and Tara O'Hara, and the great love of my life!"

Cordone bent to take a kiss from her lips, and no one was surprised at the catcalls and laughs.

"Canaan and I have decided the easiest way for you

to choose would be to simply place your mark on a simple "O'Hara or Valon" ballot listing the names of everyone within your family. It will be done electronically, and we will verify EACH of you to make sure that your ballot is the Alpha of your choice.   We will not leave this to chance. Please make sure you give us your current phone number, and make sure you are available when necessary. If not, a message will be left, and we ask that you return our call as quickly as possible. If you do not receive a call, please make sure you contact us at 1-833-555-8653. My headquarters will be at the newest location of the Seneca Publishing House in Denver, Colorado. We will also have meetings to get everyone's suggestions for the Valon Clan.   We will also have cooperative Clan meetings with the O'Hara Clan as well as others around the world. We will endeavor to make sure that we make our Clans not only equal, but cooperative throughout the years."

More applause.

"Canaan?"

"Thank you, Cordone. Now, we will announce the names of the rest of our hierarchy. Today, I announce that my Second will be Daniel Wheeler whose mate is our incredible Doctor, Anita Wheeler. And, my third will be Roland Turner. You will give to them all the respect that you afford me. They will stand in for me when I am not available. Is this agreeable to all?" Canaan asked the audience.

"Aye!" was the answer. Canaan nodded to Cordone.

"My Second will be Samuel Knight whose mate is Sarah Collins Knight. And, my third scrill be Ceasar Stefan Cecchi. Is this also agreeable to all?" Cordone asked.

"Aye!" was the collective answer.

"There will also be some other changes, of course. Each Clan will have its own council to be decided upon by Clan Members. Those who are on mine will remain, and we will elect others to fill their spots," Canaan declared. "In addition, the Master Council, consisting of Ali'on of the Elves and his mate, Sandra, along with Anteros De Angelis, my mate, Tara, and I, as well as Cordone and Kaitlan, will meet three times a year alternating each Clan location to discuss our entire supernatural world, and these will represent both males and females in everything. After the meeting, the minutes will be available on our secure website at https://wwpwev.com. After verification, you will be assigned your own, personal user name and password. Make sure you change your password when you first log on to the website. Is that also agreeable to all?"

"AYE!"

"Good. Then, we are adjourned, and I thank you all for attending the most important meeting that we have ever had."

Canaan and Cordone shook hands, and the screens went blank while the others who were in the audience began to file out of the room chattering excitedly about their future.

Strangely enough, everything worked out perfectly, because half the Clan decided to go with Cordone, and the other half stayed with Canaan. The Cordone Clan established plans to build their own town on his land, and they prepared to build businesses and homes. An annex of the Denver Seneca Publishing House was also to be built along with the other businesses.

Big changes were coming, and as Kaitlan said, "It's about damned time for a new future!"

Plans were made to hire a great many individuals for the Hall of Records to make available for research purposes. Anteros felt this was fair, and equitable. Ali'on and his mate, Sandra, were happy with everything that had happened as well. And, although Stefan had stepped down, both Jennifer and Sandra joined Kaitlan and the other three girls to make six friends, instead of four. And, they all kept their mates on their toes! In fact, sometimes the mates of the girls believed they were the target of coordinated attacks by the women! Which, of course, they were!

The world was wonderful for the supers. They still lived side-by-side with humans, unknowingly, but they were even considering making an announcement to open The Hall to all species on the planet. In fact, it was the first thing on the next Master Council's agenda. Although it was all pretty much decided, the Clan leaders in the supernatural world believed that it was time for them to make humans re-aware of supernaturals once again. Only the formalities were left, but how they were to tell the humans was another matter. It was Sarah who came up with the perfect solution. Call the leaders of the humans around the world to the Master Council to discuss it with them first.

And, true to their belief, fifteen months later, the stunned leaders of the human world - or what they had thought was a human world - announced to the world the truth. While a majority of the world accepted it as wonderful, just as in all politics, others were against supernaturals. But, that would be another problem they would address somewhere down the line. Humans were granted access to The Hall of Records so that they could learn about their history, and place on Earth.

The old stereotypes still lingered here and there, but Anita's persistence in her research went down as one of the most incredible finds ever. The vampire's transformation could not cured, but it could be stopped in its tracks by a vaccine that she had discovered. Building on her original vaccine, she discovered that by adding the ingredient, Wolfsbane to the mixture, a deadly toxin to supers, and if used right, it could almost heal vampirism. In order to test it on non-vampires, several people volunteered from each species - werewolves, elves, vampires, and humans. When refined as a powder, and added to the vaccine, most vampires were able to eliminate blood altogether, and the side effects were stunning! Her guinea pigs were given the vaccine, and then they were bitten by screened vampires. It would either stop the transformation in its tracks, or in some cases, make some immune to the bite! After her guinea pigs tested this, it stopped the transformation in at least 85% of all species on Earth. But, it still meant that 15% were turned. However, after they did turn, the vaccine worked just like it had with other vampires. Ah, but the most amazing side effect of the vaccine was that it had allowed the female vampires to become fertile as well as those who were vampires with human mates! More work needed to be done, but the discovery was so amazing, Anita was revered around the world. If she could do this, what other things could she find for other diseases around the world. Of course, Stefan was the happiest vampire that ever walked the Earth when he and Jennifer found out they were the first to conceive!

"But what about the other timeline? Did anyone ever remember what had happened?" the reader asks.

And, Dahll answers.

"Well, of course, none of them remembered it, and that was just as well," he says. Then,
"Well, I'm *lying by omission*. That's not quite accurate. Three of us do remember, because we exist beyond time and space."

"Sandra?" Ali'on asked as he held his mate tightly in bed, both panting in the aftermath of their lovemaking.

"Hmmm?" she answered him dreamily.

"Kaitlan did it." he smiled at her.

"Yes. She did," Sandra answered happily.

She was just waiting for the right time to tell him.

"I just wish I could have gotten my daughter back from so long ago, Sandra. But obviously, she was never meant to be in any timeline. I will always regret what Dan and I did to her, but I won't go back there ever again. It's time to move on, and forgive ourselves. I'll invite him to see us soon, and hope Anita will have time as well. This is a new world for supers."

Sandra kissed her mate.

"Yes, it is. I wonder if any of them still have their powers?" she mused aloud.

"Yes, of course they do."

Sandra's eyes flew open in shock, which made Ali'on laugh.

"Don't worry, Sandra. None of them will remember unless something, or someone, tries to hurt our world again. But, Kaitlan is here for one reason - to protect this world, and to unite it. She has done this in spades! Her sacrifice to take her best friends' lives to end the Nivurian and Lon McClain was the most unselfish thing anyone in our supernatural world has ever done. The Creator was greatly pleased with her, and decided to leave her with not only the powers of the White Wolf, but her elemental and wizard powers as well. More than that, Sarah, Anita, and Lynne were also allowed to retain their elemental powers."

"All of them?" Sandra was stunned.

"Yes. He decided that we just might need them sometime in the future. Hopefully never, but we all know that there is always someone who desires power over others. That means they could be needed, again sometime in the distant future."

"Oh, no, Ali'on! I hope not! We've had enough."

"I agree, but we can't count it out. The Creator found Kaitlan the most worthy of all, so he decided that forever would she possess the powers of The White Wolf, the Earth elemental, and that of her ancient wizard ancestors. She is, quite literally, the most powerful being on the planet. It was her horror at what she almost became that stopped her from gaining the power she could have had. That power could have caused her to become all-powerful, and extremely evil. Thanks to Dahll, I guess his warning got through to her when she almost lost it. It scared her to death to see what she could have become. We were very lucky. I spoke to Dahll the other day, and he was pleased with Kaitlan's choice to stop the power within her. However, the girls are never to know that they still possess these powers, and they will only appear when, or if, needed. Until then, they will be ignorant of them. And, that's the way it should be. None of them wants power, because they do not believe a person should possess that kind of power. And, that is the reason they were allowed to retain them."

"Wow! What a great honor it is to know them. I guess if one deserves power, but does not want it, it proves that the person deserves it."

"I agree. I think that's why the Creator kept their power within."

A thought came to her, suddenly, and she sat upright.

"Ali'on!"

"What, Sandra? What's the matter?"

"Their children." She stated the obvious. "Could they…I mean is it *possible* those powers could be passed to them?"

Ali'on thought about that for a moment. He had not stopped to consider it.

"While I really don't know. Perhaps if the powers have been embedded into their DNA, then I suppose it is possible."

"But, how do you keep a child from using them?"

Sandra asked.

"Best guess? The powers will not be able to be used unless, like Kaitlan, they are needed. Let's just hope that doesn't happen for a very long time."

Sandra nodded, then told him what she had recently heard.

"Uh, Ali'on?"

"Yes, my love," he asked nibbling on her right thigh.

"I just didn't know how to tell you this, but I overheard something the other day. The fallen angels are raising their heads again. Most especially one of them."

Ali'on stopped nibbling and turned to her in shock.

"What? Who? Where did you hear this?"

"Someone named Benjamin. He is supposed to be the mate to one S'alin, but I'm not really sure who she is. Have you heard of her?"

"No, I haven't. Where did you hear this?" he asked her a second time.

"A conversation between the vampire, Talosk, and the werewolf, Jheta, while I was doing research at the Hall of Records a week ago. I overheard them speaking in whispers, and that is what they said. I heard nothing else."

"Well, who the hell is Benjamin?" Ali'on asked her. She shook her head. "I hope to hell that they don't bother us for a long time, Sandra. That could be the worst case scenario, and would make Zanack look like the kindest Nivurian ever!"

Sandra nodded. She agreed with him, but she had a bad feeling that it would be sooner than later. She didn't express that to her mate, and decided to cross that Bifrost when it was time.

"I love you, Ali'on," Sandra said, feeling his hard cock lengthen and expand.

"As do I you, my love," he answered pulling her on top of him.

"Oh, one more thing?" Sandra said.

Between kisses, Ali'on asked, "Now, what?"

Sandra lifted her hips, and impaled herself on his cock, then put her lips to his ear. She wanted him sheathed deep and tight inside of her body when she told him.

"I'm going to have a baby!" she said softly.

Ali'on's eyes flew open to stare into his mate. Her smile lit up her face. His smile radiated into hers.

"Thank the Creator!" he yelled.

And, flipping her over, he proceeded to show her just how much he loved her.

~ Epilogue ~
"Life is a Journey, not a destination" ~ Ralph Waldo
Emerson ~
"~ The End ~" does not Exist in the Journey of Life ~
LK Kelley

The White Wolf ran to catch up with her mate! Feeling happy and free, the wind blew through her snow-white fur in the moonlight! When she came to a halt, she phased into her human form, and stepped upon a large patio they had built at the bluff, so that they could sit and watch the sunsets. Her clothing was on a chair next to her mate's clothing.

Putting her purple yoga pants on, and the matching purple tank top, she pulled her hair into a ponytail. Kaitlan walked toward the clearing watching the moon shining down on her mate, and her two, four year-old twin children, Canaan and Tara. They were eight in human years, and the time was going far too fast. They were running around with their Dad in his wolf form giggling. It would be years before they would make their first turn, but in the meantime, they loved riding on his back, because he was like a great big fuzzy, live, stuffed animal! Bigger than Mom, even! Even after all these years, his black fur never ceased to be beautiful, and his wolf form never ceased to excite her! His eyes were alight with mischief as he nipped at his son's heels, and nuzzled his daughter's soft skin that tickled her. Their son had inherited their Mother's blonde hair and Cordone's black eyes while Tara had inherited her Father's black hair and Kaitlan's green eyes. She was going to be a beauty, and Cordone would have his hands full!

Sitting back in a chair, she let her mind wander, wondering who her mate might be? At first, she thought that it might be their nephew, Michael - Sam and Sarah's son. Michael's eyes had recently begun to glow. That thought sent Kaitlan's head into a talespin! However, something within her told her that Tara's mate was not Michael. And, that proved to be the case. It was as if she knew that both of her children would have extraordinary abilities. There wasn't a man alive who would not want to mate with her, and not a woman alive who would not want to mate with Canaan. Kaitlan's mouth turned up into a wicked grin. Cordone would be madder than a hot-blooded, rogue werewolf if he ever found out that Tara and her mate would sleep together before she was of age. She almost laughed aloud at the thought of Cordone threatening Tara's mate.

But, Canaan? Now, he was an enigma altogether. Having already been set in stone, Canaan had already chosen Sam and Sarah's daughter, Lily, as his mate. They had seen his eyes glow when he saw her at a picnic they had held three weeks prior. Excited, Sarah and Kaitlan had hugged each other. That was their fondest dream!

Kaitlan sighed. Well, she'd leave that for another day. If he mated Lily early, Cordone would just slap his son on the back in glee, and Sam would be just as happy about it! Men were such hypocrites! She could hear Cordone now.

"Way to go, son!" Slap, slap, slap!

Oh, well. Macho men! Nope. Not gonna think about that right now. She was far too happy today of all days! She was so excited that she couldn't wait!

While Kaitlan was watching the three of them play, an odd flashback of an old dream came to her, and it made her shudder in fear. She shook her head. It was just a dream. Cordone joined her on the patio, and she waited for her mate to phase back. When he did, he dressed in his jeans with no shirt darting to his mate and pulling her to him to plant a kiss of desire on her lips. She responded in kind.

"What took you so long?" he asked her.

"Well, I had to call Anita."

"Anita? Why?" He asked absently watching his children out of the corner of his eyes to make sure they didn't get into too much trouble. They were both way too much like their parents!

"Remember last week? When the children were staying with Mom and Dad?"

"Mmmhmm?" he muttered nibbling on her ear.

If he kept that up, she wouldn't be able to remember what she had to say to him! She leaned into him. Like before, her hormones were going to be set on high for a while. Yes. Later. She pushed him away gently to his great confusion. She never did that! Ever!

"What?" he asked. Then, sudden terror gripped his stomach. Anita? "Are you OK? I mean, you aren't sick or anything?"

He was desperate to pull her back into his arms, but she wouldn't let him. She knew the crush was coming, and she needed to be ready for it. Actually, she couldn't wait for it! In fact, she couldn't wait until they put the children to bed so her mate could bed her!

Kaitlan laughed aloud at the sheer silliness of his face!

"No, my love. I'm as healthy as a werewolf!"

"Then, what's wrong? What did Anita say? Why do you have such a giddy look on your face?" he asked her while at the same time, hearing an argument break out between the kids.

"Oh, great!" Cordone muttered. "It's their annual pissing contest!"

Tara and Canaan's annual piss off was rapidly

becoming a "holiday" for the Valon household. Once a year, the two of them had a pissing contest over anything at all. Most everyone just stood around, laughed, and watched. They could be so darned funny! But, he also knew that when they were grown, Canaan would never let his sister be hurt, and Tara would defend him to the end.

"What name do you think would be good for our babies?" She whispered into his ear as she stood on her tiptoes, her hand caressing his bare chest.

"Oh, I don't know, Kaitlan. You pick. Really! You come up with the strangest things at the oddest times! Canaan! Stop teasing your sis…" he yelled, then stopped, turning slowly to look at Kaitlan with his mouth open.

Kaitlan could only grin at him, and nod her head.

"Baby? Did you say baby?"

"Yep! Right in here! Two more little Valon werewolves!" She petted her belly. "You done good last week!" she laughed in his face.

"But, we weren't even trying, Kaitlan! I don't get it?"

"Does it matter that we didn't?" she asked him stroking his six-pack abs, and moving lower.

"Oh, hell! Never mind! I don't care! I'm extremely happy about it!"

He was so ecstatic, he dropped to his knees, and placed his lips to her belly.

"Another little Valon! I'm so happy, Kaitlan. Werewolves have always been meant to have big families. And, we have many, many, many years to have more. I love you."

"And, I love you. I'll give you all the babies you want whenever you want them! All you have to do is tell me you want them!"

She held his head at her belly feeling his ear pressed against it. He listened carefully. What was that? That sounded a bit odd. Sounded like an irregular heartbeat.

Should he be worried?

"Uh…Cordone?"

"What?"

"No. There is absolutely nothing to worry about.

"Well, unless…."

"Unless what?" he asked her in alarm as he raised his head to look into her eyes.

"I did say 'babies' you know," she grinned down at him.

"WHAT?" he gasped. "YES!"

He picked her up, and swung her around and around. The children saw them, and began running to them.

She pulled his lips to hers kissing him with a passion that left him in no doubt about what she wanted.

"The children are staying with Sarah, Sam, and the monsters all day tomorrow and tomorrow night. How about a wonderful day of love?"

"Can't think of anything I'd like more! And, Kaitlan?"

"Hmmmm?" she asked nibbling his gorgeous ear.

"Did I tell you today how much I love you?"

"Yes, you did. But, you can say it all the time! I love you, too. And, I never get tired of hearing it! Oh, and by the way, Sarah is pregnant, too!"

Cordone smiled. Sam was truly an amazing Father.

"That's great! They'll be born at the same time!" he told her.

Enough about Sara and Sam, Cordone decided. Tara and Canaan were jumping up and down pulling at their Mom and Dad. Cordone looked down at them, a huge smile on his face.

"Say, let's ask the children their ideas of names?"

"OK," Kaitlan agreed.

They suddenly swept up their children in their arms hearing them squeal.

"OK. Question for you two! Your Mom is going to

have a baby. Actually, two. Twins, just like you two," Cordone told them.

Wide-eyed, they both turned their heads to their Mom.

"Babies, Mommy?" Tara asked in excitement.

"Yep."

"Oh, goodie. Just what we needed." Canaan rolled his eyes sounding bored. Or, at least, trying to sound bored.

"What we need you two to do is to tell us is what names do you like for them? We're having a boy and girl," Cordone told them.

"I like Diana, Mommy! I heard the name last week in town. Something about a goddess? Don't know what that's about, but I liked the name!" Canaan told her.

"I like Chase for the boy! I wanna chase him around!" Tara squealed with laughter.

Cordone and Kaitlan looked at each other in surprise. Out of the mouths of babes came the two most perfect names!

"Well, that takes care of that! Diana and Chase! I think I like it!" Katilan grinned.

Cordone nodded his head. He agreed. Two great names. The important things settled, it was time for bed!

"Well, kiddoes. Time for beddy bye-bye!" Kaitlan said while the kids grumbled they weren't tired.

Both children yawned at the same time, and Kaitlan and Cordone phased. The White Wolf and the Black Wolf ran with their children. The moon shining on their backs and happiness rocked the Rocky Mountains. And, well, life couldn't be better!

~Where There is a Beginning,
There is an End;
And, Where There is an End,
There is Always a New Beginning. ~

~ LK Kelley ~

The White Wolf Prophecy – Scroll of Time

Coming soon:

∼ **Children of the White Wolf** ∼

～ **Prologue** ～
What goes around, usually comes back to annoy you!

Ten years ago, The White Wolf, Kaitlan O'Hara Valon, her mate Cordone, along with her friends and their mates, Sarah and Sam Knight, Anita and Dan Wheeler, and Lynn and Richard O'Malley (aka Thor), thwarted an evil off-world wizard. Kaitlan destroyed Zanack, an evil wizard who had cast a spell wrong, and had screwed up the correct timeline for thousands of years. She and her three friends were kidnapped, and taken through a time portal by Zanack to recast the curse. They won, and he lost. End of Zanack. But…

…a whole new threat named Benjamin has arisen. He desires, above all, to rule the Earth. Who and what he is, no one knows, but he is more evil than Zanack ever was. Unfortunately, he did not get to Zanack in time to torture him in order to force him to reveal the key to recasting the old timeline to his grave. He believes that the answer lies somewhere within Kaitlan's four children, and he is determined to find it with an ancient connection called "Mind Manipulation". Only three beings on Earth have this capability. Which one of them can he trust to find the information for him? But, will they help him? It's his only chance to reclaim the Earth as his.

And, thus, The White Wolf Prophecy continues with the children…

I invite you to Read Chapter 1 of

Children of the White Wolf

~~ Children of the White Wolf ~~
~~ 1 ~~
Siblings are irritating busybodies

"*SHIT*!" Tara squealed, putting her middle finger into her mouth. Of all the damn times for this to happen! She'd torn her nail into the quick! Now, she was going to have to get it fixed, before she met the girls in town!

"Temper, temper, Sis. And, watch your mouth!"

Tara whirled around.

"Butt the hell out, Canaan!"

"Sexual frustration much?" he laughed out loud.

Tara smacked him on the arm - hard.

"Damn it, Tara! What the fuck was that for?" Canaan rubbed his arm. Man, she hit hard!

"Because you are, plain and simple, a dick! That's why!"

"You know you curse more than a fucking sailor, right?"

Canaan's patience was wearing thin with her.

"*I* cuss more than a sailor? Me? What about you?"

Canaan's hands clinched tightly. The werewolf who mated with her was in serious trouble! He pitied that poor bastard!

"And, besides! Talk about sexual frustration? You are so surrounded by it, you can cut it with a knife!"

"Watch it, Tara! You're really trying my patience!"

Tara threw back her head laughing at her brother. He was such a drama queen! She stopped when she saw his glare, and stared back at him. They were having their annual pissing contest that had been happening since their very first argument at the age of two. That was two in werewolf years, and they continued it every year from that point forward. It was always a toss-up who would win, and amazingly, the fights ended up alternating on who won each year. It would be Canaan's turn this year.

Diana bounded into the room, and came to a dead stop. Oh, hell! Good! Her brother and sister were at it again! She was always fascinated with this annual contest between them! She went to the fridge, poured a glass of orange juice and grabbed a piece of fruit.

"Let's see? What do I want this morning? Apple or banana?"

She wasn't all that picky, so she grabbed an apple, and ran back to the bar propping her butt on a stool to watch them. Their annual piss-offs were better than TV.

Hey! Great name for a TV game show!

Yeah. She imagined how the game show would begin. *"Ladies and gentlemen! It's once again time for... 'Piss-off'! The show that let's you piss off anyone you want!"* She laughed aloud at her own joke!

Diana stared at them trying to size them up to see who she would pick to win this year. Her brother, Canaan Darrin Valon, was named after their grandfather while Tara Seneca Valon was named after their grandmother. Figures they'd get the "cool" names! She was stuck with Diana Marie Valon, thanks to Canaan who named her when he was four!

Oops! She wasn't paying attention to the fight! She turned back to Canaan and Tara, and bit into the apple. She chewed as she considered her brother, first. Canaan was gorgeous - well if you were a girl who wasn't his sister that is. Diana didn't know why all the girls just swooned around him! She cocked her head as she studied him. He was as tall as their Dad, Cordone Tristan Valon, Alpha of the Valon Clan of werewolves, but he had inherited their Mother's blonde hair, and their Father's black eyes and olive skin. And, he was *buff* - with a capital "*BUFF*"! His chest was large, and may have been a bit larger than Dad's. His waist was narrow, his hips lean. And, his legs were l.o.n.g. He stood a good six-feet six inches. His blonde hair was cut very short, but long enough to leave it messy. He preferred it that way, because he hated to fuss with it. But, the girls loved it. They were all about him hoping he'd notice one of them as they giggled when he passed them on the street, and sighing at how hot he was while each hoped to become his mate. They were really dumb, but you can't fix dumb, Diana figured. She drank some of her juice, and continued with her assessment. Canaan was strong, too. Even Uncle Sam, who was the strongest of them all, couldn't best Canaan's strength! His arms were bigger than her entire torso, but right now, her brother was acting like a stupid dick, still rubbing his arm where Tara had hit him. She giggled. Tara was really strong, too!

Diana shook her head staring at her brother. OK. She had to admit! He *was* kind of gorgeous. But, just not her type. Diana had her own idea of what her mate should look like. She shut her eyes for a moment imagining him. He was darker skinned, and had black hair like her Dad's. He would have ice-blue eyes, a massive chest and arms, but only moderately tall. Oh, say…5 foot 11 inches. After all, she was only five-feet tall. But, there was nothing really set in stone about his height! He would be as sexy as hell. Sexy enough where she never wanted to be out from under his body while sexy enough where she never wanted him to be out of hers! Good thing she had kept this secret. She'd be teased to death by all three of her siblings if they knew!

She opened her eyes, and considered his resemblance to their Mother who was a beauty! Kaitlan Seneca O'Hara Valon was the daughter of Canaan O'Hara who was the Alpha of the O'Hara Clan. She and their

Dad were disgusting a lot of the time. Mates were always pawing each other and kissing. Yeesh! Get a room, already! Well, she couldn't wait till it was her turn, of course, but it was different with parents, right? Really gross!

Anyway, Diana had to admit that her Mom was a beauty with her beautiful fair skin, had the most beautiful green eyes and blonde hair she had ever seen. And, her Dad was also a hottie. Diana, though, deep down, harbored a deep secret. Diana really hoped to have a love like her parents for herself some day - a long time in the future, of course. She wanted to be free to do whatever she wanted before she mated!

Taking a drink of her juice, she moved on to Tara. The guys in their Clan couldn't keep from drooling over her, and Diana could see why. She was truly beautiful. She was an enigma with her sleek, black hair that hung to her waist, and green eyes that could stare you down for hours if she wanted to do it. Most of the time, Tara threw her hair up into a high ponytail - copying off of their aunt, Lynne O'Malley. She never fussed much with it, and the ponytail suited her best. If the guys thought she was beautiful with just a ponytail, then their tongues would hang out if they saw how much more beautiful she was in the morning without any makeup, her long hair flowing over her shoulders to the middle of her back, and it was long enough to cover her perky breasts. (OK, no more sex books for you, Diana, or I wouldn't have even given that a thought! Ick)! Her nose was small, her lips naturally dark pink, and her skin was as fair as her Mom. That's what always drew the guys to her. Tara's skin was without a flaw, and yet translucent. She was petite compared to Canaan, and was just barely five-feet, three inches tall, but her personality made up for that small deficiency. She was what her Dad called a "firecracker". And, her pink mouth was always getting her into trouble. Tara's voice brought her out of her dream state.

"Oh, hells bells!" Tara whined. "I'm supposed to meet with my friends in Denver this afternoon. We'll continue this stupid game later, Canaan. I have to get going!"

"Ah, do you have to go, sis?" Diana complained. "I mean, you guys were just getting good!"

"Quiet, pipsqueak! I have to get out of here! It's a long drive, and I have to go. Continue it later, Canaan?"

"Well, I don't know. Let's call it that I win this year since you won last year. After all, you turned away first!" Canaan laughed.

"Whatever! For goodness sakes, Canaan! We're thirteen years old - twenty-six in human terms, and adults. Isn't this annual piss-off getting a bit silly?" Tara asked him.

"Yeah. But, ya gotta admit it's a lot of fun!"

Tara glared at him. He was always laughing at her, and she was damn sick, and tired of it.

"Canaan why don't you go get your damn mate, and take your sexual frustration out on her!" She looked at her watch. "Damn! I gotta go!"

Tara turned, jumped to the first level, and ran to her room to get ready to go into Denver. She heard Canaan burst out laughing hard after her. Her Mom called it a "GRRRRRR" moment! And, right now, Tara was having one with her brother! GRRRRRR!

Diana was laughing so hard she fell off the stool! Canaan walked around the bar, and picked her up. Tears of laughter were falling from her eyes.

"You two really are better than TV!" laughed Diana trying to catch her breath.

Canaan ruffled her blonde hair.

"Sorry about that, Squirt! I'm really so glad we amuse you!"

"Yeah, well, there is one thing Tara is right about,

Canaan."

"What?" he asked as he started to leap to his room.

"When the hell are you going to mate with Lily? Don't you two think it's time you did?"

Canaan whirled on his sister giving her a look that made her step back from him. His tiny little sister of five feet, was just so adorably innocent with the curly, shoulder-length blonde hair that was always flowing riotously around her face. Her brilliant, coal black eyes of their Dad, sthat shone like black diamonds, were always wide with mischief. With the petite stature of her Mom, her skin was just as fair and beautiful as his Mom and Tara. Her mouth was beautifully full and luscious, and then he stopped as his eyes as his eyes noticed her chest. Wait! When had she gotten breasts? He hadn't even noticed, and where Tara's were a bit smaller, Diana's were voluptuous like their Mother's! OK. He shouldn't be thinking about that, but hey. He was a werewolf male, and they noticed those things. Her hips had filled out, and her waist was tiny. He could easily make her blush anytime, and he just loved to embarrass her. But, this was the first time she had embarrassed him! That did not sit well with him!

Oh, hell, Diana thought. He was going into his Alpha mode! His eyes shot back up to her face. He sure didn't need his little sister thinking he was thinking about, let alone looking at her body.

"First, it's none of your damn business, you nosey little shrimp, and second, you are way too young to talk about such things!"

She blinked at him. Did he actually just say that to her?

"Too young? What's wrong with you, you nutcase? Chase and I turn nine in two weeks! That's mating age, or have you completely forgotten that? I mean, you know, boys, mating, sex? You are just so clueless and naïve,

Big B! Geez!”

Canaan drew back in shock, looking at his little sister. Nine? She'd be nine in just two months? Staring at her, he was shocked. Oh, my God! His little sister had turned into a woman overnight, and *he had never even noticed*! OH, HELL NO! There was no fucking way he was going to let his little sister mate with anyone any time soon! As for Tara? Nope. Never gonna happen with her, either! His brotherly protection had just been triggered right along with his Alpha feelings. Both he and Tara were due to phase in seven months, but apparently, “Alpha Mode” came earlier!

“Dream on, Hummingbird!” Canaan used his old nickname for her, indicating that she was a baby, and then leaped upward to his room. He leaned over the railing staring right into her eyes.

“I have to catch the jet to St. Louis to finish my last two weeks of internship with Anita.” He paused. “Oh, and Diana? Over my damn, dead body you'll mate at nine - or ever!”

He stormed into his room, and slammed the door.

Diana's mouth dropped open.

“Yeah?” she yelled. “Well, you jerk! It can't be stopped, and you know it!”

DAMN HIM! Fighting a sudden urge to stick her tongue out at him, she slammed her glass down on the bar, and made a dent in it. She dropped her head, and closed her eyes in frustration. Her Dad was going to kill her for that dent!

“What the hell is going on down there?” asked a voice above her.

She looked up. Her twin brother, Chase, stood looking down from their Dad's office. Chase Marshall Valon was the quiet one in the family. He was studious, and always wanting to learn new things.

“Oh, nothing you'd care about, twinster! You know.

It was all about sex down here!" she grumbled back to him.

"Oh. OK." He turned, and walked back into the office. Chase was about to sit down when he stopped. Sex? They were talking about sex, and he'd missed it? He ran back to the railing.

"Did you say sex, Diana?"

Diana groaned out loud. When would she ever learn to keep her mouth shut. She knew the answer immediately. Never. Any mate of hers would really have to put up with her vocabulary, because she wasn't changing it for any damned werewolf!

Diana glanced at the clock! Oh, she was going to be late with her date with the girls in town. She leaped to her room, and ran into it to dress while quickly texting Jessica she'd be a tad late all because of her dumb sister and brother! Of course, Diana had nothing to do with any of it. She knew Jessica was going to want to hear it all. She was so happy when her parents had given her permission to tell Jessica Daylin about them. And, she had taken it really well. Well, maybe not *that* well. She had been so shocked, she hadn't talked to Diana for two days afterward, but once she got used to the idea, she called Diana. Jessica was an only, and her parents were also allowed into the secret. They took it about as well as Jessica had, but they accepted it faster than she had. Damn! She had to go!

Canaan barely made it in time for his final medical classes with Anita after a long flight to St. Louis. But, then, he was the only one in the class, anyway, and about to graduate as a Doctor for his own Clan. He had always wanted to be a doctor, and had always been fascinated with all things anatomical, including humans. But, he had a question he still needed answered. Mating. It just made no sense to him at all.

"Aunt Anita?"

"Yes, Canaan?" Anita answered as she stood up to get another book.

She had an extensive library, now, and she kept books in her office from The Hall of Records constantly. She found that there were things she still knew nothing about when it came to supers. Years ago, she had finally found the cure for vampirism's blood lust, but she was beginning to think that there was no cure for the bacteria that wound its way around the DNA strand of their anatomy. She would never stop trying, but at this point, she was not very hopeful.

"I still don't get our irrational matings, Anita. Can you give it to me in a more clinical aspect? Maybe then I'd get it. I mean, I watch Mom and Dad, but I can't seem to understand the sudden attraction when one finds their mate."

Anita shook her head. Poor boy. He wouldn't really understand until he found his mate. And, he had already found her, but he'd been avoiding her for years. Well, she'd try, again, to explain it to him.

"It's hard to explain the clinical aspects. Let me see if I can simply it for you."

She turned, and placed the book onto her desk, then looked back up at Canaan.

"When werewolves mate, the first thing that happens is the eyes glow. The same thing that allows our eyes to glow in the dark at will, also happens without our will. Do you understand this?"

Canaan nodded.

"That's simple."

"OK. Mating begins ONLY when we see each other's eyes glow, and a mate, normally, doesn't show up until the age of maturity at nine years-old. Well, I have to admit there have been cases much younger. I offer your Dad and Mom up for that one. But, I mention this in a general way. After that, all bets are off. When that happens, and when our eyes meet our mate's, it's the end of clinical. Everything else is emotional."

So far so good, Canaan thought.

"From this point forward, the emotions of our human self and our wolf join together, and become one with each other. Once that begins, we do not have control over our emotions. They are let loose, and are so intense that we cannot deny our mate. The mating instinct that is buried within our genes to procreate is so strong, it overrides our very being. It's in our genes, Canaan, and it cannot be quelled, nor can it be denied."

"Isn't there some way to stop it?" Canaan asked with a little hope.

"No. It's the way our Creator made us. And, it's a *good* thing, Canaan. We were not made to be alone, but we were made to have a mate. Only one mate. This is why we mate for life. The mixing of the blood is what causes our bodies to desire to create our first born children. The intensity during this part is unbelievably private, but totally uncontrollable."

"I get it. Not totally understanding, but I get it."

Anita's nurse came in to tell her a patient had come, and she started to excuse herself when Dan walked in heading straight for his mate. He swept her up into a wonderful kiss, then let her go leaving her breathless.

"Hey, nephew! How's it going?" he asked Canaan after he put Anita back on the floor.

"Canaan, maybe you could get a better perspective talking to Dan? You are both men." Anita left the room to see her patient.

"What's the problem, Canaan?"

"Mating."

"What? You?"

Canaan shook his head.

"No, and saints preserve me from it!"

Dan almost laughed in his face.

"OK. Ask me what you need to know."

"Why does the male have such a tremendous desire to impregnate their mate during the blood bond? I still don't get it. Isn't there something logical in it?"

"Hmmm. This is about Lily, isn't it, Canaan?" Dan asked him knowing that Canaan refused to admit his mate was Lily. "OK. Never mind I asked. Why should it be that we desire a child with our mate during the blood bond?"

"Well, yes." Canaan answered, ignoring his uncle's statement about Lily.

"It's not about logic, Canaan. It has never been about logic. It's all about emotions. Feelings. It's primal. It's instinct for our wolf to wish to give our mate our child. It's really hard to explain, but until it happens to you, you really cannot explain it. There are not clinical aspects in this. It can't be denied, and it can't be stopped. In other words, as werewolves, our wolves will never allow us to deny the feelings when we find out mates."

"Not at all?"

Dan shook his head, then smiled at Canaan.

"Nope. And, trust me, nephew." Canaan's hand touched his shoulder, and he smiled widely at him. "You won't want to stop it when it happens."

Canaan realized his uncle was telling him the truth, and he nodded his head. He didn't want to be mated to any woman. His life was dedicated to Medicine. He knew that Lily was his mate, but he had been silent on it. For several years he had avoided her like the plague. The problem was that her ninth birthday was this weekend, and after he told his Mother that he would not be attending, she told him he would attend whether, or not he liked it. He would graduate in just under two weeks, and no matter what, he would become the Doctor to the Valon Clan. He'd be around her a lot.

His plan was to avoid her eyes at all costs when he went home this weekend. He thought of another question with hope.

"OK. So what happens if a were's mate's eyes do not glow when you look at hers."

"Uh, Canaan? That is not possible. Your eyes glow ONLY for your mate. Her eyes will glow, too."

Shit! That's what his uncle Sam had told him, too! A couple of his friends had already mated, and they walked around as if they couldn't stand to be away from their mates for any length of time. It was disgusting, and Canaan had told them they were pussy-whipped!

"Thanks, Dan. I appreciate it."

"No prob, Canaan. Well, I have to go check security, and I'll see you later. We aren't going to be able to attend Lily's birthday, because Anita and I are going to Asgard so she can help Lynne."

"Lynne's about to deliver?" Well, that could put his graduation on hold!

"Yes, and Anita will need to attend her. No one on that planet has the expertise for an Elf, and she absolutely refuses to leave Richard to come here. So, Anita has to go to her. We understand duty before anything else. Give Lily and Thomas our love, and we'll see them when we get back."

Canaan stood up, and shook hands with Dan when Anita ran back into her office with a two presents.

"I almost forgot their presents, Canaan! Here," she shoved two packages in his hands. "Give them to Lily and Thomas, will you?"

"Sure, Aunt Anita. You guys have a good trip, and give my love to Aunt Lynne & Uncle Richard."

"Will do!"

After Dan left and Anita went back to her rare patient, Canaan was plotting how the hell he was going to keep from looking into Lily's eyes. He didn't want a mate,

The White Wolf Prophecy – Scroll of Time

damn it! No, he would never look into Lily's eyes!

374

www.ingramcontent.com/pod-product-compliance
Lightning Source LLC
Chambersburg PA
CBHW070759120726
47910CB00001B/229